PERMANENT
RECORD

Also by
MARY
H.K.
CHOI

*Emergency
Contact*

PERMANENT RECORD

MARY H.K. CHOI

SIMON & SCHUSTER BFYR

NEW YORK LONDON TORONTO
SYDNEY NEW DELHI

SIMON & SCHUSTER BFYR

An imprint of Simon & Schuster Children's Publishing Division
1230 Avenue of the Americas, New York, New York 10020

SIMON & SCHUSTER BFYR

is a trademark of Simon & Schuster, Inc.
For information about special discounts for bulk purchases,
please contact Simon & Schuster Special Sales at
1-866-506-1949 or business@simonandschuster.com.
The Simon & Schuster Speakers Bureau can bring authors
to your live event. For more information or to book an event,
contact the Simon & Schuster Speakers Bureau at
1-866-248-3049 or visit our website at
www.simonspeakers.com.
Book design by Lizzy Bromley
The text for this book was set in Bell.
Manufactured in the United States of America
First Edition
10 9 8 7 6 5 4 3 2 1
Library of Congress Cataloging-in-Publication Data
Names: Choi, Mary H. K., author.
Title: Permanent record / Mary H. K. Choi.
Description: First edition. | New York : Simon & Schuster Books
for Young Readers, [2019] | Summary: Nineteen-year-old Pablo
Neruda Rind is working in an upscale health food store in New
York City when pop star Leanna Smart rushes in and turns his
life upside-down.
Identifiers: LCCN 2019000541 (print) | LCCN 2019001612 (ebook) |
ISBN 9781534445970 (hardcover) | ISBN 9781534445994 (Ebook)
Subjects: | CYAC: Dating (Social customs)—Fiction. | Celebrities—
Fiction. | Asian Americans—Fiction. | Friendship—Fiction. | Family
life—New York (State)—New York—Fiction. | New York (N.Y.)—
Fiction.
Classification: LCC PZ7.1.C5316 (ebook) | LCC PZ7.1.C5316 Per
2019 (print) | DDC [Fic]—dc23
LC record available at https://lccn.loc.gov/2019000541

For my
New York family.
You're all
maniacs and I
love you.

Chapter 1

I don't care what any of the assholes I live with tell you. I don't work at a bodega. It's a health food store. Says right there on the sign: M&A JUICE BAR DELI ORGANIC GROCERY CORP.

Whatever. It's *implied.*

In any case, it's well lit, huge by New York standards, with a battalion of Vitamix blenders right up front—4K worth at least. Plus, we sell every type of rich-people fetish food. Are you in the market for organic, non-sulfur-treated goji berries at eighteen bucks a bag? We got you. Gluten-free, sugar-free, dye-free cake for your non-immunized kid's next birthday? Yep. We even have cake mix *with gluten* that's just as expensive because it's ironic. See, we're fancy, not at all a bodega, never mind that we're open twenty-four hours a day, are owned by no-nonsense Koreans, and have a deli cat named Gusto. I'm telling you: Not. A. Bodega.

Still, I just wish the damn health food store were a little closer to my apartment. Especially when the windchill mauls your face-meat to ribbons.

I slide my MetroCard smoothly—quickly—bracing for the *clang*, that hip check of an expired pass, but the turnstile clicks me through.

The reader flashes *EXP 2/13*.

Great, so my card's dying right at the stroke of midnight on the day I was born—Valentine's Day. Good thing I'm not extremely superstitious and prone to crippling anxiety. (I am.)

A can of Red Bull skitters on the tracks as a rat scurries past it. The fingers on my right hand are numb enough that watching them load up the shitty video on my phone is an out-of-body experience, as if I'm watching over someone else's shoulder.

How I got into Columbia with a free ride!

I should shove my dead hand into my pocket, but I can't. I have to know how she did it.

Because here's how I'm sick (everyone's sick in their own special way; the variety on the flavors of crazy is pretty endless, but me?): I'm convinced that the next video in the autoplay is the answer. That it'll be the antidote to my entire life. I believe (but would never admit) that watching the impossibly attractive, gap-toothed Black British chick reveal how she Instagram modeled her way into Columbia with a full scholarship will make that shit happen to me. As if reality is a Japanese horror movie where you watch the crackly footage to become the next chosen one. That is, as soon as this thirteen-minute portal to a better me would hurry up and buffer in this tundra.

College.

Any talk of it makes my blood pressure spike. It's just one topic among many that I don't broach with my mom, who is Asian—Korean, specifically. *South* Korean if you're asking. A human woman who moved to America when she was nine to improve her station in life. The way she tells it though, it wasn't her benevolent, Virginia-based aunt to whom she owes her success. It's sheer determination and a seemingly inexhaustible reserve of rage that's responsible for her becoming a doctor. Mom wanted it that bad. And it's with the same single-minded grit that she despises my job. How it looks. The optics. The *melanin* of it. She doesn't care if I'm working at a bodega, a health food store, or as a mustachioed oyster shucker in the finest farm-to-table restaurant in Manhattan. She doesn't want me anywhere in the service industry. Not even a little. She didn't move seven thousand miles to put herself through college and then med school to become an anesthesiologist at New York-Presbyterian for her firstborn to work in what she calls a first-generation job.

My dad, who's Pakistani and was born in Jersey (he'll say Jersey when you ask him and not Princeton, which is more accurate), doesn't care so much. Despite his engineering degree *from Princeton*, he's the chillest patriarch in the world. Seriously, he makes weed seem high-strung.

He's Muslim-ish, but doesn't pray five times a day because he meditates constantly with this app that's free with ads. He doesn't eat pork, but he says it's for the same reason he doesn't eat octopus, because pigs are smart and experience fear. He'll get Filet-O-Fish at McDonald's, not because it's halal but because that's what he'd get when he was a kid, and he drinks hard cider and takes Baileys in his tea at Christmastime, which is not only haram but weirdly basic.

In short, my dad's a total ABCD. American-born confused desi. By his own admission. Born and raised on the East Coast, *his* dad, my dada abu, moved in the seventies to be a humanities professor. It was a huge deal, a massive point of pride for his family who were textile workers in Lahore. Everything was going according to plan until my dad forwent grad school to work at a video-game start-up and then married my mom. We've drifted from that side of the family. Ever since auntie Naz, my dad's little sister, moved to literal Tasmania ten years ago.

But the main reason dad doesn't care what job I have as long as I'm "following my dreams" (believe me, his words) is that I could work at NASA and people will still think I work in the service industry. In fact, me and my dad have talked about how, in most chain stores, randos assume we work there. It never fails. I know that if I pull up to CVS in a polo shirt, even if it's that Ralph Lauren Snow Beach drip, more than one person will have the audacity to ask me where the vitamins are or how late we're open. It's amazing when you think about it. How racism is a wave *and* a particle since we also get followed around in stores as if we're going to steal something. I guess shoplifting's an inside job?

Train. Thank god. I snag a seat. My phone rings in my hand. Unavailable caller ID. Except I know exactly who it is. Anyone with enough juice to either have an unavailable come up or one of those 1-800 numbers that's suspiciously catchy—like 882-8888—that's a bill collector. Especially if they're calling around dinnertime.

I check my bank balance on my phone. Between credit cards, student loans, and rent, the situation is dire.

Only one of the car doors opens at my stop. Typical.

Shit. I'm late. My breath puffs out in cartoon clouds as I bolt down the platform and up the stairs. I didn't mean to be late. I never mean to be late.

"Ayo!" a kid in a red parka yells as I dash by. "Swipe me in, man."

"Please," I snap at the twerp, but double back anyway.

I haul ass down Seventh, fling open the plastic-screened door, pop a grape into my mouth from the cooler, then immediately regret it since the store's a panopticon and Mr. Kim's got CCTV eyes everywhere. Plus, I probably gave myself E. coli since I didn't wash my subway hands.

"Hey, Tina." Tina immediately checks the clock on the wall behind the register and shoots me the wild stink eye. "Come on," I wheedle. "I'm four minutes late." Tina's five foot even, with a photographic memory for numbers and grudges. Her baby hair's unruly, which is a good indicator of her mood, and there are dark smudges under her eyes. There was a time when she was fanatic about her red MAC lipstick. "It's Ruby Wooooooo," she'd coo in her high-pitched voice when customers remarked on it, but that was before morning sickness took her out. She sucks her teeth at me and goes back for her coat.

Ever since she got pregnant, Tina acts like she's my boss. Only last summer we were for real friends. We went to the beach. It wasn't a date-date, but we brought a cooler out to the Rockaways and had spaghetti with salami, which Tina said was traditional Dominican beach food. We washed it down with neon-blue nutcrackers with unicorn stickers on the plastic bottles, which of course is the traditional New York beach drink. Then we passed out cold until a gang of seagulls tried to steal our gigantic bag of Herr's Honey Cheese Curls so I threw a Timb at them, which let me tell you doesn't get any more New York as a beach activity. In any event, I miss that Tina. I get why she can't act all silly with me anymore, but it sucks.

I take my time making my way to the counter, plucking the twelve-dollar pint of grass-fed Australian yogurt from the popcorn display, returning it to the fridge. As well as the nine-dollar matcha pound cake that's strayed over by the teas. I make a big show of my conscientiousness.

Tina's not having any of it. "You're supposed to be here fifteen minutes before for put-backs, so you're nineteen minutes late, Pab." Tina pulls her gloves on so angrily she shoves two fingers in one slot.

"Ay," I tell her, ripping off my beanie. "I already saved

the company, like, twenty dollars in twenty seconds." I nod
over to the coolers. "That's two hours of work basically."
I'm wearing my XXXL hoodie, which signals the cusp of
a laundry cycle. It barely fits under my coat, so I flap my
sleeves to free my arms. "Come on, T," I plead. "How are you
going to stay mad at a man with seasonal affective disorder?
You know my people ain't built for these climates." Tina's
about ready to kill me. "I'm sorry." I shove my coat under
the counter and nudge her, but she's activated the launch
sequence.

"You always do that, try to charm your way out of situations with that hair." She stabs the air between us, on her
tiptoes since I'm a foot taller. "And that face." Stab, stab.
"I'm tired of it!" She cuts her eyes at me dramatically and
raises her red-gloved palm. "That shit doesn't work on me
anymore."

Not to be a dick, but when it comes to women, that shit
usually works.

"All right, look." I reach over and grab two gold-
wrapped Ferrero Rochers from the pile of fifty-cent candy
by the register and put them in her wool-covered palm.
They're her favorite.

"Let me work half your next shift."

I can't stand when people are mad at me.

"My Valentine's gift to you," I continue.

"And Daniel," she says, softening. Daniel's her man.
Total herb.

"And Daniel . . . even if he's a herb." I mug valiantly.

Daniel's a good dude, but a job at the Verizon store is a struggle. Then again, I work at a bodega.

"Cover me for my birthday next month too," she says.

Man, I should have seen that scam from a mile away.

"Fine," I tell her.

Tina smiles squintily, bats her lashes, and pockets the candy.

"Plus, put a dollar in the register now," she says, nodding at the candy bowl and wrapping her scarf around her face as if she's stepping into a sandstorm. "Don't forget." And then, before she leaves, she comes up to the register and hugs me. "Happy birthday, Pablito."

The screen door clangs on her way out as Gusto jumps onto the counter. Gusto's black all over except for this white patch on his chin that deadass looks like a soul patch. As if he plays upright bass in an all-cat jazz ensemble or something. He and I have a special connection. Meaning he doesn't let anybody touch him but me. That's my dude.

I check my pockets for change. Mr. and Mrs. Kim are crazy about inventory. If you saw them, you'd think they were about to play a spontaneous round of golf—all resort-leisurely—but they don't miss a trick. They know exactly how many Ferrero Rocher and Baci are in the basket along with the chewy ginger candies that to me are a rip-off at fifty cents a pop.

I pump some sanitizer on my hands and look out the window. I don't even know why I bother. It's so bright in here the glass is a mirrored sheet.

Some nights when I'm by myself, I'm convinced I'm being observed.

How I got back into NYU with abysmal grades and demoralizing student loan debt!

I watch myself looking back at me. I need a haircut. It's started to curl under my ears. And I could use some sleep.

Do I look like someone who would work at a bodega? Like, forreal forreal?

I smile. Wide. It's a genetic fluke in my family that I have perfect vision and perfect teeth. Never had braces or glasses.

I watch myself stop smiling. Who cares if I look like I'd work here? I've been doing it over a year.

I take a deep breath. Envision my lungs expand and contract. I'll find a way to get back into school. I will. I have to.

Gusto's ears perk. I look to the direction of his attention. I'm not scared to work overnight, but there are stretches where I get paranoid.

No surprises on how much my mom hates my graveyard shift. "It's not that I don't trust you," she says of my hours. "I don't trust other people. You could get robbed or jumped or god forbid somebody mistakes you for someone else and shoots you."

By someone else she means "an unarmed Black kid with a bag of Skittles."

Meanwhile, if I were pulling all-nighters as a medical resident, it would be completely different. Most people guess me and my little brother, Rain, are Armenian, thanks to a celebrity family that doesn't bear mentioning. I've gotten Hawaiian a few times too since it's every mixed kid's birthright to endure countless rounds of "yo, lemme guess what you are," for sport. Our names don't suggest much to our heritage either, and this will give you a further idea of what kind of guy my father is.

He named me Pablo Neruda after the Chilean poet, the "I want to do with you what spring does with the cherry trees" guy whose name wasn't even Pablo. His name was Ricardo, and Neruda was taken from another poet. It's confusing enough being called Pablo while not being Latinx, but personally I think it's corny that on my birth certificate it says Pablo Neruda as my first name, nothing as my middle name, and my last name is Rind. It feels dumb ESL.

My brother didn't get off easy either: Rainer Maria Rind after the poet Rainer Maria Rilke, whose sonnets I tried to read once in high school and then was like, nah. All I remember was that there were a lot of exclamations. Tons of "Os" and "Ahs" just doing the most.

At least the second part of my name isn't a woman's name—Maria. But everyone calls him Rain, yeah, like the hot Korean singer-actor dude from *Ninja Assassin* who has an eight-pack. Or, like, Leaf, Apple, Petal, some hippie celebrity's idiot kid.

Rain Smashes Tesla into Plaza Hotel
Rain Sizzles at Burning Man
Rain's Gains: The Cruelty-Free Protein Plan!
The girls call him *Rainy*, and it's accompanied by a lot

of giggling. It's gross, but a few of the girls I've seen with him definitely don't look thirteen and they certainly don't dress thirteen. I remind myself to have the Talk with him beyond me yelling that he should wear rubbers the one time me and Tice saw him posted up with a girl on the stoop of my mom's building.

My mom's Kyung Hee, but she goes by Kay. My dad's Bilal, and interestingly enough, the only time he gets tight is when white people try to call him Bill. Mom wanted to name me either Daniel or David and Rain John since they're easy to pronounce. That's where *she's* coming from. Meanwhile, the names are so milquetoast they sound way more fresh off the boat than Kyung Hee.

To round out my biography, my parents aren't divorced. Just separated since before Rain was born. So even though I don't have a single memory of ever seeing them kiss, the evidence suggests that disgusting activities have occurred between them that I never want to imagine.

I kick off my boots, set them aside, and put on the gray fuzzy house shoes that say "sport" on the upper as if that's the brand. Mrs. Kim got them for me when I admired her red ones since boots feel like feet prison during a whole shift. My pinkie toe pokes through the hole in my sock, so I try to negotiate the rip over to the side so it lands on a different part.

When I'm successful and rich, these are the details of the biopic I'll have to remember to include for color and relatability.

"Yoyoyoyoyoyoyoyoyoyoyo."

"Oh shit, it's the peanut gallery," I call out to my room-mates, Tice and Selwyn. Me and Tice are about the same height, six foot two, but he's lean where I'm scrawny. He's got a big famous-guy head and those Tupac-length eye-lashes girls think are dreamy. He's effectively my best friend though I'd never admit it to him. Selwyn the Slumlord is a kid I've known since grade school even if we weren't friends until I moved into his apartment. To be honest though, I don't know that I'd exactly call him my friend. He's got zero chill. He's that dude in the crew who'll accidentally lock eyes with the violent homeless guy on the train or who'll buy the exact same hat as you and not think it's a problem.

"Pab." Tice nods. "Hey, Mr. Kim."

I swivel around. Sometimes Mr. Kim reminds me of Gusto the way he silently materializes. He's reading the paper at the end of the counter. I have no idea how long he's been there.

"Tice," he says. "Hi, Wyn." During college (the maniac finished Hunter in three years) Selwyn started going by Wyn. He even had that ringtone "All I do is win, win, win" DJ Khaled song for a while. Total corn nugget.

Wyn reaches for Gusto's tail. The kid loves cats even though he's allergic.

"You boys staying out of trouble?" asks Mr. Kim.

"Of course," says Tice, and smiles his fullest smile. Tice's thing lately is that he wants to be an actor. He takes night-school classes and everything after his shift at Zara. Before that he wanted to be a DJ, but then again, everyone spends at least a year thinking they can be a DJ.

Mr. Kim goes back to his office and shoots me a look indicating how he's not paying me to kick it with my friends. His wife isn't so stern. She once gave Tice a free Baci even though we're not his day-to-day bodega. His regular spot is closer to the apartment and Black-owned.

"You're late," says Wyn in this officious tone, pointing to his open palm. Making as though he's going to beat my ass for being delinquent on rent. He's twenty-one going on fifty, and something in the way his Croatian mom's genes swirled with his dad's Jamaican ones makes him resemble an old man in the face. Plus, his pubes are orange, which is exactly the type of thing to make you have a different outlook on life.

"I know," I tell him. "I get paid today though." I don't tell him I'm going to be sixty short. And that's on *last* rent. Or sixty-one now after buying Tina apology candy 'cause I'm an idiot.

"This can't keep happening," says Wyn, rubbing his hands. He's got the kind of smile where it's half gums and half teeth. It's in these moments that I hate living with him. Part of me knows that 100 percent of the rent goes directly to his parents, who own the building, but I also know that Wyn only pays three hundred, where the rest of us pay about six, and I, as the last man in, fork over six hundred and forty for what's essentially a broom closet. Miggs, our fourth roommate, whose girlfriend, Dara, is our *unofficial* fifth, is a comedian. He's been there the longest and last month when he was high, he told me what everyone pays.

Wyn also has the biggest room, and it's so dumb to think about how it's not fair considering it's his apartment and how cheap it is by any New York standards, but depending on the day it makes me want to knock him around. His parents are crazy-elderly. They were grandparents age when they had him, so they think he hung the moon. *And* he's an only child. An only child with clown pubes.

"Come on, man," says Tice, rolling his eyes behind Wyn's back and urging him down the cookie aisle.

"Say," says Wyn to me after he's done gathering his provisions. I make him wait while I post a photo of his limited-edition mystery-flavor Oreos. I have a tidy little following of nineteen thousand under @Munchies_Paradise, a half-snack, half-sneaker account that my mom keeps following and unfollowing because she's torn about condoning the shit I eat.

Snacks *and* sneakers. It's basically all the Internet is good for. It's an outrage I'm not verified. I'll probably post the Oreos with Nike x ACW* Zoom Vomero 5s because the stuffing reminds me of the wedge in the back.

Wyn hands me one of his green-apple Hi-Chews.

"What are we doing for your birthday tomorrow?" he asks, chomping juicily.

"I'm working," I tell them, grabbing another piece of candy since I've pocketed one for later. "Off at six a.m., home by seven."

"Bet," says Wyn, rubbing his hands together. "Birthday breakfast."

I both hate and love Wyn. He didn't forget my birthday last year either, even though I'd moved in the week before. Kid baked brownies for me. With sprinkles. And a candle. It was adorable.

Chapter 2

As a work shift goes, ten p.m. to six a.m. is ungodly.

I make fifteen dollars an hour. It's both more and less than you'd think. Obviously the salary isn't what enticed me. Come to think of it, I couldn't tell you why I applied here. Only that I needed a job. It was a few weeks after I dropped out and I still lived at my mom's. I'd left some terrible New Year's party in Brooklyn Heights where everybody wouldn't stop talking about how "revelatory" the first semester of college was. Or else how "galvanizing." Ten-dollar words these ballsacks were bandying around as if we weren't raiding this chick's parents' liquor cabinet like we were still in high school.

I Irish goodbyed Randall, my best friend since middle school, who was home from Tufts. He'd texted me to come through as though it hadn't been since literal graduation day that we'd stopped talking for no reason beyond how we didn't really like each other that much. It was freezing that night too, and I was walking for forever trying to decide whether I was more drunk than high when I stopped in for a cup of coffee. There was a HELP WANTED sign posted for a cashier, and I figured if wandering around a bodega stoned was the one activity I was always up for, I might as well get paid for it. Cut to now. A full year and change later. Honestly, it scares me the way I end up living out the aftermath of decisions I don't remember making.

I glance around the store, then scan the CCTV monitors to the left of the lottery tickets for a grainy aerial view. I try to see it from the eyes of a customer. This used to be one of my favorite delis, but on some nights I feel the panic rise in my chest and I want to tear the skin off my arms. Every hour is interminable. I try not to check the time.

11:52.

Shit.

I count seconds (28,800 of them in an eight-hour shift), and I can't stop tapping a quarter on the counter or jogging my foot when I'm on the stool.

Be where your feet are.

That's what my mom says when I'm forecasting—or bugging out about the future. I'm supposed to let an ice cube melt in my hand or flick a rubber band around my wrist so I can, you know, snap out of it, but I don't do either. I let the circles spin.

"It's bad luck," says Mrs. Kim, nodding darkly at my restless foot. "All the good fortune escapes."

"Sorry."

I focus on keeping calm until she leaves for the back office. She gave me a strawberry ice-cream mochi for my birthday, so I'm trying to seem upbeat.

I watch another video. It's a web series called *Watershed*, about the most important moments of entrepreneurs' lives. The last one was about a nineteen-year-old millionaire who disrupted the salad industry from her dorm room, and as the next video cues up—with stats about how this creative's "street art" sells for $140,000 a piece at auction—I get a searing, acrid sensation in my throat. I know this asshole. It's that dipshit Cruzo. Yeah, *that* Cruzo. Back when I knew him in the eighth grade, his name was Salvatore Caruso and he had a spine disorder or someshit, so we called him Scolio. Whatever. Kids are mean, and it's not like they didn't try to call me Pube until I bounced a few heads off some walls.

In any case, a couple of us watched *Wild Style*, that graffiti movie from the eighties, on literal VHS, which an older brother or uncle had, and we were obsessed. We would catch tags on everything. We couldn't go into a bathroom without taking Sharpies in there and tagging over each other's names. I used to write *esco* for Pablo Escobar the drug kingpin, since he was a badass and at thirteen I lacked imagination. Plus, *esco*'s real pretty to write, which is more than you can say for *Neruda*. *N*'s are hard. Mine were these pregnant hunchbacks.

I wasn't in any danger of being good at it. I wasn't ever going to be a Jester, Zephyr, Lee Quiñones, Dondi White, or those later art dudes like REAS and KAWS, but watching this toy Cruzo is excruciating. He's shameless. I hate-watch while he keeps his face covered in a bandanna and refuses to reveal what his crew, ACDB, stands for because he's an outlaw and the vandal squad is after him. I'll tell you what ACDB means; it means all-city dickbags. A name I made up when we were high as shit at Rosario's on Orchard, which will tell you how much of a joke it was.

It's demoralizing when wins have nothing to do with talent. Take Daniel Dalton. Her mom was that model Oliver, who was famous in the nineties for having a shaved head with a cobra tattoo on it. She opened a skate shop on Crosby that me and my friends hung out at. We didn't go to the same school (naturally Daniel Dalton went to Dalton), but she and I used to be cool on some "What's up?" shit except that stopped when she got an Oscar nomination for a short she made "ironically" on a shitty camcorder. Meanwhile her dad's family's so loaded they own that one ivory building in Midtown that swoops up in a curve.

You should have seen me when she lost to a Japanese woman who made a movie about people in an old folks' home run by robots. I was so hyped. F trust fund kids for real.

Because if I had piles of allowance and parent support to "make art," I'd be up to my nipples in sculpture or "found work" or whatever it's called when you throw a bunch of crap you picked up off the sidewalk into a white box gallery. In a few years I'd have awards coming out of my ears too.

Not that that's what I want to do. In fact, I have unequiv-
ocally zero idea what the hell to pursue. I remember the
guidance counselor in high school, Ms. Miranda, inquired
about it sophomore year. Her eyes were concerned, her
head was tilted, she'd punctuate her more salient points
with these little touches to the back of my hand, but all I
could hear was white noise. Where there should have been
aspiration seeds blooming or urgent hopes detonating, all
I had in my head was a pulsing asterisk. To this day I have
no inkling as to what I care about the most. I care about
everything equally until I care about so many things I get
overwhelmed and care about nothing at all. When it comes
to the single thing I want to focus the entire rest of my life
on, it's a muscle I don't know how to flex. As if I'm a lightning bug that forgot how to turn its ass on.

"If money weren't an issue, what's the one thing you'd
do for free?" she'd asked as I was leaving.

Yeah, right. Like anyone does anything for free.

A cluster of regulars file in one after another. I try to
guess who they are from the puffy coats, hats, and scarves.
Most of the time I get it right, and I can always tell from
their purchases. The desi dude with the redheaded wife gives
me this nod to note we're on the same team. He reliably buys
two tallboys of Beck's at eight in the morning, but only on
Tuesdays when his wife isn't with him. The Black vegan
chick with a septum ring who subsists near-exclusively
on coconut ice cream no matter the season. And the curly-
haired girl with glasses who is the only other human Gusto

the cat will say hi to gets cigarettes and milk but only some-times. There's the old guy who cops a different Amy's frozen meal every night but never more than one. Plus, the bearded man with bright blue eyes and a black wire cart who buys so many actual groceries I want to tell him about the super-market four blocks over. I only know a few of their names, and they sure as hell don't know mine. You'd think there'd be a word for it. That city-living intimacy where you know the minutia of their routines, rituals, and clothes but absolutely nothing else.

Sometimes I've seen Mr. Kim give Koreans a discount. Nothing outlandish, but he never cuts a deal to this one kid who speaks Korean and does the deep bow and everything, and I swear it's because he's covered in tattoos and his ears are gauged.

"You okay?" Mr. Kim asks before he goes around back at about one. I nod. He usually stays in his office or else goes home to sleep, but he never tells me when he leaves. I'm forced to behave as though he's constantly clocking me. It's smart. How I'd play it as a boss. I put the space heater by my feet on blast because this is when the real party starts.

At three a.m. I buy myself chocolate-covered macadamia nuts for my birthday. Then create an eye-catching pyramid of seasonal heart-shaped candy at the front of the store. I'll have to mark them half price this time tomorrow and briefly consider bringing one to my mom. But my general opinion is that my birthday cancels out her Valentine's Day, which is why sons are trash.

I won't give Alice, who's saved in my phone as Alice (Tinder), anything. She's the only one I'm seeing with any regularity, but I knew from the red wine she sent back on our first date—that she *ordered at a diner*—that it's not going anywhere. Get this. She once told me she hates flowers and babies. Who hates babies? They're mysterious tiny envoys from the other side that smell of powder-fresh sunshine.

Time crawls to a standstill at five a.m., and I can hear a staticky pitch in my ears. I used to think it was tinnitus or a by-product of too-loud headphones until Miggs told me it's the sound of blood moving in your body. Apparently you can hear your own blood and organs shift inside of you. The blood is higher pitched than the organs, and the whole thing blows my mind. Thinking about what's happening in the inside of your head while you're thinking about the inside of your head is exactly what I don't need to think about when I'm by myself. Man, I hate having me for company.

I need something to happen.

Anything.

I snap the rubber band around my wrist.

Hard.

Then in a rhythm.

Ha-ppy birth-day to me.

The Stevie Wonder version since it's more festive.

Ha-ppy birth-day to me.

Happy biiiiirthday . . .

A girl walks in.

Rushes in actually.

Her chest heaves as if she's sprinted the last few blocks. Her sleeves are pulled over her hands, and she draws them close to her face to blow. She's got her hood up but no hat or scarf. Her jacket is a Supreme North Face collab from a few years ago, but at best it's a shell. She may as well be wearing a shower curtain. She looks right at me with huge brown eyes and starts, which startles me. It doesn't occur to either of us that the other is real. She's got to be freezing.

The girl up-nods so I up-nod back as the hair on the back of my neck stands on high alert. As she shuffles down the aisle, I notice that she's trailed by a long train of fabric.

Chapter 3

I watch the girl on four small screens. Late-night bodega visitors are often mysterious, and this one is no exception. I'm loopy enough that I wonder if I've willed her to appear. I'm not a tinfoil-hat paranormal goon like Miggs, but there is this thing that happened to me in sixth grade. I was bored out of my mind and channeling every ounce of my mental energy to tell—no, compel—Mr. Miller in biology to sit down and miss his chair. You should have seen my face when it happened. That split second made me believe in God, UFOs, ghosts, and reincarnation all at once. This dude goes to sit and misses. At the last second he grabs his desk with both hands and crashes into the seat with a bang that rings out like a shot. We laughed in the moment, but it was that surprised laughter where you're confused about whether or not something bad is happening. I was roaring because I thought I was a freakshow psychic spoonbender.

I don't know what this girl's story is, but she's definitely not from the neighborhood. She passes cleaning supplies, toilet paper, coffee filters, and garbage bags—anything you'd need for a nearby apartment—and heads straight for the snacks. She's walking carefully, and I see that her shoes are shiny white boots that are split, cloven in front like a pig's hoof. Beneath her oversize jacket is a Morticia Addams–type dress with jagged spikes on the tail. She could easily play the villain in a retro space-action movie.

No question she's attractive. I don't need to look at the rest of her to know that. It's the way she carries herself. It's the same way you can tell when a group of girls are hot as a mass. Hot laughter is a thing too. The hotter the group of girls, the more seductive their laughter. Sure, the laughter can be annoying or scary, intimidating maybe, but that's its own thing.

She keeps twitchily checking her phone and looking over her shoulder, but by the time she positions herself in front of the ice cream, she's locked in. Our ice cream selection is captivating. I'm personally responsible for orders, so I should know.

Whatever her provenance, I'm a fan. She peers through the glass for flavors instead of leaving the door hanging open. My mom calls this noonchi, which is Korean for "situational awareness" or "considerateness." People who lack it keep their backpacks on in crowded trains and refuse to slow down when they're walking behind old people. Which is to say they're assholes. This girl has noonchi. She's polite.

When she unloads her haul in front of me, it's highly respectable. She's probably stoned.

Salt and vinegar kettle crisps. This is the best flavor hands down. Sweet Maui Onion being the runner-up (Hawaiian brand only—not Deep River or Kettle. Sorry).

Sour gummy cola bottles, which to me is tartness overkill with the chips. As someone who's housed an entire pound of Sour Patch Kids at the movies after salt and vinegar chips, I can testify to this.

Artisanal oatmeal chocolate chip cookie dough ice cream. (No Halo Top fake-out garbage.)

Peanut butter chips *and* **white chocolate chunks** from the baking aisle, and this is where my heart skips a beat, because she's also managed to dig up a squeeze bottle of **Magic Shell**, the chocolate that hardens when you put it on ice cream. We only stock a few bottles because the dairy-free organic off-brand sells better even though its hardening capabilities are suspect.

A resealable sleeve of sliced provolone. The most unobtrusive, approachable, yet classy snacking cheese in my book.

"Hi," she says in a surprisingly raspy voice.

"Hey," I say back, ringing her up and bagging. "Strong selection. Valentine's Day party?"

"Ha." She laughs dryly. "Very much the opposite . . ." She reaches over to pull the candy out of the bag. "Plastic hurts my heart . . . ," she says, smoothing the bag on the counter. "I'll carry it out."

She smiles quickly. Ruefully.

Ugh. She's probably throwing a breakup party.

"Sorry," I stammer. "I mean, not for the bag, although apologies to the planet. . . . Sorry for mentioning Valentine's Day. I don't know your situation. Or life."

"Oh," she says, and smiles, actually seeing me now. "It's fine. I'm not sad about it. At all." She tilts her head at the food. "It's a fucking celebration, tbqh."

I can't believe she *tee-bee-que-aytch'd* me.

"Oh. Kay."

She laughs.

And then, because I'm this guy, "Can I make a suggestion?"

She eyes me. Leery. As though she senses my cooped-up feral energy and has zero idea where this is headed. "Sure."

"I admire your snack choices across the board. However, if you're doing salt and vinegar—which is an excellent way to go," I begin. "Are you completely satisfied to go sour-sour with the cola bottles? Just putting it out there that we have regular bottles, twin cherries . . . We also carry gummy frogs if you want that mallowy toothsomeness with a hit of surreptitious peach—or, and I know this is wild, but hear me out. . . ." I hold my hands up. "Would you be open to going sour cola but pairing it with Zapp's Voodoo for the sweetness even though I can't tell if the chips are somehow racist. . . ."

ohmygodstoptalking.

She tilts her head and furrows her brow. There's something

about all the makeup and this shimmery shit on her face that makes her appear CGI under the light. Objectively attractive but giving the impression that if you wiped the layer off it'd be smooth like an egg. That there'd be no features underneath.

"Sir," she says. "Hold the phone. Do you mean to inform me that those Haribo frogs are peach flavored?"

Hold the phone?

Okay. She's super cute.

I nod, clear my throat. "Yeah."

"Surreptitious is right," she says. "Thought they were apple."

I want to be friends with this person.

"Plus, little-known fact: The green gummy bears are strawberry," I tell her.

Why am I still talking? I want to cringe until my spine collapses into itself. *"Little-known fact: The green gummy bears are strawberry"*?

If sentences could reinstate your virginity, this would be a strong contender.

"Well, blow me down," she says, seemingly without judgment, and then hits the counter with a balled-up fist like a gavel. "Even still, I'm doubling down on sour-sour."

"Power," I rhyme.

Jesus.

She laughs and checks her pocket. Then she gives her skintight cave-witch chain-mail dress a hurried pat-down.

Her fingernails are painted the exact dark blue of her

dress with two of them chipped, and her thumbnail is broken to the quick. She doesn't have a purse, not even a tiny one, which is a surefire sign she's not from here. Like when dudes on the train wear adidas Sambas or Aldo sneakers—definite tourists.

"Shit," she says, and scratches her eyebrow. Then she sighs.

"Wallet?"

"Yeah," she says.

I watch her glance down at her food. Deflated.

"Apple Pay?" she asks brightly, holding her phone out.

"I don't think that's a thing with us." I glance at the register. "Do you know how that shit works?"

"You know, I've never successfully used it before in my life. Do I wave the phone over a reader or . . . ?"

"Yeah, I don't know." I shrug. "Retina scan?"

"Man," she says. "Buzzkill."

Then she shivers violently, blowing on her hands again.

"Cold?"

She grins at me and raises her brows.

"Yeah, my powers of deduction are legendary."

She laughs. "What are the warning signs of hypothermia?" she says, hugging herself tight.

My jaw hurts just looking at her chattering teeth. Her eyes are closed as if to conserve energy. "I think I'm just going to walk toward the light if that's cool," she says.

"Okay." I spring into action. "Here's what's going to happen," I tell her, coming around the counter, headed for the coffee machines. I pour a cup and hand it to her. "On me."

"Thanks," she says, drinking it black, grimacing, and then adding copious amounts of sugar and cream from the cooler. She smiles at me self-consciously and then adds even more sugar and cream and then takes another sip.

"You're a lifesaver," she says, smiling.

"Are you ready for the next part?"

"Go on," she says.

"It's kind of wild," I warn her. "You ready?"

I grab the twenty-dollar space heater from behind the counter, kick off my slippers, step into my boots, and walk the heater as close to her as the cord allows.

"Whoa," she says appreciatively. "Game changer."

"Right?"

Okay. Up close she's really, very, extra cute.

"Man, this is easily the best part of my evening . . . morning?" She shrugs, inspects her thumb, and then sticks it in her mouth. "Thank you."

I pick up the ice cream and the rest of her provisions from the counter to put them back, but the prospect of disbanding such a solid assemblage doesn't seem right.

"You know what?" I tell her. "Go ahead and keep this." I gesture to the chips and candy.

I know. Crazy. But I already knew I liked this girl when I wouldn't let her see my house shoes.

"Noooo," she says in this theatrical way, eyes bugged, thumb still lodged in her teeth.

"Yeessssss." I hand the Magic Shell to her. How could I bogart such joy?

"No way." She takes another sip of coffee.

"Seriously." I get it. New York tests you on certain days. "You've clearly traveled a long way . . . possibly many, many light-years." I nod at her dress.

She laughs as I wave my hand magnanimously, channeling Brando as Vito Corleone forgiving a loan. I narrow my eyes for effect, puffed up by my own generosity.

What's sixty short of rent when you can be a hundred?

The girl observes me. Intently. I give her a look like, *I know*. She sighs. We're the exact same type of tired.

"Oh!" she exclaims. "No, wait!"

She checks a back pocket on her jacket and fishes out a credit card and slams it on the counter.

"Yes!" she proclaims.

It's a Black Amex. The type rappers talk about and warlords never mention. The kind with no interest and no limit.

"Thank God." She loops her arm in mine and ushers me back up to the register, resuming her position as the customer-lady who has her shit together.

I ring her up again, arm buzzing lightly from her contact. She swipes the card reader, which beeps in protest.

"It's a chip, I think." Meanwhile I've never seen a Black Card in real life.

Who is this girl?

"Oh," she says, taking another sip. "Well, shit, now I have performance anxiety."

"Here." I reach over and hit yes before reinserting it. I catch the name: *Carolina Suarez.*

Carolina Suarez . . . about my age, with a Black Card.

Socialite? Gallerina? Heiress?

As I hand her the receipt our fingers touch.

Bzzzzzt.

"Let me ask you . . ."

"Shoot," she says.

"How many miles did you travel last year?" There's no way the Black Amex Centurion is a better deal than the Chase Sapphire Reserve.

"Is there a mansplain deluge in my forecast?"

"Okay, fair enough." I stop.

"Oh, come on," she says, cracking a smile. "The suspense might kill me."

This and snacks are my wheelhouse. My legerdemain, my alleyway. If you're not scamming as much money as humanly possible from institutions, are you even living? Weird flex, sure, but one time I stayed on hold with the cable company for an hour because they didn't give us Showtime for the month they said they would. I made them throw in HBO and a free ground line. I know there's a card out there that's a better deal than a Black Amex. You don't go into mountains of debt without fostering a healthy obsession with credit cards that might save your ass *if* you qualified for them.

"So, you do travel a lot?"

"A lot," she confirms.

"You fly with one airline?"

"Sure . . ."

"Delta? American?" She looks too classy to be on that Southwest mayhem tip. Virgin maybe, but it's all the same now with the buyouts.

She clears her throat then, tugging her hair out from the back of her Windbreaker. It's long, in this bewitching shade of almost neon red. The effect is spellbinding. She reminds me of the Little Mermaid.

That's when I realize who she is.

Whoa.

I'm so dumb.

Carolina.

Suarez.

Carolina Suarez is Leanna Smart.

My heart drops into my asshole.

Leanna Smart is in the store. My store. As in, the Disney star who went from a kids' show about a family of rich orphaned witches trapped in a maze to a mega popstar. When he was younger, my brother was obsessed with her Christmas Special, which they'd run into July.

"JetBlue?" I ribbit after what has to be an hour.

I attempt to swallow.

"You don't fly commercial, do you?" I ask her. She knows that I've made her but I'm not letting on.

"I mean . . . I have . . . ," she says as the blood thunders into my ears.

She gathers her groceries, and I take a half step back.

"So . . ."

"So?"

Whatever. When am I going to see her again?

"So, do private jets really cost $300,000 to fly internationally? I've always wondered."

She laughs. "Why are you so obsessed with money?"

"Isn't everybody?"

"I guess so," she says. "Even the ones who don't talk about it."

"*Especially* the ones who don't talk about it."

She goes silent.

"So, it's money and snacks with you."

"I contain multitudes."

"Sounds crowded," she says, smiling to dull the sting.

"We get by." I smile back. Wide.

Leanna Smart cocks her head, sizing me up. "Wait, don't *I* know *you* from somewhere?"

It's easily the most surreal question a famous person can ask you.

Then she claps her hands.

"You're *that* kid."

I hate this part.

Chapter 4

It's the worst.

"You're sad boy."

I can't believe Leanna Smart's seen that stupid thing.

Okay. I'll come right out and say it. I've had a small brush with fame. Teeny-tiny. Completely irrelevant in the grand scheme, but it was A Thing That Occurred.

I was Internet famous. Plus, it was the worst kind of Internet famous—meme famous—for precisely two seconds. (It's not fifteen minutes the way Warhol said; it's two seconds.) My two seconds happened in the final month of senior year in high school.

It was dumb. Beyond dumb. It wasn't a testament to any talent or intelligence or any singular or preternatural acumen. And yeah, now I'm stalling because I'm too embarrassed to admit what it was.

I was asking my now ex-girlfriend Heather to prom.

Yes, some might call it a promposal. I know. So ridiculous, but this was a few years ago. Heather was big into events and special occasions, so it was kind of a no-brainer. But the promposal was fake news since it was completely staged and required a week of practice as well as a specially built camera rig and an entire set that the AV club built. It was shot in a single take from my point of view in a packed cafeteria. You get the picture. Totally stereotypical high school scene, noise, cliques, sly acts of emotional terrorism. As the camera pans, scanning the crowd, it stops on Heather. Boom. Silence. Everyone falls away as the room fills with bright pink light, and trippy blooming flowers festoon the walls.

It was intended to capture that thunderbolt of first love in the corniest way imaginable, and it was a huge pain in the ass because sixty kids had to duck and crawl under the camera so they wouldn't be in the shot or cast shadows on the flower projections, but the end result was frickin' magic.

Right at the most poignant moment, when I basically have hearts shooting out of my eyes—the camera punches in on me—and I ask her to prom. Of course, she says no and the cafeteria becomes a cafeteria again and that's when you see the look on my face. Total devastation.

I know what you're thinking. That I completely played myself because I was publicly rejected, but honestly I didn't care. Everybody at school knew me and Heather had been together since sophomore year and I needed the extracurricular AV club credit for college, so I was pumped.

We filmed it, put it up on YouTube. Except what I didn't

figure was that it would be viewed eleven million times. People just loved the ridiculous look on my face. I was gassed when it reached fifty thousand, but then it was randomly remixed to an emo medley a few months later on Reddit, which prompted a supermodel to repost it as the final note on a gruesome breakup. It was only a matter of time before it was added to the GIF keyboard under "heartbreak" and became a GIF sticker on Instagram stories, and then it was a wrap. My fat head became the new bawling emoji. I was on the morning show on CBS for six minutes. I had to wake up at 5:15 in the morning, and my mom tried to make me put on a suit, but we settled on this stupid sweater instead. They sent a black car, which was cool, and to this day it's the main reason I randomly have so many Instagram followers for an infrequently populated snack and sneaker feed that I pivoted from my personal account.

Needless to say I didn't figure out how to monetize it, but that's what I mean by two seconds. If you don't immediately get an Ellen segment and a book deal, you're toast.

Still, you wouldn't believe who recognizes you from a thing like that.

"Yeah." I nod. "Sad boy. What every dude aspires to be remembered for in his twenties."

She smiles, peeling away the seal of her ice cream without taking her eyes off me.

"I can't tell if you look the same in real life."

"Let me ask you this," I venture. "Do *you* enjoy it when people talk about you to your face with their face?"

Leanna Smart laughs. It's an inelegant bark from the bottom of her throat and thoroughly joyful.

"I'm sorry," she says, not sounding sorry. "It never occurred to me that you were a real person. Plus, you're much taller in the flesh. Not nearly as *strapping* on my screen." Leanna Smart waggles her eyebrows like a vaudeville act.

Seriously, who is this girl? But also, is Leanna Smart flirting with me?

"D'you have a spoon I can borrow?"

I reach for the plastic ones under the till.

No, idiot. That's delusional. Abort. She just wants your flatware.

"You got a metal one? For chunk mining?"

I shake my head.

In truth I do, since Mrs. Kim only eats with steel utensils, but they're in the back and I don't want to leave my post. More than anything I'm wondering why Leanna Smart would punk me on her reality prank show at this time of night. I wonder if the crew's outside or if they've patched into the security cams.

"Here," I tell her, handing over a pair of wooden chopsticks and a plastic spoon. "For spelunking."

She smiles at me.

"Great word," she says. "*Spelunk*. It suits what it is— rocks falling into water and echoing in a cave. *Spelunk*." The word rolls around her mouth marble-like and drops on the *K*. Leanna Smart's mouth. Leanna Smart!

"Question?" she asks me.

"Shoot."

"From whence do your forebears hail?"

"Excuse me?" I laugh.

Who talks this way?

"I guess what nationalities—plural, I'm figuring—are you?"

I got to hand it to her for wording. Usually people ask me where I'm "*really* from," as if I'm going to say East Timor and not the Triborough. I'm told it's my eyes; they're this trippy hazel.

"Mom's from the city." She's been here since she was a teen.

"This city?"

"Yeah, New York. What other city is there really?"

"Fair," she says.

Wow, am I flirting?

"Dad's from Jersey, now lives in Queens. Mom's Korean, dad's Pakistani."

Leanna Smart makes to perch on the side of the low display refrigerator with the cut fruit and spies the NO SITTING! sign in Sharpie and eyes me. I shrug, so she pops a squat. You gotta figure there's a level of fame where cautionary signs don't apply.

"What about you?"

"Los Angeles," she says. "Well, outside of LA, really. Um, half Mexican. Oh, actually, I'm trying not to say that anymore—half. I *am* Mexican," she nods deliberately.

"Like straight Indio for many, many generations until my great-grandparents mixed it up. Plus—see." She raises a finger. "It's about addition and not subtraction—I'm a whole bunch of different shades of white."

"So, eggshell . . ."

"Ecru." She doesn't skip a beat. "Linen, chalk, and, would you believe, Welsh on my mother's side?"

Dang. Her brain is fast. And I love what she said about half. I'm stupefied. Ensorcelled. I am both mesmerized *and* apprehensive.

Addition, addition, addition.

Her gleaming smile is uniform *and* white. Shit. I wonder if I should have my teeth bleached.

"Do you have a trash can back there?" She approaches me, and I swallow audibly. At this range, a physical audit of her is involuntary and immediate. Her forehead is broad and her nose is rounder than in pictures, which is a strange thing to acknowledge about someone else's appearance. She hands me her chopsticks wrapper. Aside of the wads of cosmetics, I can't deduce what it is about her appearance that makes her famous. If there are biological determinants buried in her genes. Her face is an angular cohesion of panels that I've only ever seen blown up for posters, but in life— I'm not kidding—it's a perfect heart.

Leanna Smart's eyes are wide set. Cartoon fawnish. Greenish and ringed in darker brown, and I cannot tell what distinguishes her from the rest of us. Only that she's beautiful. At least *I think* she's beautiful. I want to say that attraction is empirical. Objective. But on some level you can't unknow who she is. Even my mom knows Leanna Smart.

Humans are weird. The way hierarchies are so important to us.

"While you're assessing me," she says. "Did you know that goats have rectangular pupils?"

Shit. She knows I'm staring at her.

Shit. She can see me.

Shit.

I shake my head briskly.

"My SAT prep tutor told me that right before he tried to get in my pants."

"What?" That snaps me out of it. "Whoa. I'm sorry." I don't know what else you're supposed to say to that. I bust open a Kinder Bueno for the distraction, to know what to do with my hands. "Want me to beat his ass?"

"Yes, please."

"Did he get fired?"

"Close," she says. "He became a very famous writer on an award-winning show. He's rich now."

I hand her a piece of chocolate, which she lets hang from her mouth like a cigar while she peels off the glassine wrapper from the chocolate sauce to dress her ice cream. "Of course he's successful; he was an unrepentant liar," she says with her mouth full. "Wouldn't you know goats weren't even on the verbal?"

"I am definitely beating his ass."

"Honestly, if I hadn't taken a hit out on him already, I'd allow it."

I can't believe I'm eating junk food with Leanna Smart.

"This is a good store," she says, ripping into the bag of peanut butter chips with her teeth and sprinkling it into her pint. Shit is getting precarious between the sauce and the chunks. "I didn't know you guys were twenty-four hours."

Wait. Does she live around here?

Just then her tongue sticks out of the corner of her mouth in deep concentration, and when she grabs another coffee cup and makes me a portion, the circuitry in my pelvis twangs.

She comes up to my side behind the counter to hand it to me and then stays there.

It is worth noting that Carolina Suarez IRL smells of honeyed flowers, heavy, juicy stone fruit, tobacco, and chocolate. It feels like staring into a ruby so big you forget where you are.

"Cheers," she says, raising her tub.

I raise my cup. "Cheers."

We chew in silence as I intermittently remind myself to breathe so I don't pass out.

"Happy Valentine's Day," she says.

And then we got married.

If only.

Chapter 5

"Chillchillchillchill," says Miggs, waving his hand dramatically. "There's no way."

When I get home they're waiting for me. It's barely seven, so they've set their alarms for way earlier than usual, which is dumb cute. On our crappy IKEA table is a small tower of donuts, one with rainbow sprinkles and a candle stuck in it. Around them are bacon, egg, and cheeses wrapped in foil that appear to be worshipping at the donut altar.

"Fine. Four-point-eight-two," declares Wyn, unwrapping his sandwich.

"It's *Price Is Right* rules, dumbass." Miggs rolls his eyes. The best way to describe Miggs is if you took Bruno Mars and inflated him three times bigger and filled him with wet cement.

Price Is Right rules means if you go over in your guess you lose automatically.

"Forfeit," says Tice, who grabs his sandwich, pats my shoulder, and takes it to his room. He usually sleeps until noon.

"I know that," counters Wyn. "But I'm universally beloved. Plus, I talk to every single one of my drivers."

"Four-point-four-even," says Dara, who's not even trying.

I add bacon to my glazed yeast donut. It's the only way to do it. "You need everything to be on some combo shit like you," she says, eyeing my food. It's true. Improvements are improvements. I take a picture before biting into it.

Miggs nods and calls out the rest of ours. "Pab, you're four-five-seven, Wynn's four-eight-two, and I'm four-six-six."

We pull out our phones.

This is how we are. Whenever we have a spare second, we take wild bets. The terms are for one million dollars and eternal bragging rights. Until the next bet. We've got a billion wagers going. Who'll be the first to get a standing reservation at Rao's, the Italian restaurant where rumor has it you have to wait for a mob boss to die before you can get in. Or who's going to be the first to host *Saturday Night Live and* be the musical guest. Then there's the important stuff, like who's going to get Instagram verified first.

I get my four-five-seven. "Hell yeah."

"Look at this prick," yells Miggs, pounding me on the back and handing me a blunt. It's pretty much common knowledge that he sells weed. Only weed because of his ethics, and he barely drinks or smokes. Birthdays, anniversaries, special occasions only. His routine is unwavering: work, gym, then comedy shows. There's something mad bro-ey about his setup, and if he were white he'd look high-key MAGA. But he's Puerto Rican and Dominican, which is why he's a hothead. The inner conflict he says is like being Trini *and* Jamaican.

Of course I'm still thinking of Leanna Smart. Not solely because I'm nursing a food baby from the mounds of crap I ate earlier, but because now that I'm back in the atmosphere of my home planet, filled with ramshackle plastic furniture and these loud assholes, I'm desperate to savor what that felt like. Those moments. Standing next to each other by the heater talking.

How her hair brushed my chest as she passed me to leave. How when she faltered briefly at the door and turned around, I thought it was my cue. To hug her or . . . or . . . or . . . And then, just as I was about to ask for her number, I chickened out entirely.

Truth is, and this makes no sense, I feel a little heartbroken.

"Dude, you're a monster," says Miggs to his girlfriend, sending my thoughts cratering back to this shit hole.

I watch as Dara adds mayonnaise to her breakfast. Huge lashings from a squirt bottle.

"Don't call me 'dude,'" says Dara, who we always call "dude." She then duffs him on the arm. Mayonnaise on a bacon, egg, and cheese is the whitest thing in the world, but then again, I've seen Miggs put mayo *and* ketchup on fried rice. You can tell a lot from a person by their condiment abuse.

Wynn reveals his Uber score. Four-three-three.

"Wooooooooooow," we chorus. That's embarrassing.

"This is so stupid," says Dara. "Who even cares what Uber score you have? It doesn't make the fares cheaper. Besides, if you were a real New Yorker you'd hail a yellow cab like a decent human being."

"Nah. Fuck a medallion," says Miggs. "The taxi and limousine commission's crooked."

Dara tosses her trash, kisses Miggs, and pulls on her coat to head to work, a fancy Italian spot in the Financial District that she manages. "Whatever. I'll see you idiots later."

"This shit is so biased," says Wyn, shaking his head. "How can I have a worse score than you?" He points at me.

"Why wouldn't I have a better score than you?"

"I mean, no offense, Pab, but how do you even have a score if your shit is deactivated because none of your cards work?" A greasy grin teases at his lips.

"I mean," chimes in Miggs, kissing his teeth and picking up his ten-pound key ring and strapping it onto his backpack. Miggs walks dogs and has an elaborate system for everything, to where he totes ten different types of treats according to his clients' dietary and emotional needs. "He's got a point, Pab."

Miggs picks up some envelopes from the table by the

door. "Speaking of which," he says, frisbeeing them at me. "You got more bills."

"Man, fuck you guys," I call out as the door slams. When Wyn isn't looking I pick up the mail to toss in my sock drawer with the rest of it.

I may not be in an ideal financial situation, but at least I *keep* the bills. I have every intention of dealing with them. Eventually. But the humiliating thing about my debt is that my Guitar Center credit card is the one that stresses me out most. Especially when you consider what happened. I bought turntables. I know. I know! But, like, they were Technics 1200s, and it's not as if I could let these discontinued joints pass me by. Even if now they're not-so-auspiciously collecting dust under my bed because I sold all my records on Discogs to pay a phone bill.

The worst is that their people have started calling me, and that's way harder to ignore. That makes the debt feel real.

This one guy's name is Harold. Not even a robocall. An actual man named Harold, no last name, telling me the call may be recorded for quality assurance.

"May I speak to Mr. Rind?" says Harold.

The bastard has the gall to pronounce my name right. Rind like India. Not, like, mind. I'm telling you, they know everything.

"Speaking."

"This is Harold from New York National Mutual, and I'm calling about your Guitar Center account that's past due. We're a third-party collections agency. . . ."

I wanted to throw my phone into oncoming traffic. It's so sobering when a person calls, a person who gets up every morning, kisses his spouse on the cheek with coffee breath, and wears a tie to work, whose entire job is to extract money from you.

It's Tice's stupid fault that I have those turntables in the first place. I met Tice at these parties that this kid Benny used to throw at the downstairs part of Palace, which used to be the old Alibi, which was Arca way back in the day. Benny's other hustle was that he ran a pirate radio station that used to squat on 90.1 FM and interrupt this Christian radio show out of Philly. He'd play dancehall and soca so the Bible-thumpers would have to hear about nice cocky and buff pumpums when they least expected it.

He was a riot and we looked up to him until he moved away to Miami, and it was his voice egging me on as we came upon those gleaming beauties. Tice was yammering about authenticity, which started me going about credibility, and then we got to complaining about losers with thumb drives passing themselves off as artists, which is to say that we sounded like every dork who's ever stood in this particular store in the middle of a weekday afternoon. It was a foregone conclusion.

Which brings me to an age-old rule to live and die by: Never go to Guitar Center stoned.

I clean the kitchen a little and pass out. When I wake up it's one p.m. and I've got three voice messages, a bunch of texts, and missed calls from a number I don't recognize. For a second I think I'm dreaming. I bolt out of bed, worried that the Harolds have multiplied to call in unison from different blocked numbers, but that doesn't seem right. Turns out they're from Rain's school, and I assume something terrible has happened. Until I realize the lady on the phone is furious, not concerned. And of course they've been calling my mother for an hour since she's in surgery, and my dad, who stays unreachable. Now they have to settle for me.

"Are you shitting me?" All things considered it's a restrained response. "Okay, okay, I'm sorry. Be right over." Suffice it to say PS 72 on East Fifty-Ninth Street in the city is not where I need to be on my birthday, on my day off, but I pull it together.

When I get there Principal Daley and Ms. Zapruda are certainly not kidding, and to Rain's credit he at least appears remorseful.

"Where is Mrs. Rynde?" asks Daley. He looks like the emoji version of what you'd expect from a principal, early forties, with a squishy ruddy face and a bushy mustache, wearing pleated khaki pants. "It's Rind," I correct him. Force of habit.

"Regardless," he stammers. "Where are your parents? This is a serious infraction, and we're considering expulsion."

"This could be seen as a child pornography issue," says Ms. Zapruda.

"Whoa." I raise both palms to de-escalate. Inciting child

pornography means I'm in well over my head. "No way. They're just . . ." I can't believe I have to say this word in a principal's office. "Dildos."

We all look to Daley's desk.

"Vibrators," corrects Rain, and I swear I almost grab him by the neck and throw him out the window.

"Son, where did you even get these . . . these . . . ?" He can't bring himself to say it.

"Vibrators," supplies Rain again. "And I can't reveal my sources."

On Daley's desk are six white boxes with big fuchsia lettering that reads VIVACE and next to that an unboxed one, also bright pink. It looks as if it's, well, vibrating, since it's so lurid and bright. Daley, for that matter, has taken on a mulberry hue in his face when I look at the vibrators and look back at him. They're expensive. I'm no expert, but you can tell from the packaging that it's probably more than a few hundred dollars of self-pleasure on display.

"He tried to sell one to another eighth grader," says Ms. Zapruda, who has blunt bangs as well as a teeny nose piercing. The piercing makes me think about Ms. Zapruda's life outside of being a social studies teacher in a mid- to low-grade public school. I wonder if her career is going as planned.

"Jesus." I sigh. "I mean, I'm sorry. The thing is my mother's working. She's probably in surgery, and my dad . . . Well, my dad thinks his cell phone is a cancer delivery system for the face, so he prefers to leave it at home."

Principal Daley scrutinizes me, unsure if I'm sassing him.

"Well, there seems to be a severe lack of parenting that's contributing to Rain's behavior," he says.

Yeah, no shit.

"I don't disagree with you, sir." He nods when I say "sir." If he had a tail it would wag. "It's only that I have a full-time job and I've almost saved enough money to go back to school (lies). And without a formal education at the college level I don't think I'll amount to anything (half lies), and if I have to look after my brother on top of that, well, we'll both be doomed (not a lie)."

"Rain's smart," says Ms. Zapruda. Rain smiles at her, flashing his tiny canines. "And while this is by far the stupidest thing he's ever done, we'll have to consider the wishes of the parents of the girl he tried to sell this to. . . ." Ms. Zapruda waves at the vibrators and rolls her eyes. "That said, we'll take your words under consideration, Mr. Rind."

Principal Daley nods sternly.

"He will be suspended for all of next week while we deliberate," he says.

"Got it," I tell them, and say nothing more. I have less-than-fond memories of this sort of thing from the time I got caught catching a tag in the girls' locker room. It wasn't premeditated. And it wasn't on some creeper shit. I wanted to know if I could.

Us Rind boys aren't the best at impulse control.

"Siiiiiiiick," says Rain when we're outside. The kid

flosses on the school steps like he's stoked. "I got the whole week off school. Fuck waking up when it's dark out. So, Pab, what are we gonna do today?"

"What?" I balk. He looks at me mid shoot dance and then freezes. "Are you insane?" I ask him. "Do you have any appreciation for how deep in shit you are? Mom is going to murder you. And she's gonna murder me, and then she's gonna murder dad for not having his goddamned phone on him."

"It's disconnected," says Rain, putting his knee down. "I tried calling him yesterday. See if he wants a vibrator."

"Why would dad want a vibrator?"

"Well, I wasn't going to ask mom. That's gross."

I stare at him.

"Are you caught up in a sex toy smuggling ring or something? How do you have so many? Did you steal them? What's going on? You're thirteen years old. What the hell do thirteen-year-old girls want from a vibrator?"

Between Leanna Smart and this, life is getting really absurd. I look at the sky behind my kid brother and take a deep breath. The worst thing about winter is that it's only 2:30 p.m. and I can see the light dipping.

"Are you in trouble?"

"Nah," he says.

"How much do you owe your dildo plug?"

Seriously, what a sentence.

"Nothing. I bought them with my birthday money. It was a good deal. They retail for two hundred fifty a pop, and I copped them at sixty dollars a piece. Marley's cousin

Jonah stole them from this party he was working." Marley's the girl from the next building over from mom's who's a— no pun intended—thirstbucket for Rain. "They were in gift bags or something."

The one thing I can't fault him for is his resourcefulness.

"So they're new?" Got to admit, I'm impressed. That profit margin is solid.

"Yeah, they're new," says Rain, and then thinks about it. "Ew."

"Damn. I can't believe you're out a thousand dollars' worth of pink sex toys." We start trudging to the subway. "You're never going to get them back. And you're not going to recoup your initial investment."

"What are we gonna do about mom?" he says when we get on the 4. Finally, he has the wherewithal to look scared.

"Don't worry. We'll figure it out."

The truth is, we're finished. It's going to be scorched earth when she gets home, especially if Rain's expelled. I make dinner. Which, to be honest, took a weird turn. I was fashioning a bootleg curry from turkey and potatoes and way too much Everest meat masala when I realized we were out of rice (what Asian runs out of rice?), so I served it over farfalle. Whatever. Most nights Rain eats alone and then puts himself to bed. I should come by more. He's a good kid mostly. Never thrown a party or had girls over. Nothing.

"Are you staying here tonight?" Rain asks over *Dragon Ball Z* reruns, and he looks so hopeful it hurts my stomach. "Yeah, sure." I shrug.

"Awesome," he says, headed for his room. "Mom let me get cookie butter. We can eat that for dessert."

I don't question why he pulls the jar from his bedroom, and we both sit down with that, ice cream and Linden's Butter Crunch cookies that we crush with our spoons.

"I miss dad," he says, and it occurs to me that I do too. It's been a few weeks since we went to see him.

"I can't believe that loser's phone is out." Meanwhile mine is so past overdue that I have a heart attack every time I lose signal thinking they took it away for good.

"Typical," says Rain, letting his ice cream melt into a soup.

"So typical." My kid brother seems subdued. Strangely contemplative. "We'll go see him this week." I nudge him. "Lord knows you'll be free then."

"I'm so dead," he says, and for a second he looks five. The age I was when mom first started working nights.

"Eat your ice cream," I command. Poor bastard could be eating through a straw by the time mom's done with him.

Chapter 6

Mom gets in at a quarter to seven the next morning, and I've got her breakfast on the table when she does. Rain's dead to the world the way convicts conk out like babies once they're caught.

"You're here to collect birthday money, aren't you?" she says, hanging up her jacket.

Spending time with mom's been rough. We barely spoke when I dropped out a year ago, not counting the multiple times she screamed through my closed door. It's only been since Christmas that we properly squashed it. For months it was radio silence until Rain had a meltdown and dad intervened.

"You eat?" she asks me. She looks tired, but she also looks great for her age. It's that Asian skin thing. She doesn't look a day over twenty-five.

"I made pasta." I nod at the table.

"Extortion pasta," she mutters as she goes into her room. She's right, but it's annoying the way she can't let anything slide. When she pads back over she's wearing gray leggings that are strangely the exact same shade as her scrubs. It's as though she spends her entire life in the same washed-out dove color. "Eat," she says, and I nod.

I love my mom best in the early hours after work. She gets real inside her head and quiet and there's a softness to her. It's funny to think how she and I basically work the same hours except she pulls six figures and I don't. She only ever has dinner foods for breakfast. Always with kimchi.

"What happened at Rain's school?" she asks, piling the pasta with chopsticks onto a spoon. I hand her the hot sauce, which she applies liberally. "They wouldn't leave me details on voicemail, and school was out when I called them back."

"It was stupid," I say, deciding how to play it. "He was trying to sell . . ." I avert my eyes. "Sneakers at school and they thought he'd stolen them but he hadn't."

She puts her chopsticks down.

"I mean, *he* didn't steal them." I take a forkful as a stalling tactic. "Someone in the distribution chain may have stolen them."

"Sneakers?" She eyes me dubiously. "Did he pull a heist at Champs? Your brother is not a criminal mastermind."

Screw it. I'm done lying to this woman. This isn't even my L.

"Okay, fine." I swallow and take a deep breath. "He was selling vibrators."

A creaking half hiccup erupts from her throat as she stops chewing.

"Excuse me?" Mom blinks rapidly.

"They were part of some gift bag that some party promoter was off-loading, and . . ."

"Wait," she says, and raises her hand, like, *I need a minute.* Mom shakes her head the way cartoons do when the anvil hits them. "He was selling what?"

I take a deep breath.

"Actually," she says. "I heard you. Wow. I really wish I hadn't."

We sit in silence. Her hands on the table. Mine in my lap. Nobody saying or eating anything for a good stretch. She takes a long draw of water.

And then, get this, she smiles.

"Vibrators?" Mom piles more bow ties onto her spoon.

"Vibrators."

"No wonder Daley's message was so strained."

"Mom, he was purple." I picture his bug-eyed look and the chronic throat clearing.

"They were purple?"

"No. The vibrators were pink."

"Pink?" Mom's smile cracks wider.

"Pink."

"Jeez." She sits back in her chair. "And you had to go deal with it?"

"Yeah." She's taking this remarkably well. "Daley was purple, the vibrators were pink, and then there was Ms.

Zapruda, who I swear to god Rain was flirting with while we were in there."

She puts her forehead in her hands.

"What am I going to do with him?" she asks genuinely.

"Well, he's suspended for a week while they figure out how to handle it, but I don't get the impression they're going to kick him out."

"He's so sneaky." She spits the word out like a seed. Then a short burst of air. A snort. I look up from my plate and realize she's laughing.

"How do you even anticipate that?" she hoots. "Never in a million years. Vibrators?"

"Yup." I'd be pretty happy to never hear my mother say that word again.

"Vibrators!" she exclaims one more time, joggling her head, chuckling, then returning to her food.

The whole thing's unbelievable. Mom would have sent me to Korea if I'd done something like that. That was her favorite threat when I was growing up. As if sending me to a boarding school in a country with triple-fried honey chicken, where the Wi-Fi's forty times faster, would be punishment. Never mind that me and Rain have been begging to go our entire lives. If anything, the fact that we've never visited Korea or Pakistan feels like a parental failing you could lodge with the embassy or some shit. I think about how if she sent Rain to Seoul he'd have the best time. Hanging out with all our cousins who we follow on Insta. Seriously, Rain *is* sneaky. That little bastard's like Teflon.

"If it helps, I can be around more," I offer. At this the air's sucked out of the room as she closes her eyes. Shoulders caving. Our nice moment is over.

"Where you need to be is back in school." Her jaw sets. "On that note," she begins. "Do you know what you're wearing to your meeting on March first at two thirty p.m.?"

I know what she's doing. Repeating the date and time as if I'd forget.

"Yes, I know what I'm wearing to my meeting on March first. At two thirty p.m."

"Pablo," she says testily.

I wonder how long it'll take before she brings up her boss, Dr. Houlihan. . . .

"You know what it took to get you that meeting. . . ."
And there it is.

"I had to ask Dr. Houlihan to talk to Connie and . . ."
It's all so predictable.

"Mom."

"You promised you'd go. That you'd make an effort and hear them out."

"Them" is the estimable academic adviser, one Mr. Joey Santos, who's tight with Dr. Houlihan's wife, who's on the board of admissions at Five Points University of New York. As if a school that advertises next to Cellino & Barnes on the subway is worth pulling strings for. Not to be an ingrate, but Columbia, Yale, these are the places you want juice with, but CUNY? Still, we can discuss wardrobe options if it means getting through this meal without a fight. Anything to get her off my back despite how resentful I am that she doesn't think I'll be able to get back into NYU.

"I'll wear a sweater," I tell her finally.

"Thank you."

"Under a tux. I'll even wear glasses to look extra smart. And a stethoscope around my neck."

Sighing, she walks over to the kitchen and returns with a Korean pear and a paring knife. When I was a kid I always thought she was some kind of dexterity genius because she could peel a pear in one big unbroken spiral. She carves little triangles out of each slice to extract the pits and hands one to me.

"Rain!" she calls out. "Rain, get out here. Now."

"What?" he says, coming out of his room. His hair is standing at a right angle from his head and he's scowling. My little brother eyes us warily.

Mom hands him a piece of cold pear and he takes it even though he's still groggy. It's his favorite. Two summers ago he ate four whole ones in a row and shat his pants playing Ping-Pong at Eddie Mao-Silver's bar mitzvah. To this day mom doesn't know about that. I had to cab it over to him with a fresh pair of sweats. The kid's so competitive he finished out his round with a load so he could get to the next bracket. Total maniac.

"Come wish hyung a happy birthday," she says, pulling out a small heart-shaped box of candy from the purse at her feet with an envelope in her other hand. Thank god. The fatness of the stack suggests it's at least a hundred bucks.

"I'd have thought you'd lurk around the house earlier this year," she says, handing me the candy and snatching back the cash when I reach for it. She places it on the table in front of me.

I take a juicy bite of fruit to hide my smile.

"Just because Rain is a juvenile delinquent and you're a dropout doesn't mean you don't deserve a happy birthday." She kisses me on the cheek.

"Everything else is good?" she asks me meaningfully. I know there's only one real answer to this.

"Of course," I tell her. "Never better."

"How's work?"

"Fine."

"And the apartment? You paying your bills on time?"

"Yes, mom." I keep the annoyance out of my tone since she's laced me with money. "Thank you for your concern. Besides, it's just Wyn."

"There is no 'just Wyn,'" she says. "It's Wyn's family, and I raised you better than that."

I thank her again to avoid a second fight.

"What do I get?" says Rain, eyeing my score. "It's Valentine's Day for me too."

"You get me grounding you from TV, PS4, and recreational Internet for two weeks *and* skinning you alive for Valentine's Day," she says. "And you're criminally mistaken if you think you're not going to be put to work this week. Starting with cleaning the fridge and getting groceries." She hands him another piece of pear. "Plus, I'm calling your school to find out your fate, so there's a chance you'll be skinned twice."

"Okay," he says, eyes wide.

"And another thing," says mom. "Can you two please, for the love of god, pull my air conditioner out? It's February."

It's a two-man job to wrestle mom's hulking unit out from her bedroom window. She used to go ballistic if it was still installed at Christmas since you may as well have a hole in your wall, it gets so cold. I feel awful that it's gone on this long even if it's a huge pain in the ass. The whole time you're supporting the back end of the metal box you're convinced you'll drop it all and murder a pedestrian on the street below.

"Come on, Rain," I tell him.

See? This is what I hate about going over to mom's. She's so demanding about perfectly reasonable things that provide limitless opportunity for us to disappoint her.

Chapter 7

The subway stalls out between stations for twenty minutes and everyone loses their minds. Me? I take a few steps back from my eyeballs to sit somewhere deep inside my head. Time has no meaning. I'm perfectly content. That is until my anxiety piques. On the lap next to mine is a textbook that's highlighted within an inch of its life with determined notes written in mechanical pencil in the margins.

I let my eyes travel to the face. It belongs to an Asian girl a few years older than me who checks her Apple Watch and sighs. She seems the type to kill at school. And that's not me being racially reductive; there are legit three different highlighting schemas happening. How do you get that way? Why isn't there a mandatory course on how to college before college? Like, genuinely.

Here's what I want to know about school. Everyone

assumes kids are bad at decisions, right? So why would anyone let an eighteen-year-old pick what they want to do in college? Because if you actually think about it, if you're a red-blooded American teen, the financial risk is devastating. It's the equivalent of giving a child the keys to a Bugatti Veyron and expecting it to turn out okay. Of course that hyped-up dumbass would do donuts in the parking lot at one hundred miles an hour and see if they can't Tokyo Drift straight into a check-cashing store. Nature or nurture, that much is a given.

And that's the thing about NYU. The price tag is nonsense, but if they accept you, you go, and—get this—I got in. Martin Scorsese, Donald Glover, and Jonas Salk, the guy who cured polio, they went to NYU.

So, if given the option, why the hell wouldn't I go? Of course I bought into a name-brand school. Did I mention my mother is a Korean doctor? Do you know what those expectations feel like? That's the kind of baggage that comes with those round boxes you put hats in and those hard trunks you see on trains. So here I am all through high school reading the admittance rates for good schools like, whatever, Harvard, Columbia, Princeton, and you can practically hear the laughter when you open the brochures.

So when I wound up getting into NYU, I was flabbergasted. Sure, I had phenomenal test scores but pathetic extracurriculars, and when Shane McManus's freckled hater-ass said it was due to me *not* being white, I believed him.

Of course you say yes to NYU. You say yes before they come to their senses. You say yes because you're not an idiot. You can't be an idiot—come on—you got into NYU! But then your mom, that ivy-obsessed turncoat who you thought for sure would be elated, shuts you down.

"Pab," she says. Mouth in a line. "You didn't get any scholarships."

Can you believe that? Nothing is good enough for her.

Look, I may not have known what to major in at the time. And I may not be the best at planning or deducing how loans work per se. But I'm nothing if not aspirational, so I girded myself and did what any self-respecting child of separated parents would. I went straight to dad with a sob story about dreams and he gave me his blessing and we filled out the forms for various loans to what I soon discovered is one of the most expensive private schools in the entire world.

But instead of sweating the fine print, you subsidize your expenses with extra free money that comes from credit cards that you open on your first day on campus, when they offer you zero percent APR and a nifty promotional water bottle. You take both to Stadium Goods, not to buy anything but just to see what they have, and here's where things get extra dicey. Credit cards *and* student loans? That's giving a kid keys to a Bugatti Veyron that's gone super saiyan.

I don't even know where this metaphor is going, but this money may as well be falling from the sky because credit card money is theoretical money. But when you're failing classes *and* your mom pulls out the bills from under your mattress like so much stowed away analog porn you take the path of least resistance. You're an adult. A man. You move in with Tice and Wyn in a drywall box that's technically part of the kitchen, returning home a few months later for dinner and the announcement that you've dropped out.

Let's just say it's a credit to your foresight that you don't live at home anymore when you tell her that you have a body of water and a suspension bridge that separates you from your mom's radioactive judgment because that would've made your hair fall out.

At the next stop I get up to give a woman with a kid a place to sit. Half out of the kindness of my heart and half because I can't stand to be judged by that goddamned Technicolor textbook.

When I get home I throw my clothes on a chair, wash my face, and check the rice cooker. It's a Zojirushi, which is the Ferrari of rice cookers. There's even a timer. My mom gave it to us as a housewarming at Christmas and now everyone, even Dara, who's white—well, Jewish and Sicilian—uses it. It functions the same as the coffee machine at an office. It brings us together, everyone keeps a pot going, and we chip in for the five-pound bag of good sushi rice with the rose on the packaging that I pick up at the store.

I fry three eggs, crumple up some seaweed snacks, and eat it over rice and hot sauce. I watch a few videos of yet another entrepreneurial YT series, this one called *The Architect*.

Right before the video about Ai Weiwei cues up there's an ad of Leanna Smart's new computer coding summer intensive, because of course people interested in subversive Chinese artists are also interested in Leanna Smart.

I'm so mesmerized by the way Leanna's hair moves that I don't sense Tice pulling up a chair. "Oh, you headed to coding camp for Disney kids?" he asks.

I snap my laptop shut.

He's grinning at me stupidly.

"What? You win Cash Cab or someshit?" A piece of rice falls out of my mouth onto the table and I don't even bother picking it up.

He looks happy, and in my mood it seems like a personal affront.

"We gotta go out Saturday," he says.

In New York the all-ages venues are garbage. It's always the same knuckleheads and creepy-ass forty-year-olds trawling for nineteen-year-old girls. Miggs and Dara are twenty-eight and twenty-three respectively, Selwyn's twenty-one, but me and Tice are underage.

"You too?" Wyn's been bothering me about birthday plans for days. "Why is Wyn so pumped about going to stupid El Portal or Up Stairs?" El Portal is a Salvadorian restaurant that turns into a white hipster dance party at night, and Up Stairs is a Chinatown karaoke spot that turns into a Black hipster dance party at night. Eighty-Eight Dreamers, meanwhile, is a banquet hall that's half off-track betting and half Asian cool-kid dance party, but the list's a nightmare.

"I want to take it easy for my birthday." I rinse out my bowl.

"Not everything is about your birthday, man," he says, following me to the sink. This is seriously the happiest I've ever seen him, and it's annoying.

"Okay, what is it, then?" I turn and face him. "Why so peppy?"

"Dude, I got it," he declares, arms wide as if he's about to hug me. To date we have never hugged. I'm very big on personal space, and Tice abhors human contact.

"What? What did you get? The clap? A puppy? Ten thousand dollars to distribute equally among your roommates, starting with me?" He's smiling that crazy smile again, and for a second I wonder if he's got one of those inoperable brain tumors that change your entire personality.

"I got the part in *The Agents*!" he screams.

"Holy shit!" That's a big deal. "Holy shit! You got it!"

"Holy shit!" He screams again, and we do this hug-jumping thing for a second and he's whooping into my ear, going, "Holy shit! Holy shit!" which I do back because I don't really know how else to respond. I didn't even know he was up for a part in *The Agents*, but it's way better than *Law & Order SVU*, which is the one show that reliably shoots in New York but you have to be excited about playing a child molester or a truck driver who murders people. Plus, it's insane how quickly headlines from the real news make it to air on that show. Not as fast as the reaction time on *South Park*, but the one with the devil-worshipping con who was living under the floorboards of that house in Long Island? He was still at large when we watched it.

"Man, I can't believe it," breathes Tice. "I didn't think . . ."

For a second I'm convinced he's going to cry, and I'm horrified. Thank god Wyn steps in.

"What the F, dillweeds? I was taking a nap."

"He got it!" I tell him.

"You got *The Agents*?" he says. His eyebrows skyrocket into his hairline. Tice nods, and Wyn goes "Aaaaaaaaaaaaah!" and rushes over, and the three of us do the hug-jumping thing again.

I'm the first to disengage because I need a shower and frankly all this activity is making me feel light-headed.

"We definitely have to celebrate," I inform Tice. "Really, man, I'm so happy for you."

"I'll hit Miggs and Dara and see if they want to come out Saturday," says Wyn. Miggs and Dara usually go to bars with other comedians who you'd think were funny in a pack but they came over once and they're boring depressives like normal people.

"I'm sure they're down," he says. "Which part did you get?"

"Ziad al-Abbasi," says Tice, making himself a bowl of cereal.

"Wait." I don't love where this is headed. That's the thing about *The Agents* that I didn't want to bring up, it's a MAGA-ass show if you actually get into it. "You're playing a dude named Ziad al-Abbasi?"

"Yeah," says Tice, and then shrugs.

"Word? On *The Agents*?"

"It's a small role," he says.

"No shit," I tell him. As if a character called Ziad al-Abbasi on a US counterterrorism procedural about crime forensics in New York would have a nine-season arc.

"So, what kind of background does this Ziad al-Abbasi have?" I ask innocently. "His people from Hispaniola?"

"Well," he says, and then I swear to god he gives me this look.

"What, he's a *radicalized brown* dude?" I want to ask if they requested an accent but I'm almost too scared of the answer.

"Look, I know," says Tice with a measure of solemnity. "Are you cool with that?"

I hate this shit. As if I'm holding a pass that grants him permission with Team Brown People to play a racist carica-ture on TV. Besides, I don't even know what hill I'm dying on. I'm not altogether comfortable caping for the totality of the Islamic diaspora and every Arab country because who the fuck knows what kind of basket case Ziad al-Abbasi is. But I can't believe this is a conversation I have to have with my friends. My good friends.

Wyn watches us back and forth with interest like he's expecting a fight to break out.

"Are there Muslim Haitians?" asks Wyn.

"What does country of origin have to do with religion or race for that matter?" Tice counters.

"True. Barack Obama's Muslim," Wyn says.

Me and Tice both look at him, look at each other, then laugh.

"What?" I ask him.

"Obama is not Muslim," says Tice, rolling his eyes. "His parents were atheist intellectuals."

"I'm saying you could be half white *and* half Black and be Muslim," says Wyn, trying again. "His mother was white."

Which really cracks me up.

"You're an idiot, Wyn," says Tice, shaking his head. "But wait, Pab. Are you really in your feelings about this?" he asks.

I don't know. There are a lot of aspects to it. I can't hate on dude for getting his money but I didn't think the day would come where I'd be confronted by my best friend's IMDb page being like, Tyson Scott as the jihadist.

"I don't know that I could ever play outside of my race on TV," I tell him.

"Word. Cultural appropriation," says Wyn, as if he's playing a lightning round of wokeness bingo.

"Race is a construct," says Tice. I hate fighting with him or Miggs about things like this. They live for confusing arguments. "I'm just saying . . ." I stand up, trying to figure out what I'm saying. "What if they asked me to play a Black dude *and* he happened to be a dealer or an addict or an ex-con . . . ?"

"Well." Tice gets up too and rinses out his bowl. "When the decision-making whites in the casting department at a major network television show pay you real money to play an African-American drug-dealing, coked-up, *wrongly accused man*, you have my blessing."

I don't know why I can't be purely happy for him. It's petty but I can't squelch it. Right now I would love if I had the presence of mind to be all, Well, shit, if anyone's going to get paid playing some goon it may as well be someone I love, but I can't. I can't even tell what part of my queasiness is being mad at him or being mad at me that I'm mad at him.

"You know you can't give me that blessing though, right?" I tell him, trying to find another way to talk about it. "You're not African American. Doesn't being Haitian make you more T'Challa than Killmonger?"

"What?" His eyes are bugged out. "Being Haitian makes me the *most* Killmonger. Do you know anything about history?"

I don't even know what we're arguing about at this point, but it's clear that being locked in an idiot's arms race of saying ignorant things is easier than having a real discussion.

"Are we good?" he asks, smile on his face.

I nod. "Yeah," I tell him. Definitely still mostly pissed. Not cool. At all.

"You know this is how they divide us," he calls over his shoulder before heading into his room.

"Bet," I tell him. "God knows we have to stick together since Wyn's Croatian side is clearly an alt-right nationalist birther."

Tice and Wyn laugh as I walk down the hall, shut the bathroom door, and turn on the water.

I wipe the fogged-up mirror with my hand, feeling every feeling. I understand it intellectually. I don't know what I'd do if I were faced with the same decision. Or how I'd tell my friends if something like this came up. The steam blots out my face in the mirror.

The hot water helps. Standing under the spray, I try to wash away the feeling of my skin crawling. It's the ambiguity that he wouldn't understand. Truth is, as a mixed kid, when push comes to shove, I never know if I have the right to be offended. How much indignation I'm allowed. I mean, look, it's not as if some white dude let the N word fly in front of me there wouldn't be words, but nobody treats hijabi jokes or ignorant shit about North Korea in the same way. Which, in this country, with our history, I get. I can't tell you how many times seemingly reasonable people argue that Apu gets a pass because it's the literal *Simpsons*. But when it comes to my Muslim-by-proxy kinship to family I barely know or how people don't realize there's a Korean in their midst when I'm around, I can't organize my thoughts. I want to tell them they don't have the right. That they're not their people to clown like that. But I can't help but wonder how much my people are mine. If they'd claim me in the same way I want to claim them.

Chapter 8

"You said we'd go yesterday," whines Rain in this skull-piercing tone.

"What difference does it make? We're going today."

We're on the 7 train to see dad. It's six p.m., and I woke up an hour ago with a splitting headache.

"We made arrangements!" Rain says a little hysterically. It's Friday and I can tell being suspended from school isn't the vacation he thought it would be. Mom wasn't kidding about the chores.

Off the train I steer Rain into my favorite deli by dad's. That's when I see her. Leanna Smart. Not actual Leanna Smart but a faded poster of her from a water ad a few summers ago. She's in a white cotton dress, hair mermaid long, sun dappling her bare shoulders, and her teeth blacked out with some kid's marker. I want to wring the clown's neck even if that clown could've easily been me if I'd had a Sharpie handy.

"Pab," calls Rain, glaring at me from the end of the aisle. I feel my face grow hot. As if I got busted doing some perv-shit. "Come on!" I grab some British candy bars, a fifty-cent pack of Parle-G biscuits with the kid throwing up a West-side hand sign, and a small bag of this spicy Bombay trail mix that dad put me onto, and a Coke.

We take the elevator up. You can tell it's an entire build-ing of immigrants because the hallways always smell of food. Polish food and Middle Eastern food and Chinese food and Korean food and Indian food battling for dominance. If it were only rich white residents it would smell of Tide PODS and vanilla.

"Children," says dad with his arms open. Dad is way more affectionate than mom. He cries at everything and you've got to move fast or else he'll kiss you on the mouth. The crazi-est thing about him though is that he gets more handsome the older he becomes. He's got light eyes that remind me of that Bollywood hero Hrithik Roshan, with a similar head of gigantic hair and a butt chin. When he has a beard though—I shit you not—women cross the street to try to talk to him. The thing is, he's so handsome that he looks untrustworthy. It doesn't match his personality either, which tends toward the dorky side. He once described it to Rain as having a face that other dudes want to punch. It was an entire conversa-tion about how men treat you when you're undeniably pretty, which was directed more to Rain than to me. Swear to god the kid takes an hour to get ready in the morning.

"Hey, dad," I say.

Rain gives him a big hug. "Baba!" He lets him kiss him on the cheek. "I'm sorry we're late," he says, and then shoots me the evil eye.

Me and Rain take off our shoes, which most people know as an Asian thing but that I've found is an every-one-except-white-American-people thing. Miggs's mom, who lives in Bed-Stuy, loses her mind if you drag your outside shoes into her living room with her sofas covered in see-through plastic. She'll offer you a pair of chanclas eight sizes too big, which she'll pelt you with at ninety miles an hour if you try to argue about any of it.

"It's okay," says dad, grabbing me by the scruff of my neck. "Happy birthday, Pablo."

"Hasn't it been your birthday for a month?" snaps Rain.

"Did you boys eat?"

Food at dad's is always the same. He has two grilled cheese sandwiches on the cheapest white bread with American cheese. I'm talking government cheese singles and on one side of the bread he spreads murabba, which is this jelly, and adds pickled green mango that he also buys from the store in jars. Then he has a Barry's Tea Gold Blend with condensed milk. I don't know when he made this meal up, but ever since he's lived on his own it's the same. I can't tell if it's what he likes or what he can afford. But this is what I'm saying: My dad acts as if he's a thousand years old. If he invited a woman over, I could totally picture him offering her the same sad meal. It's crazy to me that there isn't a word for "spinster" that refers to men.

Still, the experience is comforting. He's wearing a blue, buttoned sweater, and its roominess gives him the appearance of shrinking. I'm also convinced it's a woman's cardigan, but I can't remember what side the buttons are supposed be on. My father's never cared about clothes.

"So, you got into LaGuardia?" We're sitting around his tiny folding table, and he reaches over to touch Rain's cheek.

"Yup," says Rain, scrolling through his phone with one hand and eating his sandwich with the other.

"You did?" LaGuardia's impossible to get into. You've got to *literally* be Lady Gaga or Nicki Minaj to go. Leanna Smart meanwhile was homeschooled. And I know that because at this point I'm googling her so much I keep getting targeted ads for her sportswear line on my browsers.

Rain nods, taking another bite of sandwich. Ever since he was a baby he's been the slowest eater.

"For vocal."

"Well, shit," I tell him. "Congrats."

So, wait, this handsome bastard's going to be famous too? I lose any appetite for my remaining sandwich.

"Speaking of which," says dad, getting up and brushing crumbs off his lap. He puts on his glasses and hands Rain a three-ring binder. "I want you boys to read my play."

This is too much.

"I want you to read my play" is not ever a thing you want to hear from your father. It's so embarrassing. Like if you saw your dad in a flash mob or at a spoken-word open mic. By the way, both brain-bleeding events I have personally witnessed.

"A play?" I ask him, eyebrows raised high.

Rain hits my leg. "It's his latest passion," he informs me.

"I'm a playwright," says dad happily, without the self-awareness to qualify it with "aspiring" or using the words "I'm trying to write a play," which is what a normal person would do. Meanwhile, in the last few years he's been a poet, a tai chi master, a Reiki healer, and now this? Seriously, my dad reminds me of a trust fund kid with no trust fund.

"Can you send it to us?" I ask. I feel the plasticky grilled cheese clamoring up my esophagus. There's no way I'm reading my father's script in front of him.

"I'd rather not," he says. "Copyright sensitivity."

Oh, because a Russian hacker ordering Postmates from his Moscow apartment is absolutely jonesing to read my father's first stab at playwriting.

"You know what?" he says brightly, clapping his hands. "Come to rehearsals in a few weeks." He checks his wall calendar. It's red with gold calligraphy that he got for free at the Chinese grocer at New Year's. "Weekend of the eighteenth, at three p.m."

"Okay!" says Rain.

"Ah," I tell him, dejected. "I work that weekend."

"You work nights," says Rain with a glare. "We'll come."

"Fantastic," he says. "Let's take a walk."

Dad goes on these rambling constitutionals ever since he discovered from the Steve Jobs biography that the Apple founder was big on them, and depending on the day, he strolls for two or three hours nibbling on fennel seeds. Nowadays, it's what he does first thing in the morning and after meals, and in between he writes résumés for seventy-five bucks a pop. It's not a bad hustle. Dad's also not above tutoring, giving driving lessons, and performing a brief stint as the chattiest doorman in the Triborough.

"I first had the idea for my play walking down Kissena," he says reverentially as we make our way across Roosevelt on Main. Trust me, there's nothing special about Kissena Boulevard other than how the locksmith sells exotic fish in the back, which is just plain confusing. How do you even advertise for that? The park is nice, but he never goes that way.

"You learn a lot about yourself in the silence."

Meanwhile, you can hear car horns blaring and multilingual cursing even in the dead of winter.

When dad strolls, he stoops, clasping his hands behind his back in an old-man gait. Rain mirrors it. It's always been Rain and dad, me and mom. They're the dreamers and we're the realists.

"You must listen to yourself to hear what you want."

Well, it couldn't hurt. I clasp my hands too and fall in step.

It's while "hearing what I want" when, I shit you not, a cab drives by with its windows down blaring "Agonize" by who else? Leanna Smart.

I straighten up and walk normal style as if she can see me.

I follow the two of them in a daze, straight into a nondescript banquet hall with red carpeting filled with people. Dad marches across the room ahead of us.

"Dad," I whisper through clenched teeth, but he's out of earshot. Everyone's in formalwear. The shalwar kameez, Anarkali suits, and saris are super-fancy. Straight bedecked in shimmer and jewels. We follow him.

"Sunny!" says dad brightly, and this guy, I guess Sunny, who's around fifty and wearing a three-piece suit, rises from his table with twelve other guests who have clearly just sat for a meal. They've got these tight smiles as if to say, *Who the hell are these underdressed interlopers?* Still, Sunny grabs my father's hands and smiles.

"These are my sons," says dad, and then he quips in Urdu, to which Sunny chuckles. Me and Rain speak only a handful of words, along with the few Korean sentences that mom drilled into us. Dad speaks conversational Urdu and ripped some tutorials for us, but he never forced us to listen or pop quizzed us the way mom did.

"Salaam," says Sunny.

We both mumble, "Wa-Alaikum-Salaam."

"Aapka naam kia hai?"

"Rain," announces Rain, and I mutter, "Pablo." I always feel about a thousand IQ points lower when I'm talking to Pakistani people or Korean people I've just met.

And then Rain goes, "Zabardast!" in this stupid Bill and Ted voice, since it means excellent.

Sunny laughs, humoring him, and gestures to the long buffet table weighed down with food.

"We already ate," says dad.

"Dessert, then."

We grab bowls of ras malai—think super-sweet crust-less cheesecake clumps sprinkled with nuts—and gulab jamun, which is my favorite, fried cake donut holes drowned in fragrant syrup. Mom made them for us on dad's birthday one year and the oil spattered all over the place, which required an hour cleanup. Later, dad winked and said they tasted of resentment, but I thought they were great. There's also burfi and other assorted mithai for miles as well as an elaborately patterned platter of paan, these betel leaf packages of spices, sugared fruit, and other ingredients that get you hopped up as hell. Dad accidentally got himself addicted to the tobacco kind for a year where he spat up red juice constantly until we all bullied him into quitting 'cause it was gross.

There's a half-empty table in the corner, so we sit.

A different guy in a suit takes the microphone.

"Thank you for joining us again to celebrate my daughter Amina and her husband, Hamid."

The room erupts in applause.

I realize stupidly late as Rain does: We're crashing a wedding. I look around, anxiously trying to gauge where we are in the festivities. Whether the horse has come and gone. Whether I'll get pulled into dances I never know the moves to other than the one that looks like the Kid 'n Play kick-step.

"Amina, true to her name, has always been steadfast. And despite Hamid's love for the Yankees . . ." He pauses for effect. "At least he has the decency to be Punjabi. Alhamdulillah . . ."

"Dad," I whisper. Dad meanwhile is gazing at the happy couple proudly, as if they're his own offspring.

"Dad!" He looks at me.

"Who are these people?"

He shushes me. "Sunny's family."

"Who the hell is Sunny?"

"He owns the biryani place in Fresh Meadows."

"Are *you* invited to this thing?" Rain asks.

Dad shakes his head absently while continuing to beam at the speech.

"Not technically," he says. "But look around. We're welcome here. It's a celebration."

Rain cracks up.

I spoon up the last dough clump. "Let's go," I urge, mouth full.

Dad shrugs and gets up.

Rain palms a fistful of pakora on the way out, and my father takes a bite (he calls it taking a tax). We jog halfway down the block, laughing as if they're going to chase us.

When I get home, the forgotten Picnic candy bar I bought falls out of my hoodie pocket. It's ugly, delicious, chewy, studded through with peanuts, raisins, and caramel. I cut it into pieces and toss it into the bag of the Haldiram's trail mix since it goes with the salty spice and the crunch. The biscuits I save for later. I throw it on Instagram with the Kiko Kostadinov x Asics Gel-Delva 1s in the gnarliest colorway I can find because that upper's an artful hodgepodge and because, get it, it's a trail shoe at heart but with so much more.

I get ready for bed. I'm exhausted, but any time I still my mind it's as if twenty pairs of eyes inside my head spring open. I wonder what she's doing. What she's eating. If Carolina Suarez remembers me at all even if she doesn't know my name.

My fingers steer to her page. I'm racked by a startling loneliness. I return to my snack post, which has scored a few likes despite the late time, and drop a hashtag into the usual cacophony. Alongside #foodporn #foodie #chocolate #kicks, #sneakers, #ASICS, #Bulgarian, I add #spelunk.

Two days later Alice (Tinder) texts me as I'm getting off work.

Wya?

Leaving, I tell her. It's been three weeks since I've heard from her.

Come over.

Alice is an editorial assistant for a book publisher, so her grammar is always impeccable, but the tenor of the period on the end of her text pisses me off. The sureness of it. She lives in Midtown in a brand-new studio apartment with a washer and dryer, with her boyfriend, who pays half the rent since he got a job in Albany and reverse commutes for weekends.

I start texting her: Can't

Leanna Smart flashes into my head.

Stop dreaming.

I delete the text. I'm in bed with Alice by nine o'clock. On the dot.

Chapter 9

"Here," **says Alice** a couple of hours later, waving her forearm in my face. My hair's drying fluffy, and I keep patting it down since I didn't bring any product with me. She insists I shower before I even enter her room. "Subway germs," she says unfailingly, wrinkling her nose.

We're lying around, and it feels way more familiar in the daylight. As if it's the weekend in a real relationship.

"Smell," she instructs. Her slender wrist's held right under my nose. I lean into where veins cross paths and I catch the scent of fruit—plums, cherries, and raspberries so ripe they're almost ruined. Alice without makeup is so pale she has a bluish cast at the temples. Again she grinds her wrist on the rough strip of perfume sampler in her magazine, and that's when I see Leanna Smart's contorted, glossy face looking up at me from the pages.

If I were playing a Leanna Smart scavenger hunt I'd be winning. Or else I've lost my mind.

Alice's pulse points are different from Leanna Smart's, their chemistries, heartbeats, hormones, the oil deposits on their skin, and of course the way particles are relayed onto blotter paper, but I expect to smell her. The heavy stone fruit, with a dark, unnameable woodsiness underneath. It's an ad for Leanna Smart by Leanna Smart, but it's not the same.

Alice pulls on a short silk robe and tosses the offending page into her pewter trash can, which matches the chair at her vanity exactly. "You know she got seven figures for her memoir?" she prompts me. "What nineteen-year-old needs to write her life story?"

I need air.

"You want to go outside?" I ask her.

"It's freezing," she says, glancing at her window. "Do you want to day drink?" Her eyes light up. "Boozy brunch," she says. "Mimosas or, *ooooooh*, hot toddies."

She rubs her wrists repeatedly on a towel draped on a hook by her bathroom. "Ugh, this perfume. It's headache inducing. A bouquet of tween strippers. With a top note of burnt candy. Burnt candy and meth."

Alice scowls dramatically and grabs her phone. She told me once, not without pride, that she sleeps with it on her sternum.

"Jesus," she says, scrolling and rolling her eyes. "How do I have fifty-four new emails?"

Alice's favorite activity is counting how many messages she's gotten since she last checked her phone. As if the figure is a testament to how important her job is. How well she's crushing at life in New York. She has two bosses and works on both their "teams," and once, over coffee, she showed me her Slack notifications and I immediately lost my will to live.

"I'm so glad we got a day off," she says. I can't tell if she means this ironically between the pacing and furious typing. "Ugh. They're all so mad at me. I need a drink."

What I need is to get out of here. Alice is stressing me out. Granted it appears purposeful, and there's an enticing quality to the level of dedication in this unquestioning emailing and scowling. Part of me wonders if I'd want her life. A regular job. An email address that sounds legit. Business cards. Alice says there's a cafeteria in her building just for them.

I should go home and finish college applications. Research financial aid. Try to secure health insurance. Anything but watch someone else work. But the prospect of combing through fine print makes me uneasy.

"Thanks for coming over," she says, and finally looks at me. I take that as my cue and pull on my jeans.

"Do you like your job?" I've never thought to ask her directly.

"Yeah," says Alice defensively. As if her work phone can hear her. She takes a seat at her vanity and applies lotion on her arms with such vigor that she seems angry at her skin for requiring it. It strikes me as an oddly intimate sight.

"I mean, *you* know what the job market's like," she says to my reflection. Meanwhile she's never asked what I do. "I had six internships—four unpaid—and I had to beat out three other girls to get a permanent position after seven months of freelancing. I love my job. Not that I'm staying longer than two years unless I get a promotion and a fat raise."

She pauses, picks up her phone again, and smiles. "You'll see when you're ready to figure it out," she says in this treacly tone that suggests she'll want to kiss me on the forehead and pat my ass when she kicks me out.

"I gotta go," I tell her.

I scan the block when I step outside. It's freezing but bright. Glinting. The air blooms tiny shards in my nose.

The worst place in New York is easily Times Square. Ask anyone. But catch it at the right time and the manhole covers smoke exactly how they do in movies, and while there aren't wisdom-spouting, beret-topped sax players on every corner, the light can be enchanting. I thread through a family of tourists, each toting a calamity of shopping bags, glacially fording the filthy snow.

There's heavy police presence. Whenever I see multiple cops on the block in this part of town I immediately think: natural disaster. I've watched every cinematic ode to making my hometown eat shit, so if I go anywhere that smacks of the big-screen Big City—the Statue of Liberty or the Chrysler Building or the Brooklyn Bridge—places me and my friends avoid, I think of tidal waves or *Sharknado*.

There are silver barricades everywhere, swarms of teen-age girls flailing, reminding me of fish caught in nets. They crane their necks up and down the block for an update—any update—swiveling back and forth between their phones, the LED screens, and the shops.

"What's going on?" I ask a Bangladeshi hot dog vendor on his usual corner across from the TKTS bleachers. The hot dog dudes are Dominican uptown, but around here they're strictly Bangladeshi. Unlike the nut vendors, the halal chicken rice dudes, or the juice guys, who are a whole other way to stew chicken.

Hot dog dude points up. And yo, I'm not even kidding. It's Leanna Smart. A fourteen-story lit-up version of her face.

"It's the big day in the Big Apple," coos the video. As if anyone actually calls it the Big Apple. "Leanna Smart by Leanna Smart."

She holds up the architectural-looking bottle in one fist and then kisses it. It's a bugle-shaped glass shard that's rose on one side and frosted on the other.

"Today, only at Sephora."

The display dissolves into white and black sprinkles, and when it reassembles, there's a picture of a girl inside the makeup store crying and holding up a bottle.

The crowd squeals.

Then it's another girl. And yet another, not much older than eight. Everyone is going berserk at the prospect of get-ting inside, getting their bottle and their selfie with Leanna

Smart to loom over New York like a God. A vision that their envy-sickened friends outside are relegated to taking a picture of. And a video. Maybe a boomerang if they're super supportive, for which they'd better get a photo credit.

A tourist crashes into me as I spin around to cut down a different block. It's worse than when the pope's in town. The road closings mean traffic's a mess. I'm about to cross the street to get on the train when I see a guy in a bright orange work vest holding a silver-and-orange plastic sign. Something about the way he signals traffic—jovially, as if he loves his job—reminds me so much of my dad that when I see a navy sweater under his jacket I almost get run over by a cab.

I'm drenched in black slushy street juice down my leg, and even though the guy's shorter than my father and doesn't have a beard, I feel as if I've seen a ghost.

Please don't let me end up like him.

I bolt toward the train and catch one immediately, where I search Leanna's Instagram Stories for any further information.

There's a video with her holding her perfume, then tossing it onto her hotel bed with the New York skyline behind it. So she really is here.

The caption reads:

> I know it's a madcap, highly conceptual move
> to name the perfume after myself. But what am
> I if not a risk-taking lunatic?

Then I see it.

#LeannaSmart #Sephora #NewYork #Smartees #Spelunk

I hold my phone.

#Spelunk

Incredulity.

A tremor of glee in my stomach flip-flops. It's the lurch of gravity or the drop of your upper intestine when you're on a roller coaster but smaller and warmer. What does this mean? What does anything ever mean?

Chapter 10

I **double tap** without hesitation. The gauntlet has unquestioningly been thrown. Let the record show I am game.

But for what?

For three full days I contemplate the futility of a DM slide while waffling maniacally as to whether or not I should leave a comment. I decide not to. I wish there were a field guide for this. Someone to ask about the rules. Quora, unsurprisingly, is unhelpful. That's always an accurate gauge for desperation. If I'm on the Quora part of the Internet, it's a cry for help.

In an effort to exert even a modicum of chill, I do absolutely nothing and writhe in self-loathing while being extra vigilant around the deli just in case she really does live in the area. The loserish feelings have reached a deafening, skin-crawling crescendo by the time she comes back.

Which she does.

Just like that.

Leanna Smart strolls into the store. This happens in a disembodying dreamscape slow motion. I'm basically Daredevil I'm delivered so much information at once. The way she smells (different from the perfume bearing her name), the way her head bobs when she speaks, her teeth. I can't even explain how in the moment it feels impossible but entirely inevitable. Like the end of the world in certain mythology where everyone knows it's coming but you don't fully believe it until it arrives. Except of course this is different. It's a beginning.

Finally.

"Hey, Sad Boy," Leanna Smart calls to me exactly eleven days after we met. Again at an ungodly hour.

I'm stunned as thousands of windows in the browser of my mind explode to play a manic GIF of me fist pumping the sky. I am jubilant. Triumphant. I am also tempted to poke through her cheek to make sure she's not one of those freakish flight attendant holograms you get at the airport now.

This time she's wearing an enormous puffer coat with a fur collar and sweats.

"Uh, hey," I tell her. And then, "What's up, Suarez?" Since calling her Leanna Smart feels insane. Like calling someone Mickey Mouse. Or Coca-Cola.

"You know," she says. "I've eaten your food and huddled to you for warmth, but I don't know *your* name."

She smiles easily. As though we're friends. As though we've *been* friends.

Me, I'm working on a delay. I'm stuck on her lips, the way they move. Her cheekbones. The hand brushing a strand of hair away from her forehead. Her short thumbs that make better big toes than fingers. Statistics fly through my head: 345,112,459—the number of times people have viewed Leanna Smart's multiplatinum single "Tower" from her bestselling fourth studio album *Milestone.* One hundred and forty-three million—Leanna Smart's follower count across all social media platforms (rando bots notwithstanding). How her left eye's slightly bigger than her right one. Sadder. Sadder? Yes, sadder. Slightly. And the voice, *the voice, thevoice.* Deeper than you'd ever imagine. Gravelly. No, raspy. Textured. Tangible.

"I know 'at Munchies Paradise' isn't your government name," she says evenly. "Unless your parents are Frito-Lay industry plants and you're the poster child for early-onset type 1 diabetes. Plus gout."

She smiles at me, tilting her head in a way my mind recognizes as A Thing Leanna Smart Does from the hours of interview videos I've studied.

I remind myself to clear my browser history.

"Can you imagine?" I ask her coolly. My heart is thundering in my chest—*spelunk, spelunk, spelunk*—but I keep it together. "If that were what my parents ultimately wanted for my life? I'd have to tattoo junk food logos on my body like NASCAR patches."

"That would be amazing," she says. "Part SoundCloud rapper, part Nestlé ad."

She approaches with her hand extended. "You can call me Lee," she says, and I feel a warmth at the prospect of calling her anything since I thought for sure I would never see her again.

Lee. My mind furiously attempts to reconcile the syllable with building-size ads and the countless—so very many—photographs from every conceivable angle that I've absorbed. Lee. As in the title of the only-just-announced fifth studio album from one Leanna Smart. Allegedly the grown-up one. The . . .

Shit. Answer her.

"Pablo," I tell her, taking her hand. It's cold. I release it reluctantly. "And don't think my parents did me any favors. Pablo Neruda's my first name. Last name Rind."

"The poet?"

Usually I dread this. People who recognize the name ask me to recite something, as if to make them closer to a dead Chilean poet laureate. Then again, I'm happy that Leanna— *Lee*—knows who he is. Tons of people don't.

"Yeah," I say.

"Jesus. That's emo."

She's not wrong.

"So, wait," she says. "Do I call you Pablo Neruda as your full first name?"

"Nah. Pab'll do."

"Pab'll it is." She smiles goofily.

Under her coat, Lee's wearing a Big Bird–yellow sweater. "So, Pab," she says. "What've you been up to?"

"I have stood right here since you left. Contemplating mortality and the human condition. I power down when my shift's over."

"I used to think that about grown-ups," she says. "You ever see those children's books where the animals in the village had jobs? The cat was a postman. Scarry Town?"

"Scarry Town!" I remember. "Wasn't there a lion and a worm with a hat?"

"Yes!" she says. "I thought teachers lived at school and that my grandmother's priest lived at church."

"Where else would they live?" I imagine a younger version of her. Same heart-shaped face. Same seriousness. All the questions.

"But then I got into acting," she says. "Turns out, the people you see in movies and TV shows are boring real people. They're short and a few of them have startlingly terrible breath."

"Just one more reason not to work for TMZ, I guess." I can't stop smiling at her. "Meeting your heroes with suboptimal dental hygiene."

"So disappointing."

"I'd never recover."

"Speaking of teeth, mine were so sore from the sugar we ate," she tells me. "Last time. When I was um . . . here. You were there also," she adds.

Leanna Smart is stammering in my store. *Is she nervous?*

97

"So what can we offer you this time?" If this were a saloon, I'd slide her drink down the length of the bar straight into her hand.

"Why don't I take a gander . . . spelunk."

I smile.

"Spelunk away."

I watch her on the tiny monitor in her massive coat. She dawdles in health foods, and I'm the creepy voyeur watching over her until she reemerges with low-calorie seaweed and unpasteurized coconut water. Plus, a punnet of blueberries.

"I'm vegan now," she explains.

"No judgment," I tell her, ringing her up. My heart deflates three sizes.

She places her card on the counter and pulls out one of those reusable plastic baggies that tucks into its own pouch. I notice that the pattern is Yorkshire terriers, not polka dots, and something inside me comes unglued.

This time she has no problem with the card reader, and when she catches my eye we both smile.

I hand her the groceries, panic setting in about how she'll leave again and vanish into the ether of the Internet, so I do the only appropriate thing, the thing that any self-respecting New Yorker would do when faced with a vegan.

"Yo, let me buy you breakfast," I blurt.

She smiles. "*Yo*, what?"

I try again. "There's a bagel spot next door, if you're up to accompanying me. Bagels are vegan."

"No egg or anything?"

"Nah, unless you get an egg bagel." A beat. "There's egg in that."

"Yes, but is there bagel in it?"

"Trace amounts of bagel." Our faces are split in twin grins.

"When?"

I look at the clock. I'm off in ten minutes.

"Now?"

"Okay," she says. It's a date. I have a date with Leanna Smart.

"It's not going to be . . . you know, *Breakfast at Tiffany's* or anything," I tell her before informing Mr. Kim that I'm off. I grab my coat from the hook in the back, hesitating for a second that if we leave the store atmosphere this will have been a dream.

"You know they don't actually go eat breakfast at Tiffany's in that movie, right?" she says as we step into the dark street. She pulls her hood tight over her face like Kenny from *South Park*. It's got to be negative ten with the windchill, and my whole body contracts as if leaping into frigid water. The only thing I know about that movie is there's a racist Asian joke in it, because my mom hates that part.

"I thought it was *Night at the Museum* but with omelets at the jewelry store."

"Nope."

"What about waffles?"

She shakes her head briskly. "No luck on hash browns either."

"Who knew?"

"A few people."

We hit up the bagel store a block down—La Bagel Universe. Not to be confused with Bagel World or La Bagel Delight or even the Bagel Hole two blocks over. Don't be fooled by imitators; La Bagel Universe is the jam. Plus, it opens at 5:30 a.m.

"Whoa," she exclaims when we rush inside, hugging herself and shivering violently. "I will never get used to this climate."

The overhead lighting's a buzzkill, but the bacon smells good, and I give Nando, the grill man, a pound. I can't tell if he's thirty or fifty, but we give him kimchi in exchange for day-old bread, which Mr. Kim makes bagel chips from and sells. The Korean man's frugality is unstoppable.

Nando waves at Leanna, and I clock his face for a glimmer of recognition, but his wink-wink attitude has way more to do with me bringing a cute girl in at six in the morning than anything else. Besides, Nando only listens to bachata, and to him 100 percent of music is either Anthony Santos or *not* Anthony Santos.

"You know I'm not vegan," she says, squirting ketchup on the bacon, egg, and cheese she ordered.

"I had a suspicion." I nod at the sandwich. When she asked for an egg, cheese, and bacon, both Nando and I corrected her by instinct. It's so annoying to be, *Well, actually,* about a sandwich, but in New York it's always bacon, egg, and cheese. BEC. In that order. It's tradition or something.

"It was dumb," she says softly. "I thought you'd make fun of me for the health food but then you didn't and then I realized it was stupid because you'd have to put everything back so I had to buy it all even though I think unpasteurized coconut water is a racket."

At this exact moment I've taken a stupidly huge bite and can only nod and chew at the joke as Leanna shrugs and then reddens. I want to squeeze her, she's so cute.

"I have a question for you," she says, eyes affixed to the tabletop.

"Shoot."

She takes a moment.

"Um, can we split one of those black-and-white cookies?"

They're usually a little disappointing, kind of like Nuts 4 Nuts, those bagged pralines you buy off the street, but I don't tell her that. "Most definitely."

I'm pretty sure that's not what she wanted to ask me. "What else?"

Her thumb travels to her mouth.

"Did you know who I was when you offered to pay for my groceries last week?"

I play back the tape in my head.

"No."

She nods and then takes a huge bite, so I go on. "Honestly, you struck me as someone who'd had a weird night. Between the five a.m., no coat, the dress, and the mildly haunted expression on your face, you looked as though you could use a snack."

"Ha," she says. "Accurate."

"I didn't figure what was up until the whole card thing, and then I played it real cool."

"It *was* cool when you attempted to regale me with stories about superior credit card travel deals."

"Yeah. That was a highlight."

She's still squirrely with the eye contact, so I get up to bring her the cookie. We break it in half, splitting the little sheet of wax paper, and when she hands me part of her leftover sandwich, I inhale it. I'm about to burst, but when Leanna Smart gives you food, you house it. Same thing if she handed me a jar. Even if I had to take it to the back and panic-tap the lid on the side of a cabinet and tie a rubber band around it to get a grip after running it under hot water. And if that didn't work, I'd have to beg Nando to cover for me while I folded my giant body out of the tiny bathroom window and run my ass to the store to buy a replica that I *could* open.

Shit. That's when I realize how much I like this girl. Sure, millions of people are obsessed with her. Bursting into tears or passing out when they see her, but I *like* her.

Just end me.

Lee removes her beanie, so I study her hair.

She notices me noticing and tugs at the ends.

"Haircut?" It's hanging past her shoulders instead of her waist.

"They enjoy experimenting with it."

"They?" I raise my brow and sip my coffee, picturing a

troop of scissor-wielding elves sawing into it at night while she sleeps.

"The team."

"Ah, the team." The elves turn into a suit-wearing cadre of executives.

"I get typecast a lot for movie roles, so we're trying new things."

"What's the type?"

"Type A, annoying, someone who reads as aggressively white."

"Bummer," I tell her.

She crushes the foil from her sandwich into a ball, so I do the same with mine. "You know, I don't love doing the music part."

"Don't you have an album coming out?" I ask noncommittally, as if I don't know that it streets in almost exactly three weeks.

That's when a piece of cookie flies into her windpipe and she erupts into a coughing fit. I spring to my feet so fast my chair falls back in case she needs the Heimlich maneuver, and her eyes are wide. She covers her mouth with one hand and flaps the other to signal that she's okay.

I sit back down, cracking open her coconut water, which is kicking around in the bag by her feet, and wait for the spasms to desist.

"Whoa," she breathes, taking a small sip. Eyes streaming. "So embarrassing."

Holy crap, my adrenal system can't handle hanging out with this girl.

"God," she breathes. "Don't you wish you could throw a 404 error message up for the other person to look at while that shit happens?"

"I confess it's not a side of you I thought I'd see."

She laughs, wiping her eyes. "I guess we're both too cool for life."

"So before you almost died . . ."

"Before my entire life flashed before my eyes . . ."

"You were saying you dislike music?"

"Not all music," she says. "My music."

It's never occurred to me to have an opinion of her music. It's perfectly inoffensive. Infectious. Breathy. Mostly she sounds as though she's cooling hot food in her mouth as she sings.

"It has nothing to do with me," she says.

"It's working at least," I try to reassure her. Leanna Smart's music is not wanting for exposure.

"I don't have a Grammy."

I wonder how life would feel if that were a legitimate concern of mine. The not having of a literal Grammy.

"Would a Grammy make you happy?"

She shrugs.

"Before my first record came out, I was so nervous. I couldn't sleep for weeks. Total mess. 'What if they hate me?' 'What if they only want to see me on TV and don't care?' 'What if I peaked at nine?' All of it."

"And when that didn't happen . . . ?"

"Honestly, it stunned me. Billboard, Spotify, YouTube, everything . . . The numbers were so insane."

"That had to feel good though, right?" I think about my own puny moment when the entire Internet seemed to be looking at me. It's a high that only becomes poisonous once it starts to taper off.

"Totally," she says dully. "I have no right to complain."

"You can complain."

"It's just . . . First off, I don't write my own songs. Luca, my manager A&R's the whole thing, so he picks the tracks, the songwriters, the topliners, the producers, does the sequencing, mixdowns, first single, second single."

I know about half these terms, but I don't interrupt her.

"He holds these things called writing camps, where he gathers the best music people in the whole wide world, the writers and producers responsible for your favorite songs, who convene for weeks and make hundreds and hundreds of tracks for you to choose from."

She takes another sip of coconut water.

"Then you go into the studio and you're auto-tuned to death," she says. "They cherry-pick the best few *seconds* of your voice from every take and frankenglue it together."

I wonder whether Lee's even in the room for this part.

"Do you know what uncanny valley is?"

"Sure," I tell her. "It's when the robot dances so much like a person that the human gets grossed out."

"That's exactly right." She laughs dryly. "That dancing

robot is basically my life. When I hear my song on the radio, there's this burst of recognition. I have a jolt of place. I'm like, 'Oh cool, that's me.' But then I realize, Wow, I'm the most expendable part."

"That can't be true," I tell her, wondering if it's true.

Leanna Smart sighs as if she's a million years old.

"At times I can't even feel myself in my own body," she says. "It doesn't help that I never know where I am." She shifts closer to me.

"What do you do when you're not at work, Pab?"

I love when she says my name. I don't tell her I saw her in Times Square. Or that I bought a magazine from the newsstand expressly with her ad in it so I could smell it.

"Are you in school?"

It takes me only a second to decide to lie to her.

Chapter 11

"NYU."

"Ugh, jealous," she says. "I got into Berkeley but deferred. I daydream about it all the time. My phantom other life. This cute apartment in the Bay with good light and hardwood floors."

I'm struck with a vision of her in such a space—by the window holding a blue mug—and how badly I'd want to be beside her.

"What major?" I ask, hoping she won't turn the question back on me.

"Something ridiculous," she says. "Philosophy. Or poetry."

"Chilean obviously."

"Obviously," she says, nudging my shoulder with hers.

Lee takes the final bite of her cookie and brushes the crumbs from her hands. "It's more sponge cake than cookie."

"It's not our best work."

"It's disappointing," she confirms.

I love this girl.

"It's one way of many that New York fools you."

"What are you doing for the rest of the day?" she asks me.

"I don't know. Take in a little culture, maybe go to the Met, observe some art. Hit up the farmers' market, make ratatouille."

"Really?"

"No. My exact plans were to huddle in the dark while listening to my one thousand roommates argue about basketball."

She studies me openly.

"Okay," she says. "Want to play rock, paper, scissors?"

I wonder where this is going. "Sure."

"On three," she prompts. We bob our fists together. "One, two . . ." But before three she blurts, "*Why* do you love your dad more than your mom?"

"What?"

"Three," she calls. I throw down scissors, which she beats with rock.

"I knew you'd do scissors," she says.

I'm stunned.

"Ask an invasive question and your opponent will go for scissors," she says. "It's a defense mechanism."

I look down at my hand, betrayed.

"It's in the phrasing," she says. "It doesn't matter how true the statement is. If there's a fraught relationship with either parent, it makes people want to cut you. Hence the offensive. Or scissors."

"Wait. My turn." I hold out my fist again and we go. "On three," I say.

On two I ask her: "Go out with me."

She pulls out paper and wraps it around my rock. Her hand is hot. A little damp.

"That's not a question," she says softly, looking right at me with an intensity that makes my breath catch.

Whoa. Is this swooning? Do dudes swoon?

Reality feels unreliable.

"You're right." I clear my throat. "Will you go out with me?"

"When?"

"How about now?"

She looks up at me. "Okay."

I search my mind for things to do in the early hours of the morning in frigid weather and the list is unsurprisingly small.

"Come with me," she says suddenly, palm still hot on my hand.

"That's not a question either."

"I know."

There's a challenge in her dark eyes.

"Okay," I agree.

"You don't even know where we're going," she whispers.

"Kinda beside the point, isn't it?"

Her lips are parted. Slightly. We're openly staring.

There's a stray eyelash on her cheek, and I'm tempted to pick it up, to show her, to ask her what she'd wish for, but it's all too corny and too confusing. This is not a movie.

She leans in close enough that I realize we're both holding our breath.

Lee removes the hand enveloping mine and says one word, "whoa," and then maneuvers us into a handshake. It's so dorky it makes me smile.

"Deal," she says, nodding crisply. I wonder if she'll want to spit on it.

"Deal," I tell her as she smiles wide.

Dang. It's a gutshot the girl is so pretty.

"Um . . . just don't murder me," I add. "Wherever it is that we're going."

"Pablo Neruda Rind, don't tell me you're antsy about a little homicide." She tucks her hair behind her ears. "I thought New York dudes were tough."

Wheels up at 2:30pm ET.

I get a text, not from Lee but from someone who makes it a point to say, This is not Lee, and introduces herself as Jess. I save her as "Jess Not Lee" on my phone. In the shower I can't decide if I'm nervous, which is a surefire sign that I am, and by the shampooing stage of the wash I'm at DEFCON 1 that my passport's expired. This is the headspace that everyone in my life dubs "Pulling a Pab." That one-track, panic-fueled mind that spirals furiously until I can locate some pertinent scrap of information. I whip open the shower curtain, tiptoe into my room, bare-ass, wet feet, puddles everywhere, dampening all my socks and underwear in my drawer to pull out my passport. Thank god. Meanwhile I don't even know if we're leaving the country.

"Wheels up" is such an intense statement. Like "stop the presses" or "release the hounds." A term you're almost guaranteed to never hear if your life is spectacularly dull. On the topic of dull, I need to find a way to tell Lee or Jess not Lee that I have to be back at work the day after tomorrow. And that I have that meeting with Joey Santos from Five Points to decide my scholastic fate. But then again, how presumptuous do you have to be when a girl asks you to kick it and you tell her you have to be out *two days later*. This is fine. It's the dog-in-the-burning-house meme, it's *so* fine.

I'm sent a foreboding Escalade with illegally tinted windows. The whole operation looks suspicious as hell, and as I text the roommates that I'll be gone for a bit, I wonder when I'll return.

The car seats, for the record, are heated.

"How's the temperature, Mr. Rind?" the driver asks. He's a pockmarked guy about my dad's age with silver hair and a goatee, wearing a three-piece suit and wraparound sunglasses.

"It's great," I tell him. "Amazing." My haunches have never been toastier.

"Very good," he says. "There are phone chargers and water." When he gestures behind him, I see that he has a gold ring on his pinkie.

Sure enough, there's a discreet compartment filled with an assortment of cables, even the old thirty-pin flat-paddle iPad charger. I'm in the swaggiest class of Uber ever.

It's congested on the road, so I expect we'll take the long way to JFK Airport on Atlantic, past Barclays Center, which resembles a postapocalyptic coliseum. But when we loop back into the city to take the Lincoln Tunnel into New Jersey, it occurs to me that I'm getting on a plane with someone I just met. When my metal-encased body goes careening through the sky engulfed in flames, I'll be a cautionary tale. But at least I cleared my browser history.

I take a deep breath.

"Yo." I lean toward the front seat. "What's your name?"

"Basim."

"What's up, Basim? We going to Newark?"

People hate on Newark, but it can't be worse than JFK or, good lord, LaGuardia, the most embarrassing parcel of public real estate to greet visitors from. I can't imagine smiling tightly at Lee in that horrible bowling alley overhead lighting, air dripping with fake-butter aroma from Auntie Anne's.

"Teterboro."

I look up Teterboro. Oh, right. We're flying private. Oops.

Teterboro, in keeping with most things in New Jersey, is remarkably unremarkable. It's fine. Nice. A student union building or a doctor's office. I didn't know what to expect, but I guess even famous people's waiting areas are overly reliant on neutrals and lacquered wood. A Hudson News store would tie the room together, but no such luck.

I take a seat on an armchair and act like I belong here.

There's a couple, both blond, four coffee tables over to the left. I recognize them without specificity. They have that veneer of famousness where you can sense their vigilance, that expectation of being noticed. She's wearing leather pants and reading a paper with sunglasses on, which looks conspicuously absurd. As if she's missing a trench coat and fedora for her espionage outfit. Her companion's slouched low, also in sunglasses, feet propped on a coffee table, arms crossed. His head lolls as if in mid REM cycle, except he's playing a Nintendo Switch with black AirPods. His sneakers are those UNC blue Off-White Jordan 1s and he's wearing a matching sweatband that makes his dirty hair appear sewn into it, and that's when I realize who he is.

Dyland Nagl. The erstwhile French-Canadian Olympic snowboarder turned rapper turned actor. Needless to say, the ladies love him. I don't know who the woman is, but judging from their body language she's either his girlfriend or his mom.

I check the time. Again. I wonder if we're going somewhere far. How long the flight will be. The conviction that I'll get airsick rappels into my brain, and even though it's never happened before, I'm anxious that today is the day I'll start. Puking in front of Leanna Smart in close quarters would be a very specific nightmare.

I check Lee's social. No new updates since she was at the gym earlier.

I review my own math. I've lost five followers. Shows what they know.

I zone out at the beige floor and wish I could kick my shoes off and post up, lie down fully with my face touching the human skin particles and dust mites on the carpet. Catching a bum nap right now would feel glorious, but my self-respect wouldn't allow it. Plus, my mom would administer tetanus shots to my eyes.

"Pablo?"

"Yeah?" I can't tell if I'd fallen asleep for a second. I clear my throat and sit ramrod straight.

A tall, light-skinned Black girl with hair in twists to her hips extends her palm.

"I'm Jess. Jessica Longworthy," she says. "I'm Lee's chief of staff—not to be confused with her assistant." I figure her for about my age.

"Okay." I shake her hand. "Consider me confusion-free."

Jessica's wearing a mint-green crewneck sweatshirt and matching sweatpants with the F&F black KAWS Jordan 4 Retros, and carrying a pastel aqua Goyard. Meanwhile, there's salt-studded gray slush on the ground outside. Either she's extremely wealthy or out of her mind. Even with a general release I've seen them on StockX for two grand.

"Great," she says, and smiles warmly. The canine on the right side of her mouth is ringed in platinum and studded with a tiny diamond. "Then we'll get along perfectly." I wish Tice were here. Jessica Longworthy is the embodiment of everything positive about the Instagram Discover page.

Jess checks her phone and pats my arm. "Can I get your ID? And when do you need to be home?"

"Tuesday," I tell her, and hand over my passport. She nods crisply, sends an email, and takes a picture of it. "Great," she says. "You'll get a confirmation shortly." Her eyes scan behind me. "Lee's here," she says.

Chapter 12

"Hi." Lee brightens when she sees me. I get up.

"Hi." I don't know whether to hug her or . . .

"Hey, Cam, Dyland." She waves breezily at the languid couple, who spring into action. The formerly comatose dude bounds over to us.

"Hey," he says as they hug. The woman, Cam evidently, removes her sunglasses and air kisses Lee three times. Her sweatshirt's the cut-up Gosha Rubchinskiy combo hoodie from a few years back.

"Thank you for everything," says Dyland, bouncing on the balls of his feet. "I'm so pumped. This tour's going to be epic. It's gonna be a *movie*."

"Seriously, thank you," says the woman. I half expect both of them to start bowing they're so deferential.

"It's going to be fun," says Lee. I wonder if she'll introduce me, but a nod and a pause signal Cam and

Dyland to retreat, which they do.

"You came," she whispers, smiling shyly and tugging at my shirt.

"You didn't think I would?"

She's wearing a white sweat suit and the unbranded blue Celine Air Force 1s so box fresh my heart skips a beat. She perches on my armrest, smelling so good. Vampire fruit all over.

"I didn't want to get my hopes up," she says, leaning in for a hug.

I feel another rush of cold air as the doors slide open. Lee stiffens and pulls away. It's a short brown-haired man, in his thirties or forties, wearing an orange and blue Knicks beanie.

"Hey." He up-nods the room with his eyes on me. "Who's this?" He's super tanned, smiling wide, and as he marches toward us I see that his teeth are bleached almost blue at the edges. He's one of those dudes who dick-swing by displaying an outlandish indifference to personal space. Plus, he talks like he has earbuds in.

"His name's Pablo." Lee's thumbnail makes its way to her mouth.

I dislike him immediately.

"Pablo," he booms, patting me on the shoulder as if I'm a long-lost cousin. He's a half foot shorter than me, with crunchy shellacked hair and crinkles around his eyes. He's wearing an unseemly amount of silver man-jewelry—ropy bracelets and *Game of Thrones*–type rings. "What's up, brother?" His hands are bright red from the cold. "Lucas-Sebastian." He grabs my palm and pulls me close for a half-in man-hug.

The sad thing is, I recognize the guy. I didn't put it together that Lee's manager Luca was Luca Loops. There was a time in my life when I would have been high-key pumped to meet him. Luca Loops is the award-winning songwriter who founded Waribashi Records when he was sixteen, back when Pharrell and the Beastie Boys and them were into anything Japanese. I nod at him coldly since he's coming in hot and don't say anything else.

"You see that shit against Dallas last night?" he asks affably. As if my silence passed some sort of test.

Okay, fine. As a long-suffering Knicks fan, if anyone wants to talk about dread-watching with a hole in their heart, I'll allow it.

"Season tickets," he says, shaking his head after we commiserate for a moment. "Courtside. I'm a true glutton for punishment. We should go to a game."

I am confident I will not be attending a sports event with this man.

Luca claps me again on my arm.

We travel by golf cart to the private jet parked not thirty yards away and I know I'm supposed to be impressed, but the size of the tiny plane on the horizon freaks me out. It doesn't become demonstrably larger the closer we get. When you're taking off in a massive commercial flight with hundreds of people you can at least sense the collective heft of humans and luggage and fun-size bottles of liquor rising into the sky. It's reassuring. You feel safer, insulated if only psychologically, as if a thousand packets of pretzels will pillow your fall. When you're hurtling through time zones in a passenger-van-size metal tube, where you can see its dimensions end to end, its smallness, the lack of mystery in the machinery, feels rinky-dink. When we board, we're met with ostentatiously creamy leather seats that strike me as flashy in a doomed way—the *Titanic*'s chandeliers to lifeboat ratio.

"You're awfully quiet there," says Lee, leaning over to poke me as we reach cruising altitude. I realize I don't love flying. We're each seated in a La-Z Boy–size recliner, angled so that no one's facing the back of anyone else. Jessica's with Luca. Dyland and Cam are strapped into a love seat in the back.

"Can I offer you a drink?" asks a petite blond woman in a prim navy suit.

"Just a water for me, Nina, thank you," says Lee.

I do the same and then change my mind. "Wait, Nina."

She turns around. "Yes, Pablo?" Okay, *that's* pretty cool. She knows my name.

"Do you have unpasteurized coconut water?"

"Yes, of course," she says.

"That's my jam," calls Luca from behind us.

"Okay, in that case I'll take regular water."

Lee smiles.

"I've always felt unpasteurized coconut water was kind of a racket," I say quietly.

"Total racket," she agrees, and pokes me in my thigh.

I want to talk to her, but a silence takes hold, ballooning to fill the interior of the vessel. Lee crosses her legs. I check my phone but don't want to ask for the Wi-Fi password, so instead I flick through my photos, even though I know exactly what's in there.

I delete photos religiously. Transfer and organize any keepers on an external hard drive. The folders are labeled by date and named by subject. Certain memories are better cordoned off if you don't throw them out entirely. My mom's the same way. Sometimes I wonder if this is a sign of a character flaw or a type of pathology.

I put my phone away, feeling awkward. At least in massive flights everyone agrees that we're together but not together. How in New York restaurants you can practically be sitting in your neighbors' laps but you ignore each other as a courtesy. The rules for private planes are odd. You feel the need to be quiet because it invokes the social contract of an elevator, but if Tice, Wyn, Miggs, and Dara were onboard there's no way we wouldn't be running around like hooligans shooting IG Stories with Drake captions.

"Care for a little music?" Lee asks, retrieving an ovoid speaker from her bag.

"Sure."

I wonder how Lee's tastes skew, if she's completely random, deeply into obscure rap or Afrobeat or, possibly, country. I hear an ominous wind-blowing sound. A lead into a song I haven't heard before. Halfway through I realize it's her.

"It's called 'Insecurity,'" she says unselfconsciously.

The song's on the long side, and I'm surprised she'd play her own music given that she's admitted to disliking it. I figure maybe she didn't intend to play the track, that this is how her Spotify launches. But then I realize autoplay is alphabetical. We're listening to this on purpose.

She's observing me as I listen, so I smile awkwardly and wait to see what follows. That's when I hear the rustling again. I glance at Lee, who's swiping through photo after photo *of herself* on her iPad, wondering if she notices the repeat. Maybe she's desensitized. The way you say your own name over and over and it ceases to have meaning. But when her song comes on for the third time and we listen to it from start to finish I wonder if this is her way. That she's like this in front of other people. That she loves her music and lied to me out of false humility.

I want to crack a joke about whether or not she's wearing a T-shirt of her own face under her sweatshirt because that level of egocentrism is absurd to the point of hilarity, but by the fourth time the song plays the knot at my gut corkscrews. Truth is, I do not know this person. No matter how familiar her face is. Lee looks at me, smiling sweetly, touching my forearm to inform me: "This is the acoustic." Sure enough, there's a guitar track where the singing's stripped down.

"Isn't it *fascinating* how it fits any mood?"

"Really versatile," I say emphatically.

"You know, I have a poster of me framed in my bathroom,

and it doesn't matter where you stand; my eyes track you. Certain artifacts inspire that kind of draw. That unassailable magnetism."

I nod. Mute.

Okay. This is the moment I'd start screaming at the dumbass in the film to get the hell out because there's a sunken place in his future or some *Saw*-type torture about to go down. I glance at the door. My attention skitters to Jessica, who's checking her phone, and I can't make out Dyland's or Cam's expressions—not that I'd put anything past those freaks. They seem game for some light cannibalism or tossing me into a cage match for entertainment.

"Instrumental's next." Lee picks up her jam box and places it closer to me. On my lap so it serenades directly at me.

This is it. They're going to take turns wearing my face.

"Cool," I say, holding the speaker steady with both hands. "Is it out yet?"

Lee bounces in her seat. "Not yet, but soon."

We listen and she smiles again, so I smile back. Then the corners of her mouth jerk upward—wiggle a little. I hear Jess crack up before Lee loses it.

"I'm sorry," she says, hand to heart. "You had to know I was kidding."

I close my eyes for a moment. Try to regulate my pulse. "How would I know you were kidding? I don't even know where we're going."

"Oh my god. Really?"

"There wasn't a whole lot of time for questions," I tell her.

"LA," she says. And then she rests her hand on my arm. "I'm so sorry." She starts laughing again, tossing her head back, the curve of her throat exposed.

"Honestly, Pablo, I was beginning to wonder about you," says Jess from behind.

"You weren't going to say *anything*?" Lee asks me.

"We've been listening to fucking 'Insecurity' for literally twenty-six minutes," Luca chimes in.

Lee throws on Whitney Houston.

"How long were you going to ride it out?"

"I made a fifty-minute playlist," she says, eyes wide. "If the Spanish-language version were out, it would have been seventy-five at least." That makes me laugh.

She smiles, pleased with herself, tilting her seat back.

"The thing is," I tell her, adjusting my seat to match hers. "If you really were that person, I wouldn't blame you. I'd be a monster in your shoes. Demanding they play my song wherever I go. Supermarkets. Restaurants. Lounges."

"Lounges are very accommodating," says Lee.

"It would be the only music I'd hear. I'd be all, 'Wow, I can't believe everybody loves my art *this much*.' I'm everywhere. And *my* chief of staff—no, my *chieves* of staff . . ."

"Is that like culs-de-sac?"

"Exactly. Anyway, my *chieves* plural, when I'd be all, 'Everyone is obsessed with me,' *they'd* be like, 'I know, riiiiight?'"

"You sound so abundant and grounded."

"Grounded because the twelve-piece band that follows me around to play my song would take up too much space on the PJ."

"Would it be your ringtone too?"

"Obviously," I tell her. "My alarm, push notifications, everything."

"I believe it," she says, shaking her head. "The shit I've seen . . . It would turn your hair white."

Lunch is grilled chicken, salmon, and a quinoa salad thing with beans that's served buffet style on a low table.

The couch in the back's been converted into a fully flat bed, with Dyland playing video games lying on his belly, sunglasses and shoes on.

"Landy," trills Cam over her shoulder, hovering over the chicken. "I'm going to do white meat for us. You have that shoot tomorrow."

Dyland shrugs, and I watch Cam spend the next five minutes using the miniature salad tongs to pry chicken skin off a segment of bird. And then another few minutes attempting to negotiate it into smaller pieces by shaking it listlessly.

"Need help?"

Cam looks at me startled that I'd addressed her directly. Up close, her skin is creamy with a fine layer of peach fuzz catching the light, and the hollows of her cheeks are so pronounced that her puffed-up lips give the impression of a person eating their own face from the inside. Her skin's so taut she reminds me of a burn victim. A super-expensive burn victim. Immolated but fashion.

"Oh my god, yes?" she says in a baby voice and shrinks her body down into a rigor of helplessness. "Maybe cut this in half? Why do they make them so big? It's organic though, right?"

This is what I mean by people thinking I work here.

Her eyes are beautiful. Bright green. And her lips have been painted beyond the contours of her pout.

I grab a knife and fork and wend into the glistening flesh.

"Jess," Luca calls out. I hear the juicy smacking of his full mouth. "Get Pablo to do that thing."

"Sure," she says, producing an iPad from her purse.

"You're over eighteen, right?" she asks pleasantly. "It's a formality mostly."

Cam leaves without so much as a thank-you and I return to my seat.

The formality is an NDA. As in nondisclosure agreement. As I scroll through, I see that it's 121 pages. My appetite's vanished, and I'm trying not to get hung up on how Lee's suddenly ignoring me.

I nod.

"You want to take a second to read it through?" asks Jess casually.

I take more than a few seconds.

The long and short of it is that I can't use social media

around Lee or take pictures or write a memoir or say anything remotely defamatory about her or the people around her or use her likeness in any way for anything.

I can't buy her gifts because of the contractual obligations to her sponsors.

I cannot discuss anything I overhear that relates to her or her work or her music or her affiliated projects and collaborations.

I cannot describe any of her physical attributes or review or comment on unreleased work in any media, including social media.

Technically I can't even use the name "Leanna Smart" in anything that even insinuates to promote anything else since it's copyrighted and trademarked.

Similarly, Smartees is trademarked. With a whole clause devoted to "Smarties" and the North American rights for the wack, pressed pill sweets as opposed to the international rights for "Smarties," the hard-candy-enrobed chocolate. A skirmish even I hadn't ever considered.

Farther on, I'm gag-ordered in mentioning the nature of my relationship both professional, personal, and otherwise (what would otherwise account for?) with "Leanna Smart."

Any violation will result in an upward of ten-million-dollar fine. This makes me involuntarily smile. It reminds me of *Austin Powers* supervillains, it's such a ridiculous number.

Basically, if I tell any of my roommates or my family, I could be sued to kingdom come and so could they.

Plus, get this, I have to agree to a background check

and a series of interviews as part of an "intimacy contract," should we engage in such a relationship. Meaning if we sleep together. She owns me. Forever. Nothing like the promise of being slapped with a civil suit for damages to entice you to want to make a move on a lady who also happens to be a multinational conglomerate.

And there are three additional pages devoted to if our relationship extends beyond a year. Or two. And three or four or five years. The next level up is seven.

In essence, with every page requiring an initial and date, no matter what happens between me and Leanna Smart, there is paperwork governing every permutation of possibility. In perpetuity. Anywhere in the world. Clauses to rein in the highs, safeguards for the lows. Lows that a very fancy law firm has good money on being virtually unavoidable.

The list goes on to say that I can't divulge or even insinuate how I had to sign an agreement or that such an agreement exists.

I can't discuss anything we've ever done, talked about, and I can't have an opinion on it either.

I wonder if thought crimes count.

If I sign this, there's a binding contract between us that out there in the world I cannot claim to even know her.

"I'm sorry," says Lee quietly. Finally. "I wish it weren't necessary. I've learned over the years that it keeps things cleaner. Or clearer, I guess."

Behind me Cam erupts into giggles. They're play wrestling and making out.

"You know, I didn't even tell anyone where I was going today," I whisper. "About any of this."

"I didn't think you would," Lee says, and sighs. "I wouldn't have invited you otherwise. I know it's annoying . . ."

It's beyond annoying. It's insulting. This document hanging over my head like a permanent record in high school. My college transcripts. My credit card debt. Is there an arena in which people aren't eternally keeping tabs?

"No sweat," I tell her dispassionately, signing with my finger and handing the iPad back to Jess.

She checks it. "Did you have any questions?" she asks.

"Nah," I say as she pulls up a page to show me.

"You forgot to initial this one." She pats my shoulder. "Morality clause sounds worse than it is. Just don't leak your nudes."

Chapter 13

Upon landing, Lee pulls her hat low and slides dark sunglasses in place. Another black car scoops the two of us straight off the tarmac to sail through LA streets. The palm trees are backlit and the sky's a keening pink. It's a tacky airbrushed vista so surreal it reminds me of a green screen background.

I'm itching to open the windows to experience the atmosphere so I don't feel as though I'm in a video game. But there's probably a provision against cross breeze in the booklet of contracts I signed. I want to take her hand for the assurance, to confirm to myself that I'm here. To prove that we're real and doing this, but I don't.

On the highway we're stuck behind a silver Prius. And when I notice an identical one to our right, a wooziness takes hold. I tilt my head to glance at the rearview, confirming the silver Prius behind us as well, and hold my breath. I look left and thank god it's a teal SUV.

I pull my hood up to lean my head on the glass, and I must have dozed because the next thing I notice is that we're pitched at a ridiculous angle going uphill as we pull in to a private driveway that emerges from a wall of ivy.

"We're here," she says. "I got us a hotel."

Hotel?

"It has three rooms," she mentions as she exits the car and clears her throat awkwardly and cartoonishly.

I clear my throat to make fun of her.

"Three rooms *achhhhem*?"

"Yeah, not two," she says. "Less than four. Three *achhhhheeem*."

I wonder if she'll want me in my own room.

There's an alarmingly handsome Sikh dude in a dusty-rose paisley turban and a black suit waiting for us.

After a barrage of kindnesses—whether Lee needs to be watered or attended to in any way—the door's closed firmly.

"Hi." I face her finally. Nervously.

"Hi," she says, and pulls me in for a hug. We melt into each other, and I put the contract out of my mind.

"We did it." I raise a fist halfway into the air in a small cheer. "Woo."

"We did."

I place my hands at the small of her back, conscious of the warmth. She tilts her head to me, gazing up. If there were ever a time to kiss her it's now.

I lean in, halving the gap between us—

"Is there anything that you . . . ?"

Oh no.

I realize too late, her mouth was forming a question.

"Um," she stammers, pulling back.

"Wow."

I release her, shoving one hand extremely suavely into my pocket and registering the other raking my hair as my soul leaves my body. "Yeah, I'm sorry if I . . ."

"No," she says, alarmed. And then, "I was trying to . . ."

Fuckfuckfuckfuckfuckfuck fuuuuuuck. She thinks I'm an idiot.

"Crap," she says, brows knitted, fist to mouth. It's the universally human reaction to watching someone eat shit.

Oh god, she feels sorry for me.

My heart constricts.

"I didn't mean to . . ."

Eyes wide as saucers. She clamps onto my shoulders, hoists herself up to kiss me with so much force our teeth make an audible knock.

Now it's my turn to be surprised.

She covers her face with her hands. "God, I just head-butted you."

"Okay." I take a deep breath. "Let's pause. I've been wanting to kiss you since the moment you came back to the store."

"Same," she says. "Well, since the moment *I* came back in the store . . . Christ, why am I still talking?"

I laugh.

"You know, we're spending two days together," she says. "I need to discern our compatibility in this arena."

"Agreed."

"So can we both stop talking?" she asks.

I nod in assent. Mouth shut.

She nods. Then licks her lips.

Her hands return to my shoulders.

I angle toward her, and for a moment her lips wriggle into a smile, but when I brush my thumb on her jaw, she quiets and . . .

Holy shit.

Do you guys do this? When that first kiss is so historic, so ruinously good, so ingredients-scrambling that you black out a little?

Apropos of truly nothing, I'd been convinced that Leanna Smart would be a terrible kisser. How could she not be? Lee doesn't *need* to be a good kisser. Elon Musk or Marie Curie aren't required to be good at sex either. It's so not the point. That's not their contribution to civilization. Besides, what guy would willingly volunteer to be the one to inform Leanna Smart that she needs to monitor her saliva output or watch her tongue girth or any of the other mechanical factors that the rest of us have to be leery of?

Thankfully, blessedly, all the noise evaporates. I forget to remember who she is beyond Lee. The warm, soft, incredible-smelling, hilarious girl in my arms who is allowing me to rush headlong into this tunnel that is so consuming that it would blot out the sun. All the usual insecurity and shrapnel that whizz around in my brain stills. For this moment I'm not the worst. In fact, I'm accomplishing something worthwhile.

Which is to say that we are highly compatible in this arena.

"Thank you," she says in a tone that makes me laugh. I half expect her to high-five me.

As I compose myself, the molecules of the room we're standing in assemble to call for the attention it deserves.

This hotel room is bananas.

The entrance opens into a gleaming white-and-silver kitchen on the right, an island separating the lounge area on the left, a huge living room with low minimal sofas, beyond which are sliding-glass doors with a fire pit twinkling outside.

"Nice digs," I tell her. "I never say 'digs,' by the way."

"I dig that you're digging the digs," she says, taking my hand and leading me in, past the enormous white coffee table to flop onto a bed-size pale-gray sectional.

This hotel has nothing to do with the carpeted beige boxes I've visited when mom had medical conferences or when I looked at schools. This is a whole apartment. With an entire second floor.

"Do you stay in hotels a lot?" I want to ask her where she lives, but I probably don't have security clearance for that.

"Yeah," she says, kicking off her sneakers and gathering

her legs beneath her. "My house is far from here." She adds nothing more.

Stretching her arms above her and yawning, she could be anyone I went to school with, and it occurs to me that she has a mortgage. Possibly several.

"Want water?" she asks.

"Sure, but I'll grab it." I get up, pull the charger out of my bag, and head toward the kitchen.

The cabinets are stocked as if you're at someone's house. Wineglasses. Mugs. Mason jars for hipster hydration.

"Get a bottled from the fridge," she calls out as I run the sleek faucet. "Unfiltered LA water's barely potable. And it's not alkaline at all."

Alkalinity has never before been a concern of mine, but something tells me my life after today may barely be recognizable.

I open the fridge. It's no shitty little dorm-room hotel fridge either but a proper big silver one that fancy murderers from movies have. Clearly someone hit the Whole Foods before we arrived. There's eggs, yogurt, fresh cut fruit, and coffee creamer. I grab a Smartwater and plink it with my fingernail. Get this, it's in a glass bottle.

"Whoa." I pull my phone out and shoot a video plinking it again. "I didn't know a glass version was even a thing."

"Oh, you should check out the whole pantry. The snacks are out of control."

The snacks are decent, if uninspired—Terra chips, two

kinds of M&M's, and king-size candy bars for *twenty* bucks a pop, according to the discreet placard resting on the basket. A small reminder that we're in a hotel.

I always thought stocking minibars would be a dream job. For this place, I'd go high-low with wasabi peas, Hot Cheetos, Funyuns to be crazy, Ritter Sports, every Hi-Chew, chocolate-covered Hawaiian macadamia nuts, mini Altoids for the chips, saltwater taffy from Santa Cruz, See's Candies, and those It's It ice cream sandwiches made with oatmeal cookies that I tried to carry at the store back home, but the shipping costs were devastating.

Mr. Kim usually lets me dictate the snack stock if I can talk him through the logistics. I take a picture of the snacks and then delete it and erase the water video. I'm shook that they somehow violate some legal clause I barely remember agreeing to.

"Want one?" I wave the water at her.

"Yeah," she says. "You know what I thought of that's so dumb?"

"Tell me." I kiss her quickly again, stoked that we broke the seal. The sofa's so big we could both lie down without touching.

"I miss my Brita," she declares. "I had a clause for tours that I'd only drink out of my reusable water bottle until I realized they were refilling it with, like, two or three of those tiny Fiji Waters. I'm so tired of living out of suitcases. First-world problems, I know," she says reflexively. "But I actively miss shitty tap water that's been filtered in a plastic pitcher with charcoal particles that I bought from Target in a glass that belongs to me. Shitty tap water from the Valley that my nutritionist swears is making my teeth porous."

"I'd miss New York water for sure," I tell her, inanely happy that she shops at Target like the rest of us. I love Brooklyn tap water. It tastes extra refreshing and bright to me.

"Let's sit outside," she says, and I follow her onto a deck chair. Even in the dark, the chair's warm to the touch from the afternoon sun and it heats up the backs of my thighs. I take off my hoodie gratefully, pull up my sweatpants to reveal my chicken legs, and stretch out.

She takes the seat next to me. Her feet are bare, and I can make out a tiny tattoo on her left ankle that reads 2.22. She brushes her leg with mine and lets it stay there. "Thanks for coming."

"And thank you in advance for not murdering me," I tell her. She laughs. "And for not murdering yourself but making it look like I did it, because I've seen that Netflix special and the brown guy gets it."

She laughs.

"I'm brown too, remember," she says. "Ish."

"Welsh-ish, too."

"Yesh," she says, and we both groan.

Lee leans back, her T-shirt riding up to expose the swell of her belly. She yawns, and then chortles as if she's found her own joke funny again. I love when this girl laughs.

"What do you want to do tonight?"

"Oh, right," she says. "I was going to ask you. Have you ever been here before?"

I shake my head.

"Wow," she exclaims. "I'm drunk with power. On a scale of one to ten, how touristy are you?"

"As in, do I want to see the Hollywood Sign and the Walk of Fame?"

"Yeah."

"Hard pass," I tell her. "For what it's worth, I wouldn't take you to the top of the Empire State Building either."

"What if I really wanted to go?"

"Then we'd fit it in between a guided tour of Times Square and the *Sex and the City* bus."

"Ha. I would never," she says. "Okay, how offended would you be if we watched a movie and ordered room service until the end of rush hour and then reassessed?"

"Zero percent offended."

She yawns again.

"Good. Because I don't feel like causing a riot tonight."

I can't tell if she's kidding.

"Do you have work tomorrow?" I ask her.

She nods while yet another yawn racks her.

"At least in the morning," she says. We wordlessly settle back on the couch. She selects an animated werewolf movie that I've been too lazy to Torrent, proving that it's destiny.

Lee and I are meant to grow old together. She grabs the menu and calls in for salad and soup, while I eye the hummus, which I figure has to be the cheapest.

"Don't worry about the tab," she says. "Snacks, too. The company picks it up."

I order steak frites and bust open the Terra chips as an app.

Chapter 14

The food arrives, and when we rearrange on the couch she invades my side under the auspices of stealing fries, then drapes her body on mine and lingers. Her hair is soft on my neck. I love how she locks into my side, comfortably, lazily, as if we've done this a thousand times before. The anxiety of the day melts away as I realize how tense my shoulders are, how rigid I've been the whole way over. It's hard to reconcile this girl with the paperwork and the billboards, the supple heft of her, the weight, the inconceivable smallness of a body that I can fully wrap my arms around. I feel protective, able, yet completely and utterly awed.

After a while her breathing deepens, becoming rhythmic, which is when I let our food grow cold because she starts snoring softly. It's so endearing, I want to wake her up to tell her about it.

Turns out the werewolf movie's a real tearjerker. I get

choked up because the whole time the baby lycan's trying to find his parents and finally go home. He's caught between the wolves and the humans, not realizing he's the last of his kind. For the entire second act he's searching and searching when the whole time what he wants doesn't exist. But home isn't a place, he comes to realize; it's wherever you find acceptance and support. The kid's voice in the opening musical number sounds so much like Rain—who I guess really must sing like an angel—that it gets me misty-eyed. Poor, doomed preteen werewolf.

As the credits roll Leanna wakes up and smiles sleepily.

"Damn," she says, stretching. "I'm killing it as a tour guide, huh?"

She eats a cold fry and looks at me sheepishly. "Was I snoring?"

I shake my head, but I'm cheesing so hard we both know I'm lying.

"So, where all have you visited?" I ask, the theme of the movie kicking around in my head. We grab our food and travel to the kitchen.

Watching her check the bottom of her bowl to make sure it's microwave safe and then nuking it with a napkin over the top to prevent spatters does something weird to my heart. It reminds me of her coughing fit. I love moments like these. We eat her undressed salad with our hands, crunching on romaine and plucking out croutons, talking all the while.

"Everywhere," she says. "Switzerland, Japan . . ."

"Egypt?"

She nods.

"You see the pyramids?"

"You can't miss 'em."

"What's the verdict?"

"So bizarre. They're astonishing, but they're also just *there*? Most people in the area treat them as a regular part of the scenery. Then there's the tourists who are so hell-bent on getting a selfie with the entire pyramid behind them, cropping out the fast-food restaurants for authenticity." Lee makes a scrunched face, holding her hand out front. "It's straight double chins and backlighting. The real heroes are the selfie-stick hawkers. They make a killing."

I heat up my steak slices on the stove.

"You cook?" she asks.

"Sometimes." I want to manage her expectations around how I think Maggi sauce fixes most culinary shortcomings.

"It's attractive," she says approvingly as we eat the meat with our hands.

"How well do you know New York?" I imagine where I'd take her if we were hanging out.

"I've been there so many times without seeing it that I don't know how to answer that."

I think about this a lot. The difference between watching and seeing.

"Isn't it wild how you never appreciate anything that's

right in front of you?" I've never been to the Guggenheim, that spiral-shaped museum that resembles a drill bit, and I can't remember the last time I went to Central Park as a destination.

"Oh totally," she says. "Take the Alps. Crossing into Italy from Switzerland, you're staring up at these looming, altogether-indifferent snow-capped ecological monuments, and yet most locals bitch about tunnel traffic around the holidays."

She dips a piece of meat into the side of salad dressing, and it strikes me how pleasurable it is to watch a girl eat. I would happily feed her forever. "Plus, show me any tourist who's ever actively enjoying the moment . . ."

"People aren't ever in the moment," I chime in, imagining the hordes who travel trillions of miles only to lodge a screen between their eyes and the very thing they've crossed oceans to experience. "We have to plan and scheme and shop the best deal, and when we arrive, the first order of business is to collapse the experience and stuff it into our phones. Instant gratification isn't good enough. We have to save it for later since we're sooo busy."

Not that I don't do it too. Last summer at a music festival, me and Tice practically got cramps in our arms filming. "Sometimes I miss when I was capable of being bored. Where your brain goes when it's empty." I clear my throat, "I didn't mean to monologue you. . . ."

"No, I agree with everything." She leans over to kiss me.

We settle back into our nap spots.

"Do you ever think about how things don't disappear anymore?" she asks.

I never know what she's going to say next.

"Like how energy, mass, everything is conserved?" she continues.

"Are we talking about death?"

"No," she says. "Although that would be so us to talk about becoming corpses."

I warm at there being an "us." Even as it relates to cadavers.

"You ever think about what the cloud is? What happens to these selfies and videos of pyramids or road trips and concerts and weddings we never look at again?"

Lee leans into me. Little-spoon style. Folding my arms across her chest.

"It's not that mysterious," I tell her. I can say this because I Pulled a Pab on this very topic two months ago and had to google it before my brain let me sleep. "The cloud sounds ethereal, but it's a mess of analog-ass server farms that overheat and contribute to global warming. They get so hot that Facebook has a data center by the arctic circle in Sweden. And Microsoft has one inside the literal ocean."

"I believe this with my brain," she says. "But I want to see them."

"You want to vacation at a server farm?"

"Why not?" She shrugs. "Take a selfie and be part of the problem." She turns around to kiss my chin. We are officially at the laissez-faire chin-kissing portion of this deal.

I'm pumped. I'm also not above rubbing my chin reflexively to check for stubble or, god forbid, pimples. "Have *you* been to a lot of places?" she asks.

I'm self-conscious answering given who she is, but that's stupid. It's a short guy forbidding his wife to wear heels as if the entire world around them isn't a dead giveaway. "Not really. I've been to Canada."

"Where would you go if you could go anywhere?"

I give this some thought.

"I guess Korea. Or Pakistan, but I'd need a visa."

"Seoul's great," she says. "I've never been to Pakistan."

"Well, I haven't been to either," I tell her. "We were supposed to visit Korea when I was a kid, but my mom had a huge fight with my grandparents and then they died within a year of each other."

"I'm sorry," she says.

"It's sad. It's bizarre how much we don't talk about it," I continue.

I don't know why I'm telling her this, but it's easier that she's not facing me. "I was in eighth grade when my halmoni—my grandmother—died. I asked my mom why we weren't going to her funeral, but she didn't want to talk about it. My mom's mysterious that way. Or stubborn, I guess. When her dad died, I didn't ask. It was too sad. And the way she pretended everything was fine was somehow sadder. She started working a lot around then."

I'd never made the connection before. The timing on her schedule ramping up like that.

"Families are a trip," says Lee. "You think you know them so well that you stay wrong about each other."

It's true.

"It wasn't until I lived on my own that my mom and dad became these other people to me," she says. "Not that whole, 'Oh, my parents are flawed humans' thing. I've known *that* for a while. My dad has never been a regular fixture, but it's only recently that I can accept that without being mad at him." She shifts in my arms.

"That's what I mean by *other people*. It's not my responsibility to get to the bottom of why my mom's so unhappy. Nor is it on me to teach my dad how to parent. I love them and I forgive them, but I don't go to the hardware store looking for orange juice and I don't expect them to give me things they don't have. I give myself permission not to spend time with them. Thank god for abuela, though. I don't know what I'd do without her."

She sounds smart. Wise. Meanwhile, I don't know what to do with the shame I feel about the way my dad's life turned out. Or the guilt of ignoring my mom. "How'd you figure this out?"

"Therapy," she says. "But once I knew, it made so much sense. This was a huge tell: My mom doesn't ask me questions. Ever. It's just statements like, 'You sound good.' Or else, 'I saw you on *Late Night* and I liked your shoes.' She never once has asked how I'm doing or if I'm okay."

"I guess not a whole lot of people think to worry about you."

"Exactly," she says, turning her head to look at me. "It's so lonely when no one worries about you. Not even your parents. You start to wonder what's wrong with you."

"Okay," I say, squeezing her. "From here on out consider me moderately to gravely concerned about you at all times."

"Thank you," she says. "I know it's absurd, but hearing those words actually means a lot."

At last my championship fretting skills are getting me somewhere.

"I'd love to go to Korea with you," she says, clasping my hands. "Asia's fun. Tokyo, Shanghai, Hong Kong, Seoul, they're so fast. And I love the time difference. Asia's so future. I love cities. The thrum. New York has that too. And the audio! It sounds so amazing. I make voice notes of street sounds whenever I can. But most of the time I ruin them."

"How?"

"The people saying my name."

I remember the screaming girls. How deafening and disorienting it must be if it follows you.

"I'm there but I'm not there," she continues. "It's what you were saying about the selfies. In every town, no matter what's going on, I never get to immerse myself in it. The environment looks so inviting, but the second I appear it changes to accommodate me. I'm blocked off from reality. Suspended in these glass towers or these cars, and it's as though I'm vacuum sealed or in a terrarium. No, a diorama.

"The food doesn't change since my chef travels with me.

And I'm usually on a diet set by my nutritionist. It used to make me crazy, but it's become a necessity. I don't have to make any decisions. I show up and smile through the same interviews with the same approved answers." She sighs. "You know, I used to kill myself making these unique responses so I wouldn't sound fake, but then you discover that all the questions are the same and no one notices or cares.

"So while I'm there lip-flapping the same three singles on some stage, I can see the beast of the city in the distance. The one that everyone else gets to live inside except me, and I want that. I long to be the one taking a ride inside of a giant."

The way she puts it makes me picture her as the lead in a Miyazaki animation. I want to break the hex and set her free.

Still, I'm reminded of how reluctant I was to ask where we were going, as if Lee is a current or a force of nature not to be questioned. "What you do . . . who you are . . . it has its own gravitational pull or distortion field, I guess."

"I see that," she says. "But I'm a cog in the machinery too. People are so startled when I voice an opinion. It doesn't occur to them that I read books or watch movies or have allergies and get heartburn." She places a hand to her sternum and grimaces.

"Do you have heartburn?"

"Yeah," she says. "Your fries are trying to assassinate me."

"Well, I'm honored to see this rare and tender side of you," I tell her.

"You are very welcome," she says, and lets out a burp. "Excuse me," she says, laughing.

"Do you want to go to the pool?" she asks.

Do I want to bob around in water in minimal clothing with this girl?

"Sure, okay."

Chapter 15

When Lee sidles out from the bedroom, a towel's fastened at her armpits and her hair is in a topknot. Unsure of the level of my own anticipated nudity, I'm wearing trunks that I thought to pack at the last minute and an entire bathrobe with a belt that I don't stop messing with until she emerges.

"Hi," she says shyly.

Be my girlfriend.

"Hey."

I follow her to the pool, our feet padding silently. Unmoved by the clearly marked sign not to dive, she knifes smoothly into the water, a flash of white bikini. I wade in since a cannonball is my go-to. She swims toward me, and I marvel at the slope of her shoulders. I'd been worried about our bodies. Concerned that she'd be scarily, celestially beautiful or disastrously, worryingly thin. The reality is gentler, warmer, curved, and impossibly inviting.

She swims in a practiced stroke, testifying to lessons. There's so much I don't know about her and want to. It's hard to imagine that it was *this* morning that we had bagels. That we're in the same day by some trick of magic.

Lee's head pierces the chrome surface of water and the lights lend a dreamy phosphorescence. I'm trying not to stare. It's a baffling tension to have seen her body before but only from afar. Despite the countless appearances and photo shoots, you only ever see Leanna Smart in parts. Even her own music videos focus on tight frames. Most of them rendered digitally. You're trained to batch process a celebrity. As if they're diagrams of livestock with dotted lines to indicate cuts of meat. Portions dictated by price. A face in a cosmetics ad, hair in a shampoo commercial, arm in billboards for watches.

I wonder if she's appraising me similarly. I lean in the dark, pool tile cold on my back, hoping to appear rakish. Thinking of her thinking of me makes me anxious. I'm unsure what to do with my hands.

"Where'd you learn to swim?" I ask her.

"It's the one thing my dad taught me."

"Does he live here too?"

"Yeah." Then silence. The pool burbles.

"I don't know how to ride a bike though," she offers after a while, saying nothing more of her father. "I am, however, an accomplished equestrian."

"Naturally."

In the pool, floating at the same height, our heads are

tantalizingly close. She's slippery as I wrap my hands around her waist. The temperature of the pool is comparable to the inside of a mouth.

"And I can do a backflip," she whispers, thigh brushing against mine, chest pressed on my forearm.

"Same," I tell her.

I taste a garlicky note on my tongue. I'd kill for a piece of gum right now. I brought gum. And mints. I also have condoms in case the gum and mints lead to anything. They're all helpfully located in my bag back in the room.

"I'm also a mean juggler," she says.

"Impressive."

She wraps her legs around my hips as I hoist her up.

Her face is inches from mine.

"Carolina Suarez."

"Yes?"

"What exactly are your intentions this evening?"

She smiles. A flash of teeth.

"Moral corruption and induction into Team Smartees."

Right. *Team* Smartees. Registered trademark. A logo. A legion.

The paperwork flashes in my brain again. The contractual language that holds dominion over us both. I remind myself that this is Lee. And that Lee feels as much a captive to this colossal outfit as I do.

Still, the thing I realize belatedly is that I want some assurances of my own. I want to know how often she does this. What bodies lie in her wake. Whether the statistics are in my favor. I want a clue on how I'll feel in the future. Tomorrow. A week from now. In a month.

I ignore it all and kiss her.

Blackout.

There's nothing else for it.

Leanna Smart kisses me back.

Sweet oblivion.

Fuck it. If I'm a pawn in Leanna Smart's quiet ongoing campaign to defile unsuspecting youths from bodegas nationwide, so be it.

When we tread back to the room hand in hand, we don't say a word.

Dripping pool water on the kitchen floor.

I'm wedged by the counter. Her fingertips slide under my waistband.

Her mouth is salty.

"Is this okay?" I ask before tugging on a bikini string. She nods; it loosens.

"Wait," she says. Pulls away.

"Okay." Hands by my sides. Instantly. As if stung. My heart is hammering, and I take a deep breath. It's a Herculean effort to deactivate various physiological sequences.

"Sorry," she says, retying her swimsuit.

"No, I'm sorry." I shake my head quickly to clear it. "Are you . . . ?"

"I'm fine. It's okay," she says, and then she takes a deep breath. "Whoo."

We collect ourselves.

"I need to ask you something," she says. I scan my entire sexual history. A pregnancy scare with Heather, the HIV test after a stupid hookup, the coat-check girl at El Portal last fall who ended up being married, Alice (Tinder) whose HPV phobia means I've learned absolutely everything there is to know about the human papillomavirus, including how it's not called the human papillomavirus *virus* despite the big *V in HPV*. I think about the number of people I've slept with and if the number's a lot or too little. I'd always thought it was exactly in the middle. But what do I know?

"Ask me anything," I tell her.

"I need you not to google me," she says.

"What?"

"Don't go searching for news on me," she tries again. Since the numbskull in front of her doesn't know what the googles are.

"Wait, is this a question?"

Her posture slackens as if a vital bit of scaffolding's buckled. "There's so much crap out there on me. My family. My friends. What I eat for breakfast. I can't anticipate what people are saying, because most of it's bullshit, so I need you not to go believing things I can't keep track of."

"Makes sense." It honestly does. "Of course."

"Not 'of course,'" she says. "It's not as easy as you think. I need to minimize your exposure to fake news."

"No alternative facts."

"So no deep dives of who I'm sleeping with, my elective

surgeries, my multiple pregnancies, if I have neck cancer . . ."

"Neck cancer?"

"There's no shortage of weirdos out there."

"I promise."

"It's hard for me to trust anyone," she says solemnly, a storminess in her expression, as though she's thinking of someone in particular.

"I won't give you any reason not to trust me," I tell her.

The sheen of her eyes catches the low light in the room.

"It makes it easier if you don't pry."

"Okay. Media blackout instated."

"And if you ever have any questions, you'll ask me?"

"A hundred percent."

She returns her hands to my waist. "So, now that we've installed a prophylactic force field between you and the gossip jackals . . ."

The pause is interminable.

She undoes her bikini top herself and catches the fabric with her hands to hold it there.

"One more thing," she says. "It's not a question either."

"Okay."

Lee's hands fall away to expose her breasts. Except they're smoothed over by a matching set of fleshy cups, her torso resembling a mannequin's or a Barbie doll.

"Whoa."

"Yeah," she says, peeling one off, scowling. "You may as well see this side of me too. I almost rip my nipples off every day."

"Jesus." I wince. The way her skin stubbornly clings to the adhesive looks terrible.

She drops one, then the other onto the floor. "Ahhhhhh," she breathes, massaging her chest.

"Did you bring condoms?" she whispers.

"Yes," I admit.

"Perv," she says, and laughs softly, pulling me toward her.

Chapter 16

Okay, what I don't know about rich people could fill a book. Same goes for famous people, but forget what you heard about lobster mac and cheese and bottles of Moscato, because if there's anything that separates the one percent from the rest of us it's the mattresses. Expensive-ass pillow tops, slippery, cool sheets, plus blackout curtains that ease you into a quality of sleep where nightmares are too low-rent to touch you. I roll over, and Lee's red hair is fanned out on the smooth white sheets. Some time during the night she's put on my T-shirt, and this kills me. It is, without a doubt, extremely clichéd in romantic comedies, but it's wonderful in real life. I kiss the back of her neck, put on some shorts, and head downstairs to make coffee.

It's after eight, but it feels much later, and while searching for mugs I idly daydream of how if we lived together we'd split time between New York and LA. I could go on tour with her and survive out of suitcases. Become a groupie. Take care of our vaguely beige kids who'll speak every language and eat any kind of food. Maybe get a man-bun.

God, what is happening to me?

I despise myself for believing it as I think it.

"Thanks for letting me sleep in," she says, hugging me from behind. I startle, paranoid that she sees my gold-digging fantasy. I hand her an Americano. With enough sugar to promote instant tooth decay and gobs of cream. Just how she made it when we first met. She takes a sip and tilts her head up for a kiss. Part coffee, part toothpaste. "How's LA treating you so far?"

"Five stars, would visit again. Subscribe."

I can honestly attest that there's no LA-specific activity I'd have rather been doing last night.

"I'm going to take some calls," she says apologetically.

"Do your thing," I tell her.

She dumps out a handful of cases of AirPods from her bag onto the counter and eyes me watching her. "I'm constantly losing these," she says, and smiles before taking her coffee outside. "I'll be quick but do you want tacos after?"

Yep, definitely want to marry this girl.

I kiss her. "Always."

LA's incredible. People on the East Coast go on and on about seasons and the turning of leaves, apple picking, whatever. But fuck what you heard; none of it beats sunshine. It makes no sense that this temperate paradise is attached to the same country as New York. Having a car at your disposal is chill too, and there's a beat-up silver Nissan pulled into what I guess is our private garage. It's well guarded by leaves, and the only camouflage that would make it more effective is if it were a Prius.

"It's my secret car," she tells me, pulling on a hat, a wig, and sunglasses as we get in. "One of a few beaters I use. This one's my grandmother's." In the same way that it's unfathomable to see Leanna Smart naked until you do, it's absurd to watch her assume tasks as pedestrian as driving a car. On some level I understand that this person who stirs her foot as she sleeps also sells out arena concerts worldwide, but sitting next to her careening into traffic like a bat out of hell breaks my brain.

In twenty minutes we pull up to a remote gas station where there's an airbrushed taco truck with a line snaking in front.

"My favorite spot doesn't open until after sundown," she says. "But this one's legit."

She texts someone, and in moments a dude in an apron and black tee approaches with a huge smile on his face.

"Ay," he says. Lee leans out of her window and gives him a hug.

"This is Hector," she tells me. "Pablo." He shakes my hand and passes her a delicious-smelling white paper bag as she palms him a hundred-dollar bill as seamlessly as if it were a drug deal.

They chat for a while in Spanish, and I can tell she's

shit-talking because of her tone. They hug again before he heads back.

Within minutes we're tucked safely behind a car wash and we've got meat juice dripping down our chins and we're moaning. We've got the doors cracked open and our legs hanging out while we shovel tiny pork tacos into our faces.

Lee's hat's crooked and her sunglasses are sliding down.

"Isn't this good?" she asks, mouth full.

"Spectacular," I tell her. "It's awesome that you speak Spanish. I don't speak any of my parents' languages."

"I'm nowhere near fluent," she says. "But I'm so pumped we're finally doing Spanish songs for the deluxe edition. I don't know if I told you but my next record's called *Lee*."

"Oh, rad." Meanwhile, I've been fed ads of it for weeks based on my search history. "You sound excited."

"I guess I am," she says. "Don't get me wrong. I'm still over it . . . the music stuff . . ."

She fishes out a slimy charred pepper slice from the tinfoiled packet on the dashboard and plants it onto my taco. "Did I tell you that Hector"—she nods back at the truck—"usually charges for grilled onions and jalapenos? But of course I get them gratis." She blots her fingers on a napkin.

"He's been here twelve years. Isn't that amazing?"

She hands me a napkin and points at her cheek, then laughs as I fail to wipe whatever food is on my face.

"Here." She swipes.

The tender action hits me right in the solar plexus. This

time tomorrow I'll be back home. Worse than home. I'll be seated across from a guidance counselor, pleading that he find enough value in my future to grant me the privilege of going into more cataclysmic debt at a school I don't want to attend. I breathe deep.

"Thank you for bringing me." I gesture at the beautiful weather and the resplendent tacos. "This is the dream."

"You're so cute," she says. "You keep thanking me for everything."

Neither of us mention me leaving.

"What do you want to do for the rest of the day?"

I'd be happy doing anything with this girl.

"I don't care," I tell her.

"Same." And then. "God, you know what I really want to do? I want to see my fucking abuela."

"So let's go see your fucking abuela."

"Really?"

"Really."

"Seriously?"

"Look, I'm super down if you're okay with it." At this point there's not a whole lot I wouldn't be down for.

Lee chews on her thumbnail before breaking into a wide grin. "Fuck it," she says. "Let's go."

The drive to Moreno Valley takes over an hour, and I wonder who decides what neighborhoods in Los Angeles get to look like. They remind me of wallpaper with door-ways or bookshelves painted right on them, because the landscape doesn't seem quite real. Honestly, the unbroken loop of fast-food restaurants, lavanderías, donut shops, and gas stations seem the work of an uninspired graphic designer—*control V, control V, control V.*

"Do you know these neighborhoods?"

"Not really," she says as it flits past her profile. "I wish I did." I try to see the ten-mile stretches with different eyes— zoning out, warm air on my face, letting the colors bleed together. All the signs are sun-bleached as if sent through the wash too many times.

"LA doesn't work that way," she tells me. "I've been to a few spots." She points out a gas station. "But unless a friend lives here or there's a crazy-good restaurant someone tells you about, you mostly drive by."

"I guess LA takes a while to let you in."

"Totally," she says.

Meanwhile, New York swallows you whole.

"I'm so glad you're coming with me."

"I hope she likes me," I tell her. My palms sweat.

"She will."

"So she doesn't think all Muslims 'did 9/11'? Or is she going to be disappointed that I'm not in a K-pop super-group?"

"What?" Lee eyes me as if I'm having a stroke.

"You never know what the expectation will be with older people," I tell her.

"You don't know a lot of older people, do you?"

I think about my grandparents and how they're not in our lives. "I guess not."

"I mean . . ." She smiles. "Abuela's hard-core Catholic, so whoever isn't on that team is going straight to hell. But I'll make sure to ask her how racistly she feels toward you."

"Tight."

"I'll make sure to do it in English too, as soon as we get there."

"Perfect."

Lee's abuela lives in a gated community off another nondescript patch of scrubland. It's pink and gray and right next to a church.

It reads SUNSET CLIFFS in cursive by the guest parking lot, and I see that it's an assisted living facility but the upbeat kind.

There are Easter decorations hung up throughout the lobby, and signs point to a pool and a spa. As far as I can tell it's the Disney Cruise Ship of homes.

"There's a four-star chef here," Lee says as we sign in. "Not that she lets anyone touch her food."

I follow her into an elevator, wondering if she pays for the place. Probably.

"Abuela!" she exclaims when a diminutive woman with pitch-black hair and a slightly curved posture greets us in the darkened hallway, wearing a dark dress. I jump a little since she's *right there* as soon as the elevator doors open. I wasn't expecting anyone, let alone an emaciated woman with bead-shiny eyes.

But then she smiles, features disappearing into her wrinkles as she pounds me on the back.

She hugs Lee, and there's another flurry of Spanish. Her grandmother calls her *Carolina* with the trilly *r* as we follow her to her apartment. Abuela walks surprisingly fast and talks even faster, and I recognize the word "novio" for boyfriend even if I only learned it from a J Balvin song. It sucks that I don't understand any more despite taking four years of Spanish in high school. Ask where the library or shoe store is and I'm golden.

The apartment feels crowded with the three of us standing in it. Granted Lee's grandma is under five feet tall and could probably breakdance in here if she wanted to, but my living room is bigger, which says a lot. Even still, her enormous flat-screen TV, mounted to the wall, is the size of a chalkboard. You could catch motion sickness playing video games on it.

"This is Pablo."

I shake abuela's hand awkwardly since she's holding a balled-up napkin, and while I take care not to crush her papery bones, abuela shows me she's no slouch in the handshake department. Her grip is cold and firm, purply veins darkening.

"Pablo," she greets me. "Pleasure. Sofia," she says, tapping her chest.

"Pleasure," I repeat. I never say "pleasure." "Thanks for having me."

Chapter 17

A table is set up in the middle. It's small, printed to resemble marble, and is covered in a layer of thick, see-through plastic, laden with tiny bowls of food and Tupperware containers opened up. There's an orange cut into segments resting on a rubbery pink lid. A handful of chopped onions in a squat plastic tub. There are little green things that appear to be pickles but not made out of any vegetable I'd ever recognize. Beans in a dish. And a saucepan so small its belly rivals the capacity of a good-size mug. The pot contains meat in a scarlet sauce where the layer of bright oil rises a half-inch above. The hodgepodge speaks to bits and bobs left over from a hundred meals, and it reminds me of my dad and how if you bring a snack to his house, say, a ninety-nine-cent bag of peanuts, you'll find it two months later in the back of a cupboard with a chip clip.

"Are you hungry, Pablo?" she asks me.

I nod with enthusiasm.

"I'm starving." Lee brushes past me to sit down. She kisses her grandmother on the cheek and animatedly chatters in Spanish, her grandmother calling her *Lina, Lina, Lina.* The conversation involves a lot of lip-smacking from Lee as she cracks jokes and sticks her tongue out as the punchline. With the three of us gathered, Lee claps her hands to survey the table. She looks so happy. "I told her I haven't had a home-cooked meal in months."

We eat the pickled green things, which wind up being cactus salad, and spicy beans smeared on tortillas and rice, and Lee and her grandmother are so busy catching up and translating and putting things on my plate and passing me containers with radishes and peppers and crumbly cheese and cilantro that I lose track of what we're eating.

"Do you eat goat?" Lee asks me, and I nod. "People are weird about goat," she says.

"Not my people," I tell her as she spoons the stew onto my tiny mound of rice. I go to take a bite and she stops me.

"Ah," she says. She hits it with a sprinkle of chopped onion. "Now."

I pile some more cactus onto it for good measure, the slippery green-beaniness contrasting with the richness of the meat. And balance a nugget of white chalky cheese on top for luck.

"Nicely played," she says.

I chew, and it's delicious. Her grandmother nods her approval.

"She says you're a good eater," Lee tells me, smiling. I've never been fussy about food. There are stories of how I ate bits of kimchi rinsed in water from the time I had a single tooth.

With a mouthful of meat and chili, I grab a brown, flat circle from a Styrofoam plate and put it in my mouth to discover it's sweet. Chocolaty.

The women laugh. Her grandmother cracks on me.

"That was dessert," Lee says. "Her neighbors brought those over." And sure enough, I discover it's a Ritz Cracker covered in chocolate.

Genius.

"It's so good." I'm slightly embarrassed. Lee spoons some rice and sauce into her mouth and pops a chocolate chaser to try it.

"Real good," she says, and makes her grandmother do the same, and we all agree that the sweetness excellently counteracts the spice.

"Like mole," says her grandmother to me, which makes Lee go, "See? Mexicans thought of everything already. You didn't invent shit." When she laughs, a piece of food goes flying out of her mouth and lands directly on my forearm, which cracks her up even more. And at that moment—that precise sliver of time and the myriad decisions that led me to sit in front of this girl and her grandmother in the middle of a town I've never heard of—confirms that no matter what happens, this is where I'm meant to be.

I've never been more sure of anything.

I remind myself to remember it. Will myself to record

this. Log it for keeps. Access it again and again whenever I need something good and true. I don't know what brought Lee to the store the first time. Or what compelled her to return. If it was by luck or by design. But I decide then that it doesn't matter. Whatever benevolent conspiracy gave me this, all I need to know is that Leanna Smart's got nothing on Carolina Suarez.

We retire to the living room, as in, we take a half step from where we were seated. Me and Lee shove the dining table into the kitchen so we can make space. Abuela pours us instant coffee. The kind that my dad keeps around with the sugar and nondairy creamer mixed right into the plastic sleeve. Lee sits on the floor and reaches for a bookshelf as abuela sits on the love seat.

"Check this out," Lee says, grabbing a red leather-bound photo album.

I join her on the floor. Baby photos and pictures from school. "Lo-fi Instagram."

"I haven't looked at this in years."

We pause on a blown-up shot of Lee as a toddler in a rainbow bathing suit wearing clown makeup. She's staring right into the camera.

"Whoa . . ." It looks haunted as fuck.

"I know." She traces the makeup on her baby face.

She's in the backyard with blurs of other children, half in, half out of the blue plastic kiddie pool. There are adults as well. Knees mostly—total kids'-eye view—but Lee's the only one facing us.

"Why clown makeup?"

"Why am I the *only* one wearing clown makeup?"

"Whoa . . ." It's true. No one else is painted that way.

"I know," she says. "To this day I have no idea about what was going on here. My mother doesn't remember even being there."

She flips the page. Newspaper clippings and announcements. Local pageants and small parts in Moreno Valley theater productions.

"Abuela collects everything," she says. "Always has."

"My mom is the least sentimental person I know," I tell her. "She opens the mail with one foot on the trash can pedal and says, 'aw' and then tosses it. Christmas cards. Newborn announcements. Everything. 'Aw' and done."

"Efficient," she says, and leans over to kiss my cheek. On instinct I check abuela for any signs of disapproval, but she's smiling beatifically into her coffee cup.

We keep flipping. There's a series of Lee at varying ages in frilly dresses and big hair. In one of the shots the lens is fogged up all dreamy, reminding me of glamour portraits of pageant babies.

There's a picture of Lee at four with a sash and crown. A thin brunette with really skinny eyebrows, presumably Lee's mom, bends down as her hair falls directly into her daughter's face. Lee meanwhile is grimacing, swatting at the obstruction.

"Me and mom's relationship to a T," she says, and I laugh. Lee's trying to make a break for it.

"Where's she from?" There's something in the huge hair that could either be San Antonio or Staten Island.

Lee snaps the book shut with a kind of finality.

"Here," she says. "But that's the thing about Southern California that you forget. It's the American South."

A contented sigh escapes from abuela. So far my Los Angeles visit has been composed of a hotel so grandiose it will torment me for life, a taco truck so delicious it will do the same, the interior of a car that doesn't belong to Lee, and an old folks' home. I think of Tice snapping on me for not going to Malibu or Melrose, but I love this trip. It's a version of Los Angeles that's real to Lee. One I had to be invited into, hidden from the street driving by.

"I can't believe I have work tomorrow," she says into my shoulder. For a moment I'd forgotten. What all this entails.

I do the dishes to take my mind off what kind of life I'm returning to. I had to fight abuela's vise grip as she blocked me from the sink, but soon enough I'm washing, Lee's drying, and her grandmother's watching telenovelas on her TV with the volume set to eleven.

"Sometimes I dream of getting a house for me and my grandmother, but she won't have it. She says I'm always running around the world and that she'd be too lonely living in a big house all by herself. This is the best I could do. Plus, she picked that out." She nods at the TV and laughs dryly, gazing out of the window as her smile fades. That's when I see it. Right across the street, as if the zoning ordinance has a twisted sense of humor, there's a funeral parlor.

We say our goodbyes, abuela handing me a few chocolate Ritz Crackers in a Star Wars Ziploc where the twin moons of Tatooine have faded off from reuse. But when we reach the car, I check my phone to see the roommate group chat's blowing up.

Where the F r u?

Wyn's offering any roommate twenty bucks to shovel the walk. The Greek chorus is trying to ratchet the bid up to a hundred.

Shit.

Shovels.

I scroll.

"Whoa."

The first text is our front door covered in what has to be at least two feet of snow.

"What?" Lee asks me.

"Blizzard." It never occurred to me to check the weather in the perpetual seventy-degree chill zone that is LA. In New York, however, there's a meteorological event called a bomb cyclone. A nor'easter with winds so intense the snow's falling sideways. It's not letting up for at least another day.

Lee's phone lights up. "Yeah, your flight's canceled," she says. It's Jess.

Fuck. Fuckfuckfuckfuckfuckfuck.

Joey Santos. The meeting. Five Points. Dr. Houlihan and his wife. I'm never going to hear the end of this.

"I have to get home." All the food in my gut revolts.

"Jess says she can get you on a red-eye tomorrow night, but you won't get in until seven the following morning. All the airports are closed."

My heart jackrabbits. This is it. I'm canceled. I'll have to work at a bodega for the rest of my life.

Shit. The Kims.

"I have work tomorrow."

"I'm sure they'll understand," she says sympathetically. "It's weather."

Given my lie about NYU, I can't tell her everything I'm concerned about.

"Plus, you know what this means, right?" Lee ventures a smile. "We get another day." She raises her fist.

She's right. Through an act of god, we have another day.

"Another day," I repeat. I'm numb, but she's grinning, poking me in the ribs, wheedling me to celebrate.

Lee unclips her seat belt, lunges, and kisses me, both hands on my face, staring deep into my eyes. "I knew the story wasn't going to end tonight," she says. "I had a feeling."

I kiss her back.

"One more day!" she declares, both arms raised. Victorious. "One more day!"

"One more day!"

"Fuck work!" she says. "Fuck responsibilities!"

"Yeah," I chime in. "Fuck it all."

Lee's here. I'm here. How could anything else even chart?

. . .

I read in the *Post* that it costs a million dollars for every inch of snow that falls on New York City streets.

I have to figure the going rate of halting the entirety of Leanna Smart productions for an hour is similarly staggering. No salt, sand, or hard-hatted men battling ice to clear roads, but the calls are endless.

"I'm sorry," says Lee.

It's six forty-five a.m., and by my count Lee's apologized to at least a thousand people. To her credit, she handles it smoothly. Professionally. As if she's just doing her job in informing you that what you wanted is no longer happening. And that *your* only job is to accept it.

"I know," she whispers, closing the glass door behind her to walk barefoot on the patio again in my T-shirt, again in the hotel room. I can't hear the rest of it, but the face of bad news is pretty universal. Even if that face is Leanna Smart.

By seven thirty Jessica comes over with an assistant. Dora or Cora. Short haired. In smart black jeans and a black blazer. Nobody introduces me to her. I retreat to the bedroom, relegated to the kiddie table.

I shut the door to call Mr. Kim. I've never called in before. Ever.

"I had to travel to California last-minute." The self-loathing bursts in my chest. "For schools. To visit. I'm going back to college." None of this makes sense, but I hope he'll relay my excuse to Mrs. Kim since school cancels so many sins.

I search for my mom's email about Mr. Santos with his contact in it. I plug mom's name in the search bar and scroll. Zip. I search "Santos." "Five Points." "Meeting." Nothing. I thumb frantically until the dates roll back a few years and I start at the beginning. He's going to think I'm such an idiot.

I call Five Points, where an automated number asks if I know the extension of the party I wish to contact. I check the time. By now it's noon in New York. I'd have to leave in fifteen minutes to take the F into the city to meet this guy. Scratch that. I would have to leave immediately for train delays. That is if I weren't three thousand miles away.

S-A-N-# I mash into the phone once I reach the faculty directory. The phone goes dead. Then a dial tone. Perfect. I hit redial when Lee knocks.

"Good morning," she says, pushing the bedroom door open.

"Hey," I call out. I feel as though I've been caught doing something shady. I hang up as it rings.

"Sorry," she says. "Were you on the phone?"

"No. Just finished up."

Then I get a load of her.

Whoa.

If I *were* home I'd miss this. In the last half-hour Leanna Smart has changed into a red sports bra and matching leggings that are soaked through. "Hi," she says, tilting her head so her long ponytail flops to one side.

How am I this lucky?

She takes my hand, and we go downstairs to meet a man

so uniformly tanned he looks as though he were rolled in paint. He's wearing a white singlet with CALIFORNIA airbrushed onto it. I have a long-standing belief that advertising the name of any state instantly implies you're not a local.

"Pablo, this is Marco." I shake Singlet's hand. His palms are rough.

"I'm sorry you couldn't train with us this morning, Pablo," he says in a European Spanish accent.

"Coffee?" Jess nods toward me.

"Thanks." I grab a mug.

Marco leaves because a man in his fifties named Jerry's arrived. He's wearing a suit. And his sternness and expensive aftershave fills the room. He and Lee walk outside to talk. The temptation to read lips is stunning.

"Sleep well?" asks Jess, who looks up from her phone. Rather phones, plural. There are three on the kitchen counter. One facedown with the phone number printed on a white label on the back. More AirPod cases beside them. I wonder if she's angry with me. The interloper. The interference that's wreaked havoc on her plans.

Jerry's back is turned, but something he says makes Lee laugh.

"Not really." Unlike the first blissful night, my dreams were plagued with the anxiety that comes with giving up on your life to run away with the circus. "What about you?"

"Well . . . ," she says, and smiles pleasantly, though it never quite reaches her eyes.

"I'm sure the change of plans isn't easy for you," I acknowledge.

"Oh, it's fine," she says primly. Switching phones. "The timing isn't optimal, but these things rarely are."

The coffee's bitter. Probably laced with arsenic.

"The last time she took off last-minute like this she had shingles," Jess says serenely. "July, 2014."

One of the phones ring. She checks the number. Sighs. "Just don't tell me you're going to Disneyland," she says. This time she really does smile. "I know it's cute on TV, but I'm in no mood to assign a security detail to cover your asses on Space Mountain, okay?" She gets on the phone.

"Hi, Fatima!" she coos, collapsing on the couch. "I'm so glad you called."

Chapter 18

"**Just remember that** wherever you look is where you'll go."

This is not the greatest idea, but it was the only one I had. It's not Disneyland either, for what it's worth. If anything, it's shaping up to be a huge mistake.

"I don't think we have insurance clearance for this," Lee tells me dubiously, glaring at me from under the enormous graphite helmet on her head.

The bike we got at Target.

Well, I got it. She waited in the car after conducting an exhaustive Internet search. Ironically, we also discovered that a Leanna Smart branded bike does exist. It's rainbow with neon streamers and a basket, but they were sold out. On the box is a terrible Photoshop job of Lee popping a wheelie.

"The only difference between knowing how to do it and not knowing is to learn!" she exclaims. Lee's said this to me at least four times in the last fifteen minutes.

We're on a quiet residential street a few blocks below Pico, which I guess is LA's version of Houston Street but way longer. Lee drove us around for ages.

"Too hilly," she says on a street called Rimpau.

"Too many cars," she says of another. It's a game of residential Goldilocks.

"Bad juju," she says of Keniston because, "Jess used to mess with an evil guy who lived here."

After circling for twenty minutes, Lee parks. "This is it."

Before we get out, we run through our plan.

All the best YouTube instructionals say it's best to learn how to balance first without even putting your feet on the pedals.

"So it's balance, balance, balance," recites Lee. "Then, when I feel confident enough, I lift my legs, placing my feet on the pedals, and then *boom*—I'm riding a bike."

"Boom," I tell her. "You're a polymath who knows how to tame horses and juggle. I bet you learn this in ten minutes."

"It's the final frontier," she says. "This and falconry."

She looks so serious in her starter bike helmet, elbow and knee pads. I can't help but kiss her.

"No, Pab," she says, swatting me away. "I have to focus. You know the only difference between knowing how to do it and not is to learn."

The first few trials go disastrously.

She's too quick and skittish. At the slightest wobble her feet reach for the ground.

"You've got to be traveling at a certain speed to keep it upright," I tell her. I get on the bike to demonstrate, but of course it's describing a color you've invented to someone over the phone.

"Are you engaging your core?" she asks after I zoom down the block and back. It's amazing how suburban parts of Los Angeles are a few blocks from a major thoroughfare. Both me and Rain learned how to ride bikes at my mom's friend's summer house on Long Island.

Lee tries again, sailing clear down the block with her feet stuck straight out and her knees locked. "Bend your knees!" I yell, racing after her. "Pedal!"

Just as I say "pedal," she falters, slows, and skids into the pavement.

Lee topples onto a grassy patch, an inevitable but comically slow fall, legs tangled in the machinery.

I bolt toward her. Lungs burning.

"Better," I tell her, grabbing my thighs, hunched over, desperate to catch my breath.

Lee lies there. Blinking. Not looking up.

"Why are we doing this again?" Her gray T-shirt is drenched in sweat and my shin splints are killing me.

It's a good question. Part of me imagined that we'd reenact one of those commercials of mutual funds. That the instant my hands came away from the back of the bike, she'd glide effortlessly through the terrain, realizing at the last glorious moment that she's got it, that she's doing it, that she's riding a bike all by herself.

The reality is that in the last forty-five minutes I've never been more stressed out.

This is not your average teenage human trying to learn how to ride a bike. Leanna Smart is precious cargo. She's basically a person-size diamond she's so valuable. Though not nearly as indestructible.

"Come on." I hold my hand out. "We'll do five more times each way. You're so close." I don't know why I'm challenging her. Or what I'm trying to prove.

Lee picks up the bike and stares down the street to where we parked.

"Can't I call a Lyft?"

"Five more times."

"Nah. I'm done," she says, letting the bike drop.

Something in me catches fire. I'm desperate for her to have this. I want this to be the thing she'll remember me by. A singular gift I was able to give her.

"Don't quit." I realize I sound like my mother. "The only difference is learning!"

I reach over and pick up the bike.

I slap its still-warm seat.

"Come on, Suarez. Don't fail me now."

"No," she says, and smiles tight. I know it's a wrap. "I'm done. Admit it. This whole thing was a bad idea. I don't want to do this today."

I check the time. Two fifteen. We have mere hours before I have to leave for my new flight.

Still, I can't let it go.

"Don't you want today to be different?" I ask her. "It's our bonus day. It's leap year, or if we moved to New York from Taipei forever and got a whole day free. It's time we weren't supposed to have."

"So, let's enjoy it," she says, trying a new tactic. "Are you enjoying this?" She takes off her helmet. Her hair is matted onto her forehead. "Forget it, Pab."

"Wow," I tell her, shaking my head.

"What's the big deal?" she counters.

"When are we ever going to have the chance to do this again?" I know I'm being a hypocrite. I love quitting as much as the next guy, but it's increasingly clear to me that I'm not talking bikes anymore.

"I'm never doing this again," she says. "And thank god."

"Well, it's my day off too, and we've already sunk so much of it going to Target and finding the right street. Why give up now?"

"I don't know what to tell you, pal," she says calmly. "But I get badgered enough by the men in my life and I'm done here."

I run my hands through my hair, saying nothing. I try to envision a drag-out argument with this girl. How the mechanics would figure. No matter how down-to-earth and real she seems in fleeting moments, I can't imagine there's much getting the upper hand with Leanna Smart.

"Dude, you're not my dad. Would you want me to teach you how to drive right now?"

I think about it. I've had fantasies about driving, and whatever you're supposed to do with your hands and feet seem intuitive. It can't be that different from *Grand Theft Auto*. But the idea of Lee barking instructions at me finally lets me see her point.

"You're right," I tell her. "That would be deeply unsexy."

"Thank you," she says, hands in a prayer. "I have never felt more unsexy in my life. Also, sweaty."

"What are we going to do about the bike?"

"Forget the bike," she says, placing her helmet next to it. "Some kid will take it. Let's go eat asada fries and make out."

The bathtub in the hotel has claw feet and is deep. Lee drops a black bath bomb into it, and it detonates into a cloud of murk.

She hands me a bathrobe. I pull off my shirt and put it on before removing my shorts and boxers.

"I've had maybe two baths in my entire life," I tell her, eyeing the water. My mom has a shower stall, and while we have a tub at the apartment, it's too communal. Too petri dish.

"Okay," she says, perching on the side of the tub. "I have another confession to make."

"What was the first confession?"

"The fraudulent boobs."

"Hey, they are not fraudulent. Your boobs are a blessing

with whom I'm psyched to hang pretty much anytime you'll let me. With or without a squishy padded adhesive layer. Dealer's choice."

"Okay, then, this next part is similarly personal," she says.

"Jesus, are you going to molt?" I think about that eighties movie *Cocoon* where the old people shed their skin and turn into balls of extraterrestrial light.

"Sort of," she says. Lee digs into the base of her skull, and for a good second I do imagine her unzipping a flesh suit and how I'd get home after that. She removes a patch of hair and places it on the side of the tub. Another one. Still another.

Her hair is choppy, around chin length, red still but much shorter.

"This is actually my hair," she says. "My resting hair. My naked hair."

"So when a dude goes, 'send n00dz,' you shoot him a picture of you throwing a peace sign in full scuba gear with this hair?"

She smiles shyly. "Exactly."

"It looks great," I tell her encouragingly. It does. Her features are enormous now. Expressive.

"It's so overprocessed," she says, running her fingers through it. "I can't believe I got in the pool with them." She shakes her head. "But, if it means anything, I'm pretty sure my fake hair is real Asian."

"Aw," I tell her, taking a step toward her. "That makes me feel so much closer to you."

"It does, right?" She dips a toe in the water. I spy the tattoo again. 2.22.

"Two twenty-two," I ask her. "What's it mean?"

She removes her robe and gets in. I follow her.

The bath bomb smells of expensive oils and flowers, and the water reaches all the way to our clavicles.

"February twenty-second was when I was legally emancipated from my parents. The number symbolizes both unity and division." She traces over it with her thumb. "Two sides for all things. It's weird. Everything's way more complicated than you'd ever imagine at the time."

She doesn't volunteer any more and I don't press her.

"Remember when we were talking about music?" she asks, expression unreadable. The water's squid ink.

"You mean the conversation we had forty-eight hours ago?"

"God." She sighs and then smiles. "We were so young then."

"Practically babies."

"Infants!" She laughs. "Well, I think I figured a way to get out." She continues. "There's this movie I want so bad I can't stand it. It's terrifying how much I want it."

"What is it?" I fold my legs in so my feet aren't invading her area. We're facing each other, and I'm as scrunched up as I'll go.

"Here," she says, turning around to slide her back to me so I'm big spoon.

"So much better, thank you." I kiss the nape of her neck

while quickly readjusting my dangling bits from bobbing into her.

"So it's called *The Big One*. It's an indie, and the script is incredible," she says, settling against me. "It's about a small-time heist in New York."

New York. The possibilities of Lee in New York. With me.

"It's *Bonnie and Clyde* meets *Sid and Nancy* meets *Dog Day Afternoon* set in Bushwick. I read for the main guy's sister because Luca doesn't want me taking a break from tour. It's this tiny part, but there's this scene that guts me. It's in a diner and it's the last time they'll see each other and it's devastating. He's addicted to heroin and strung out and she's a mess but trying to save him because he's her big brother and he practically raised her. Anyway, I did this quick self-tape and had them send it."

"And?"

There's no way they wouldn't want her.

"*Then* I decided I really wanted the lead. So I made another one and sent that, too." Lee scoops water into her hands and rinses her face. I can't see her expression, but I can imagine it's the opposite of the glassed-out, unseeing one she gets when she talks about music. "It's so embarrassing. They're going to think I'm insane."

"Have you heard back?"

She shakes her head.

"When did you send it?"

"A week ago."

A week. Is that a sign? Who knows? I realize with a

sinking dread that I'm allowing myself to root for it. Lee telling Luca to go take a hike, quitting music, buying a nice spot in the city.

She turns around to face me. Sweat mustache, eyes wide.

"What do I do?"

I'm equal parts flattered and stunned she'd ask.

Honestly? If it were me? I'd take the silence as guaranteed rejection and slither away into a corner to die in the fetal position. But this is Lee. Everything's possible for her.

"I think you have to allow yourself to truly want it and believe you'll get it. Who's the director?"

It's not a name I've heard of.

"The main guy is Teddy Baptiste though." That name I know. A few superhero movies, an Oscar contender. And . . .

"Shit, that guy's beautiful."

Lee laughs.

"Wait. I thought you said it was an indie." I wonder if there are sex scenes. A Gollum-like covetousness unfurls within me. I'm never going to watch this movie if there are.

"A tiny British company's producing," she says. "But they have an amazing track record, and I'm telling you I've read a hundred scripts and this one is no joke."

"Would you shoot in New York?" I pull the trigger.

"I don't know," she says. "God, I can't remember the last time I wanted something like this." Her longing for a Grammy echoes in my memory. "It's so uncomfortable not to know how it'll turn out." If she does film in New York and works nights there's a chance our schedules will align.

Another flash of Leanna sitting by a window with a blue mug. Not in California this time.

We sit in stifling, steamy silence. The air is thick with a tension I can't name. Is it stupid that I want us to be together?

She shakes her head, hair flicking water into my eye.

"Ow," I say in a tone that reveals more hurt than I'd intended.

She turns her head and cups my cheeks lightly with her hands. She kisses me quickly. "Does this bath feel the least bit conducive to cleanliness for you?"

"As in, do I feel as if we're marinating in our own sweat-gravy?" I want to get out. I want to shower, cleanse myself of these feelings I can't untangle.

"Exactly." She gets up and turns on the shower. "Let's rinse off."

"Ugh, thank you," I tell her.

"I love that we're always on the same page," she says, turning to kiss me.

Meanwhile I'd give anything to know what page that was.

Chapter 19

When it's time to go, I pull back the curtains and the setting sun hangs brilliant, bloated. Lee's downstairs, getting dressed for a dinner. And the bedroom looks different, anonymous, without her in it.

"Bye, room," I say, quietly. It's sentimental, but I take a picture of it. The bed, sheets mussed, comforter rolled into a fat grub.

Jess arrived an hour earlier with a stylist, hair and makeup in tow. Robbing me and Lee of the chance to say goodbye in private. They're all posted up in the kitchen when I come down, chatting about the next few days.

"We'll be in the car," says Jess, giving me a hug. "Get home safe."

When it's just us, Lee's thumb travels to her mouth and she looks at me.

"Hey," she says, sounding as miserable as I feel. "I'm sad."

MARY H. K. CHOI

"It's sad."

"Will you call me?" she asks.

"Of course." I hug her again. She smells correct. Exactly as she should.

"Thanks again," she says. "For coming with me."

We gather my bag and my hoodie, and as I close the door behind us my heart is despairingly heavy.

I watch her get in the car. I get in mine and wait.

If she rolls her windows down it means I'll see her again.

Her Escalade with its cold blackened glass remains apathetic.

Come on, Lee.

A line. Then a sliver. When her eyes emerge, my insides sing.

I can't get mine down fast enough.

"Bye, Pab!" she says, waving madly. "I'll miss you so much."

On the plane ride home I'm dazed. I need sleep, but the din in my skull won't let up. I'm flying first-class and wish I had the window seat to watch the sky but that honor goes to a curly-haired kid whose Yeezys don't reach the floor. He's about six. I wonder what the rest of his life will feel like if he's flying first-class now. In fact, I wonder how the rest of *my* life will be.

I rub my neck. The pressure of the past two days' intimacy is knotted at my shoulders. So many new people and situations. Does Jess like me? What about Lee's abuela?

Dyland, Cam, the assistants, trainers, that lawyer-looking dude in the suit who gave me the once-over, Jesus, even Luca. It matters to me what these people think. Never mind what Lee thinks of me.

Good god, Lee.

I wonder how I did. If I passed. The weekend feels like the longest job interview of my life, and honestly, I think I did okay. I only wish I could tell Joey Santos and the Kims about it. I wish the credits transferred.

"Pablo, I need to talk to you."

Another black car picks me up on the New York side and delivers me straight to work. I'm relieving Mr. Kim for the day shift since Tina and he worked the night before. He's waiting by the registers when I get in. This is not a good sign.

"Sure. What's up?"

I check the clock. I'm almost forty minutes early. Even with put-backs.

"Come into the office," he says, unsmiling. My heart sinks.

I follow him to the back, where the shiny beige epoxy flooring ends and the grimy nonslip rubber mats begin, a demarcation of us versus them. What's private and public. We weave through the stacked boxes, beyond the walk-ins. You'd never get a sense for this warren of crannies from outside, but it's almost as big as the store itself. A shadow version. I remember the first time I realized a stock person replenishes sodas in the refrigerated case from the back. It never occurred to me that it's human hands at work. Same with the first time I saw a vending machine refilled as a kid. Or a subway ad being replaced.

Mrs. Kim's in the tiny office, and I love how her husband never fails to give her the courtesy of a knock even though it's only ever the two of them. Mrs. Kim's in a spotless black apron and smiles without meeting my eye. She exits but not before squeezing my forearm. This is not good at all.

I'm glad I called, but I'm expecting some fallout. I almost violated their no-call, no-show policy since I'd only given them a half day of notice. I'd expected to catch hell from Tina but hadn't mapped out how a confrontation with Mr. Kim would play out. I'm glad it's just us. I couldn't handle Mrs. Kim's disappointment.

Mrs. Kim is among my top three humans. She reminds me of my mom but gentler. No exaggeration, I'd take a bullet for her. I fantasize about it occasionally since her sons, Michael, who's a snob, and Alfred, who's younger and reminds me of Kim Jong-un with that high skin fade, rarely visit.

Mr. Kim sits down at his desk. I take the stool next to him, where his wife usually sits when they're having meals. I can smell the kimchi from breakfast since there are no windows in the tiny room.

"Are you okay, Pablo?"

That he's opening with concern thickens my throat.

"Yes. How are *you*, Mr. Kim?" I ask lightly.

His shoulders settle lower as he sighs.

"I got a call," he says. Not sounding angry exactly, but his mouth is firmly set.

"A few," he continues. "Your mother, for example."

Shit. So they've talked. The Kims know I wasn't visiting colleges.

"She was looking for you," he says. She's left me two voicemails since texting about the Joey Santos meeting. But I never thought she'd call here.

"I told her I didn't know where you were," he says as he puts on his glasses that are attached to a black lanyard. "The other call was from a collections agency," he continues, consulting a notepad. There are doodles all over it. Little interlocking squares. "They said they are going to sue you for nonpayment."

I notice that the roots of his black hair are stark white. A skunk strip that my mom gets when she skips appointments. Mr. Kim dyes his hair. The mortality is astonishing somehow. I picture Mrs. Kim with plastic gloves attending to it, and the image is so intrusive I feel a flush of shame.

"It's very serious," he says.

I clear my throat. "Okay."

"Pablo." He sighs. "They say they've been calling you many, many months. And sent so many letters."

I nod and notice how no matter how much time he spends on his feet Mr. Kim always wears dress shoes— black, leather businessman loafers. And they always look freshly shined.

"You must contact them. Okay?" He says this softly. "I asked my son Alfred and he said that if you call them you can ask for a payment plan. He says talk to them directly."

"Okay."

I can't believe bill collectors are suing me. I'm getting sued. I'm too young to get sued. Lawyers and courts are for adults, and right now I'm a far cry from one. I can't adult. Most days I can barely human.

My blood runs cold thinking of the avalanche of letters I've flung into the dresser drawer without opening. I can't stand that Alfred knows about any of this.

"He says you will be okay."

When I finally bring myself to make eye contact with him I can only nod. I'm hit with a pressure behind my eyes, the sudden and overwhelming urge to cry.

"I think you'll be okay too," says Mr. Kim, patting my leg once. Gruffly.

"I'm sorry." I don't know what else to say.

"Don't have to be sorry to me," he says, eyes so kind I want to die. "But you contact them today, okay?"

He copies the phone number from his notes onto a clean piece of paper and hands it to me.

I put it in my pocket. Numb.

A few hours ago I was watching in-flight movies and drinking my first mimosa.

As Mr. Kim leads me back out to the front I want to apologize again. For disappointing him. For lying. For being a mess. And getting the messiness on him. He's given me clear directions on what to do. I have to call and face it all, but part of me knows that I won't. That I can't. At least not today. I'm so spent that my head feels inside out.

I change my shoes behind the register. There's a vacuum where my heart should be. I let my mind wander to the footage in my head. How it was only a few days ago that Lee and I both stood here. As excruciating as it is to miss Lee, it's a welcome distraction from my life. The debt. This job. School. I close my eyes, compiling a list of things I want to tell her.

I want to ask what her favorite nut is. They'd served warmed hazelnuts on the plane, which was a power move.

I want to say that I googled how long it takes to hear back from an audition and that it's like asking the length of a piece of string.

I want to know if the no-search rule applies to her social media. I would plead the case that I don't think it should.

It's incomprehensible how the lure of my thumb to her Instagram is so constant.

I wonder if Lee's ever been sued. I get the impression that she may be the one usually doing the suing.

The Kims give me some distance, and the shift passes in a dispirited daze. Sometime around noon Mrs. Kim hands me a lunch box of rice and bulgogi. It makes me emotional.

"Ma-sshitge-deh-saeyo," she says, bowing slightly, using the honorific for "enjoy your meal." She's always trying to talk to me in Korean and to Jorge the stock dude, too, who's picked up a surprising amount.

I bow back.

"Gamsa-ham-nida," I tell her, thanking her for the food. She reads my eyes and pats me twice on the cheek. It's the twin gesture to her husband's but softer, her small hands cold and calloused. "It'll be okay," she says, smiling. I know she means it, but my only thought is, *How could you ever know that?*

Chapter 20

I haven't worked a day shift in over six months, and it's a trickier beast by a lot. Customers are relentless, way chattier than the nocturnal crew, and I'm prickly that I can't get paid to mostly watch videos with Gusto. I check to make sure I still have the phone number Mr. Kim gave me in my pocket.

Maybe litigation is a rite of passage. I wonder if Lee had to sue her parents for emancipation. I'm suspicious of my lack of immediate hysteria around the bills. Maybe I'm crazy now. Maybe I've entered a state of psychosis. Maybe after meeting Lee there's only so much suspension of disbelief the brain can take. I only wish that she'd call.

An Asian woman with a happa baby plonks her basket down. "Hi," she says, "I brought my own bag." She pulls out a nylon carryall, like Lee's, and even though it's cats, not dogs, it pains me. When her total comes to eighty-six dollars, I'm flabbergasted. I peer into the bag. Oh, right, that's what happens with twelve-dollar ice cream, fifteen-dollar yogurt, and multiples of the twenty-dollar coffee. Why do things cost what they do in New York? How am I expected to survive here?

I admit the turntables were a mistake, but the rest of it seemed unavoidable. It's not that I went buck with the cards. It's that I used them a hundred times for tiny things. Death by a thousand cuts. Complicated coffee orders. Deli runs. Whatever happens at Duane Reade that makes you spend fifty dollars when you go in for Q-tips. I didn't know that credit cards were so powerful. They sounded harmless when the dude with the clipboard in non-ostentatious Flyknits explained it to me on campus. Plus, that free water bottle really *was* cool. Even though I don't know where I left it.

All I'm saying is that the fact that anyone can get a student loan bill and three credit card notices and a phone bill on the same day makes me question who designed it this way. I know it's my fault. But seriously, how am I supposed to learn how to do this when I'm already in the type of financial ruin that metastasizes this violently?

Moving out was a necessity. I was peeling years off mom's life with our fights. Because guess what? Even when you enroll in paperless billing, those credit card assholes send you bills about how they emailed you bills and then send you letters to make sure you got them.

Plus, it might not be the best course of action to learn how to defer student loans from a free video tutorial, but when I started getting notices that read THIS IS NOT A BILL, I figured I was good. Except six months later they start sending real bills in identical envelopes, which honestly feels like kind of a trick.

While I ring up the customers one by one, I think about how much money each of them owes—schools, the IRS, the government in general, medical bills, credit cards, the whole thing. Even in this rich-ass neighborhood, I suspect we're all pretty much fucked.

The tattooed Korean kid comes in and buys a plastic tub of pre-peeled grapefruit segments that cost six bucks. I can't stop thinking about how I've returned from a state where actual citrus fruit casually grows on trees by the side of the street.

Basically, fruit now reminds me of Lee.

Tacos too. White bikinis.

It's been eleven hours. I break down and text her.

Tell me anything.

Then silence.

I should have known it would be this. That the second I text the howling free fall would be horrific. What am I supposed to do while she doesn't respond?

Die.

I check Jess's socials.

Selfies mostly and surprisingly few of Leanna Smart. It would seem that Jessica Longworthy is her own thing. She's launched a consulting agency, an LGBTQIA-inclusive cosmetics line, and as I google, I vaguely remember her backstory.

Jessica started out as a rank-and-file Smartee but was so effective at rallying organizational support in the early days that Leanna Smart levitated down from Mount Olympus and hired her. Right in the middle of Jess's junior year at Emory. It's the stuff of social media legend. Jessica Longworthy's now amassed 4.3 million followers on her own merit, with a competition reality show coming out next year that's *Shark Tank* for teens. Fittingly, her career trajectory's inspired every third Smartee who believes they can thirst their way onto Lee's cabinet. For what it's worth, I know I'd watch a YouTube video on how she did it.

I land on Luca. There's no real lesson here beyond how being a child prodigy is extremely convenient. He dropped out of Skidmore after skipping two years of high school. He's one of *those*. His parents, both teachers, live in Long Island, which explains his devotion to the Knicks, but it was a chance meeting with Lynette Harrisberg while throwing parties in the city as a literal child that made him start working as an A&R. A stint with some profoundly accessible music software and he was packaged as a genius at making simple, wickedly catchy beats. His estimated net worth is fifty-one million dollars. And he's remarkably well preserved for a forty-three-year-old.

Then there's Teddy Baptiste, Lee's leading man if all goes well. The autofills that come up are as follows:

Girlfriend

Height

Speaks French

Workout

Oscar

Nudes

He's Black, multilingual, single, tall, shredded, rich, accomplished, and there's a few leaked stills from an alleged sex tape that doesn't so much land him in a compromising position as it does testify to his ridiculous assets. I wouldn't know. Even I'm not enough of a masochist to click through.

Another rush of customers arrive to torment me as I check my phone under the counter every two seconds. I like this crowd though. The ones that hit at nine p.m., stumbling, starving, compiling struggle meals from canned soup and cereal since they skipped dinner and roared into happy hour.

A regular, in a long-sleeved red dress and matching tights, leaves a pair of spare keys with me for "this Bumble asshole" who's coming by. I'm tempted to tell her she could do better, but I don't know that for a fact, so I inform her that we have grilled salmon, the only flavor Belle, her Scottish Fold, deigns to eat. She goes, "Fuck that cat," smiles wickedly, and storms out.

The desi guy's redheaded wife comes in—or Freckles McGee, as I call her in my mind. She's wearing sweats and buys contact lens solution and ice cream. When she pulls her coat aside to grab her wallet, I notice she's pregnant. I want to congratulate her, but it doesn't seem appropriate.

One dude, a youngish white business-suit man I've never seen before, picks up duct tape, two packs of bacon, two jars of twenty-dollar Italian tuna, a plunger, and asks me if I have any small Vaselines.

"The tube kind? The ChapStick?" I look at the assorted pharmaceuticals behind me.

He shakes his head impatiently. "The mini tub," he says, pinching his fingers an inch wide.

"Nah. Sorry, dude."

He leaves without buying any of the other stuff.

I wonder if they ever wonder about me.

I check my phone after they leave and it hops down from 38 percent battery to 11 percent. Fuck. It's definitely going to die on my way home.

Around midnight Mr. Kim dismisses me, and I listen to the crunch of snow under my feet. My black and cement Jordan 3s are getting demolished. I should have wrapped my feet in plastic bags to preserve them but I'm too tired to care.

Rent's due in twelve days. My birthday money's long gone. They're coming after me in court. Never mind the student loans.

Is this how people become bankrupt? How does this work? How am I being sued? These bastards will spend more money getting it than the amount I owe. I'm like how a penny costs more to produce than it's worth.

The apartment's empty when I skulk into my room and flop into bed. I drink a three-day old glass of water as my phone buzzes alive.

I've got a text.

My heart jolts.

It's Lee.

I did something dumb, she writes. And then, I'm so sorry.

Suddenly my phone goes haywire with notifications. Another text from Lee comes in, but the wall of notes flooding my screen are coming so fast my OS can't keep track. Stupid inherited 6S. I turn off all my push notifications and finally get the texts to open back up.

Emoji with the gnashed teeth.

She sends a screengrab.

It's my most recent Instagram post, of Tapatio Doritos paired with the Chicago orange Huarache Run Qs.

Leanna Smart liked it.

And added the licking-lips emoji.

I go into my account and scroll way down, and there it is.

Leanna Smart blue checkmark is now following you.

That's when the shit hit the fan.

The next infinite scroll worth of follows are from Leanna Smart fan sites, gossip sites, more bots than I can imagine, and anyone with even an ancillary interest in ex-Disney pop stars.

I don't quite know how it works. If they have spies squatting on the "Following" activities page or what, but when Leanna Smart likes any post of yours, evidently it's seconds before Smartees figure it out. They have a sixth sense for any online interaction she has. The comments are hilarious too. More licking lips. A torrent of thinking emojis, which is the Smartees sigil. Countless, *Hi Leannas*. And *ILY Leannas*. And a ton of *Lb*'s for *like back*. There's also an absolute cacophony of different languages since it's two a.m. Eastern Standard, which is breakfast time in Europe and Africa and afternoon in Asia.

Whoa, I text her.

I know, she types back after a while. And then:

Ugh

In thirty minutes I net two hundred new follows. And here's the worst thing: I love it. I notice myself loving it. I'm catching myself rehearsing. Responding to interviews about how we met. What we did on our first date. Whether or not Doritos are an inside joke. I'm contractually free to answer these fantasy questions because there's updated paperwork for when we're happily married.

I lean into my own grossness. I'm giddy with it. I'd spent the last day steeling against never hearing from her again, so now that there exists a tie that binds us I'm thrilled. I go through my whole Instagram history. There are only a few selfies in the early part of my feed. I wonder if I should delete them in preparation for my new life.

Social media spurs the most unslakable thirst in all of us. I love that people know that Leanna Smart knows me. That the world now knows what I do. Partly, it's proof I'm not going crazy, but it also makes me proud.

You should probably turn your notifications off, she says. I unfollowed you. I've never done that before. I'd meant to hit you from my burner account.

Oh.

Turn off Facebook too.

I deleted it. I don't want to complicate things for you. Smartees are judgy.

Okay, I text her.

I scroll through my posts again. Mostly food and sneakers. I delete my selfies and then click through to every image I've been tagged in. I'd untagged myself on Heather's feed when she got a new man because who wouldn't. But there's a picture of me and Tice that Wynn took where we're rap squatting in front of a murdered-out G wagon with a vanity plate that reads: BODEGA. I untag that too.

Still, part of me wishes there was a flattering picture of me out there for them to ferret out. Not a thirst-trap per se but something.

I save the screengrab of the comment that she sent me. Just to have.

This is not my most attractive headspace.

Okay. At least we're texting. Do I call her? I can't remember the last time I had an actual Telephone Call with someone I was interested in, but I want to hear her voice.

After much deliberation I practice heroic restraint and send a single emoji.

The corn emoji.

Chapter 21

What the fuck was I thinking with the corn emoji? What does corn even represent? That I'm a genetically modified Monsanto fanboy?

When I wake up the next morning, Lee still hasn't texted back and I'm beside myself. I should call her. It's not as if normal texting or terrestrial dating rules apply to the stratospherically famous. There is no risk in betraying my interest because literally everyone is interested. Millions of people are interested. There are droves—droves—of her fans whose entire bios are the date they met Leanna Smart and whose avatars are of Lee. I've seen them. I've checked. Three thousand of them follow me now. Some have commented. Not solely about Lee either. The hibiscus Dough donut post with the Mizuno Wave Rider Phoenix is doing remarkably well for the fact that it's almost a year old.

Maybe I should email her.

What if Leanna Smart's email address is Carolina_ Suarez@gmail.com? Ha. That would be amazing.

I want to poll my roommates, but I don't want them thrown in celebrity NDA prison. And besides, things have gotten weird in the last week. I'm a horrible liar and they know *something's* up. I didn't even respond to Tice's texts of: Yo u alive?

I creep out of my bedroom and it's quiet.

Why did I pick the corn emoji????!!! Emoji in general are safe, but I should have sent the black heart. It's less a heart-heart in the love sense and more just a badass pictograph that shows how much I care without seeming like a sap. But I've just always liked the corn emoji. IT'S A GOOD EMOJI.

But is it adjacent to an eggplant? Oh god, or the hot dog? Or anything remotely phallic? Maybe I should have sent the curling rock. That's always a crowd pleaser. CD-ROM?

I go to the freezer and grab an ice cube and hold it in my palm. As the sting eases, I calm down. It's what my mom does when she's bugging out, and I am completely bugging out.

I blot my hand, throw on my coat, put on my boots, and go outside.

The cold is a vise grip of metal around my head. I shift my beanie off my ear and call her.

Like a man.

It goes to voicemail.

I almost burst into tears.

Like a man.

As I'm about to head back in, she calls me.

"Cornmoji?" she says by way of a greeting.

"Cornmoji!" I tell her. My heart's going bonkers.

"Hi, hi, hi, hi! I miss you!" she says, and it's her. Not Instagram Leanna Smart. Not the Leanna Smart with her Lb Lb cohorts. It's Lee. My Lee. We're back.

I walk down the block, keeping my eyes on my feet so I can avoid the black ice. The gray snow embankments on the sidewalks are packed tight and high, up to your thighs. I watch as a woman in a fur coat gingerly makes her way through the shoveled pathway. Taking her sweet time even as a line forms behind her.

I plunge my left Timb in a puddle, and the frigid water instantly soaks my sock. "Shit."

"What?"

"Nothing," I say. "Just got my sock wet."

"Ugh. I hate that."

I am unconvinced that Leanna Smart has ever in her life gotten her sock wet in street water. "What's the weather over there?"

"Eighty-two degrees."

"Fuck you."

She laughs her raspy laugh.

"What'd you do today?" I ask her.

"Too much. I meant to call earlier."

I smirk at a passerby who scowls at my good humor.

She meant to call earlier!

"In fact, I'm leaving for a dinner," she says. "I'm sorry about the Instagram thing. I'm off my game. Jess gave me an earful about it. Between taking days off work and that, she thinks I'm losing my marbles."

I stroll around the block and make my way back. I love that I'm having this kind of effect on her. It's only fair since I'm a total basketcase.

"Hang on a second. I gotta get in the car," she continues. I hear muffled *Hi*'s to her driver.

"Hey," she says. And then, "Sorry. Hold on?"

She's talking in the background.

"Pablo, I'm going to have to call you back." She pauses. "I miss you."

"I miss you," I reply, and then she's gone again. I run upstairs.

A half hour later, long enough that I've made Wyn call me to make sure my phone works, she rings.

"I have possibly five minutes," she says. "I'm literally calling you from the bathroom."

"Hi."

"Hi."

"How do you emotionally feel about FaceTime?" I ask her. I'm dying to see her. "As a communication tool?"

"Emotionally?" She laughs. "I feel better about WhatsApp since it has end-to-end encryption." She sing-songs the last bit, despite the connotation.

"Let's do that this week, then."

"Cool beans."

That makes me laugh. "Nerd."

"I believe we're called savants?" she corrects. "Colloquially known as Smartees? Shit. Hold on." She covers her phone again. "Wait," she says helplessly. As though I'm the one who has to go. "Tell me anything," she says, and I smile at her recall of my first text to her. "Tell me three things you're doing this week so I can imagine them," she says.

My mind takes the opportunity to draw a complete blank.

"Tell me about the store," she says. "Tell me about Gusto the cat. Tell me about your classes. Tell me about your dad. You said your mom is a doctor, but I don't know anything about your dad."

She's pleading, as though knowing my dad's job is the cure-all for the wretchedly terminal disease of not having enough time to talk on the phone.

"He's a playwright," I say. "At least he's trying to be. My brother got into LaGuardia, the school that any famous New Yorker went to—ugh you probably know that—and, um . . . this guy at the store tried to buy bacon, duct tape, a plunger, and Vaseline, but we didn't have Vaseline so he left without getting anything."

"What a murderer!"

"Total murderer."

"Thank you," she says, and I can hear the smile in her voice. "I'll talk to you soon?"

"Encrypt-chat soon."

Not ten seconds later she sends me a screen of corn emojis.

I send her a screen of black hearts.

When I toss my keys on the sideboard I see new mail. Shit. An envelope addressed to me from King's County Court clerk's office and it's fat.

I leave it exactly where it is.

A few days later I hit up dad's rehearsals with Rain. We're almost forty minutes late.

"Calm down," I tell him when I pick him up. He's doing this pee-pee dance, which gets on my nerves. "Yo, seriously, you know we're not in the play, right?"

Rehearsal's at a public high school, and when we open the door to the classroom, there's a knot of people of varying ages and races huddled around a table reading what I assume to be copies of my dad's script. Everyone's wearing their coats and hats, turning pages in gloves, since dad's debut production is so momentous the building didn't bother switching on the heat.

Dad holds his finger up to his lips and shushes goofily, which irritates me. We take stools closest to the door.

Dad waves us over. "How will you hear it from there?" The assembled actors swivel around. "My sons," he explains.

Rain makes his way over just as I blurt out, "I'm all set."

My idiot brother shoots me a look, as if I'm the one being embarrassing. I move closer.

"So, what's the distance between your true self and how people perceive you?" asks dad, and the sincerity makes me inwardly shudder. I regard the assembled randoms. Honestly, we may as well be on a crosstown bus. Do these people believe that this guy is a playwright? I can barely look at my father as he dishes encouragements and dissects "artistic process."

I check my phone. Cringing to consider what Lee might think of all this. She'd be supportive, but I'd sooner die than have her bear witness to this fraudulent pantomime. I glance at the slouched shoulders in coats. If you've got Hollywood's idealized New York, this isn't even cable-access New York. This is bathtub-in-the-kitchen, laundry-strung-out-of-the-window-of-a-seventh-floor walk-up, tenement-museum-come-to-life New York. The collected humans smell vaguely of soup. The Chinese guy who plays the lead has got to be at least fifty-five.

The sky outside is wooly and gray and I can see only a portion of it since there's condensation on the pane from all the mouthbreathing inside.

Rain's chuckle pierces my thoughts. Leaned in toward them, a half smile glued on his face, the little kiss-ass appears to be enjoying this.

From what I can gather, the play is about a Chinese bicycle delivery guy. He lives in this boardinghouse somewhere deep in Queens, knees arthritic and short on options. His restaurant is squeezing him out, except then he wins the goddamn lottery.

I look at the dude. How am I supposed to believe a guy like that would win the lottery?

Rain laughs again. And when dad's eyes flit to both of us, I manage a weak smile.

My father calls for a fifteen-minute break as a woman with a buzz cut and neon pink scarf switches a radio on. Just as I'm looking at my texts, I hear her voice. "Hey, Smartees, this is Leanna Smart, and you're listening to 98.1 FM. Where pop pops off." I hear a vaguely familiar acoustic riff as her voice talks about omens and what she didn't know.

Rain is humming along and saying "highway, highway" even though the third time she's clearly saying "byway" or "by the way."

"*This* is Leanna Smart?" I ask him.

He shoots me a look of purest *Duh* and keeps humming.

It's not that I didn't know the song. I recognize it from last year. Or the year before. It's the type of tune that may as well be carpeting in certain rooms—a given—a sound that's built into select months wherever you are in the world. It's one of those ditties that's vaguely familiar, where you never bother to learn who sings it because it expertly mimics every other major hit that came before.

I realize I don't know which songs playing in passing taxicabs are hers. Or the tinny emanations from random earbuds in the train. Never mind the brain-bleeding dub-step mash-up iterations that waft by me when the doors to fancy gyms open and close in my face. She might be all of them.

It dawns on me what Leanna Smart™ means.

I'm sitting here shitting on the idea of a Chinese dude winning the lottery when I'd have better odds attempting to date Jesus than Leanna Smart™.

I listen to the lyrics for the first time. The song is about this moron who's stupid enough to let her drive away. I'm not going to let that happen. I'm not going to murder my life twice.

The rest of the afternoon passes in a crawl. It's hard to sit inside of myself. I have secondhand embarrassment *for me.*

When rehearsals are over, I can't break out fast enough. But of course Rain dawdles.

"What did you boys think?" dad asks in front of everyone. I clear my throat. I can't deal with pop quizzes right now. "I thought it was great," says Rain brightly. "It's nice to see old people, no offense"—he pats the Chinese dude on the arm—"as the fleshed-out characters and the kids as caricatures. It's very refreshing."

"Totally refreshing," I mutter.

"Do you think mom would enjoy it?"

"*My* mom?"

His expectant, hopefulness curdles my insides.

"She's my mom too," covers Rain, smiling. "And I think she'll love it. It's great, dad. Honest."

Dad looks back to me for confirmation and I can't get it up.

"We're late," I tell him instead. "We gotta go."

Chapter 22

That night I dream about accidentally posting a selfie on Lee's Instagram stories. A bleary, ugly smear with one eye closed and my mouth ajar.

It's humiliating how unimaginative it is. I swear I'm getting stupider.

The worst part wasn't the act itself. It was the aftermath. I was trying to rationalize to her that it was an accident, convinced for some reason that it was my dad's fault. Lee gets angrier and angrier because she can't get a straight answer, and I wake up feeling as though I'd had a fight with my mom. The Freudian implications make me want to hurl.

I know my mom deserves an explanation about Five Points, but I add it to the list of things I am completely incapable of handling right now.

Over the next week Lee and I talk every night anywhere from ten seconds to hours when neither of us can sleep, but otherwise it's a montage of getting up, going to work, going home, opening the rice cooker, getting made fun of by my friends, blowing off Rain, seeing Rain when I know my mom's at work, going to bed, and getting up again. Rinse and repeat.

Tice texts me, go outside it's nice, but I sleep through both the message and the afternoon, and by the time I make it into the world the warm weather means nothing more than the slippery, hardened ice floes giving way to disgusting slush puddles.

His text is as much as we've talked in weeks.

When I join the roommates, minus Dara, in the living room to watch Tice's character get killed, I nurse a low-grade hostility but eat the celebratory pizza anyway.

"Man, they really let you cook this episode," says Miggs. We're transfixed as Tice is obliterated in John Woo slow motion.

"Yeah," he says, smiling, eating his pizza with a knife and fork off a plate on his knees. We're way past making fun of him for it, but tonight I'm tempted. "I was supposed to get doused with Novichok nerve agent in the first five minutes, but they extended the arc a little."

A calendar alert chimes on my phone. I swipe it away. I've been doing it for the past two days.

One week until my application for Five Points is due, with or without Joey Santos's cosign. But even more pressing, as far as my heart is concerned, is that I have three weeks to apply for summer semester at NYU. Two months after that to figure out how to pay for the $8,706.00 in tuition and fees for six credits if I get in. I wonder if I remember my log-in for Albert, the NYU computer system.

As the camera punches in to Tice's bloodied face, I wonder how much he got paid for everything. A few hundred? Thousands?

I swear if this dude got thousands of dollars to play a stereotype on TV . . .

I wonder if I could be an actor. Isn't it easier to get into college when you're famous?

I lean back in my seat. Tice looks over, expecting me to say something, but I smile tightly and make like I'm wiping my mouth on a paper towel. I wish I were less of an asshole.

I wish I could get back into school.

I just need one look.

The look that gets me on the map, because the alternative is unthinkable.

Like, you ever hear of Earl Lamb?

Really sweet Polish and Nigerian kid who decided to his detriment that he had to be a rapper. If you hung around that hipster deli in Greenpoint with the benches in front you'd know who I was talking about. Anyway, extremely talented human being.

He did all the right things. To a point. Had a minor hit on Pyrite Records, shot a video in Berry Playground in South Williamsburg, where we all made our cameos. Ran up some decent SoundCloud numbers and landed a major deal, and we thought that was it for him. That he'd won and it would just be a matter of time before we'd flood him for favors and sneaker run-off, but then a year passes and it's crickets.

Earl stops going outside, and we figure he was in the studio with his head down, total demon, but then his socials didn't feature anything other than these workout videos. It was this constant running joke that he was turning into a juicehead, so the comments would be like, "Where's the album? Where's the album?" With the musical-note emoji over and over.

Still no music. We figure the label's got to be pulling their hair out. Then the kid dies of an embolism deadlifting twice his body weight one morning and no one finds him for another three days, and the worst part isn't that there was a roach eating his face. It's that there was an album on his hard drive and it was finished. It hadn't been touched in eight months. His manager puts it out and it kills. There was even talk of a hologram tour, but I don't remember what happened with that.

It's called *Hidalgo Crescent*, and the even worster part is that it's incredible. Actually, empirically excellent. The music reviewers who when Earl Lamb was alive were locked in an asshole contest to ignore him to death called him— get this—a *genius*. Genius! And they went on and on about how "relevant" he is, which is the highest compliment any of those scumbags can pay anyone. It's so sad. Meanwhile, I'm dying to ask the kid why the fuck it's called *Hidalgo Crescent* since it doesn't exactly roll off the tongue, but I can't because he's dead.

I think about Earl Lamb all the time. How I don't want to be him. I have an album in me. I know it. A body of work that's dying to get out. And NYU's the catalyst that will unlock it. I got to get a do-over. Not everyone gets one.

"Ay," Miggs protests when I mindlessly grab my third slice of pie without checking in. The five of us usually get two slices each for two pies, and then the hungriest pair shoot a fair one for a third. I take a bite while the credits roll. There it is, Ziad al-Abbasi—Tyson Scott. The roommates cheer. "I don't know," I tell him. "Your acting was great, but I still can't tell if you're supposed to be a Middle Eastern dude."

I wasn't trying to be a dick, but it sucks the air out of the room. Tice shakes his head.

"That hot Agent Salinas didn't care what kind of dude you were," says Wyn, slapping Tice on the back. "That was some chemistry right there."

"That's what I'm saying," I butt in. "This show's implausible. How the hell are you going to be a love interest in two minutes? A dude on a suicide mission would be too focused. Besides, how are you going to wear Vans?"

"Man, shut up," says Miggs, nudging me hard. "I'm tired of listening to you complain. We don't see you for a month. Zero explanation about where you are or why the fuck you're so depressed. You're sitting here eating the man's pizza, watching him on a fucking real-ass, big-time TV show, and you can't be happy for him. I'm sick of your salty attitude. Go run around the block."

"Bet," I say, getting up. "Congratulations," I tell Tice, tossing my pizza crust back in the box and heading to my room.

"Fucking selfish," I hear Miggs say as I close my door. I text Lee a heart to let her know that I'm thinking about her. If she texts me back within the hour it's a great day. If not, well . . .

My mom calls again and I send it to voicemail. But then both Rain and dad start in on the group text. Finally I agree to go over there for dinner, and when I arrive at mom's on Thursday I'm on high alert. I wish there were push-ups you could do to train up for a mom-guilt assault. I kick off my shoes and see that there are take-out Chinese containers on the table, still in bags.

"I'm home," I call out, but no one answers. I dump my laundry in the wash and then peer into the kitchen. I'm trying not to be a total jerk, but a knuckle-dragging part of me is annoyed that my mom harassed me into coming over for a hot meal only to find out it's Seamless. You'd think I'd get a home-cooked dinner before she homicides me.

I resent that our apartment never smells of food. No caramelly sautéed onions. The rich earthiness of roasting meats. If the spot features any scent at all, it's mom's perfume combined with those smelly sticks jammed into jars of air freshener that give me a headache if I get too close. Mom redecorated when I was in high school, so everything's beige. There's even an artsy dish in the middle of the dining table that used to contain fruit, but nowadays it houses Rain's comic books and a stack of *New Yorkers* mom has no time to read.

I grab a plate to help myself, buffet style, without unpacking the boxes into serving bowls, which is how mom typically does it. I'm slightly nauseated by the sautéed noodles and glistening duck as I pop the sweaty lids open. I don't know if I have it in me for a fight. Only that I want it to be over quick.

"God, what are you doing?" Rain comes out and plants a bony elbow in my ribs. He arranges the boxes and sets the pewter dish on the sideboard. I throw him in a headlock.

"Stop," he says, writhing out of my grip to grab dishes.

"Mom," calls out Rain, rolling his eyes at me. "Eat." And then, as if to warn her, "Pab's here." Mom emerges from her office, formerly known as my room, with her glasses on.

"Pablo," she says, mild surprise on her face. She smiles and then frowns when she sees that I'm eating a noodle with my fingers.

"Pab," she pleads, more a sigh than my name, and checks her phone. "We're waiting for dad."

"Dad?" I swallow. I glance at my brother. He's either as confused as I am or an even better actor than he is a singer.

Mom's face remains maddeningly impassive.

From the chaos of emotions, panic, shame, frustration, a streak of protective anger whips out into the forefront because my mom has no business inviting my father over for dinner. I cringe again at the memory of my dad asking if we think mom will like his play. Suddenly I'm furious at everyone.

"Dad?" I ask again. "Really? You know he's going to be late as hell."

"I texted him again," she says, and even though I'm tempted, I don't tell her that his phone is probably cut off since covering for dad is a conditioned response.

He arrives as the food begins to congeal and mom's unimpressed, but some other mood hangs between them too. They hug, which I haven't seen in a while, and it devolves into that heinous, *Whoops, who's head is going which way?* stop-and-start thing and they nearly kiss on the mouth. I realize they're nervous.

"We got mapo tofu with minced chicken," says mom. It's his favorite.

I watch her hand him a plate, trying to deduce meaning. Tasting little of my own food as I shovel it down. Dad's wearing the same women's cardigan from last time and chews slowly, tentatively, the way Rain does; it's as if they're infirmed.

I wonder if dad has cancer. Mom would be wrecked. Still, of the two I'd rather dad be sick.

I know that's messed up, but it's purely from a practical standpoint.

Mom would be able to recover eventually and he wouldn't stand a chance. He's the type to die a month after and the autopsy report would reveal a cartoon broken heart. Besides, if Rain has to live in dad's tiny apartment, he'd probably get scurvy or rickets from the lack of nutrients.

Mom brings out a fruit plate and puts on tea.

I google whether scurvy and rickets are the same thing. One's a vitamin C deficiency and the other is D. Who knew?

"Rain," says mom. "Can you give us a minute with your brother?"

He shoots me a look and I nod. Rain goes into his room. Normally he'd pitch a fit, whining about how he's old enough to be in on all family business, but this time he doesn't. He's probably in on it. The rat. Wait, *do I* have cancer?

"Pablo," mom says.

"Mother." I grab a clementine and hold it. If it's not a terminal disease, I give her ten seconds before she says either *Houlihan* or *Santos* or *responsibility*.

"We're just . . . ," begins mom. Okay, this is scaring me. The two of them haven't been a "we" in well over a decade. "We're worried about you. About what you're doing with your life."

"Your mother and I," says dad, as if he's giving me a white-guy lecture about substance abuse.

I lean back in my chair. Seriously, where the fuck does this absentee-ass, sorry excuse for a patriarch get off telling me anything?

"We want you to think seriously about your future." He gives me this wet look.

"Future?" I pop a wedge of fruit into my mouth. It's not at all sweet, but I chew it insolently. Like gum. "*You're* going to talk to *me* about the future? Have you forgotten about the last ten-plus years of your life?"

Dad crosses his legs and tucks his hair behind an ear.

"Pablo," warns mom. It doesn't matter that they don't live in the same house. Both would kick my ass if I went after the other. They take the united-front thing seriously.

"What?" I ask her. "Him? You I'd understand. You can talk to me about my future and jobs and fiscal responsibility, but not him."

I know I'm being a dick. But there's zero mystery as to where I get my recklessness from.

"Fine," she says, drawing a breath. "Look, when you blew off the meeting at Five Points, I was furious. But you don't call me back for weeks to explain, and that's not like you."

"Are you kidding? What about the six months when we didn't speak?"

"Pab," she says. "You still checked in with me. Any time I asked you a question, you'd respond. And when I put a heart on your Instagram, you'd heart me back. We never go this long without a word. In twenty years there's never been total silence. If it weren't for Rain, I would've been convinced you'd gotten into an accident or something happened to you at work."

"Fine," I tell her, but Miggs bitching about my absence rings in my ear.

"And you promised you'd seriously consider summer enrollment. You swore to me. Did you at least finish the application?"

Dad taps mom on the knee just as her voice takes on this strident edge.

"This isn't solely about school," he says.

"It's about everything." Mom massages the meat between her thumb and forefinger. She does this when she's about to get a migraine. "But school's a big part of it. What are you going to do? The rest of your life is a long time."

She nudges dad.

"I know you think I'm a hypocrite," he begins.

This fake-sneeze erupts from the back of my throat. The tracheal equivalent of an eyeroll. I don't know where the hostility is coming from. Just that there's so much of it.

"But this is a larger issue," he continues. "If you can believe it, I'm the one who called your mom to talk about this." He looks to her, then back at me. "We're worried because you don't seem to enjoy anything anymore. You were always such a talented kid, but with you the challenge was that you were pretty great at everything you ever tried."

The compliments are a decoy. I become entranced with the shrill color of the mandarin peel in my hand.

"I asked you to rehearsals to see if maybe the theater would inspire you," says dad. "And it's fine if it doesn't, but we can't help you until you actually engage in your life. How do you want to leave your mark on this world?"

Heat builds behind my eyes. I envision ping-pong and the Happy Painter. Diverting my attention to neutral, soothing visions as when dealing with a No-Apparent-Reason Boner on public transportation. I block out my parents. How weary Mr. Kim appeared when he lectured me on the collections agencies. How Mrs. Kim's been feeding me extra, as though we're at a wake for my future prospects. I can't look at my mother's face. It takes monumental effort not to burst into tears. Everything is humiliating.

"Are you depressed?" dad asks, and I realize I've been staring at him. The temptation to tell him everything is enormous. I have never been more exhausted. I want my parents to help me.

Mom leans in across the table, looking as if now *she's* about to cry.

"Do you have trouble getting up in the morning?" she asks. "Do you feel irritable? Do you find it difficult to concentrate?"

She's going through the clinical depression checklist in her head. I can't burden them with my shit. Mom will absorb it all as a personal failing. Neither of them has the tools to deal with this. I'll have to figure it out on my own.

"Guys," I say finally. "I appreciate your concern. I do. But I'm not depressed."

"But you act like a different person." She inspects me intently. "You know people don't always know they're depressed when they're depressed."

It dawns on me with sickening clarity that she's right.

"Guys," I tell them, attempting a smile. "Hand on heart." I put my hand over my heart. "I promise I am not harboring fantasies of self-harm. . . ." At this mom sighs as if she's been holding her breath. "I'm not depressed. I'm not doing drugs. . . ."

"Honey, nobody said anything about drugs," says mom

defensively, which is when I know I've made the right decision. She proceeds to tell an imaginary live studio audience of jurors, "I think I would know if my kid were on drugs."

"I'm experiencing a setback." I uncross my arms and lean toward them. The picture of even-keeled mental health and fearless honesty. "I have a plan."

Even my father looks dubious.

"I'll snap out of it," I tell them. What other choice is there? "And I will get back on track. You'll have to trust me."

I pass my mom the rest of the clementine, which she finishes peeling and wordlessly splits with dad.

"Just give me a few more weeks."

Mom studies me as if she can diagnose mental illness with her gaze. "This plan is going back to school though, right?"

"Mom."

"Well, Pab," she exclaims, eyes wide. "You can't blame me for asking. The track record for your plans hasn't been encouraging. NYU was your grand plan. Moving out when you can't afford it was also your plan. Signing up for credit cards when . . ."

"Kay." Dad touches her knee.

"I patiently await details on the Plan," she says. I can tell it's killing her not to throw air quotes around it.

Dad taps the back of my hand and winks as mom eats the fruit and then grimaces. She takes dad's portion back, gives him some grapes instead, and tucks the offending orange into a napkin.

"Your plan has you staying in New York though, right? Don't do anything crazy, Pablo Rind, or I swear to god . . ."

"Mom!"

We both take a breather.

"Yes, I'm staying in New York."

"Okay." And then she says to dad, "Feel free to jump in at any point here, Bilal."

"I think you both did as well as could be expected."

Mom and I roll our eyes. He's the worst.

"Rain!" she yells over my head. "You can come out now."

Rain rushes back into the room, picks up an apple and hands it to mom for cutting, and then sits really close to me. Last borns have no sense of personal space.

"If you do leave New York," he says, "can I have your BAPE x Knicks jersey?"

"Oh totally," I tell him.

Mom looks about ready to murder all of us. She hands me a slice of apple on a toothpick.

Chapter 23

After my dad leaves and mom and Rain are watching a movie, I throw my clothes into the dryer. Despite all the agita, it's nice to be back here. Free food. Dryer sheets, which I never buy at home. Plus, I usually snag a roll or two of mom's toilet paper because she gets those trillion-ply double rolls that are eight bucks for a four-pack at Duane Reade. It feels good to be a kid again. Even momentarily. Even if all through high school I never felt as though my parents, my girlfriend, or most of my friends ever knew me.

I wonder if my friends know me now. Or if I know them. The thought leaves me restless.

I lock the door to mom's office and lie on my old bed, which is still pushed up against the wall. It's wild that I lived here just over a year ago. I don't remember anything about the first two months at NYU. It's all missing footage. That guy would never have believed I could know someone like

Lee. Thinking of Lee in my bedroom at my mom's house is strangely disquieting. I wish I could tell everyone that at least one aspect of my life is going well. Better than well. Inconceivably well.

I call Lee. Breaking my rule of not calling her back-to-back if she doesn't at least text me in between.

When she picks up, I'm flooded with a mixture of alarm and gratitude.

"Hey," I say, smiling into the phone.

"Hi." I start pacing in about three feet of space, suddenly nervous to have the attention.

"So . . ." I try a jaunty tone. "My parents literally interventioned me."

"What?"

"Yeah, they voiced some concerns about my future." I sit down at my mom's desk and mindlessly open all the drawers. I realize I expect Lee to reassure me somehow. Tell me I can't be that bad.

"Stop," she says.

"I know." Mom's top drawer, the one with the lock, opens easily. It's filled with pens and pads from the hospital. A few rubber bands.

"Why'd they do that?"

I grab a sushi-shaped eraser from Japan that's never been opened. You'd think my parents lived in a fallout shelter, the way they save everything. Mom will regift anything remotely indulgent and use wrapping paper at least twice.

"I don't know."

"Are *you* worried about your future?"

"What is that supposed to mean?"

"I guess, is there anything bigger you want to do with your life?"

"Bigger?" I put the California roll eraser down.

"Well, not bigger necessarily. I wasn't trying to imply anything."

"Well, I'm not going to work at a bodega for the rest of my life."

"Pablo, it's a *health food store.*"

She says it in a valley girl voice, which lightens the mood.

"I guess 'meaningful' is what I meant . . ."

"Meaningful, huh?"

Why did I bring any of this up? Talking to Leanna Smart about my career aspirations couldn't be any more emasculating. In the fantasy version of this, when she prompts me, I'd have a hidden talent. An undeniable and preternatural skill that we uncover together. Maybe I'm supposed to be a poet like my namesake.

"You love snacks a lot," she supplies.

"Enough about me." I continue to snoop. "What have you been doing? Tell me anything."

Under a leather day planner from 2009 (unused) there's a stack of papers with my name on them. Bills from two years ago. Organized by date with tiny scratchings in my mom's awful handwriting, tallying up various sums.

"There are amazing culinary programs in New York," continues Lee. "I don't know if your schedule . . ."

On the topic of school, the room feels as if it's filling with water. I've had plenty of opportunities to come clean about NYU, but I divert her every time.

"That's true," I conclude. "I'll take that under consideration. Tell me three things you're doing this week that you're excited about."

There's a meeting for some sneaker collab, a shoot for a magazine, and a flub with travel arrangements.

"Even though we have TSA precheck and CLEAR," she says, and then after a pause. "This isn't interesting."

"No, of course it is," though I'm barely listening. Instead I'm thumbing through the rest of mom's paperwork. "How do you feel about it?"

"Fine," she says. "I'm mostly nervous about getting ready for tour. Hold on a second?"

I turn my attention to mom's filing cabinet. It's unlocked because it's mom. This is a woman whose passwords are all QWERTY123.

Inside there's a New Mexico license plate key chain that she bought at the airport with my name on it. She buys one whenever she sees a "Pablo" since there aren't that many of them out there. Rain's never been lucky in that department either.

Lee mumbles, then laughs. A male voice laughs with her. "Who's that?"

"Dyland," she says. "My *fiancé.*" She's kidding, but I hate hearing the label. "According to the news, we've been engaged for six months except that I'm cheating on him with someone from my past. Honestly, Pablo, some days I think it's my own PR team creating dirt to sell concert tickets."

"Well, it is called the Intimacy tour," I tell her, testiness creeping into my tone. Some of the black-and-white posters do nothing to contradict the hookup rumors.

"Gross," she says conspiratorially. "Believe me, I'm not getting any D from that D-bag. I'd sooner gouge my eyes out than diddle Dyland."

I laugh. Sometimes I miss her so much I hurt.

In mom's cabinet I find a sleeve of old passport photos of her. A small uncomfortable smile affixed in place. Face unlined. Hair permed huge but pulled back tidily from her ears.

"I miss you," says Lee.

"Same."

"It's so infuriating. Of course Dyland never gets any of the backlash. And people don't even know about Cam."

"How old is Cam?"

"Unclear."

"And they've been together how long?"

"Since he was seventeen."

"Whoa. Also, ew."

"How old is Dyland?"

"My age."

"How old are you?"

Lee laughs.

"You told me to go to the source," I tell her.

"Guess."

"Hell no."

She laughs again.

"I'm twenty-two," she says. "But the Internet says I'm nineteen."

"Wow, an older woman."

"See?" she says. "See how much I trust you?"

"What else?"

"I'm meeting the director next week."

I return the packet of photos to the drawer. I take my mom's watchful eyes as a sign to stop intruding, but then I notice her files. They're meticulously organized. Color coordinated and chronological. Begging to be nosed through.

"They must have liked the audition tapes," I tell her.

"Or they're only meeting me as a professional courtesy and think I'm delusional," she says. "I'm doing everything I can to not be a needy trash-monster. I'm having dinner with Teddy and his people tonight."

My stomach drops. I know it's a business meeting, but I envision the candlelight, the wine, the tinkling laughter, his seemingly harmless touch on her forearm.

"That's great," I manage.

"I'm so nervous."

"They'll love you."

"God, I hope so."

"I miss you," I blurt. And then, "I guess I already said that."

"Me too," she says. "Anyway . . . it's happening."

"I wish I could see you."

"Same."

I'm dying to ask when.

"Hey, before I go," she says. "Do you want to talk about what happened with your parents tonight?"

"No, I'm okay."

"You sure?"

"Yeah."

"Okay, I gotta go."

"So go."

I keep snooping to have something to do.

All the folders are organized in months, and in each is a stack of bills. The same scrawling that enumerates various expenses, dad's insurance bills, Rain's phone, allowance, school supplies. In the February folder from this year there is a minus two hundred dollars for my birthday. I recognize "Pab" phonetically in Korean only because it's my name, but the half-Korean, half-English handwriting is virtually illegible. Never intended to be read by anyone but the person who wrote it. A ledger for every scrap of worried, lonely counting she does for us. To keep us safe.

I sit on the floor. She could help me. I could bring her all my mail. The bills. The scary letter from the county. More than that, though, I wish I were more like her. That I had the mind to organize and account no matter how frightening and overwhelming it is. I don't know that I know what depression feels like, but most days if I'm honest I wake up with a hammering in my heart and unless I'm talking to Lee I don't see the point in being conscious.

The dryer buzzes in the living room. It's time to go.

I can barely look at my family on the way out.

A few mornings later Tice catches me in the kitchen as I'm emailing for a password retrieval for NYU. It's unclear whether or not I'm even still in the system and I'm annoyed to have him breathing down my neck. Lately, Tice has been getting up earlier than Dara because he has a new job with three days of shooting at seven a.m. in Gowanus. That's in South Brooklyn by a canal that has a gnarly rat problem in the summer but also features artisanal small-batch ice cream.

Brooklyn's wild. In my lifetime it's been akin to watching a time-lapse video of a self-respecting town turn into douchebag wonderland complete with organic macrobiotic restaurants and single-source pour-over gazillion-dollar coffee. Tice was saying Gowanus now features flanks of brand-new condos and a huge Whole Foods with a beer-garden roof deck, which as a dude working in an independently owned store pisses me off. It's how when 7-Elevens started popping up in the city I became irrationally angry. Any true New Yorker should be ashamed to be frequenting a 7-Eleven instead of their bodega. I don't see any of those bastards extending credit to regulars or holding your spare keys and FedEx boxes for you anytime soon.

"Come on, you're not going back there," says Tice, looking at my screen while pulling out his revolting, sugar-free flax cereal from the pantry.

I've still got a week and change before the deadline.

"Summer semester, baby," I say, slapping my laptop shut so he can't clock that I'm locked out of my account. I feel my cheeks heating up. "Just got to finish up, talk to my adviser, and I'm good to go."

"They said that?"

"Basically," I mutter. "I'm practically legacy or whatever."

A spoonful of cereal stalls on its way to his mouth. "You know that's not how legacies work, right? Dude . . ." He shakes his head, and his spoon clatters back in the bowl. "If you've been out longer than two consecutive semesters, you're back in the big pool with incoming freshmen and transfers. It's NYU. You know that shit has only gotten harder and more expensive to get into. Also, are you sure summer semester's even a thing? Isn't that for high schoolers and international kids?"

For a college dropout who's six months younger than me, Tice sure has a lot of opinions on guidance counseling.

"Look," I tell him. "You do you and I'll do me." It feels like years have passed since it was effortless between us. Getting high during the day, staring at our phones, jawing about world domination feel like distant memories.

I check the time on the microwave.

"Aren't you late?"

Tice shovels the rest of his breakfast into his face.

As he turns to rinse his bowl, I notice that he's wearing his nice sweatpants. The damn-near hundred-dollar joints with the seams on the legs that he wears on dates and hangs on clippy hangers. It's as if he's a different person now.

"Work going well?" I feel guilty that I haven't been asking about it.

"Yeah," he says, slinging his backpack over his shoulder. "I'm getting paid for extra this week even though they could have squeezed my scenes into a single day. I mean, the call time's a bitch, but there's a trailer with heating and craft services—we call it Crafty—so there's free food even if you spend most of the day waiting."

Hearing him talk about call times and trailers and "Crafty" makes him seem older somehow. Professional. Like he's started a new life that I don't know anything about.

I force myself to say something nice. Supportive.

"What kind of snacks?"

"Oh, you'd love it," he says. "Everything. Those little toasty coconut chips we like. Twix. Whatever. Full charcuterie board sometimes. You know, they're looking for a production assistant next week. I'm sure it's a decent day rate to re-up snacks and do Starbucks runs. Could be perfect for you."

No way in hell am I doing Starbucks runs for Tice.

"I'm straight." I don't need to be an actor's butler while I figure out my life. "But look, I've got a more important proposition for you."

He sits at the table to tie up his boots.

"It's crucial," I warn him.

"What?"

"Who you bringing to the Oscars? Me or Wyn? You can't bring Miggs because Dara would kill him if he went without her."

Tice laughs. "Stupid." He gets up to head out.

"It's me, right? I look way better in black tie!"

"Pab," says Tice, all serious like some tax-paying adult. "Think about the PA gig? And . . ." He hesitates but fords on. "Maybe think about what you'd do if you *don't* get back in?" He nods at my laptop.

I make my face super serious, as serious as his, and break into a smile. "Promise you'll take me to the Oscars over Wyn first."

"Fine," he says, shaking his head, and closes the door.

Chapter 24

Swear to god I'm going to die in this health food store.

I don't know what it is, but each day is more soul-numbing than the last. And I know this sounds paranoid, but I swear the cell reception is weird in here because Lee calls me way less often than when I'm at home. At least that's how it feels.

When I get off work it's been a full twenty-four hours since I've last heard from her. My mind's racing as I swing by the bagel place for a pick-me-up.

I pause before pulling the door open. If it's Nando at the grill, Lee will call me by noon. If it's Seppi, the younger fobby Sicilian dude, Lee's eloped with Teddy Baptiste after their dinner and it's quiet for me.

I almost French kiss Nando I'm so happy to see him.

"Bacon, egg, and cheese?"

"Why don't you add *extra* bacon," I tell him, feeling celebratory. "On a sesame bagel. Not toasted."

Toasted bagels are strictly for schmears in my book. "They're fresh, right?"

Nando looks at me.

"You're right," I tell him, hands raised. I should know better. "My bad." Of course they're fresh. It's La Bagel Universe after all.

I've got my earbuds in and I'm cuing up a new video when I feel a pat on my shoulder. I turn, fully expecting to chin-check some impatient putz, so it takes me a second to register the face.

Luca.

"Ay," he says, smiling wide and pulling me in for a hug.

I hit pause on my phone. "What are you doing here?" He's with an Asian chick wearing thigh-high boots and this blousy shirt even though it's five degrees out. Clearly they're both dressed from the night before.

"This is my spot," says Luca. I look around as if I don't know where I am. None of this makes sense.

Nando passes me my sandwich and I stare at it.

"Ay," says Luca to Nando, up-nodding him familiar-like.

"How long are you in town?" I ask him.

"About a week," he tells me, then orders. "But I stay out here. I bought a place around the corner. The brownstone. Weird castle-looking joint. With the tower."

"Is Lee with you?"

"Nah. She's in LA," he says.

"I'm gonna go wait in the car," says the girl, who waves quickly to us and takes off.

"At least I think she's in LA," he says. "We're not heading out again until Wednesday." Luca eyes me quizzically. "She put you up on this place too?" he asks. "She said the bagels were bomb but to steer clear of the black-and-whites."

Right. Because they're disappointing.

The rest of the words go in and out.

"You all right there?" And then, "Oh, are you still wasted from last night?" A congratulatory pound on my back. "Ah," he says as if it's all coming together. "Walk of shame." Another meaty thump on my shoulders.

My peripheral vision blurs, and I swear to god it may as well be that scene from *The Matrix* where everything's white and Morpheus is telling Neo that reality is a fallacy.

"Word to the wise, Pablo," he says, pulling me toward him. "Maybe don't go to the bagel spot your girl told you about if you're visiting your *other girl*, know what I mean? She must be fancy if she lives around here. She older? I mean, this is a close call if you think about it. Lee could've easily been . . ."

The puzzle pieces that have stumped me since the beginning fit together. Why Lee was in my store. Of all places. At five in the morning. She was with him. At his house.

"Whatever, man, I get it. I love her to death, but you know how she gets . . ."

It takes me a second to register that Nando's waiting for me to pay him.

"Oh, I got this," says Luca, pulling out a twenty from a roll of cash as thick as my arm. I pipe up to protest. But then I see it. As Luca grabs his change, the cuff of his sweater rides up on his wrist. 2.22. The same tattoo Lee has on her foot.

That night the roommates and I go out at my insistence. Before we leave I get absolutely demolished on a bottle of Dara's Bacardi, which earns complaints from Miggs and a concerned look from Tice. I check my phone. My voicemail's still full from mom.

Lee texts me a black heart, and for the first time I ignore it. I have a huge text a mile-high that I haven't sent. A block of words that describes how I'd run into Luca.

What I know.

Except what *do I* know?

That Luca lives nearby.

Lee has ample reason to be at Luca's house.

Without Jess though?

Sure. He's her manager.

At five in the morning?

Yeah.

Twice?

I cut and paste the text copy to notes and close out because the prospect of sending it by accident chills my soul.

I take another swig of rum, no chaser. It's disgusting.

"Yo, let's go," I yell to the house.

The first function is a bust, so we head down Wythe to the next. Individually we're in weird headspaces, that seasonal cabin fever that comes from being cooped up for months in the cold. We're in the part of winter where you'd swear that sunlight was a hoax.

I want to have a good time in that determined way that never turns out right. As with Halloween or New Year's, expectation is a surefire jinx. We're all frozen solid from trooping four blocks, and as soon as we get in Dara grabs a corner booth by aggressively dumping her coat over a pile and sitting on them to stake her claim.

I'm itching for another drink, but I'm assed out. I really should get a fake ID, but it feels pathetic to lie about that final year and it's not as if being a year older means I'll have more money. Just as I check my phone again, this time to make sure I definitely cut the text from the message box, I see her. Tabitha. My high school ex Heather's younger sister. "Pablo!" she squeals, throwing her arms around me and stumbling. She's clearly had a few. "Hey, Tabs." I peel her off as I catch Wyn giving her a skeezy once-over. "Oh my god, your hair's so long and luxurious now," she says, running a hand through it.

Tabitha's a wild card. She was liable to walk downstairs in nothing but underwear when I was over at the McAllisters'. Not that I would ever try anything with her. You have to be a real bottom-of-the-barrel scumbag to scheme on your ex-girlfriend's little sister.

"Fellas." I point to the guys. "This is Tabitha. My ex-girl Heather's *very much younger* sister.

"Tabs, this is Tice, Wyn, Miggs, and Dara." Dara waves from her perch.

"Nice to meet yoooooou!" she squeals, and then whispers to me, "Get me a vodka sugar-free Red Bull? I got my ID snatched at Mr. Cerulean."

"Nope," I tell her. She's stunned. I can actually spy the gum wad in her open mouth. I wonder if I'm bearing witness to the first no in her life.

"Tab, I'm twenty."

"Ooooh," she says, and then bats her eyes at the rest of the guys. The crew look to their phones or the ceiling.

"That's cool," she says, and practically sits on top of Dara, who says, "Excuse you," to which Tabitha responds, "Oh my god, I'm obsessed with your eyebrows."

She pulls me down in the booth with her, but I immediately distance myself. "So, how are you?" she asks, retrieving still more gum from a glittery purse the size of a deck of cards.

"Good," I tell her. "How's Heather? How's Tufts treating her?"

Tabitha nods. "So good," she says. "I miss her so much. She's in France for a year to study abroad. Her new boyfriend . . ." Tabitha gauges my expression, which I leave purposefully blank. "He *does* hospitality in Paris, and they're having the best time. It's on their IG highlights."

First of all, I haven't checked for Heather in almost a

year, let alone lurked her man, and secondly, Tabitha says *Pareee*, which reminds me of Heather and her habit of dropping French words into sentences for no reason.

"How's NYU?" asks Tabitha. "I want to go to Tisch School of the Arts." She says the full thing too: Tisch School of the Arts.

"Great," I tell her.

I zone out. There's a girl with super-short curly hair and these square glasses who's made the power move of wearing a baggy sweatsuit to the club. It's the type of flex that's so much more attractive and confident than any designated "going out" clothes. It reminds me of the story of how my dad met my mom. It was eight in the morning and she was eating chicken wings on the train in scrubs like a savage, and everybody was shooting her the dirtiest looks.

Few people have the gall or gumption to eat on the train, let alone during a morning commute, when a bag of chips is about as far as you can take it or maybe a bagel with cream cheese but definitely no egg.

Everybody was giving mom and her fried food a wide berth, as you do when you catch a homeless person in your particular train car or the dude clipping his nails, but that was it for my dad. He *had to* talk to her, and when she said she was busy and that she'd worked a thirty-hour shift at New York-Presbyterian, he knew he was going to marry her.

I look back at the girl who's only got eyes for the person she's dancing with and only then do I notice that it's another girl with short locs. They make out.

". . . not that moving to LA will fix that," screams Tabitha over the music.

"What?" The LA part gets my attention. I have opinions on LA.

"LA!" she screeches directly into my ear.

The crowd's bathed in a red glow, writhing, and I'm struck by the feeling that I'm watching a movie I've seen before.

I wonder what Lee's doing. If she'd be jealous if she saw me and Tabitha. I feel stupid for even questioning it. As if Lee could ever be threatened. Besides, Heather's lapped me in life, so it's no wonder I'm talking to her younger sister. If I'm stuck here talking to Hailey—Tab and Heather's fifteen-year-old sister, in a few years—I will leap off the Manhattan Bridge.

Tice comes over. "Let's go."

Wyn's behind him and nods. I grab my coat. How did I let myself forget that going out sucks? Every night is exactly the same. Boring and expensive. I don't even know what I spent money on, but I know the sixty dollars I got from the ATM has unceremoniously evaporated in my forty-dollar jeans. It's so predictable. I feel worse about the Luca run-in, not better.

Tabitha lurches to her feet, face glowing from her phone light.

"Pablo, come with me to Happy Valley," she says with her eyes closed. She's wasted.

"I'm all set, Tab."

She squints at her phone. "What about Six Sixteen Mott? Or there's an afters at Lucien."

"I'm going home," I tell her. "You should too."

"Noooo," she says, swaying. One of her fake eyelashes has come unhinged. It swings as she grins in this clownish way that reminds me of a line from *The Sopranos* where Tony refers to crazy eyes as "Manson Lamps."

"Where's your jacket?" I ask her.

"Over there," she says, gesturing vaguely into the darkness. She leans in and talks into my chest. "Where are you going?" she whines.

"I told you. Home."

"Can I come?" she asks. "I have weed."

I look around. Nowhere in this cluster can I spot anyone who's concerned for this girl.

"Nah, but I'll wait until your car gets here if you want," I tell her. Just as Wyn calls out, "Yo, Tabitha, you tryna slide through?"

Tabitha passes out on my shoulder in the cab and normally I'd be flustered about a girl seeing the apartment, but it's Tab so it barely counts.

When we get home, the first thing I do is pour another shot and pound it. "Easy, killer," says Tice, taking the bottle from me. Wyn, of course, is in rare form. I swear his favorite part of the night is when we're back home after going out.

He has the worst insomnia, so he loves when we're all up late together. This is the witching hour, when I work my magic with the Hot Snack.

"Hot Snack!" he declares, rubbing his hands together. Hot Snack™ are a specialty of mine, and the thinking is that after a night on the town we're deserving of a truly enticing food experience, unlike garbage regular snacks, which would be chips or cookies.

For Hot Snack™ Wyn plays sous-chef and raids leftovers in the fridge and sets them on the counter so I can get to work. It's usually a hodgepodge of our favorites—kimchi fried rice, Miggs's childhood fondness for ramen flavor packets and elbow macaroni, Tice's love for anything curried, and Dara's mom's ingenuity with baloney. It's a joint peace treaty in the after-hours. It's even deepened my respect for mayonnaise, that white-devil condiment, because if you apply it *and* butter liberally to the outside of any sandwich, it browns like you wouldn't believe.

The only time I wasn't around to make the Hot Snack™, Tice stepped in and served stewed chicken over Tater Tots, which Miggs said brought tears to his eyes. But he got an assist from his mom, who dropped off the chicken in a Tupperware. Ethnic mom Tupperware as a ringer is definitely cheating.

There's leftover Chinese—some Singapore fried noodles— enough that I fashion a large pancake layer on the bottom of a pan. I nuke some Trader Joe's frozen breakfast sausage, cut it up, sprinkle it on top, and add some beaten eggs with smoked paprika, some all-purpose seasoning mix that doesn't have celery salt in it because that shit is nasty with eggs. Then I pour the mixture over the top to form a noodle frittata that I'll serve in wedges. Grated cheese, sriracha, sour cream, and we're good to go.

Wyn grabs all the other condiments because you can never tell what a Hot Snack™ will need until you dig into it, and I notice that Tabs eats like she hasn't been fed in weeks. For dessert I whip up bootleg affogatos, vanilla ice cream plunged in Bustelo coffee with dark-chocolate M&M's and crushed-up Violet Crumble honeycomb. And this is also where the Parle-G biscuits come into play.

By the time I add the salted-pretzel pieces, Miggs is champing at the bit, but I make them all wait while I shoot a quick video for reference. I have a full archive of Hot Snack™ footage. I'd watch the shit out of a cooking show where all the recipes were leftovers or ingredients you could get from the bodega. Especially if it had a gonzo, public-access look to it since glossy stuff always looks like an ad to me.

When we're done, Dara brings out her mini bong and even lets Tabitha hit it right before she passes out.

Tab's curled up on the couch with her feet gathered and I throw my coat over her, but then I have a crisis of conscience.

"Yo, Tabitha." I shake her a little. "Tabs."

She sleepily opens her eyes. "I'm so tired, Pablo," she said. "I haven't slept in two days."

"Come on," I tell her. I make her take off her shoes and give her a T-shirt and basketball shorts. Then I go brush my teeth so she can change. On my way back Wyn pokes his head out and gives me this questioning smile. All Cheshire cat–looking with his stupid grin practically glowing in the dark.

"Don't be an idiot," I whisper. "She's twelve years old. And trashed."

He nods rapidly a few times. "Word," he says. "Mutual affirmative consent man. You can't compromise a girl's agency."

I slug him in the arm. Sometimes he's an idiot and other times he comes at you with this fully formed truth kernel.

When I get back to my room, Tabitha's snoring on top of the bed. Over the sheets and the comforter. Everything.

I roll half of the covers over her in a burrito, grab a pillow and my hoodie, and hit the couch.

I try to sleep but can't. Flashes of Luca's tattoo shudder into my mind when I close my eyes. I thought for certain getting hammered and high would serve as enough distraction. At least to pass out. But my thoughts tunnel vision to what this means.

It's stupid and I shouldn't do it, but my thumbs go rogue and I start searching. Luca, Leanna Smart, 222. Then their names and February 22. Luca, Leanna, love. But every search ties Lee with Dyland or a handful of other Lotharios who are rumored to have dated or slept with everyone. Leanna, emancipation, parents also yield nothing. I wonder if Lee has enough juice to alter the Internet. Or if what she told me was remotely true.

And because I'm not disgusted enough with myself, I ransack her Instagram. And her Twitter. Snapchat. It's all perfume, new album, and shockingly absent any revealing admissions of how she's infatuated with her manager that geotag to his Brooklyn house.

In the morning, I've got a crick in my neck and I'm pissed. I'm hungover from the weed and booze and the late-night data binge in equal measure. Why the fuck did Wyn have to invite Tabitha over so that I can't self-soothe to the point of self-harm in my own bed? That's twenty-eight dollars in rent. If Tabitha slept in Wyn's bed he'd be out seven bucks. I'm cheap enough to pull the phone out for calculations.

I return to my room. Tabitha's still asleep.

"Tabitha. Get up. I got work."

She grumbles, nods, and swings her legs to the floor.

"Can I borrow this?" she asks, plucking at the T-shirt and yawning.

"Yeah," I say. I'm never gonna see that shirt again. I silently add it to the tally of resentments against Wyn. "Not the shorts though."

"Thanks, Pab," she says, puddling the basketball shorts on the floor and stepping out of them. I turn away. "Thanks for hanging out. It was fun."

She carries her heels. Her dress is draped on her arm, and she's about to head out pantsless.

"Do you need cab fare?" I ask her out of concern. Not that I have any to spare.

"Nah," she says, eyes glued to her phone. "I called a car."

It's probably a hundred bucks to her house from here.

"All right."

"Bye, Pab." She kisses the air by my cheek and shuts the door. She smells of unwashed hair. A new pile of envelopes catches my eye. All addressed to me. This could be it. A new morning. The first day of the rest of my life. I grab the stack and head into my room. It's practically radioactive in my hands. I open the drawer, greet the rest of them, and toss the pile in.

With a dry throat and a metallic taste in my mouth, I do what I always do.

I text Lee back.

Chapter 25

Over the next few days I develop a cold with a cough so raucous it sounds as if broken lawn chairs are rattling in the vacuum cleaner of my chest.

"Good god, Pab," says Tice, steering clear in the hallway with his sweatshirt pulled up over his face. "Will you get that shit looked at?"

I have my comforter draped around my shoulders as I shuffle back from the bathroom.

"It's a cold," I tell them. I never get a flu shot. "I'll be fine as long as I can get some sleep."

The thing is, it's an impossible proposition because of the racket inside me. And because I might have a hairline fracture in my ribs that would explain the sharp radiating pain on my left side.

"Bone pain or muscle pain?" asks Tina at work with a disgusted look on her face, as she keeps a safe distance.

"Bone pain," I tell her, sniffing so hard I see stars.

"Yeah," she says, shaking her head. "You gotta get that shit looked at."

"Go home," commands Mr. Kim, creeping up behind us. We both jump a little. He pumps hand sanitizer on his palms as if looking at me is contagious. "You're going to get customers sick."

I stumble to the CityMD, the walk-in emergency clinic on Seventh, hugging myself in an effort to keep warm. I wish I could call my mom with symptoms, but I'm back to avoiding her. The blast radius of her rage would annihilate me if I told her my big plan was total paralysis and reapplying to NYU and nowhere else. My pockets are filled with tissues—sweatpants pockets, hoodie pockets, and coat pockets. The insides of my mouth are sliced and metallic from lozenges, and I can't see that far ahead of my face.

I fill out forms in triplicate on a clipboard with a logo'd pen that writes so smoothly I pocket it. I wait fifty-five minutes for a thirty-five-minute appointment. A twentysomething woman with a pinched expression weighs me, eyes flickering down to the big toe sticking out of the growing hole in my sock when I kick my shoes off. I'm a mess. The nurse asks questions, listens to me breathe, and refuses to give me codeine. They hand me a gown and I slip out of both sweatshirts and shiver. When they've left me alone in the room for fifteen more minutes with no further instructions, I put them back on.

A changing of the guard. A slender Indian woman in

her thirties or forties with freezing-cold hands. When I flinch, she rubs them together for warmth.

She asks me whether I got a flu shot.

"No."

"Why?"

I shrug. I'm twenty going on twelve.

Another fifteen-minute wait for a five-minute chest X-ray. No broken bones. Not even a little bit.

I text Lee, but she's distracted and sends the frowning emoji. We had a phone call this morning, but my cough was so gnarly I was too embarrassed to speak.

One hundred and eleven minutes of time. One hundred and thirty dollars for the appointment. Three hundred and sixty dollars for the X-ray. Four hundred and ninety dollars added to the thousands and thousands and thousands—and change—that I owe the universe.

"Let's do . . ." At the front desk my fingers hover over the fake, but ironically fake, LV wallet that's split along the side, a testament to the state of my finances. "This one." I fish out a card and hand it to the heavyset receptionist with a bowl haircut and thick black glasses.

She has the decency to try it twice before handing it back.

"You might want to call your bank," she says kindly. Instead of: "The shit was declined because you're broke."

I hand her the other Visa. The one for emergencies. The good one that I've been responsible with. The one I keep in an entirely separate compartment of my wallet because I don't want the others tainting it. It still has an introductory APR of 8 percent that I could transfer old balances onto except that of course I haven't.

"There we go," she says, and hands me the receipt to sign. I gank a second CityMD pen. They have ergonomic grips.

They give me a prescription for benzonatate pills, but the Walgreens doesn't carry generic so I get the fancy Tessalon Perles that cost eighty-eight dollars for a two-week supply. I'm so traumatized by now I hand over the good Visa and pray.

I wish I'd stayed on my mom's health insurance, but she kicked me off when I moved out and left school. Meanwhile, my father remains on it.

When I get home Wyn is on the phone. Without addressing me, he pushes me into a chair and shoves a steaming mug of ginger, lemon, and honey into my hands. It's brewed so spicy that it stings my eyes and burns my throat. Clasping the mug so it warms me, I think about how I've spent over half my rent in an afternoon on the worthless skinsuit that is my broken body. I take another sip.

Wyn, phone on face, brusquely takes the mug and replaces it with a massive saucepan of scalding water with a bunch of herbs floating in it.

"Breathe as deep as you can," he tells me, patting my shoulder. He throws a towel over my head. The steam clings to my cheeks as I shut my eyes. When I open them my eyeballs burn and I can barely make out my features in the reflection, a dumb shadowy blob of head. I close them again and imagine the persistent pressure at my sinuses as an angry black knot that loosens and dissolves. Wynn speaks in Croatian behind me and laughs. I understand the word "marjoram." The heat and moisture coat my linings. It's the warmest I've been in months and the longest I haven't coughed in forever.

"Thanks, mom," says Wyn from somewhere above me. "Volim te."

I feel so awful I can barely stay upright. I watch reruns of Lee's show, trying to figure out if her teeth look different. There's an episode with Dyland from way back. I'm watching ground zero for the rumors about their romantic relationship.

In my diminished state it's hard not to see the chemistry.

Last week Lee complained about him for an hour on the phone.

"He's such a prima donna."

"Tell me." I'm a fiend for any tour details.

"Okay, so he's on a crazy diet."

"So predictable."

"I know," she says. "And get this, he keeps screaming 'sub ten' and doing push-ups because he wants to get his body fat below ten percent."

"What a freak."

"Completely reprehensible."

"Also . . ."

"Go on . . ."

She laughs.

"Wait. I gotta make sure the coast is clear."

The day before, we'd made the mistake of trying to have phone sex while she was mic'd. It wasn't out-and-out phone sex per se, but things were getting suggestive when Mike, the sound guy, knocked on her door.

"Okay, so he drinks this special drink that he calls—I shit you not—Opulence. It's Diet Sprite mixed with coconut Bai."

"Opulence?"

"Opulence."

"Get the fuck out."

"I'm serious. It's always in a white Styrofoam cup with a straw. I'll get to rehearsal and it's waiting there for him. A stupid white cup with a plastic bendy straw and that tiny tube of paper at the top so he knows that his pristine drink is untainted."

"It kills you that it's in a nonbiodegradable container, doesn't it?"

"I want to murder him every time."

"You know Diet Sprite and coconut Bai sounds delicious."

"It is. He let me try it and it was objectively tasty, but you don't understand; one of his three assistants have to be able to hand it to him whenever he calls for it."

I picture him play wrestling with Cam again and believe every word.

"Pab, he calls them 'assistant' even when they're all

three right in front of him. Assistant singular. I don't think he knows their names."

"Do you know *your* assistants' names?"

"Okay, firstly, they're lady's maids, and of course I do," she says. "They wear name tags."

A beat.

"You know I'm kidding, right?"

"What about everyone else?"

"Like who?"

Luca, Luca, Luca, Teddy, Luca.

"Oh, I don't know," I say blithely as I hold my breath.

Silence.

"You mean like does anyone else have fetishistic peccadilloes beverage-wise?"

Or, are you in love with Luca?

"Remember when Luca wanted unpasteurized coconut water on the plane too so I said never mind?" I ask her.

Another silence.

"Yeah, that was funny," she says noncommittally.

When Lee and I next find time to videochat, she's mobbed.

"Ayo," says Luca to me from behind her. If I could lunge into her screen and garrote him with Dyland's headband, I would.

"Stop." Lee shoos him away. "Sorry I'm running late." She's calling me from her laptop. She reconfigures and I'm swung to a wall and then the back of a chair and then she's in picture. There's a pair of arms hovering above her head. "We can either do this while I'm in glam or I'll call you super late tonight."

"Nah. This is fine."

"Hi, Pab," says an adenoidal voice.

"Hey, Chase," I call out to her hair stylist.

From the waist up I'm wearing a decent-to-good sweatshirt; on the bottom I'm a duvet Jabba the Hutt. I've positioned the lamp in my room so the light doesn't betray my sallowness. I clear my throat.

"Still sick?" she asks me.

"Yeah."

"I'm sorry, babe," she says. "This flu season is no joke."

"Did you get a flu shot?"

"Of course. I got one trillion B12 shots too. I am also basically composed of oregano oil and ginger."

Lee pulls out her phone right as Chase's tattooed elbow covers the laptop camera.

"God, I can't wait till tour's over."

Lee has twelve more domestic dates and then a week off and then she's in Europe for three weeks.

Chase grabs a lock of hair and twists it into a knot and secures it with a clamp.

"Babe, can't we do the braid again?" Lee asks behind a fog of hair spray.

"Nope," he says. "They only love you with your hair down. You're shooting promos for"—he riffles through a sheaf of paper—"Japan, China, and South Korea, babe."

"*Babe,*" I butt in. "But I thought China only liked you in pigtails."

"Huh?" Lee's engrossed in her phone.

"Nothing."

"Sorry," she says, putting it away.

"Don't worry about them," says Chase, working a massive brush through the crown of her head. "It's a smear campaign. It'll blow over."

"Smear campaign?"

"Chase," snaps Lee.

"What will blow over?" I pipe up. Out of guilt I've been cooling it on the searches for a few days, and of course this is when news breaks.

"All of these hater-ass Dummees," he tells me.

Lee jerks her head forward and glares at him.

"I'm sorry, but it's trending as of this morning," he says. "He can't *not* know."

"It doesn't matter," she says.

"It doesn't matter," repeats Chase, chastened.

Sistine comes in and starts on her eyebrows. Watching Lee get ready reminds me of those NASCAR pits, where it takes four people six seconds to complete two tire changes and a refuel.

"Hey, Pab," she says.

"Hey, Sistine, what's the smear campaign?"

"Isn't it when one person insults another person a whole bunch? In politics? Right? Mudslinging or whatever." She gets right in front of Lee for a second to check her hand-iwork. "Are you running for congress, Pab? We could use you."

"No. Who's leading a smear campaign against Lee?"

"Oh, fuck the Dummees," she says dismissively, dabbing a tube of shiny paint on Lee's cheek. "Can you think of a *less* original name? Why would you call yourself a Dummy? I guess it's meta, or maybe non-ironic ironic since they're stupid."

"Lee?" I ask her pointedly.

She sighs.

"Okay, purse your lips for a second for me, babe?" says Sistine, taking her sweet time with the liner.

I wait.

"And cue elaboration!" I call out to Lee when they're done. "Who are the Dummees?"

"I'm sorry." Lee sighs again. "This is too hectic. Can I call you later?"

I google it. What choice do I have?

This time, breaking the seal is wonderful. I don't even feel guilty about it. In fact, it's the satisfaction of popping a thousand yards of Bubble Wrap at once. Or when your scissors glide while cutting wrapping paper. Googling Leanna Smart is deeply gratifying. I gorge on her whereabouts, actions, and, yeah, why not, even her outfits, *clickingclicking-clicking* like a fiend in the shameful darkness of my bedroom. It's glorious.

The Dummees, though, aren't that rewarding. In fact,

this is when the shame hits. The Dummees suck. They leave me feeling entirely cheerless about the human condition. The whole thing started as a moderately populated Reddit page about how she's not Latinx *enough*. How she only dates white guys. That her music fell off when she stopped opening her heart up to Christ and started taking off her clothes in concerts. Someone posted a photo of her from when she was six where she—regrettably—had her hair in cornrows. For no reason it only just went viral. A streetwear designer made an allover print of it and put it on a skateboard that showed at Art Basel. Truthfully, it's exactly the sort of thing Tice and I would want on beach towels or socks if I didn't know her.

Binging on the Dummees makes me want to take a shower with all my clothes on. There's another site too that's helping to signal boost the anti-Smartees movement. It's entirely dedicated to scrutinizing every single image of Lee to dissect whether or not she's had surgery. Aggregated before and afters of what they claim to be photoshopped images. The "real" Lee references are unflattering candids or red-carpet photos where her body's contorted.

I now know why Lee didn't want me to do this. It's assaultive. It's betrayal.

I understand why she armors herself with the prosthetic boob adhesives and the hair. Why she mumbles and talks too much when she's nervous and why she seems so unsure of her self-worth outside of the music industrial complex. The conviction that she's replaceable makes sense.

I want to stop out of decency, some sense of honor and ethics. But I devote another sixteen minutes to conspiracy theories about 2.22 and add to the traffic of the seediest underbelly of the Internet.

Still nothing.

The first signs of a migraine claw up the base of my skull and cling there. I push on the meaty part of my hand. It doesn't help.

Chapter 26

"**I'm headed to** Canada," she announces the next day as I'm staring at the blinking cursor on the document on my laptop. Her call is a great excuse to bail on the résumé I'm taking a stab at. It's not that I want the job that Tice offered, but it's maybe a good idea to finally have one.

"Canada? Why for?"

"Search me," she says.

I hit save but realize the only part I've changed from the template is my name. I'd thought about calling dad for help, but that would require a whole conversation on hopes and dreams and I don't have it in me. I've been staring at the *Pablo Neruda Rind* on the top for so long it's ceased to have meaning. The way when you say "iguana" a bunch you stop thinking about the reptile. I add my address. Center it all. And then change the type to Futura Heavy Oblique because it's the Supreme logo font.

"Isn't that close to New York?" I save it again, shut my computer, and open my window for a gust of crisp air. I put on my boots and climb out onto the fire escape. It's the best part of having a bedroom that used to be in the kitchen.

"Is it?" she asks.

"It *feels* close."

She laughs.

"It does *feel* close. Northerly and overthere-ly."

"Where in Canada?"

"I didn't look. They hang on to my wallet and my passport and I get herded like meat. I haven't carried a set of keys in years."

"You make it sound like a hostage situation."

"My feet barely touch the ground."

Sometimes when Lee describes her life I may as well be talking to a member of the royal family.

"I can't believe winter lasts as long as it does." It's been five weeks since Lee and I have seen each other. I wonder if Leanna Smart has ever written a résumé.

"I miss New York," she says. And then, "Shit. I gotta go."

"Yeah, me too," I say reflexively, and then take an urgent three-hour nap.

"Just kidding!" Lee tells me the night after. "I'm in Melbourne."

"How are you in Australia?"

I'm arriving at my shift, and it's unfathomable that since the last time we spoke, I've traveled a single subway stop and she's on a different continent.

"It's only nine hours from Hong Kong on the direct."

"I thought you were going to Canada." Meanwhile I didn't know she was in Hong Kong.

"Same difference."

I laugh. I don't know why.

"How'd that happen?" I ask her.

"It has to do with tabs and files and an intricate series of . . . I misread it on the thing."

"Relatable."

"Ugh," she says. "So picture my little red dotted line having flown Australia-ward, not due Canada, on a map of the world."

"Yeah, I don't know any of these directions really."

"Why is everyone so bad at geography? I at least have a general idea, if only because I had that map shower curtain when I was a kid."

"Remember globes?"

"Vaguely?" she says.

"Isn't it wild that there was a time when *that* was all the information we had on the world."

"You mean the good old days."

"Ha. Exactly. Now we know every single awful thing that's happened to anyone anywhere ever. All the natural disasters, scandals, privacy crimes, and when an Instagram influencer gets pregnant. We've watched polar bears die in real time. It can't be healthy."

"All of this can't be good for us," she says. "Remember

when people got points for memorizing phone numbers? Those days were good too."

"Do you think there's a person out there who that was their entire talent, memorizing phone numbers?" I picture a slender man named Neville.

"I bet his friends wouldn't hear the end of it," she says.

"Maybe he didn't even have friends he was so boring and annoying."

"And repetitive."

"God, what if he memorized his parents numbers' and then a mess of strangers' contacts to keep his numbers up?" Neville lives in his parents' finished basement with a foos-ball table and an aging ferret. "This guy's the worst." I try not to picture how close I am to being a Neville.

"I don't know," she says. "I like this guy now. He sounds lonely."

"G'day, Leanna. Are ya havin' a rippin' good arvo?" I respond when I see the unknown caller right on time at five thirty a.m. Lee said she'd call after the show and a luncheon some-place. Dead air. I wonder if I've made a tactical error. Maybe my awful accent is culturally insensitive.

"Hello?" I try again. Gusto jumps onto the counter, sens-ing turmoil, and waves his tail right under my nose to show me his butthole. For solace I guess. I pet him anxiously.

"Hey," she squeaks, and then takes a ragged exhale, and I can tell immediately she's crying.

Unease races up my spine.

"Hey," I say quietly. "Are you okay?"

Silence.

My heart thumps.

"What happened?"

A sharp intake and another ragged breath out.

"I'm sorry."

"Don't be sorry."

My insides coil.

It's partly how far she is. And how isolated she seems in this moment—without the background chatter. I'm going from zero to sixty for fight-or-flight responses, and I'm ready to pulverize a crew of thugs or hop aboard a plane with a "very particular set of skills." I have never been more ready to run a thousand miles to locate the trunk of the car that this girl is trapped inside. I pace behind the counter.

"Please tell me what's wrong," I say, glancing at the clock again. That she's fourteen hours in the future makes her seem extra far away. "Are you okay?"

"Yes," she says after an eternity. "I am. It's dumb, but I had the worst fight."

"With who?"

I clear my throat to downgrade the mania I hear in my voice.

"Luca."

2.22 flashes in my head.

"But it wasn't even about him."

"Okay. What was it about?" I automatically summon

visions of Luca pawing at her. Of them kissing in his multi-million-dollar brownstone.

"He's just . . ." She sighs again and blows her nose. "No, never mind . . ." She whimpers.

"Lee, please tell me." I soften my tone. "Remember when I promised that I'd worry about you? Well . . ." I try for levity. "Color me extremely concerned."

More silence.

"Lee, what did he do?"

"It wasn't anything that he . . ." Another deep sigh. "God. Honestly, I'm just exhausted. I can't wait to go home."

"Lee, what happened?" I press on.

"This is going to sound ridiculous."

"Try me." I scratch the spot behind Gusto's ear. He's purring, and the vibrations of the tiny motor in his neck have a self-soothing effect on me too.

"Do you know what meet-and-greets are?" she asks.

"I'm sure I can get it out of context."

She laughs softly and then blows her nose again.

"There are so many this tour. And I get it; it's a lot of money. People pay thousands of dollars to take a picture or say hi and whatever, but once they're in they act so entitled. It's like they've bought you. It's supposed to be one photo and they take thirty *and* they shove you in a video and want you to sing for them or give a friend of theirs a shout-out or wear a stupid company logo hat that they literally take off their own heads. It's like, there's not enough hand sanitizer in the whole world. . . . There's just so much touching and pushing and everyone here is super polite and so nice, but . . ."

Another shaky exhalation.

"But tonight there was this woman and she was maybe fifty. She and her two friends were spectacularly hammered and she grabbed my boob."

"Whoa."

"Yeah, and when security stepped in, she kept laughing and screaming in my ear, saying she wasn't gay but that she couldn't resist. Then she broke free as they were ushering her out and she grabbed my ass except I was wearing a skirt . . . I know it's not a big deal . . ."

The more she plays it off, the more protective I feel. "It sounds awful."

"It wasn't painful . . . just mortifying. I was so stunned."

"What did Luca do?"

"That's the thing—he didn't do anything. He used to go crazy about that kind of stuff when I was younger, but he couldn't even pretend to care. He was on his phone the entire time. Didn't even look up. Just told me to soldier through and get it over with."

I fantasize about rappelling into his house under cover of night and beating him senseless.

"What did you do?"

"Nothing. There's been so much bad press lately, and I didn't want to seem difficult."

"That's assault, Lee. You could have canceled—"

"Pablo . . ." She laughs a hard little laugh. "The girl

behind that woman was wheelchair-bound. I couldn't cancel. Not now."

Okay. She's right. The Internet would have had a field day with that.

"Yeah. I was *so close* to shutting it down. Tell everyone to hightail it home, and there she was. Setsuko. Eight years old. Leukemia."

"Wow."

"I know. It's like, what's the one thing that could really take the wind out of your complaining sails?"

Apparently, it's Setsuko.

"She was from Kumamoto. Which is famous for their oysters and its impressive distance from Melbourne. And she was very cool."

"This story is an emotional roller coaster."

"Pablo."

"Yes, Lee?"

"I was her Make-A-Wish Foundation wish."

"Damn."

"Yeah. Her final wish was for me to sing 'Highway' even though I was ready to crawl into a ball and die."

"Die figuratively."

Lee groans.

"Right. Die *figuratively.* Unlike Setsuko." Another exhalation. "Is there a layer beyond first-world problems? Where you're even more despicable for complaining? I disgust myself."

"Better out than in," I tell her. "Listen, I'm on your side

and Setsuko's side in this." I don't know what else to say.

"And get this . . ."

"What?"

"She told me straight to my face to break up with Dyland. That he wasn't good enough for me because he— and I quote, again from a eight-year-old icon—'lacked character.'"

"Lacked *character*?"

"Oh yeah."

I imagine Setsuko sizing me up and saying, "Needs work."

"She had a translator, a very nice woman, also extremely chill. Evidently there's an aspect to facing mortality at such a young age that makes you wise."

"Evidently."

"Actually," says Lee abruptly. "That's not entirely true. I've met plenty of Make-A-Wish kids who prove jerks get cancer too. Believe me, not all children with terminal illnesses and disabilities are magical beacons of inspiration and hope for us typicals. Some are mean as snakes. But, man, Setsuko specifically was cool as hell."

"I'm glad a dying child could be there for you in your hour of need?"

"Oh jeez . . ."

Gusto bats my hand because I've stopped petting him. Deli cats don't play second fiddle to anyone.

"Thank you," she says.

"For what?"

"For the perspective. And listening to me without judgment."

I keep petting.

"Of course."

Okay. This is it. I should trust her. If there was ever a time to ask about Luca it's now.

I give Gusto a really big scratch for courage and he goes nuts.

"I have a question," I begin.

"Shit," she says. "Wait. I forgot to tell you the best part. I'm coming to New York!"

"Really?" I push Luca out of my mind. I'll ask her in person. "When?"

"A few days. There's a thing. I wasn't going to go, but then . . . I don't know, Pab. I just miss you too much."

"Thank god," I tell her. "I'm dying to see you."

"I know," she says. "So dying."

"Figuratively."

"Jesus, yeah. Figuratively."

Chapter 27

On the Wednesday she flies in I'm anxious and my leg tapping is at an all-time high. Mrs. Kim can't stand next to me I'm too nerve-grating. She *tsssk*s and goes around back. The night is slow, and I'm compulsively checking my phone for any morsel of a Lee update. I can't wait. In a few hours I'll actually get to see her. I'm meeting her at her hotel after I shower and change. She's checked in as Frieza Marron.

"They're *Dragon Ball Z* characters that I pick at random," she tells me. "Or *Pokémon.*" It's wild to think how well she'd get along with Rain.

Just when I'm about to bore a hole in the clock and my shift's almost up, pandemonium breaks loose.

Mr. Kim rushes to the front, followed by Mrs. Kim. Even inscrutable, unflappable Jorge appears vexed. *It's bad,* he mouths, shaking his head.

"The back freezer's broken," Mr. Kim tells me. That is bad. Real bad. The back freezer's the big one with the stores of the super-expensive vegan frozen entrees and the twelve-dollar tubs of Italian ice cream. It's extra cold. Mrs. Kim is on the phone with an emergency repair guy, and me and Jorge get to work consolidating the food into the other freezers or even fridges so we can salvage what we can.

As I'm stacking the gluten-free pizzas together I notice that the cardboard is sodden, which is when we realize that it's not only the back freezer. Both big freezers are out.

It's past seven a.m. Lee texts that she's landed, but I tell her I have a work emergency. I want so badly to bolt out of the deli, but it's all hands to negotiate as much of the food into the remaining freezer. I'm not leaving the Kims. If we move quickly we won't have to throw too much out. Hopefully I can still make it out of the door by nine, be showered by ten, and Lord willing at Lee's hotel for lunch. Anxiety clambers up to my shoulders, and I slam a coffee that only fuels my restiveness. I want to get to Lee as fast as possible.

We put signs up telling customers not to open the freezer doors. I check in with Mrs. Kim. I don't want to bail, but maybe I can get an idea of how long it'll take.

I've got three texts from Lee asking where I am and two missed calls.

I call her back. "Hey. You okay?"

"Yeah," she says. She's whispering. "I'm in a car."

"From the airport?"

"No. I couldn't check in," she says. "We're trying to find another hotel, but it's a mess."

I hear Jessica in the background letting someone have it. "Sir, as I said before, four suites on a vacated floor." And then with a hint of hysteria, "What kind of Mickey Mouse operation are you running here?"

"What happened?"

"Nothing," she says in a weary tone that suggests otherwise.

"Lee . . ." I hate how quickly she forgets how much better she feels when we talk.

"Cabrón!" yells Jorge, shooting me a look, like, *Really?*

I plead with my eyes. "Lee," I try again. "What happened?"

"It was a security issue," she says darkly. "Nothing serious. A formality."

"Pablo, man. Come on." Jorge sucks his teeth. I keep moving, phone sliding off my shoulder.

"Wait, where are you?"

"Driving around."

I groan inwardly. Midtown at this time of day is a parking lot.

"Are you off yet?" she asks hopefully.

"Kind of." I eye the hundred boxes we've yet to migrate.

"Can I come over?"

"To my house?"

Hell no.

"Please?" she says. "I have friends I could stay with, but I didn't tell them I was coming. . . ."

I picture Luca grinning and calling me *brother* with his hand wrapped tightly on my upper arm.

"Where are you?"

"Forty-Seventh and Sixth," she says.

Christ.

"Okay. Circle around the block a few more times and then head over." I give her my address. She'll think I'm pathetic. She'll think I'm a squatter. She'll think . . .

Sweet Jesus, never mind. What will the roommates think? I hope Jess has enough hundred-page NDAs for all of them.

I catch up with Jorge and Tetris boxes of food together as fast as I can.

If I leave in ten, twenty tops, and run home I can at least toss my laundry in the hamper and wipe down the bathroom. I try to imagine how the bathroom looked this morning and can't. It must have been gross. It always is.

My adrenaline is through the roof. I finish emptying out the freezer, grab my coat, and check in with Mr. Kim.

"Can you stay for another few minutes? The repair man showed up."

It's almost eight.

"Please." He looks pained. Whatever this is going to cost, it's not going to be cheap.

"Absolutely." I stow my coat under the register.

I text Lee that she might beat me home and call Tice.

"Yo," I say.

"What up?"

"You home?"

"Yeah."

"Something very weird is about to happen to you."

"I don't enjoy surprises, Pablo."

"Okay." I try to find the best way to explain this. "Do you know who Leanna Smart is?"

"Sure. Her music sucks. Other than the track with Three Stacks."

"Valid."

"Why?"

"She's coming to the house."

Silence. Then a drawn-out, "Okay . . ."

"With her friend Jessica. Jessica, by the way, who is so supremely a person you would fall in love with, so please take this as a warning."

"Duly noted, but also . . . what the fuck are you talking about? It's early as hell. I'm trying to go back to sleep and you're telling me cryptic messages about fantasy shit."

"Tice!"

"Of all places, why the hell would . . . ?"

"I know," I tell him. "It's a perfect storm of fuckshit. Listen to me," I say this in a calm I don't feel. "I am stuck at work. Leanna Smart is headed to our house. She came into the deli a while back. We stayed in touch. I went to LA those days I was out of town—I was visiting her. She's incredible, and for the love of god, I need you to clean. I need you to not let her in my room. I need the house to look the way you'd want if a girl you had an inconsolable crush on came over. I need you to help me. Please, man. It's urgent. Please make them a cup of coffee and don't let anyone bother them or look at them. I need this from you."

"Oh shit. Deadass deadass?"

"Yes. Deadass deadass."

"Oh shit," he says. And then. "Yo, if you're fucking with me, I will murder you."

"Fine! Please, do all of the things. And make sure my laptop is closed. Fuck."

An hour later Mr. Kim's still in the back and we're slammed with the morning rush. The juice and smoothie orders are relentless. I want to scale the walls I'm so panicked.

I text Lee that I'm sorry, and when she doesn't immediately hit me back, I'm convinced she found another safe house, maybe Luca or Dyland or that model dude from her video who's licking her neck or whatever he's doing in the part where they're underwater and slithering like merpeople. Oh god or Teddy. Fucking Teddy.

"Yo, Pab." I hear Wyn, but don't immediately see him behind the lady who wants her corn muffin toasted and buttered.

"You know it's not vegan anymore if I butter it, right?"

"Yes," she huffs. "It is gluten-free though since it's corn?"

I stare at her for a second and check the packaging.

"There's wheat in it," I tell her.

"Pab," says Wyn again.

"Well, then, I don't want it," she says, and continues

to check out with her Nutter Butters, which are also not gluten-free but I know to be surprisingly vegan.

I hand the corn muffin to Wyn. "Eat this," I yell at him. I'm beginning to feel the lack of sleep and the extra three hours on my shift.

"I'm sure if you ask him nicely, he'll put sunflower-oil spread on it," says a voice, and it's Lee in a blond wig and sunglasses and a dad hat. In front of me. In real life.

"I hate that stuff," says the lady, who snatches the muffin back anyway and rolls her eyes. Lee laughs and I laugh and then I come around the counter for a big hug. She's wearing jeans and a hoodie, and she jumps into my arms. She smells exactly of her. I've missed it, and I make a mental note to snatch a piece of her clothing so I can smell her whenever I want.

"Hey, Pab," says Jess. Her hood is pulled up and she's wearing sunglasses.

"Yo, Unabomber much?" I tell her.

"It's been a stressful morning," she says, tipping her enormous lenses low. I can see the fatigue. "And *someone* in your apartment wouldn't let us in yet."

Mrs. Kim looks up from rearranging fruit.

"You can go," she says, waving me off since the bedlam's died down some. She looks beat.

"You sure?"

Mrs. Kim nods in that *I'll deal with my husband* way. "Thank you, Pablo," she says.

"Guys, this is Mrs. Kim," I tell them, throwing my coat back on.

They wave.

She waves back.

"Slow your roll, Romeo," says Wyn. "Your *friend* Leanna Smart," he continues under his breath. "She wanted snacks, and Tice sent me down to bring them here."

"Where is Tice?"

He shrugs. "He was acting crazy. Wouldn't let the girls up, said he had something to do."

"Wyn here was introducing us to the concept of a Hot Snack . . . ," says Lee.

"Trademark," says Wyn. "Hot Snack trademark."

Jess rolls her eyes like, *Is this guy serious?*

"Trademark," Lee continues. "It's Munchies Paradise–caliber stuff." She winks at me. "We got on the subject of how you all are totally shortchanging the hot-to-cold-to-freezing snack as a category. Which in my personal estimation is the perfect post-flight-straight-into-breakfast meal of choice. Except that it requires a little preparation."

"What the hell is a hot-to-cold-to-freezing snack?"

"That's what I asked," says Wyn.

"Amateurs," says Jess.

"Hot-to-cold-to-freezing-snack trademark," says Lee. Wyn laughs as he gives me the *I like this girl* head tilt.

"It's a surprise," she says. "But that's why we're here. I'll be right back."

I watch her hit the usuals. The baking aisle, the cookie aisle, and then she hesitates at the freezers, which are on lockdown.

She rushes back. "Your freezers are broken?"

"Yeah," I tell her. "That was the emergency."

"Catastrophe," she says. "I need ice cream."

"We have it at the house," I tell her. I want to get out of the store as quickly as possible while the getting's good.

As we exit I notice Lee doing a scan for cameras or unwanted attention, and when the coast is clear she links her arm in mine and snuggles closer.

"God, it's good to see you." I want to eat her I missed her so bad.

It's sunny and crisp and I consider kissing her in the street, but I don't. It's odd, but I will probably never get to kiss this girl in public. Unless we're in Guam. And even then . . .

"Can you be out here?" I ask her. "All loosey-goosey. Aren't people going to see us?"

Lee laughs, but she glances around again.

"All that TMZ footage makes it seem as though you're mobbed wherever you go," says Jess, "but most of those irrelevant losers tell the cameras where they'll be or go where they'll be spotted."

I've stopped searching for Lee news, but the mention of TMZ fills me with guilt.

"I have a confession." Lee squeezes my arm and narrows her eyes. "We're not technically *loosey-goosey*." Jess herds us across the street toward two black SUVs. "The second one's for Isaac and Big Huge—my bodyguards."

Whoa. Big Huge. When the scale of a person trumps

the temptation to call a large dude Tiny, he's got to be impressive.

We pile into a car, and when we reach my apartment and get buzzed in, I die of embarrassment with every footfall that composes each staircase and every landing that signals yet another chapter in the never-ending turmoil that is our fifth-floor walk-up. It's a trek I curse every day of my life.

"Goddamn," breathes Jess at one point, and it's Lee's polite but labored silence that makes it impossible to look at her. The whole time I'm praying, hoping it's only Tice who's home, but of course it's a full house. I duck my head in and Miggs is having coffee in his tighty-whities, ironing a T-shirt of all things, and I can hear Dara's blow-dryer in the back room.

"Miggs," I call over to him with the door ajar. "Yo, put on some damned pants. Jesus, didn't Tice talk to you?"

"Wha-happened?" he asks, scowling like it's way too early for this. And then he kisses his teeth. "No. You put on some damned pants. What the hell is up with everyone? Tice was running around yelling and vacuuming and you're turning into a never-nude?"

"I have guests," I say, refusing to open the door all the way.

"So tell your guests to put on some goddamned pants," he says. "This is my house."

"Fine," I announce. I swing the door open and we file in. First me, then Lee, then Jess, then Wyn.

"Nice codpiece," says Jess wryly, and I watch as Miggs realizes that my guests are women. Attractive ones.

"Thank you," he says and—get this—continues to iron.

God love him, he's such a maniac.

Wyn looks at me, then looks back at Miggs, who is clearly leaning into his nakedness. Just doubling down.

"Would either of you ladies care for a cup of coffee?" Miggs offers. At this point I can't even tell if he knows who he's talking to.

"That would be great," says Lee.

Jess nods as well.

"May I take your coats, ladies?" offers Wyn, bowing deep, auditioning to be Lee's personal concierge.

"Don't mind if I do," says Lee solicitously, handing him her blond wig first, which makes him laugh. She's wearing a mesh hairnet, which she also removes, and her red hair dangles down to her waist.

"I'll just . . ." Wyn arranges the bob on the arm of the couch, and I think about how Lee wore a wig on top of what is essentially a wig.

"Why, thank you, kind sir," says Jess.

These girls are so rad.

"How about I brew a new pot?" says Miggs, puttering, fleshy back toward us.

"How about you do that," says Jess. "But maybe not, you know, *teabag* the coffee."

Miggs laughs and goes to his room to put on pants, and I know he's blabbing to Dara because her blow-dryer shuts off and they're in there for a good five minutes.

I stay in the kitchen and try to imagine my living room/

couch area/dining room plus kitchen through Lee's eyes. I will commit hara-kiri if a roach pops out from somewhere to say hi. Where the hell is Tice?

"This is cute," lies Jess, looking around. "Babe, look," she says, pointing to the kitchen. "You have the same guy."

I follow her gaze to the neon green soap dispenser that I bought, which has a caddy for a scrubbing brush.

So weird.

"Do you have a loaf tin?" Lee asks, rolling her sleeves up in the kitchen.

"We do," says Wyn, snapping to attention.

"I know what you're making," he says, surveying the ingredients. "I've seen a video."

"What are you making?" I ask. "What is the hot-to-cold-to . . . ?"

I don't finish before Miggs returns, this time in sweats, collared shirt, and Dara in tow. I swear if Dara curtsies or does anything embarrassing, I'm going to throw her coconut cashews and her hundred-dollar porcelain blow-dryer into the street.

"Good morning, freeloading roomie," I say to her while she stares openmouthed at Lee.

"This is my friend Lee," I say.

Lee waves. "Hey."

"Lee's making a highly sophisticated snack," I tell them, relishing the expression on Dara's face.

"This is Dara."

"That's my cousin's name," says Lee.

"Get the fuck out." Dara's eyes bug as if it's the *wildest* coincidence.

"How long are you in town for?" squeaks Dara in an octave only dolphins can hear.

"Few days."

"Are you staying here? You're more than welcome to stay here. You both are."

"Why the fuck would they stay here?" Miggs asks his girlfriend.

"Well, what the fuck are they doing here?" Dara asks. It's a hell of a point.

"Shit," says Lee. "Ice cream?"

"It's mine, but you can have it," says Wyn. Sure enough, when he pulls it out it's labeled *W* in black Sharpie, which is so college-life and mortifying.

Then Tice walks out of the bathroom, and if he's been in there this whole time blowing it up with one of his legendary morning poops, I'm going to fight him. In fact, I might fight every single one of my roommates at this rate.

"Hey," he says to the girls.

"Well, if it isn't Tice in the flesh," says Lee, giving him a hug. "I've heard so much about you. Were you putting your face on or something? Why wouldn't you let us in?"

"I had some things to attend to," he says smoothly. "Welcome."

Tice's face remains impassive, whereas Dara, Miggs, and Wyn's attentions are darting around like cats clocking a laser pointer.

Jess rises from the sofa.

"Hi," she says, going for a handshake. "Jessica Longworthy. I'm Leanna Smart's chief of staff, and I'm mad at you for not letting us in sooner."

Lee raises her brows at me for a nanosecond. And I flash her the same signal. There's no doubt in the world that we'd be the cutest double-daters ever. Even if this is possibly the girliest thought I've ever experienced in my life.

"Hey," says Tice, shaking her hand. "Tyson Scott. I'm sorry I made you wait. It was unavoidable." Then he smiles his best smile. The nuclear-option smile. Like, I've seen this kid shoot Chrissy Teigen this smile at a Christmas fundraiser Dara catered.

"Wait," says Tice, appraising Lee's ingredients. "I know what you're making."

Finally, I look at the assortment. Wafer fingers, milk chocolate, creamy peanut butter, condensed milk, coconut oil.

Lee plonks the can of sweetened condensed milk into a saucepan of boiling water and breaks up the chocolate into a bowl.

"Here, let me help," says Dara, commandeering chocolate duty.

"Do *you* know what I'm making?" Lee smiles at me in a way that causes a commotion in my chest. I walk over to give her a kiss. I can feel all four pairs of my roommates' eyes scorching holes into me, but I don't care.

"No idea."

"A Big Kat!"

Turns out a Big Kat is a ginormous Kit Kat made in a loaf tin.

"It's a hot-to-cold-to-freezing trademark snack because you have to melt the chocolate to cover the vanilla and chocolate wafers in alternating layers of peanut butter and caramel. It's freezing because you eat it with ice cream," she says. "The peanut butter and caramel are my additions because I'm a master."

As she assembles, I excuse myself to wash up. The smell of deli bacon's embedded in my clothes.

I lock the bathroom door and run the water. The house sounds full and loud in a way that I love. Heaving and alive. Celebratory. Like a holiday. In certain moments roommates feel more like a boisterous family than my own family, and I wonder why that is. I love watching Lee hold court. Goofy. Slightly messy. Obsessed with snacks almost as much as I am. I imagine her buying into our stupid roommate bets. Piling onto the couch to eat some deranged sizzling casserole after a night out. Food is magical. Having Lee hang out with some of my favorite people is magical.

That's when I notice that our bathroom is sparkling. Where there are usually water-warped, four-year old *Fader* magazines and Eastbay catalogs on the toilet tank, there's a little yellow candle that smells of vanilla. I know it's vanilla because it's brand-new and there's a sticker on it that reads VANILLA with the dollar-store price tag still on it, which I peel off with my thumbnail.

In place of the biosphere of sour, moldy towels that typically live on every available surface, there's only a clean one left out. It's hand-towel sized, a ceremonious unit of towel we never bother with, the top sheet of towels, and it's startlingly presentable—forest green with a cream stripe, and I've never seen it before in my life. I pull back the shower and the grout is pristine. I'm so moved that I actually put my hand on my chest.

I pop my head into my room and damn if my bed isn't made. The socks and dirty underwear have been squirreled into my laundry hamper. The windows are flung open and the atmosphere smells of freshly sprayed Febreze. Meanwhile, our last communal bottle had been diluted so many times it's inert, so I know he's looted his own stash.

I come back out and squeeze Tice's forearm with so much gratitude he says, "Ow," before he says, "Bet," and then nods because we both know I owe him one so prodigiously big I probably won't be able to afford it for a while.

Once the Big Kat's in the fridge, Miggs sparks one and hands it to Jess.

She pinches it between her perfectly manicured fingers and takes a baby puff, then hands it to Lee.

"Wow," says Lee, taking a hit and grimacing. "Analog weed, huh?"

Jess laughs.

"Chill." Miggs sucks his teeth. "What, you Cali heads only vape or what?"

"I assure you my man only holds the highest quality,"

says Dara, who won't stand for anyone disrespecting her dude's stash. Not even Lee.

"I mean . . . ," says Jess, pulling out a small, light-gray pouch from her purse. It could easily be a sunglass case but shorter and thinner. She snaps it open and rolls out five identical-looking pens.

"Wow," says Tice. "A cornucopia?" We take turns passing them around. Blunts of the future. Elegant. With rounded edges. As if a Scandinavian designer made them to be sold at the MoMa store.

I catch Tice staring at Jess, trying to impregnate her with his eyes.

"These are beautiful," he says.

Even Miggs has to admit how cool they. "May I?"

Jess nods. "A hundred doses in each."

Moments later we're smacked on medical-grade fancy-pants California digital weed.

Everything is hilarious.

We hand slices of Big Kat around with a scoop of mint chip ice cream. You'd think it wouldn't go with peanut butter, but it does. I make coffee. The Big Kat is cold and crunchy yet smooth, and the hot liquid's bitter and sluicing through the sugar and cream.

"That's why Instagram's trash," exclaims Miggs while we're bouncing off the walls and talking about, what else, surveillance and privacy issues.

Dara, Wynn, Tice, and I collectively groan. This and

the collapse of capitalism are the only things he wants to discuss when high.

"No, wait," says Jess, standing up to stretch to her full height with her arms up above. "I agree with him. Those inputs mess with your attention span. And they're spying on you." She sighs, snaps her hands to her hips, and folds over. "Oh my god, this is amazing," she warbles, hanging upside down.

Suddenly, as with a yawn, I'm compelled to copy her.

I rise, the blood rushing to my extremities, vision blurring slightly. I touch my toes, letting my head hang.

"Oh god," I moan.

"Sure," says Tice from behind me. "But that whole 'oh the Internet is giving us ADD' argument is so tired."

"Have you ever kept a dream journal?" says Lee sincerely. And then, "What are you guys doing?"

I look up. Three of us are contorted into odd shapes. Jess in downward dog, me folded over, and Dara with her hands behind her in a complicated pretzel.

I sit back down.

"Dream journal?" I ask her, eyes blurry. Lee's backlit from the kitchen window. I can't see her face, but her teeth smile back. I love this girl. And caffeine. And weed.

Leanna Smart is in my house. With my friends!

"Hi." The Lee shape with teeth waves and then laughs.

"Sorry." I wave back, total space cadet. If it weren't for the audience, I'd confess that her nearness confuses my

Wi-Fi signal. "Wait. Are dream journals the same as 'morning pages'?" I ask her. It's that thing where artists write three pages of thoughts down upon awakening.

I've tried that, writing letters to the universe, and worry lists. Honestly, ask me anything about brain hacks to which billionaires attribute their success and I can tell you the details. I've abandoned at least a hundred.

"No," says Jess. "Morning pages are where you write down ideas longhand. A dream journal tracks your dreams first thing in the morning longhand." Jess folds her legs into a lotus position.

"I know, huge distinction," says Lee, who rolls her eyes for our benefit, then elaborates. "But me and Jess did this experiment last year where we wrote down our dreams, and I swear to god Instagram is Taco Bell for your head."

Jess nods emphatically.

The rest of us are already smiling.

"No," Lee says, palms up. "Hear me out.

"Instagram is Taco Bell because it's the only thing your brain wants to eat once it's had it. And"—she eyes me to see if I'm following—"if that's all your brain eats, that's all it poops out. And by poop I mean your dreams. If all you do, all day long, is binge-eat social media, at night you'll have explosive diarrhea. It's an anxiety and garbage bomb because you didn't consume anything meaningful or nourishing or nutritious. Feel me?"

Lee stands up, making big dramatic hands in the circle we've formed. "And if all your dreams are occupied with porcelain shredding wreckage every single night, well then, when, I ask you, when can the muse strike? You know?"

Miggs looks almost compelled to clap. Lee sits back down and takes another hit of weed and shrugs. Eyes in slits. "So, yeah, me and Jess don't use social before bed. It's poison."

"Poison," confirms Jess.

They're high as fuck.

"All of it's toxic," continues Lee. "Going outside is toxic. Fame?" She shakes her head and snorts. "Trash. Honestly, if I had my way, I'd live in ratty leggings with Netflix asking me if I'm still watching a hundred percent of the time."

"Deadass, B," says Wyn dramatically. "That Netflix prompt is the source of so much insecurity in my life." He says it so seriously we crack up.

I watch Lee pat him on the knee in solidarity.

I wonder if I believe her. I mean, the Taco Bell stuff makes sense. That's just science. But Netflix? Would she be satisfied with a normal life? Leanna Smart has the best life. I've been on her plane. She has a small funeral procession of black cars stalling for her downstairs as we speak. In fact, if anything, she's patient zero for most kinds of insecurity in millions of people.

Lee grins at me happily.

Maybe she would leave it all behind, though. Go to college the way she intended. Quit touring. Work on a handful of movies every few years. It's not as if she needs the money.

"Shit," says Dara, shaking her head as if she's coming to. "I'm so late for work."

"I'm leaving too," says Jess, yawning extravagantly. "I'll go ahead and check into the new spot and shower. You coming?"

Lee looks to me and looks back to Jess as I run highly complicated calculus on how I feel about Lee seeing my room.

"Nah," she says. "I'm gonna . . . *you know* . . ." She nods at me, which makes Jess swat her arm.

"All right, then." Her chief of staff stands and grabs her coat. "I'll let you . . . *you know*. With . . . *you know*." Jess waggles her eyebrows, hugs my shoulders, and kisses the top of my head.

"Stop," says Lee, laughing.

"Keep it classy, Pab," she says as my ears burn.

"Thanks."

With that the door closes but not before we hear Jess mutter, "Jesus Christ, these fucking stairs."

Chapter 28

I sit on my bed, and Lee sits beside me. Suddenly I'm back in high school with a girl visiting me at my mom's house. The collision of nervousness and excitement is astounding. We've been hanging out for hours, but it's different in my room.

Has my bed always been this creaky? The light this bright? The weed paranoia kicks in: Does she hate my room? Is she quiet because she's repulsed?

My eyes dart to the enormous Sade poster over my dresser. I wish it were framed instead of binder clipped and thumbtacked so the pins don't prick the paper.

Does she hate Sade? Who hates Sade? That's so messed up that she hates Sade.

"So, this is your room," she says.

"Yup." I wonder if I sound defensive.

"Did it used to be part of the living room?" I look around for the answer as if I don't know.

"Yeah," I tell her.

She laughs. "Did you have to look around to confirm it?"

I laugh back. "Yeah." I rarely think about that anymore. How my room's drywalled into what's effectively a coffin shape.

There's a weird triangle of dead space at the head of my bed where my pillow always falls.

"Is it rhomboid?" Leanna Smart was tutored since middle school, and whatever they say about homeschooled kids is patently false because she retains all manner of obscure facts. From how a bill becomes a law to different types of cloud formations and which countries comprise Central America. Things I haven't had to remember since I got a phone.

I look around again and shrug.

She hugs me hard and we fall onto our sides.

Leanna Smart is in my bed. My bed. My actual bed.

"Life is so weird," I tell her. Our faces are inches apart.

"How so?" she asks innocently.

I focus on her eyes.

"How are you, Pablo Neruda Rind?"

"Splendid," I say hoarsely, and kiss her.

She slips her sweatshirt over her head, and I do the same. I can't wait to feel her skin on mine. Her chest is pressed up against me, and I'm filled with relief and whatever hormones are released when you hold someone. My chest feels tight my heart's so full.

"I love this," she says. "I'm recharging."

"Same."

"Bzzzzzzzzzt," she says at the contact, and it's so cute I can't deal.

I can't explain exactly how this is more intense than the time at the hotel, only that it is. LA was a fantasyland. This? This is New York. This is Brooklyn. My hometown. At my house. In my bed.

We climb under the comforter, which is soft and has been washed a million times, and soon we're both completely naked and it's impossible to admit but the whole time we're not kissing we're staring straight into each other's eyes. We're usually horsing around, trying to one-up each other on stupid callbacks or dumb jokes, except now, in person we're quiet.

"Hi," she says after our heads part for a second in between what could very well have been seventeen years of making out.

"Hey," I whisper. When I told my ex I loved her it felt like the right thing to do. There was an expectation to it. Call and response. She'd said it first. She'd made it easy. I know if I told Lee right now that I loved her it would be wild and inappropriate and a sign of dementia, but I feel something big. Huge and profound and unmanageable.

I try to transmit everything I'm thinking and I swear to god maybe she knows, because instead of saying anything more, she nods. As if she's heard me.

Lee leaves and I fall asleep. When I wake up, Dara and Miggs are having dinner in the kitchen.

"You eat?" Dara asks. "We made Sloppy Joes."

I peer into the saucepan and groggily take out a plate.

"You're welcome," she says. Miggs keeps an eye out to see how much of his potential leftovers I'm scamming.

"Thank you," I tell her sweetly.

"So *that's* what you've been up to," says Miggs between bites. He always eats with his hands guarding his food as though he's in prison. It makes sense. He grew up the second youngest of five boys.

I shrug. But then break into a smile. I can't help myself.

"Look at him," says Dara. "All googly and shit."

"Come to my show tonight," says Miggs, and I inwardly groan. "I'm on early. Slide through before work. It's right off the F."

Comedy is ballsy stuff. I've seen Miggs pull a room back from the brink of absolutely despising him, but I've also seen him bomb and it's the type of humiliation that reduces everyone to animals. There's zero confusion about who the loser is. Plus, there's the Darwinism of it. The whole room wants to snap the runt under the spotlight's neck to put him out of his misery. It's too much humanity.

"I'll think about it."

"Well, don't kill me with your enthusiasm," he says. "I know it's not a Leanna Smart concert."

I take a bite of food. I love how Dara makes Sloppy Joes. Sweet and sticky but also a little tart. The sauce is mostly ketchup.

"Leanna's cool," says Dara. "Funny."

"You know, I don't think I knew she was *that* famous," says Miggs. "Did you know she has more followers than Cristiano Ronaldo?"

"The fashion designer?" says Dara.

"What?" Miggs puts his sandwich down. "You didn't just ask me that."

"Whatever. I'm not surprised that she has more followers than *whoever your mans is*," says Dara. "Leanna's been famous her entire life."

"I don't know a single Leanna Smart song," says Miggs proudly.

"Of course you do." Dara smacks him on the arm. "That one, *highway na-na-na by the way . . . ,*" she croons. "They remixed it like crazy last summer."

"They're all the same to me," says Miggs, shaking his head. "I'm washed. This whole time I could've swore Leanna Smart was in the movies with the orphaned emperor. The one in space."

"Nah, that's Tinsley Dahmer," corrects Dara. "She's in those movies with the curly-haired kid with the pencil neck. Where he's blind in one dimension but a soothsayer on terra firma."

"Oh, yeah," says Miggs. "The books were better."

"I saw the fourth sequel on a plane," says Dara. "Coming back from It-ly."

The non-Jewish side of Dara's family says It-ly as if the "a" doesn't exist. They also call pasta of every shape "macaroni."

"I don't know why, but plane movies always make me cry," she says.

I feel dumber for having heard any of this. It's like accidentally overhearing a subway conversation about mixed martial arts or microbreweries.

"Oh," says Miggs as if it's finally dawned on him. "So Leanna's the one dating that French rap kid."

"Who?" asks Dara.

"You know, the rapper." Miggs puts scare quotes around "rapper." "Maybe he's Canadian."

"Wait, the short one with the small face that pretended he was on a private jet but then he got caught at Walmart with the geotag so we knew he was lying? That one?"

"No," says Miggs, forking the air between them. "The one whose regular face you want to sit on. That one." Miggs makes floppy hair action with his sandwich-free hand.

"God, Dyland! Man, he's hot." Dara gets this faraway look.

"Come on!" exclaims Miggs, sucking his teeth. "How are you going to be at a table across from me imagining yourself sitting on that kid's face?"

He finishes inhaling his food.

"What kind of name is Dyland anyway. Dy-LAND. You know his dusted-ass parents just went with the typo. Like this kid I went to middle school with. Sibon. Deadass Simon with a b."

"Dyland's my free pass," says Dara to me. "I'm allowed to sleep with him and Miggs can't get mad."

"That kid's a twerp." It slips out, and before I know it both sets of eyes are on me.

"Tell me everything," gushes Dara. "You met him? Is that who you were with? Tice says you went to LA."

"He's dating his publicist who's twenty years older than him." I know I shouldn't say more, but surely the contract doesn't cover Dyland and Cam.

"Hell, yeah, I knew he'd be into older women," says Dara triumphantly, kissing Miggs on the cheek.

Her boyfriend scoffs.

"In any case, bring your girl to see my set," he says.

"I'll ask her," I mutter as my phone buzzes. It's Rain. I send it to voicemail.

My phone buzzes again. Rain. Texting.

Yo

"You need to come," says Miggs. "You haven't in months. Even Tice pulled up last week."

Rain texts again: 911.

"I said, I'll let you know." I shove the rest of the sandwich in my mouth. The mush takes on a nauseating treacly quality.

"Wait," says Dara, tapping my forearm, eyes wide. "Did she make you sign that thing?" She turns to her man. "She apparently has this eighty-page Love Contract that she makes her *lovers* sign. . . ."

It's over a hundred, I want to tell them.

Rain: Help. It's mom.

My stomach lurches, and I get up to call him.

301

"You know who my free pass is?" says Miggs somewhere behind me. "Selena. Selena Quintanilla is a goddess."

I call Rain, and when he doesn't pick up I call mom. I call and text both of them a million times as I run for the train. For some reason the image of her passport photo flashes before my eyes. The grim determination in her face. I will never forgive myself if she died thinking that her deadbeat son is an irresponsible loser and that . . .

As soon as the elevator doors open I hear her yelling. For a full minute my adrenaline is in overdrive, but at least she's alive. I almost break my wrist trying to yank the locked front door open. There's no sign of a forced entry.

No broken glass, zero spilled blood or EMTs anywhere. No one in the living room or kitchen, but in the hallway stands my brother wearing basketball shorts, no shirt, in front of his room.

Relief washes over his face when he sees me.

Chapter 29

"Seriously?" I scream at him. "I've been calling you!"

"Pablo?" says mom from inside the room.

"Mom." Rain turns to plead with her. He tries again in Korean. "Umma."

I brace myself for the worst. My normally rational mother has pulled out every dresser drawer and upturned it onto his stripped bed. She's sitting in the middle of the floor on her knees, dressed in scrubs, purse at her feet, and she's pulling out books from Rain's bottom shelves and flipping through each one.

"Take off your shoes!" she screams at me. I look down, kick off my sneakers, and set them in the hall.

"What is going on?"

"Oh, finally!" she says, throwing a book at my feet with an air of pure derangement. "Well, thank god *you're* not dead. Where the hell have you been? Does anyone care about anything around here?"

"Okay, I'm here now." I crouch slightly and make slow movements into the room. "What's happening?"

"Your brother"—mom's voice trembles; her face is streaked with tears—"is on drugs." Her hair's pulled up into a messy ponytail, and I can see that there's a shock of white at her temples. "It's my fault," she says, standing shakily and then sitting on his bed amid the books and clothes. "Oh god," she says, palms open in her lap, as she starts to bawl.

Rain and I stare at each other. I've only ever seen her cry once, when Rain was six and he caught a viral infection when he had his appendix out and almost died. He was weirdly pleased when I told him but to this day I don't think he's ever seen her cry. Dad's into the waterworks and kisses. Mom's a tougher nut.

"What drugs?" I whisper to him.

"Just weed, man," he says with a drawl on the "man," posing as a burnout. "She came home early." He shrugs, and suddenly my thirteen-year-old kid brother has turned into just another arrogant, shitty teen.

"You were smoking in the house?"

"So?" he says.

I slap him upside the head. "Dumbass!"

"It was one time," he says.

Whatever. I get it. I'm still shaking off my residual hangover from Jess's turbo cannabis. But you don't do that stuff at mom's. You have your white friends stash it since most of their ex-raver parents smoke weed with them anyway. Especially since they'd "rather have it under their roof than having kids sneak around." Meanwhile my mom is the type of highly wound individual who only lets us drink soda when we order Chinese food, and even then we have to split a can of Dr Pepper three ways. She calls it a "Doctor's Appointment" and pours it into three cups with plenty of ice, as if she's serving scotch. With the number of ODs she's seen, when my dad drinks a second beer she starts talking about the opioid epidemic.

"Mom." I inch down toward her and get to her level. "I'm sure it won't happen again," I tell her. "Right, Rain?"

"It definitely won't happen again," he says, coming into the room. "Look at this place. This"—he gestures around—"is not worth it."

Mom sighs as a fresh crop of tears dribble down her cheeks.

"What the hell," she wails plaintively as if struck by unfairness. Her shoulders slump, and I'm relieved that the crisis seems close to being over. I hand her one of Rain's T-shirts. "Thanks," she says, and blows into it.

"Hey," protests Rain.

I glare at him.

"That's my box logo tee," he complains.

Mom dabs at her eyes, her makeup blotting the red Supreme on the cotton.

"It won't happen again," she continues. "Because I won't allow it." She looks at Rain. "I'm sending you to military school."

What?

"Mom, don't be crazy."

"What about LaGuardia?" asks Rain quietly.

"LaGuardia's high school," she says, groaning to get up to her feet. "Grow up and take responsibility now and at least you'll be ready for college.

"God, I can't do this by myself," she says to no one in particular.

Her eyes are wet, but her fists hang by her sides. Periods on the end of a sentence.

"Someday you'll thank me," she tells Rain, and stoops to pick up a single book among the thirty or forty on the floor. She places it on his desk and strokes the cover once to ask for forgiveness. "Matter of fact, you don't have to thank me."

"Mom!" yells Rain. "Pab, you've got to talk to her."

Mom stares at me robotically.

"You can't send him to reform school," I tell her. "They'll eat him alive."

Rain looks at me terrified.

"Rain." I motion for him to leave.

When we're alone, mom sits on the floor, against the bed, knees drawn up. I sit beside her.

"Mom." She won't meet my eyes, but she nods. "Those kids have serious issues. Sending Rain to a place like that . . . It'll change who he is."

"I *need* him to change," she says. "First he almost gets expelled for selling sex toys at school. Then he starts dating this Rachel, who's two years older. She's practically middle-aged, this girl. And ever since he got into LaGuardia he's been so scattered."

Mom takes sips of air, catching her breath.

"I want him . . . I want him to be more than talented," she says. "I want him to be successful. He's smart and funny and sensitive and charming, but he needs a goal. A purpose. It's not easy for boys like you to win in this life. It's not fair that you're competing with kids whose parents are big deals, who have trust funds and important last names, but this life isn't fair. You *know* that. I raised you and your brother in New York for a reason. You can't be good. You have to be exceptional. Only an education will level the playing field."

She leans over to pick up another book. Dusts it off. Chastened. Mom's the type to lecture us on disrespecting books. How leaving them on the floor isn't good for their spines. That they don't like it. She threatens to donate our comics to Goodwill constantly.

"I can't have both my boys end up like . . ." She falters, eyes flitting up to my face and then looking away.

The moment tells me everything I need to know about the way she sees me.

We sit in silence.

I think back to our first fight about school.

I'd been so pumped when I saw the acceptance letter. I'd been maniacally checking my spam filters for weeks and had gotten into St. Francis and Queens College, but when NYU came in, I almost passed out. I called everyone. Dad first. My girl. All my friends. But mom? I wanted to tell her in person.

I went out and bought flowers, marinated steak, forced Rain to vacuum, and when she got home the next morning, I had everything laid out. Even had the letter loaded up on her iPad so she could see. I'd gotten to enjoy twelve hours of believing she'd be proud of me.

"Getting into NYU without any scholarships isn't getting into NYU," she'd said. Then she pinched the top of her nose as if she were getting a headache. This I wasn't prepared for. Not a bit. I was shattered. For some reason I remember that she still had her purse on her shoulder. She hadn't even sat down. In an instant my mother joined the ranks of all the kids who believed I'd gotten in on a technicality. A fluke. By default. A mistake.

Even if that were true, you'd think my mother could lie to me at least for a second.

I don't know that things have been the same between us since.

Mom reaches for my hand and squeezes. Her hands are always cold. She says if she hadn't gone to med school she would have made a great pastry chef since butter wouldn't melt in them.

"Rain has a real opportunity here," she continues. "But let's face it. Singing is a hobby. I'm worried that LaGuardia will limit his choices. I don't want him to be so lost." She picks up Rain's T-shirt to blow her nose again

"I know it's not been easy for you," she says. "Not knowing what you want to do. Getting confused by all the options. That's why, with Rain, we have to take action now. Give him the direction and encouragement he needs. Hyung ee-ni-kah." Because that's what big brothers do. She squeezes my hand. "He needs our support. . . ."

She takes a ragged but determined exhale.

Rain at least is salvageable. Me on the other hand . . .

I get up.

"Mom." I think about how if my twenty-year-old kid was fucking up, I still wouldn't count them out. And how I'd never send my thirteen-year-old away to an upstate prison camp. "Your faith in school and discipline borders on superstition," I tell her. "'Direction' is not the answer for your shortcomings as a parent. And reform school, even the really nice kumbaya ones, will ruin Rain. But if you think sending him away isn't you making the same mistakes with him that you did with me, you're wrong. What you're call-ing a hobby could change his life. And if it doesn't, that has to be okay. You have to forgive him. You've got to let people mess up and you've still got to help them. You have to talk to them and support them while they make decisions, even if they're the wrong ones. That's how people learn, mom. Umma-ni-kah." Because you're the mom.

I head to the door.

"Ground him for the rest of his life." My voice is shaky, but I don't care. She needs to hear this. "But you can't make a sadist with a god complex raise your child because you feel guilty about not being available. I know being a tyrant is exhausting, but you don't get to shut down."

When I swing open the door, Rain's on the other side, eyes wide. He follows me through the living room.

"You're leaving?" he whispers incredulously.

My phone buzzes.

See you soon?

It's Lee. We're meeting at the hotel before she flies.

"Yeah," I tell him. "I'll see you later."

Rain smacks me on the arm, alarmed. "You can't leave me with her like this."

My phone continues to buzz. "Just give her some space," I tell him. "I'll come back tonight." I muss up his hair as he jerks out of arm's reach.

"When?"

"Late, but I'll be here."

"Promise me." He looks exactly as he did when he was five. As if he believes I can fix it.

"Dude, I gotta go." I shake him off.

The train downtown is packed with a gaggle of middle schoolers coming back from some field trip. The thirty-odd kids are loud as hell. Screaming, really, with their dazed minders looking as though whatever salary they're collecting is nowhere near sufficient for this fresh hell.

I can't believe I thought going to college in my backyard would be chill.

It was disarming somehow that the NYU Academic Resource Center was a few blocks south of that sneaker store Flight Club. I'm a native New Yorker. I've been taking the train alone since I was five. Why did I ever think know-ing the city would demystify school?

The program I got into was called Gallatin and it was like NIKEiD but for college majors. You built it the way you want, and I didn't want to take math prerequisites. I thought I was getting away with murder, so I don't know when I lost the plot. Probably from the moment I sat down in my first-year interdisciplinary seminar. Do you know how it feels to be the only one in a room full of freshmen who has no idea what they're doing?

I swear, you should have seen this class. We had two kids who'd been on the lecture circuit since grade school. Another who'd outlawed plastic bags in her state and yet another who'd launched an app by the time he was eight. Wouldn't you know his mom was employee number six at eBay? It was me and seventeen pairs of eyes that shone and twitched with promise and calculation. They knew exactly what they wanted to make of themselves and how they'd get there.

Meanwhile, my gormless ass felt as though I were reading street signs in a dream. None of the words made sense. You had to create your own curriculum with a list of books that you select from the millions of collected tomes of knowledge that exist in the whole world. How though?

I consumed the entire Internet in search of what I was supposed to want to do.

For what it's worth, don't google "What should I major in?"

And if you do, don't spend half a year reading what it says.

Day after day I'd put off meeting with my faculty adviser. A great lady who was patient but couldn't tell me what I wanted to study either. Students around me who'd come from all over the world had real plans. This one kid got a bunch of credits teaching poetry in prison. They had internships at the White House, journalism fellowships, they'd secured seats on advisory committees for museums. I'm telling you, I was competing with fucking cyborgs.

There was no way I could keep up. I should have switched majors. Found structure. But after everything I'd gone through with mom—filling out the paperwork behind her back, taking out all those loans, I was frozen. Every passing moment it became clearer and clearer that I was a glitch. A rounding error. I had no business being at this school. The students around me knew. My advisers knew. My mom knew. It was a testament to my sublime ignorance that it took me almost failing out to know it too.

Chapter 30

I rush into Lee's hotel. Thoughts roiling. She's got two rooms booked. One under Jess's name and the other under . . .

"Eevee Blastoise," I tell the front desk clerk, a tall Asian chick with swoopy eyeliner. She smiles as if we're in on it together. "Actually, Mr. Rind." She pronounces it perfectly. "Ms. Blastoise asked me to have you meet her in the car. It's waiting for you at our back entrance on Park on the south side of the street."

I'm led to a Chevy Suburban, and the door flings open.

"Tell me anything," Lee says as I slide in for a hug. She's wearing a skintight black turtleneck dress, light jacket, her legs bare, and I realize that when you're Lee, the only weather you have to dress for is the insides of planes and cars.

"I'm so glad to see you." I breathe in her particular smell and close my eyes. "Where are we going?"

"It's a surprise." She pulls me in for a kiss and smiles as we ease into horrendous traffic.

I text Rain. **Everything will work out,** I tell him.

Promise.

There's a small black dog on the street, waiting at the light in a red sweater. The dog's fur has fallen over his eyes, and I can read the writing on his back. EMO SUPPORT ANIMAL. I glance up, and sure enough his owner is a hipster kid in a tiny leather jacket.

"Do you think emotional support animals get enough from us?"

Lee's arm is linked in mine and she squeezes it. "Please elaborate."

"Just that . . ." I think about it. "I get the mutual benefit. If I'm a dog, I try to be cool so that my owner will feed me. But emotional support? That's above and beyond. That yawning vacuum of human need with an anxiety whirlpool in the center of it. I wonder if they get stressed out."

"No way," she says confidently. "They live for it. We're like gods to them."

The car jerks and we move another four feet.

"But a dog can't be an inexhaustible well of good humor and self-sacrifice."

"You don't know that," she says, leaning into me, resting her head on my shoulder.

I smell the top of Lee's head. The dog trots happily across the street.

"I guess not."

Still, it strikes me as a crummy deal. How the Giving Tree in the children's book depressed me.

I kiss her deeply, and she kisses me back.

"I feel so lucky," I tell her.

An hour later we're in Midtown. It would have been fifteen minutes on the subway. And for the first time I get what she means. How logistically inconvenient it is to be around her. Everyone knows Leanna Smart's in New York. She posted a photo of herself eating a Salty Pimp cone from Big Gay Ice Cream in the West Village. I know because she tagged it *spelunk*. It's as thrilling as the first time it happened. Or the other time, I guess, since it's only happened twice. Still, I wonder if I'll ever be able to post a picture of us. Together. Being the us I know us to be.

"We're here," she says, popping open the door. We're greeted by a chorus of designer names emblazoned on gleaming buildings—Burberry, Chanel, Miu Miu, Armani, YSL—with the tourists seemingly under the impression that shooting the Gucci store makes it a Gucci-brand photo.

"In and out," she says. I scan the glass facade of the boutique before two black jackets block my view. "This is Isaac and Big Huge."

I finally have the pleasure of meeting Lee's security. Isaac resembles Matthew McConaughey if you'd injected him full of growth hormones at puberty, and Big Huge is exactly what I'd expected, the human equivalent of three linebackers standing on each other's shoulders.

We shake hands, and it's a miracle my metacarpals are intact.

"You ready?" Lee grabs my hand and leads me inside.

The entire store is wallpapered in embroidered silk fabric. It's as if we're cradled in the interior jacket pocket of an incredibly swaggy giant.

It's the four of us flanked by four salespeople with smiles plastered on their faces, cheesing with such force they may as well be covering for a hostage situation.

A slender Black dude with aqua hair and insanity cheekbones approaches us.

"Would you care for a drink? Coffee, tea, champagne, sparkling water?"

Lee smiles at me. "Do you have unpasteurized coconut water?" she asks.

"I'm sorry," he says. "We don't. But we can source some."

"No, no, no sweat," I tell him. "I'm good."

"Me too," says Lee.

"What are we doing here?" I whisper.

This is exactly the sort of New York establishment that makes me uncomfortable. That I'd never set foot in willingly. This, Lincoln Center, the Cloisters, and the Met. They don't have anything to do with me or my life. The only exception is the one time me and Miggs went to the 40/40 club to see if Jay-Z was there. Which is to say I don't stay long in the sorts of places I expect to be kicked out of.

I clear my throat.

"Let's go upstairs," she tells me. "I had Trev pull a few looks for you."

The second floor is the men's department, with another four, impeccably well-dressed people waiting to be activated. In the front there are sunglasses, logo wallets, bags, and to the side by the glass is a mirrored wall of shoes. I follow Lee toward the back, where there's another floor-to-ceiling embroidered room with an exactly matching couch camouflaged against the wall. She happily lowers herself into it.

"Mr. Rind," deadpans a pale woman whose waist is the circumference of my leg. She hands me a flute of sparkling wine and gestures to the row of hangers to her left. "These should be in your size."

"I wanted to see," says Lee gleefully, tipping the glass of tipple into her mouth. "Do the leather first."

On the rack closest to me hangs a brown motorcycle jacket. The coat is smooth and buttery, so alien to any leather I've ever felt before, wholly unlike the rubbery tack of the pleather couch in our living room. I immediately flip the matte black hanging tag to see how much it costs. There's no price, and the absence of a number is somehow scarier than if it spelled out "one trillion dollars" in blood.

"It's custom," says the woman silkily. "Calfskin." The way she says calfskin convinces me she's a vampire. I wriggle out of my nylon bomber and pull off my sweatshirt as she helps me into the sleeves. "Price upon request."

I almost want to clap my palms over my ears in case she

blurts it out, but we're in no danger of being so gauche.

The silk lining feels cool and slippery. My arms slide in as if oiled, and as the weight of the shoulders ease and latch on to mine, I instantly understand what hundreds of years of designers and New York Fashion Week and every magazine ad and billboard is talking about. I appreciate what's actually being sold here. The seduction is irresistible.

Forget college. I should have been buying leather jackets.

"Whoa," breathes Lee, sitting up. That's when I realize I'm wearing a larger, cognac version of the exact jacket she's got on.

Whoa is right. The coat feels alive. Cool atop my T-shirt but warm as a jacket. As if the really expensive stuff has a distinct climate-control system far superior to the one you come with.

"Tony Stark would be waitlisted for this jacket," she says, smiling. "You're beautiful."

I watch myself. Thrusting my arms in to grab a wrist and look again. I put my hands in my pockets to see if I'll look any cooler with my hands in my pockets, and guess what? I do. I pose as if for album artwork because in this jacket I am plausible as a human with an album cover.

Lee hugs me from behind. And as she hitches her chin onto my shoulder, I watch the two of us.

"We're so cute," confirms Lee. With our dark hair, dark eyes, and her heart-shaped face and my angular one, we do look cute. I decide then that I want to grow a beard.

"Now try the white one," she breathes into my ear.

I emerge from the embroidered fitting room in an over-size blindingly snowy parka that swallows me whole with a pair of matching pants that would be sweatpants if they weren't quilted and made out of some kind of high-tech wool. I am every inch one of those assholes who gets hunted down by street photographers, and when I ask Lee if my Timbs look appropriate she says they're not quite right, and a flurry of activity breaks loose so they can locate the correct shoes.

"You look so expensive," says Lee, pulling up my white sweatshirt to check out the pants. "I would kill for your hips."

We both laugh. It's the giddy, head-thrown-back cackle of the one percent.

"Now do the suit."

I do the suit.

It's midnight-blue, almost black but not quite, and when it catches the overhead spotlight there's a sheen that appears almost ultramarine.

In it, with a crisp white shirt unbuttoned at the top, I look taller. If I updated every social media avatar with this, my enemies would choke.

I've never been a fashion guy and certainly not a suit guy, but clearly I was the wrong type of guy before this moment.

"Holy shit," says Lee, fingering the lapel of the jacket appreciatively. She kisses me square on the lips in front of everyone, and again we study our reflections.

"I want a picture," mirror me tells mirror her.

"Oh, you have to," she says, grabbing my phone, backing away. "Wait, I gotta get the shoes." It's true. She does. They're crushed velvet.

I want to correct her. That I'd wanted a picture of both of us, but I can't admit this. If she smiled tolerantly and said no, I'd die.

She shoots the picture with her tongue sticking out slightly.

I kiss her when she's done, and she wraps her arms around my waist.

"Isn't this fun?" The curved awning of her eyelashes almost reaches her eyebrows.

"Completely." I feel a pang of guilt about Rain but squash it down.

"Good," she says. "Let me get this for you."

"No way," I scoff, sliding out of the jacket.

Leanna Smart is not buying clothes for me.

"Come on," says Lee, grabbing me before I back into the dressing room.

"Thank you but no," I tell her gently but firmly.

"Pab," she says. "What if I told you that we could get either this ridiculously smoldering ensemble or the leather jacket—whichever—with no money down and zero additional payments until forever?"

"Lee." I slide it back onto a hanger. "You're not my mom."

With that I shut the fitting room door.

I press my forehead on the cool length of mirror and take a deep breath, fogging it up.

Quietly, surreptitiously, I put the jacket back on. I need a private moment with this suit.

Holy shit.

Again, I'm transformed. I'm a parallel-reality Pablo who has won. It's a lie so convincing I can almost believe it.

Making sure my phone's on silent, I take a selfie. Then another one. Okay, I take more than a few. The photos Lee took are entirely serviceable, but a fitting room-selfie in a boutique is canon. It's shit-eatingly blasé.

I open up Instagram, briefly considering adding it to Stories, when I see what she's done.

Lee posted the suit photo to my Munchies account with the tag #snack. And #spelunk. I know it's funny, that she meant it as a joke, but it feels like anything but. I consider deleting it, but something stops me. Possibly because Lee did it. Most likely because of vanity. I slip off the jacket and finally check the hangtag as I do.

The crash-land back to earth is a bruiser. Four thousand dollars.

What does four thousand dollars mean? Months and months of graveyard shifts. A drop in the bucket of what I owe school. What am I doing? Why doesn't money make more sense?

I take a step back. In my undershirt and the narrow suit pants, I look at my reflection. I appear extra naked. Exposed. As if I've removed a suit of armor.

I delete her picture from my feed.

On one hand it's no surprise that everyone makes more money than me. And on good days, the dead-end aspects of my job feel punk-rock. Me, Nando, Jorge, and Sylvan, who does the deliveries for the bagel spot, are on the same humble level and I like it. We crack jokes about the neighborhood snobs. It's why we hate the Kims' kids. But Nando has children to support, Jorge sends most of his money back to Puebla, plus he's got a plan—to become a famous guitar player with his death metal band, Cabra. Letting my girlfriend dress me is not my professional destiny.

A chilling thought crosses my mind quicker than I can unthink it. Is it so wrong to let her give me this suit? Given the NDA, seeing as there's no other artifact or evidence that this is real life? Shouldn't I get a memento?

Maybe I was led to this suit for a reason. Is it so deranged that I'd get to keep something this nice? The doors this suit could open . . . I can't deny how much I want it. How I'm scared Lee will see how much I want it and buy it for me. Thing is, part of me knows that if I had this suit, nobody could say shit about me being with Lee. We'd make more sense.

God, I wish I didn't know about this feeling, these clothes.

I feel sick by the time I slither into my sweatshirt and notice a stain on the sleeve. I want out of this store, out of this moment, out of my skin. I need an elastic band to snap around my wrist. I rub my eyes until I see stars. I rub them again as if I can scrape the horrible, weak-willed pipe dreams from my brain.

By the time we troop downstairs in silence, I can't command my face to smile or my shoulders to straighten. We're blindsided when a voice calls Lee's name. "Leanna!" barks a man, and as I turn a flashbulb goes off in my face.

"Shit." I hear her, but I can't see her. More flashes. Lee slips her hand from mine and grabs sunglasses, but not before another flurry of exploding light.

"Leanna? Who's that? Pal, can you give us a smile? Lee, you know how this goes. Give us the shot, and we'll get out of your hair." There are four or five men of varying ethnicities, ages, and sizes swarming us. "Where's Dyland?" they want to know. "What about Luca?"

Look, I've seen the videos. All the GIFs of celebrities punching paparazzi out at the airport. I'd assumed it was the tax of being famous. The cost of being rich. But when you're in the scrum, smack-dab right in the middle of the action, it's scary. You're pushed with such force on all sides, and the worst part is everyone has these glassy smiles on their faces. They look—hungry.

"What's your name, buddy?" His face is obstructed, but his gravelly, nasally voice is all New York. I feel vaguely betrayed.

Another, a Middle-Eastern-looking man in his forties gets right up to Lee with a camera and mic.

"Lee, Lee," he screams. Lee's sandwiched between me and her security with her head pitched down, hair in her face. "Who's the boy toy? Where'd you get him? You giving him a makeover?"

At this she swivels and cuts him a death stare as he keeps filming.

The pap grins wide, loving the attention. "I could use some new clothes if you're giving them away," he says, and then he smacks his lips inches from her.

"Back off, dude," I explode. We're mere feet from the car, but even with Big Huge and Isaac clearing a path, we're penned in. Isaac cuts right in front of me while I'm dying to take a swing at the guy.

"Leanna!" A high-pitched voice. Small hand in a coat sleeve jumps up and down waving. An older woman, probably her mother, does the exact same thing with her phone up. "Leanna!" she calls out. "She's your biggest fan! Can we get a selfie?"

Other Smartees materialize. It's horrifying to watch in action. It's the aerial view of every fast zombie movie ever.

"Me too," screams another. "Please!" Everybody's closing in with their cameras posed in selfie mode backing into us. An older man takes a picture with his iPad. "You're famous?" he asks us in a German accent, and snaps another picture before we can say anything.

Suddenly we're in the car.

"Shit," she says.

An elbow lands heavily on the window to my side and I jump. I'm flushed with adrenaline as I pull off my coat and put on my seat belt. Through the tinting, even this close, the people outside don't seem real.

"Are you okay?" I take her hand, but she pulls away.

"I have to make a call," she says shakily.

"Hey," she says, and then listens for whoever's talking. "Not great." A dry laugh. "Worse than usual. It was Paolo, Bruno, all of them."

She nods, waits. "Yeah . . . someone must have."

Nods again.

The car begins to move. I check my phone.

Shit. It's eight thirty. I'll have to leave for work as soon as we get to the hotel. And I didn't get to see my brother.

"That's what you said last time," says Lee into the phone, and then she finally smiles. "I know you do. Thank you. You're a lifesaver."

Lee hangs up, closes her eyes, and leans back into her seat.

I have zero idea what's going on in her mind.

"How are you?" I ask her. "Tell me anything."

A beat. Eyes remain closed. Another sigh, and then she looks at me and attempts a smile.

"Fine," she says tightly. "How are you?"

"That was crazy."

She nods.

We ride in silence.

Rain calls. I hit ignore. Something in Lee's temperament has altered, and I can't tell how. I'll call him back.

The car stops. I pull her seat belt toward her.

"Seat belt," I say lamely.

"Thank you," she responds, but I can tell from her glazed

expression that she's gnawing on something in her head.

We're stuck in crosstown traffic again.

"Lee, are we going to talk about what just happened?"

It's a fair question.

She tilts her head as if sizing me up.

"What is there to talk about?" she asks.

Her cold tone surprises me.

"I guess, what's going to happen? Can I get *some* debriefing?" My tension escalates to match hers.

"Nothing's going to happen."

The lack of details again is maddening.

"But the photos."

"Pablo." She takes my hand and kisses the back of it. "Please," she says, as if I shouldn't trouble my simple head with any of these intricacies.

"Lee . . ."

"I don't want to fight," she says, and smiles. It's the smile that sets me off.

I didn't want to fight either until the option to fight was vetoed without discussion. I'm fuming. Unbelievably frustrated. To go from wanting to split the skin of my knuckles on those photographers' faces to being completely shut out.

"Look," says Lee, again in an alienly mild tone. "I know this is difficult," I almost expect her to shush me. "Being with me comes with challenges, and if you can't do it, I completely understand. I would miss you so, so much, but . . ."

While she recites the words, as if from a speech she knows too well, I watch the strands of her red hair cling to the car window from the static and quaver there.

Rain texts again. Shit.

Lee's eyes flit down to my lit-up screen and back at me. Her hair's still sticking out of her head and bobbing behind her. I realize then that if I leave this car I'll never see her again. Coughing Lee. 404 error message Lee. Recharging Lee. Bath time Lee. Bicycle Lee. Static-cling Lee.

"I'm going to be in Asia for the next few days. Maybe it's good if we both take time to . . ."

"Wait a minute," I tell her. "Wait." I carefully smooth her hair down and touch her cheek with my hand.

She'll take her smell with her when she goes.

"Pab," she says, and the sadness in that single word pierces straight through to my chest. "How long can this go on for?"

She takes my hand in both of hers. Panic seizes me.

What is this really about?

I should have let her buy the jacket. I should never have provoked the paparazzi. None of it.

Please don't let this be happening.

I trace her jaw with my thumb. She closes her eyes and leans into me.

I kiss her.

This doesn't make sense. All the feelings are still right here.

"Do you really want to take a break?" I ask her, voice catching.

"No," she admits, and I kiss her again.

"Come with me," she says, and smiles sadly.

I think of Rain. My mom. My shift at the Kims' that starts at ten.

"Okay," I tell her, and nod.

"Stop." She pulls away. "Pab, I'm leaving in an hour."

"Where are we going?"

"I'm leaving for Seoul."

Seriously?

"I've heard good things about Seoul," I tell her.

How could this not be a sign?

A slideshow of visiting Korea for the first time with Leanna Smart plays in my thoughts. It's intoxicating. It's not real, and I miss it already.

"What about work? What about school?"

"Look," I tell her, and when she kisses me again I can feel the shift in her mood. "When I'm lying on my deathbed contemplating my life, this is something I'm going to want to see."

"One more day," she chants, tiny fist bobbing. Grinning.

"One more day," I respond.

"Do you think if we send a driver to your house, one of your roommates could give them your passport?"

"Wyn would do an endless assortment of verbs if you ask him nicely."

I text him in a daze.

"Are you really coming?"

An eighteen-hour flight is no picnic.

No matter how Lee attempts to make it one. At some

point in the middle of the interminable twilight of a transpacific flight, Lee shakes my leg.

When I lift the satiny sleep mask from my eyes, she's looking at me, smiling, like a little kid at a slumber party. I yawn, covering my mouth so my corpse breath doesn't knock her out.

The novelty of a sleeping pod on a private plane wore out at least six hours earlier. When she goes to the bathroom, I avail myself of the Wi-Fi, and sure enough there's no press yet on me and Lee's boutique excursion.

"Want to know the best part about flying to Asia?" She yawns as she comes back, pulling her hood up and crossing her legs.

"The embolism from being suspended at this altitude for what feels like a calendar year?"

"Close second," she says. "The first?"

She presses a small button and a flight attendant materializes.

Instant noodles. The answer is instant noodles.

"They make your fingers swell up from the sodium," she says as the spicy kimchi steam bathes my face and alleviates some of the dryness in my nose. "But tell me this doesn't hit the spot."

She's right. The cup ramen is the best part.

I'm not aware I've passed out until a discreet light softly illuminates somewhere below me, and while I'm half in the grip of an unsettling, entirely textbook dream where my mom or Mrs. Kim has her back to me and refuses to face me no matter how much I shake her, I hear my name.

"Pablo, look," says Lee, lifting up the window shade and kissing my shoulder as we fly into Seoul airspace while the sun rises. Skyscrapers I don't recognize, that don't belong to me the way the Woolworth Building or the Empire State does. I'd never seen the Twin Towers from an airplane, and it squeezes my guts that I can't tell my mom about this. That Rain isn't here with me. As with so many things in my life, I'm doing this wrong but I'm doing it.

It's six a.m. Seoul time when wheels touch tarmac. When I see Luca and Jess, also in hoodies and sunglasses, deplane, I'm startled but too tired to punch him on the temple as I've fantasized for weeks. I steel myself as we move through a separate, private line for customs, wondering what will greet us on the other side, but there are no screaming fans and photographers camped outside the glass. Instead a man and a woman in stylish monochrome outfits greet us in excellent English, bowing deeply. I bow from the waist as I've been taught by my mom and expect them to see, to remark that there's something in the way that I bow that betrays how much I'm like them. But they don't. Another black car.

This is going to sound unbelievably ignorant, but as we course through the highway it blows my mind that all the cars around us are filled with Korean people. It makes me giddy. On the high street, I stare at the blocky letters on stores and restaurants and will myself to be able to read them.

The hotel is on a hill, since the rich love a view, and as we crawl up the winding roads, I'm struck by the meaning of what Lee's told me. How sealed in you feel. Seoul may as well be a VR headset so far.

"How are you?" asks Lee.

"Good." And kind of blue.

We enter the lobby, pass a resplendent breakfast buffet with guys in foot-long chef's hats manning station after station representing every country under the sun—French pastries, muesli, waffles, noodle soups, congee, miso, grilled fish, dim sum, biscuits, roasts, and an Easter ham.

My mom would have a field day with her dinner-for-breakfast preferences, and I push thoughts of her to the back of my mind along with the rest of them.

Lee squeezes my hand, nodding at the spread. I'm too disoriented from the flight to eat, but when she throws my arm over her shoulder and smiles up at me in the elevator, it's all worth it.

"I'm so glad we got out of all that," she says when we're led to our rooms. I still can't believe the photos won't leak. That it won't be a matter of time.

The room is palatial, draped in tasteful champagne-colored fabric with a stunning view. Of course there's an adjoining living room and multiple bathrooms.

We kick off our shoes and collapse into bed.

"I have to work today," she says, flipping over to prop herself up on her elbows. "In fact, I have to get ready soon."

"How soon?"

She rips off her hoodie. "Soonish." Lee tugs at my sweat-shirt. "Quick, quick," she says. "We have to recharge."

We clap our bellies together, which makes me smile.

"*Bzzzzzzt,*" she grumbles.

"What's on the schedule today?" I ask her.

"Meetings but not that many. I told them to cool it."

"Did you actually say 'cool it'?"

"The exact words were, 'Listen up, sheeple, cool your jets.'"

"So you'll knock off early and show me the town?"

"Totally," she says. "It's going to be fun. They have malls here that open at two in the morning. And these twenty-four-hour hole-in-the-wall restaurants that sell the best fried chicken you've ever had in your life and, baby, they have these rice cakes. You gotta know about these rice cakes. The fat chewy finger ones with the spicy red sauce."

"Dduk bok ki? Yo, those are my actual favorite." The last time I had them was over a year ago.

"That's what I'm saying," she says. "They have corndogs studded with french fries here. This is your snack-food her-itage. We're going to have the best time. I'm so glad you're here."

Her tummy's warm on mine.

"When do you have to go?"

"In a half hour," she says. A protest bubbles up in my throat, but I remember her coldness in the car.

"Okay, so we have thirty minutes," I say brightly. I kiss her on the temple and take her hand. "Thirty minutes is a long time if you think about it. Consider all the boredom you can achieve in thirty minutes when you have nothing else to do."

She kisses me. "Thanks for understanding," she says. "But we have two days. Well, thirty-eight hours."

"An embarrassment of riches," I tell her.

"Yeah, we're lousy with time." I can't believe I almost let this girl break up with me. "I'll be done at noon," she says. "Will you be okay here?"

The prospect of a nap in this padded palace has its appeal. "I think I'll cope." I pull her in for a bear hug. I can wrap her frame in mine completely. It's agonizingly face-melting.

She relaxes into me, her full weight easing at my chest.

"We can take a stiflingly ineffective bath after," she whispers.

"Can't wait," I tell her.

Chapter 31

I **wake up** groggy. Flat on my back in the pitch-black, it takes me a moment to register that I'm not at home, that I'm not even remotely close to America, let alone New York. A sense of vertigo swings through my senses as I grab my phone. It's 1:22 p.m. My body tells me vehemently otherwise.

"Lee?" I croak, reaching out into the endless expanse of bed next to me. I get up and pull the curtains aside as the sunlight bores into my retinae. We're surrounded by a surprising number of trees.

I get back in bed. Did Lee say she'd be back later today or tonight? All I know is that we leave the morning after, and while I want to sleep for another twelve hours, I can't miss this.

My stomach growls, recalling the towers of food downstairs. The baked goods, the meats, the army of capable chefs.

But wait. Is breakfast included? Am I allowed to get room service? Who's paying for all of this? Lee mentioned that "the company" foots the bill when we're in LA, but I'm increasingly convinced the company is Leanna Smart Multinational Conglomerate Enterprises Corp and she's picking up the check. I'm not above eating on a girl's Seamless dime if she's treating and I'm certainly not conservative when it comes to disrespecting my own credit cards, but I don't charge to tabs without asking.

I go to my texts, and a message from my phone carrier pops up to say it's ten bucks a day for international roaming, with additional fees that may apply.

I call the front desk.

"Good afternoon, Mr. Snorlax," says a woman in mildly accented English. "How may we help you today?"

"Uh, yeah, hi. I had a stupid question. . . ."

Silence.

"Yeah, so is the breakfast buffet included in the rooms?"

"I'm afraid not," she says.

"How much does it cost?"

She tells me in won and converts it to US currency, and let's just say, it's in the ballpark of thirty perfectly hearty breakfasts at La Bagel Universe.

"Is there an ATM downstairs?"

"Of course," she says, and then, "Just beyond the ballroom."

I locate my shoes. I know Lee's going to find all of this ridiculous. I know she doesn't care. But I also know that if I called to ask for permission it would be tantamount to asking my girlfriend for pocket money. Never mind the whole, *Are you fucking kidding me and interrupting my Very Important Bajillion-Dollar Rainmaking Deal to ask about small change?* aspect of it.

A whole-body cringe radiates through my bowels.

I wash my face, throw on my clothes, and make to head out when I realize I don't have a key card. It's a virtual guarantee that I'll regret leaving the room, but my joints feel tight with unspent energy and my anxiety only increases with the general annoyance. I bite the phone fee and text Lee and Jess. By now my hunger's less a low boiling expectation but a panicked piercing alarm. I waffle for another half hour, drink a bottle of water, discover that none of the windows open, pocket my charger, and make my way to the elevator.

No dice on Jess. Of course no dice on Lee and unfortunately no dice on the ATM. As in, they have one. Past the ballroom as promised. And I even have money in my checking account, but it won't let me at it. There are three identical buttons that say DOMESTIC CARD on one side of the screen and three buttons with FOREIGN CARD on the other. I press a FOREIGN CARD at random. It asks me for a pin code that isn't my ATM number. I have no idea.

I stick a credit card in to see what happens and it asks me if I'd like a cash advance.

The google results for what a cash advance involves scream in all caps not to do it.

Shit.

"Hi." I ask the front desk clerk if there's a convenience store nearby. He's a kid, about my age, in a smart blue suit. His eyes flicker up and down, and I register how I must appear. That the New York uniform of Timbs, sweats, hoodie, and an MA-1 bomber doesn't necessarily indicate "Totally normal college dropout whose mother is a doctor."

I wish I spoke Korean.

"There is a bus," he says. "The walk is about thirty minutes."

I take my chances, palming an apple and a banana from a bowl by the door, and wolf them down once there's enough distance from the hotel that the staff doesn't think I'm a fruit-stealing vagrant.

The hill burns my calves, and as the wooded view from the room implied, there doesn't appear to be stores or restaurants for ages. There are, however, homes with impressive brushed-steel gates, ivy-covered walls—all the telltale signs of the super-rich—but there are little to no other pedestrians.

I check my phone again. It's past three. I'm getting hot under my coat, and when I hear footfalls behind me, I turn. A college-age kid in headphones. I slow down so he can overtake me. There's a fork in the road, but I follow him since he's wearing varsity red Foamposites, which is about as trustworthy as those get, besides which he seems to know where he's going.

Finally, a clothing boutique. It's closed, but farther down

there are several cafés with outdoor seating, a few signs in English, a crepe place, another restaurant that seems to specialize solely in "Japanese cheesecake," and gloriously, a beacon of hope hailed as a GS25. The sign says it's FRIENDLY, FRESH, FUN, and of course it is because it's a bodega.

I'm home. Inside, it's a parade of brightly colored snacks, dried fish, chips, and tiny cookies packaged in candy-colored boxes. Plus, a cartoon wonderland of vacuum-sealed chicken drumsticks, and fish balls on sticks that are stored at room temperature and remind me of those fake plastic bowls of noodles outside of Japanese restaurants where the chopsticks appear suspended in midair.

I take a video of the lot.

The most promising section is the refrigerated display of lunch boxes served on cafeteria trays, shrink-wrapped, tray and all. Some handy-dandy conversion math tells me that it's only four bucks for the one with cheese, corn, rice, three pink sausages that look like emoji, a tangle of red stuff and a yellow wedge that might be egg. I poke the wedge with my thumb. It yields zero additional information as to what it could possibly be. Probably egg.

Each lunch box has a sticker featuring a Korean lady with bleached teeth and a perm. They look nothing alike, but I'm immediately reminded of Mrs. Kim. I tried calling on the way to the airport but no one picked up, and then my entire shift was spent in the air.

I know I'm fired. I left them no choice. I've let them down so colossally, not even having the decency to quit to their faces. At least I'll try to call Rain when he wakes up.

I pick up a squat plastic bottle of banana milk and walk purposefully to the register. My card beeps in menacing protest.

We try my other card. The good one. That beeps too. The pale young woman in glasses hands it back, saying, "Sorry," then covers her mouth and laughs, embarrassed. It's not malicious, but it adds insult to injury. The last thing I ate was pot noodles a thousand years ago. I recall the Easter ham from breakfast and break into a sweat. I'm so hungry I see double.

Back out in the street, the prospect of climbing the hill ends me. I know people have better things to do, but I'm convinced they're staring at me.

This is not how I pictured it. I thought my first time in Korea would be a kind of homecoming. Part of a myth I'd concocted where the trace metals in my blood would recognize its origins in the soil. I expected to experience a fundamental kinship. Thought people would teach me phrases and laugh at my pronunciation, some Crayola-rendered egocentric fantasy I must have cooked up as a kid. But this place is just a city. I'm about as special here as any wackjob rolling up to a New Yorker on the subway expecting an enthusiastic reception.

I wish I could find my cousins.

I keep walking farther down because heading back up is still too daunting, and admittedly, I wouldn't be mad if Lee returned and worried about where I was. I approach what has to be a main thoroughfare. There are signs in English, for a women's university and row after row of clothing stalls outdoors, sort of like how on St. Mark's they're more market vendors than boutiques.

I find a subway station, but I have nowhere to go.

It's almost five by the time I reach the hotel, and I spend the next two hours in a lobby armchair attempting to make myself as inconspicuous as possible. I'm even reluctant to pee since I'm partly convinced they'll kick me out.

I start to text Rain, but I don't know what to tell him.

I want to recharge my phone, but I don't have the adapter and can't help fantasizing about how the hotel people would treat me if they realized who I was by proxy. This, unsurprisingly, depresses me further.

My phone rings. I pounce, but it's not who I'd hoped.

It's five a.m. in New York.

"Dad?"

"Babbu!"

He hasn't called me that in ages.

"What's going on? You okay?" I ask him.

"Yeah, yeah, everything's fine. I couldn't sleep." He pauses to slurp his tea. "Are you at work?"

I look around. "Nah," I tell him. "But I'm up. How come you can't sleep?"

I hear a deep sigh. "Nerves, I guess. Play's a mess."

Right.

"I'm sure it'll turn out great," I tell him, rubbing my face.

"I hope so," he says. And then, "Are you okay? You sound . . . I don't know."

The care in his voice. The knowing tone. Something in me crumples.

"Yeah, I'm okay," I say quietly.

"You're coming to opening night though, right?"

"Of course."

"Good." Another slurp. "And you're sure you're all right?" His concern travels at the speed of sound clear across the world.

"Yeah. You should get some sleep, dad."

"You too," he says.

"It's going to be okay, dad," I tell him, and he chuckles.

"I have the exact same faith in you, you know. This part of your life will work out, babbu."

"Thanks, dad."

As the hotel sets up an extravagant dinner buffet, I feel as though all of this is happening in a dream, especially when, behind the ice sculpture of a pirate ship, I see her. A flash of white fur coat. With Luca and Jess and a cluster of suits. She's on her phone and laughing with a smile that dies as she sees me. I look away. Flustered to be caught watching her. Out here. Exposed.

I've rehearsed this moment hundreds of times, my reactions varying from casual to levelheaded to a monumental fight. By the time she approaches and I can confirm she's real, I'm so relieved I choke up.

"Pab?"

"I got locked out," I tell her, not meeting her gaze. Lee tells the entourage she'll see them later.

I have waited for this woman now for thirteen hours.

"What do you mean you couldn't get back in?" She slides out of her coat. She's changed since this morning. Into a scarlet satin suit. Pajama-like but fitted—a leisure tuxedo. Or a Christmas present.

Back in the suite, back in comparative safety, the rage loads first.

"Where have you been?"

"I'm sorry," she says. "Nothing went as planned today. Had I known you were locked out . . . Did you eat?"

"Lee, where were you?"

"Pablo," she says. She's looking at me, but her thumbs are still tapping on her screen, which sets my teeth on edge. "I'm sorry. So many things are up in the air right now."

"Is this about the pictures?" I ask her.

She seems angry with me again.

"The ones outside of the store?"

Lee tilts her head, removing a dangling feathered earring from her right ear, and smiles faintly. "You don't have to specify which photos," she says, methodically rubbing her lobe. "And believe me," she scoffs. "Those photos are not a priority today."

"But what happens?"

"I told you it was handled."

"Yeah, but what does that mean?"

"Pablo, why do you need to know how the sausage

gets made? Favors are called in. Pictures disappear. Search results are buried. I'm sorry. Call me crazy but you seem disappointed about this."

She glares at me accusingly.

I don't know what to say. I *am* disappointed. Part of me would love if it got out.

"Can you even fathom what a pain in the ass I've spared you from?" she asks. "I handled it to protect you. All of you. Your mother, your father, your brother, all your room-mates. You've seen the swarm. Well, multiply the frenzy by a thousand, and that's the level of intrusive bullshit that will descend upon you and everyone you love in a hellfire of pestilence. It's not fun, Pablo."

"We didn't even discuss it." The question that's teased my mind all day is this: I want to know if she's embarrassed of me.

"What is there to discuss?" she fumes, throwing her hands up. "Pablo, do you know why I had to come to your house from the airport?"

I vaguely recall a security issue.

"I asked you, but you wouldn't—"

"There was a package at the hotel. Addressed to me. Nobody was supposed to know I was there and I certainly didn't send myself anything, but there it was. Do you know how creepy that is? Shit like that scares me, Pablo. I've had credible bomb threats at shows. I once had a stalker live inside of my house for six months while I was on tour without me knowing. She slept in my bed, wore my clothes, cooked in my kitchen for half a year. I don't tell you about this stuff because it's better for you not to know. Bad enough that I have to."

I'm stunned by how this intellectually makes sense. That I'd *known* about the stalker—I'd read about it like everyone else—but I didn't consider the effects it would have on Lee the person. I realize with finality and utter mortification that she hasn't thought about the photos all day. Why would she? I admit that part of me wondered if she was punishing me by leaving me in a hotel. But that's a fantasy. Another self-important delusion. She's not embarrassed of me. That would acknowledge that I factor anywhere in her life. She's not hiding me because there's nothing to hide. I don't chart. And how could I really? Look at her life. Then look at mine. This is the deal. This has always been the deal.

She pivots to sit on the bed. Her feet and calves are framed by the bedroom doorway.

"Look," she calls out after a moment. "I'm sorry it took so long. We were meant to meet here, but then the guy canceled. He owns basically every movie studio in China, and if he doesn't come to you, you go to him. He's the one who flew us here in the first place and when he sends another plane, you go. Believe me, it was the last thing I wanted to do."

I walk over to her. "You were in China?"

She's starfished on the bed and staring at the ceiling.

"Pablo, I said I was sorry. It was out of my hands. And honestly, you couldn't have come anyway. You'd need a visa."

I stand over her. She closes her eyes as if to create distance.

"You left me in another country?"

Silence.

"You were in China?" I ask again. I picture the red dotted line of her. Traveling. Away from me to an entirely different country. I can't wrap my mind around it. This is where the entirety of my understanding halts. The fear grips me retroactively. That I was even more stranded than I was aware of.

"It's a two-hour flight," she says softly.

"That's not the point."

"I know it's not the point," she says, sitting up. "But you could have ordered room service. I told you we'd hang out tonight."

"It's been thirteen hours," I tell her again. It dawns on me all at once. The cost beyond the time. I had work today. Rain. College applications. I dropped it all the second she beckoned, and for what? "I texted you."

"You know what would be great right now?" she says. "If you could ask me how my day went."

In any other time-space it would be a nicety I'd be capable of. Still, I say nothing.

"Because it wasn't great. My album release is bungled. The market's flooded with counterfeit perfumes. My single is barely making a blip because a nine-year-old who vaguely looks like me said the N word on Instagram and that's the story. I understand that you had to wait for me today. But you want to know how many times I have to wait for me?"

Her eyes are aflame.

"Try every day. Try however many hours there are in fourteen years. This is what I'm talking about. How no one worries about me. You think any of this stops for me ever? I eat, sleep, fly, *fall in love* in the snatched time—hiccups really—between Master Tour day sheets of hurry-up waiting that dictate my entire life." Her voice cracks.

"I know you don't get it. And I know I don't get to complain. Everyone assumes that I've leveled out of problems and pain, but I'm a person. And all of this is hard. I'm tired too."

I can see she believes everything she's saying and there was a time I wouldn't think to question it. But as much as I care for her, I'm not so sure about her words. Not long ago I could vividly imagine how disorienting it must be to exist in the inner sanctum of this huge life that radiates out from her. The loneliness of the girl in the bubble. So expensive and special that she's never allowed to steer, the cargo of her own body being too precious. But the wizard behind the curtain, the one with the controls is Lee. And I know that now. I can't un-see it.

She pads shoelessly to the minibar and cracks open a bottle of water. Her silky pant legs swing as she walks. Her life is exemplified by what she's wearing—both pajama and suit. This is a woman, no matter how guileless she likes to appear, who is CEO of the entire operation. The sole player in the organization who cannot get fired no matter how many other fiefdoms operate on her behalf. Jess runs her kingdom. Dyland opens for her shows. Luca. Even Luca is her envoy, not the other way around.

"I wish I could waltz out of here after a few measly hours, but I can't," she says. "There is no going home for me. There isn't a difference between going to work or coming home from work. There's only work. Because that's what it takes."

Lee takes a long slug, and water drips down her chin to land on her shirt. It darkens a deeper red, as if she's been shot.

"Takes to do what?" I finally ask her. "Admit it. You want this. You wanted everything, so you got everything. You won. What else is there? You say you're going to quit music, but we both know that's not true. *You* could stop all this. Go to college. Major in poetry. Act in all the movies your heart desires. You keep telling me you miss New York. Well, move to New York. You could do it if you wanted. You can't pretend to be the passenger in your life. You are the puppet master. You choose this every day. Every last part of it."

"Well, what about you?" she roars. "How are you of all people going to cross-examine me on how easy it is to do what you want? You have all this support. Your parents tried to intervention you they cared so much about your future. But what are you doing with it?"

She's crying now. Her face is crumpled, beet-red and wet, and she keeps slugging long gulps of water as if she's trying to replenish as she goes.

I take a step toward her, but she shies away and it crushes me.

"Do you know how many choices you have?" She's not done lighting into me. "You live in one of the greatest cities on earth. In fact, you didn't have to get there. You were born there. Yet you choose to do nothing. Every day. You're going to die in that bodega if you don't change things, Pablo. You have so much potential."

Potential. God, I hate that word. I take a deep breath and shake my head.

"Look," I tell her. "We're both tired and . . ."

"You don't even go to NYU." She tosses the blue plastic bottle top on the ground, and I watch as it bounces in slow motion.

It's a blow to my windpipe.

Of course.

How stupid could I be?

To think she wouldn't know.

So stupid.

"I used to," I tell the carpet. Even her socks are red. They're thin enough that I can see her toenails, which are of course also red.

There's no way the background check wouldn't be exhaustive. Certain information follows you everywhere. Metadata that appraises you no matter where you are. My grades, my credit, social media standing, and so many other taxonomical brackets that prove I don't count.

"I didn't really need to be told. It was pretty obvious."

"Why didn't you say something?"

She shrugs. "God. You know, I thought this would be easier," she tells me. "I've tried being with artists. Actors. But before you I never would have considered being with a normie. I don't care what you do. Where you live. How much money you make. But I need to be with someone ambitious. I want to be with a man who wants something. Who's driven and passionate. Our chemistry is undeniable, Pablo. I know you feel it when we're together. But when we talk . . ." She shakes her head dolefully. "Sometimes there's so much under the surface you want to tell me but you never do."

I open my mouth to speak and then shut it.

"Why don't you trust me, Pablo? I know you can't, but it's all I ask." She attempts a smile.

"Are you sleeping with Luca?"

She sighs. The earring she's left on, the purple one, reminds me of the dress she wore when I first saw her.

"It's why you came to my deli, isn't it? You were at his house."

She says nothing.

"Were you with him this entire time?"

"Pablo." She crosses her arms.

"You're never not with him, are you?"

She bites her thumb.

"You have matching tattoos."

Again Lee falls silent.

I wait it out.

"It's the day I signed with him," she whispers after a while.

"I'd moved out of my mom's six months before. She had this sketchy 23-year-old boyfriend and they were tearing through my money. Luca was nice to me. He was hanging around the show since he'd signed another kid. He introduced me to his lawyer and they helped me. When he wanted to sign me to his label, it was a dream come true. He knew I wanted to sing. And he had this beautiful studio in his house. By then I was sick of living in hotels so when he asked me to move in, it made sense. It was business. And I didn't want to be the dumb kid who was too scared to say yes. He was all I had. I was fifteen when I signed that contract, Pablo. It's not a contract I'd sign again."

It comes into sharp focus. The fights. How they talk to each other. The way he looks at her.

"We haven't been together like *that* in years," she says. My relief is immediate but her eyes are closed off to me now. Dead. "But he knows everything. Where the bodies are buried. And he owns everything. The night you and I met, after my show, we'd been fighting for days. My contract's up but I don't know if I can be without him. I don't know if he'll let me."

I sit where I stand, numb and reeling.

"I wish I didn't have to wait for me all the time either," she says, taking a seat across the room on the floor. And then, "I'm sorry I made you wait. I wanted Korea to be good. I hope you believe me."

There are so many things I don't know how to do.

Countless flaws. Configurations of words that elude me all the time. But I'd give my entire life if only to know what to say in this moment.

I feel her gaze.

I fail me as I always do.

"We'll get you a flight," she says from somewhere above.

I nod mutely as tears wet my hand.

Chapter 32

She leaves moments later, and the background shifts without my notice. It's day and then night. Another plane. I eat something. I don't remember what it is. Somewhere over the Pacific my alarm pings. The NYU deadline is up in twenty-four hours. Of course. If you're going to fail, you may as well do it spectacularly at everything at once. The shame blots out my senses.

For all my resentments at Lee for ghosting me for a day, I realize it's what I've been doing to everyone for weeks. Months.

I try to sleep, suspended in a twilight where my body's numb, slow—so slow—but my mind won't stop racing. My self-hate is tidal.

No girlfriend. No school. No job. No money. How will I reassemble this?

The smell of exhaust. Lights. Cold air. Another car. Back

at my door, there's a jumble of emotions. Relief. Defeat. A finality. I've been spat out of a dream I'd been deemed unworthy of. I stagger up the stairs blindly, collapse into my room, and cry. Horrible, unmanageable sobs. I sleep for hours and wake up with a tiny reprieve that shatters when I realize where I am. My alarm rings again in the fog. The school deadline has passed. I experience grief I am not entitled to.

I am lost. Irretrievable. I abandon myself to the vacuum Lee's left behind. It is the black of the sky after fireworks. So much darker for having been bright.

"Ay, Pab," says Wyn at my door. I'm grinding my hot eyes with my fists.

"What?" I scream.

"Open up," he says. "Where you been?"

"Sleeping," I bellow. I blow my nose on my sleeve and take off my socks. I've lost count of how many days I've been wearing them.

"Doesn't matter," he continues. "House meeting."

Unbelievable. I grab a dry pair, and as I shove my foot into it, I realize it's the sock with the hole. I whimper audibly, crying again. Wyn knocks a few more times.

I rip the sock off, dry my face, and open the door. "What?"

"Jesus," says Wyn. "You look like shit."

"Thanks."

"Are you getting sick?"

I peep down the hall. Miggs and Dara's door is wide open and their bedroom is flooded with light.

"I thought you said it was a house meeting."

"It's a 'you and Tice' meeting," he says. "Seriously, where the hell were you?"

I roll my eyes and push Wyn out, but he throws his shoulder into it.

"Just go talk to him," he says.

I hear Tice drop something. His room is across from mine and the acoustics work out that I hear him better than Wyn who's right next door.

I peel off my sweats, which are so dirty I almost want to burn them, and throw on my bathrobe over my boxers. I rinse my face. My eyes are ringed in red. I blow my nose and knock on his door.

"Yo." It's bizarre but for however much time we spend together I've been in his room like three times.

Tice is wearing a red St. John's hoodie, and I wonder if he'll get back into school before I do.

"Ay," he says, sealing a box shut with one of those packing tape guns that screech as it dispenses.

"What's this?" It's pretty obvious.

There are boxes stacked up to his waist and a few more still flattened up against the wall.

"Moving out," he confirms, starting on a new box.

"Damn."

So that's the news.

"What, are you going Hollywood on us now? Moving to LA?" The envy sears through me before he can respond.

I sit on his desk chair and try to swivel, but there's not enough space without my legs hitting a box.

"Close," he says. "Williamsburg." That makes me smile. "Yiiiiikes."

"I know," he agrees. "Pass me that stack by your feet." I get up to hand him a pile of identically folded sweaters.

"Man," I breathe, suddenly gutted. It's the end of an era. "What did Wyn say? Did he cry? I can't believe you're breaking up the crew."

"Nah. He was cool. Except about the deposit. Little slumlord's trying to say I broke the towel rack in the bathroom two years ago."

"Ha." We're eight days out from rent being due and I have no idea how I'm going to pay it. I'm owed one last paycheck from the deli, but I'm too shook to pick it up.

"Off Bedford or what?" I imagine Tice living it up at the twenty-dollar salad spots, drinking fifteen-dollar juices.

"Nah. Too hectic. I'm moving in with this girl from school. Further south. I'm not trying to live that L train life. It's chill."

"How much?" There's a black lighter on his desk that says A24 in white. I flick it a few times and think about stealing it. "I bet it's a grip. What is it, two grand a piece? That's almost fifty K a year. Not even for a mortgage. I'm right, right? Williamsburg gotta be at least that much."

Over my shoulder Tice makes this teeth-sucking noise and I catch him roll his eyes. I smack the lighter down.

"You know that's the first question you've asked me in months?" he says, head cocked as if he's done with me. "That's the only thing that's piqued your curiosity—how much I'm paying in rent. And the *question before that* was whether or not I'd take you to the Oscars."

He shakes his head and grabs another box.

"Oh," he exclaims, pointing his tape gun at me. "I guess there *was* the time you called me to clean up your filthy bedroom and the bathroom. But does that constitute a question? Or is that more a rhetorical directive? Because you knew I'd have to do it?"

"What's got you?" I lean into his chair, stretching my crossed feet out, using his boxes as an ottoman. "You're moving out because I wasn't the founding member of the Tyson Scott fan club?" I try to smile at him. "People get busy. Also, come on, fam. You know why I've been busy. You met her."

Tice kicks my feet off his boxes and sits on his bed.

"Look," he says to the tape gun in his hand, eyes downcast. "I don't know what you've been going through with this Leanna chick. I don't really care. I want to talk about you. You've been a dick. First, you act salty as hell about a job that I'm excited about. And for the record, I'd understand if you felt some type of way about *The Agents. And* I acknowledge the role was deeply problematic, but I also asked you about it and you didn't say shit. Instead you avoided me for weeks."

He shakes his head again before looking at me. Tice and I have argued plenty. About dumb stuff. But he's never been genuinely angry with me before. Moody? Sure. Pissy about us drinking his orange juice? Absolutely. But this is different. In a way I don't like. It's making me feel things.

"Plus, and I don't know if it means anything to you," he says. "But I stuck my neck out for you asking my production manager for a job. I'm brand-new and a total nothing on that set, but I asked."

"Well, thank you," I snap, not sounding at all grateful. "But nobody told you to do that. I'm good. I don't need to follow you or your people around asking if you need a trenta latte or some Raisinets. I have to work nights so I can go back to school."

I look away. Tice doesn't need to know I screwed over the Kims, too.

"I swear to god, Pab, sometimes you have amnesia about your own life. First of all, you've been trying to leave that job since summer. And school? Really, dude? Yo, NYU is not happening. It is not financially plausible, plus you're not going to get in. You've got to move on."

The concern borders on pity, and for that I want to destroy him.

"Wow," I tell him. "You get one bit part on a high-key racist show and now you're a clairvoyant motivational speaker. Cool TED Talk, my guy."

Tice makes another box. I can tell he's trying to decide whether or not to keep talking. It's a staring match he'll lose. There's no way I'm leaving his room at this point. Hell, now I'm in the mood for a fight.

"That's the other thing. Since when can't you be happy for me? Did you know that I'm in the Screen Actors Guild now?" he says. Another streaky tape squeal and then, "That's a big deal. Happened last week. I've been working toward it for two years. And I wanted to celebrate but I didn't make a big deal of it because I wasn't sure if *you* could emotionally take it. Lately, you're so bitter about everything. It's all fucking incredible when Leanna Smart is around or when you're talking to her or whatever it is that you do, but then it's back to regular programming with your mopey ass acting as if the world owes you something."

My phone rings in my room.

I shrug. It's probably bills.

"Remember that kid Rooster St. Felix? Chubby kid with the glasses who used to work as a graphic designer for Acetate?"

This is when I know I'm in for another Tyson Scott meandering life lesson.

"Sure," I say. I hear the bitchassness in my tone. "We used to see him at record fairs at PS 1." He had a hot sister.

"The one with the sister," says Tice.

I nod.

"Remember when he quit making allover-print sweatpants to literally make cheese upstate?"

"No."

"Well, he did." Okay, now that he mentions it, I do have a dim recollection of making fun of him.

"So?"

"Everyone thought he was nuts. Black kid from Staten Island goes from becoming the next Jerry Lorenzo to goat cheese. And here I am thinking anyone with any type of melanin is lactose intolerant."

"Oh my god, get to the point."

Tice glares at me.

"This is what he devotes his life to. Cheese. I ran into him a month back. In four years, your man has a little chèvre sampler at Whole Foods with his own cheese that he makes with his hands. He's got six kinds now. Six."

I still don't know where this is going.

"That is the saddest thing I've ever heard," I tell him, because it is.

Tice shakes his head as if he feels sorry for me.

"That's what's wrong with you." He gets up to start another box. "You think everything's supposed to be big and easy. Meanwhile, I've never seen Rooster this happy. I've never seen a lot of people this happy. He was so happy I realized I had to get my shit together. That's what made me want to move out. I stopped smoking weed, started eating right. I work out every day now. Life's hard, man. Trying to get better at the thing you want to be the best at is humiliating. You think what I do isn't challenging? You think it's not humbling to try to be an actor in New York? It's corny as hell. I know I'm that asshole trying to make it. Sometimes worrying about what you'll think actually sets me back. It's ingrained in my head from when we were trying to be DJs and you refused to do shows."

"Man, those set times were at nine p.m.," I remember. "Who the fuck is coming to see you at nine when the main act is at two?"

"But why the fuck would you, a total nobody, be on at any other time?"

"I'm not trying to make that my life," I tell him. "That's working harder, not smarter."

He squeaks another box shut with tape and seals it with a flick of his wrist. I'm so exhausted the screeching feels like it's coming from inside my skull. "Did I tell you I was up for a role in a J. Escobedo movie?"

I sit sullenly.

"It was literally a part about a kid who drops out of St. John and throws away a basketball scholarship after a failed drug test, and *I* didn't get it. There isn't a role that's ever been more autobiographically perfect for me, and I still didn't get it. And the worst part is? I know I nailed it. I know—for a fact—that I gave it my absolute best, and it wasn't good enough. But I keep throwing myself at it. You, though? You're not even in the game, man. And this girl is the same as whatever craziness you thought NYU would be. They are not plans. They're delusions."

I pull my dressing gown closer to me, an old dame caught in a draft. When Tice finally stops talking, I notice that I've been scorching the hair on my thigh with the lighter. It smells as acrid as my insides feel.

"Yo," he says. "Come on, man. At least *pretend* to be happy for me."

I want to be happy for him. I do.

"You're right," I tell him. Staring at my feet. "I've been acting like a dick. I knew I was being a ill asshole to you."

I feel his eyes on me, but I can't look up. "I'm sorry. It's my shit, but I gotta tell you, sometimes it's like an out-of-body experience. I don't know why I do half the shit I do. I can't even tell you how tired I am of feeling sorry for myself. But I'm not like you. I have no idea how to turn this around."

"Pab," he says, sitting on his bed so we're at eye level. "You're not going to change your life in a day. It took two years and antianxiety medication for me to stop getting overwhelmed about even getting out of bed. Do the next right thing and don't worry about anything else coming down the pike. You don't have an audience. No one's judging you. Do the work."

I can't sit in here anymore. Tears are blinding my vision, and pretty soon my nose is going to run.

"You should have a housewarming," I tell him, clearing my throat, gaze still pinned to the floor. "Get some sexy plants. And don't forget that lamp's Wyn's." I point to the twenty-dollar IKEA floor torchère. "He'll charge you for it." I walk out with his lighter in my hand.

Back in my room I cover my face with my pillow and bawl until I can feel my heartbeat in my teeth.

Chapter 33

"It smells weird in here." Rain's only ever been over once, so when I buzz him up, he surveys the premises. "I'm still mad at you," he says, staying by the door, but that he's here telling me to my face is a good sign.

"You look terrible." He's wearing my old polo rugby, which is brazen since I'd asked if he'd seen it and he said he hadn't. Still, we both know I'm not going to say shit about it now.

My kid brother didn't take my calls for three weeks, which is a record for him.

"I'm sorry," I begin. I've apologized in a voicemail and over text, but saying it in person seems important.

Finally he kicks his shoes off, dumps his stuff, and joins me on the couch.

"It's a miracle I'm alive, fuckface," he says. "She was

this close to ending me." He pinches the air. "You know she made me clean the whole house? I didn't know vacuuming curtains was a thing, but apparently it is. She screamed on me until four in the morning that night. And where the hell were you?"

"I got held up." I decided on his way over that I wouldn't involve him in my Leanna drama.

He rolls his eyes. "Why do you do that?"

"What?"

"Lie," he says plainly. "You lie about the stupidest things without any agenda. If you don't trust your brother who are you going to trust? Or do you think I'm so stupid that I won't know that you're being sus? Someone texts you and you run out, and then you're ghost for three days when I need you the most? I know you got held up. Knowing you, you got held up doing something dumb. I do dumb shit all the time, but I tell you about it. So I'm asking you again. As a man. Where were you?"

"It was a girl."

He rolls his eyes with his entire body. "Seriously?" He shakes his head. "You sold your brother out for a lady?"

"I was in love with her."

"Huh," he says, and frowns as if he's mulling it over. "Honestly, I thought maybe you were a drug dealer or something. Like a really unsuccessful one. Or maybe had a gambling problem. That seems like some shit you'd be mixed up in." He leans back in his seat. "So, what happened?"

"Well, she's real busy." A flash of Lee lifting up her sweatshirt to plop her belly against mine. And ambitious. She travels a lot. . . ."

"She an Instagram thot or what?"

"No!"

Rain laughs.

"She's smart and good at life, and I don't know . . . Honestly . . . the timing didn't work out, but I thought I could force it. I think I was jealous or something. Of how much her job required of her."

"Whoa," he says. "That's stupid. But I get it." He leans back.

"What's going on with you?" I nudge him. I'm trying this thing since Tice tore me a new one where I ask people questions about their lives. "Mom said you had a girlfriend?"

"Yeah," he says. "I tried it. But . . ." He shrugs his bony shoulders. "She was out of my league."

"Ha." I think about how this is what truly unites us. My dad, my brother, and me. We love women who best us by miles.

"So it's over?" I ask him.

"Yeah." He nods dully. "What about you?"

"Yep."

"So you're depressed or something?" Rain asks me.

"I guess. You?"

"I don't know," he says. "How are you supposed to know if you're depressed?"

That's a question for the ages.

"Well," says Rain, leaning over to his backpack and unzipping the front pocket. He pulls out a black plastic bag and tosses it at me. "These are from me and dad. From the Irish deli in Woodside."

It's a milk-chocolate Tunnock's Teacake, a bag of salt and vinegar Hula Hoops, pickled onion Monster Munch, a Flake bar, and mint leaf fruit slices.

I pick up the bag of ninety-nine-cent green wedges and raise a brow.

"Dad," supplies Rain. As if I need to be told who's responsible for the old-timey candy of the bunch.

Most of the time his obsession with war foods—the peanuts and the condensed milk, the dried-up old Maria cookies—the fact that you could cop any of his favorites with food rations in 1945 annoys me, but this time I find it sort of sweet.

I open up the bag and give it a shot. Rain leans over and grabs one too.

We chew, give it the gas face, and spit it out in unison.

"Nasty," says Rain. He's right. It's as if you rolled toothpaste turds in cat litter.

"Gummy mint is not a real candy experience," I confirm while pulling my phone out to shoot the sack of struggle gummy. "It's like cinnamon. Spices are cool, but we have blue raspberry and orange Creamsicle now."

"Strawberry's always the best," says Rain, reaching over to examine the teacake.

"Word. Mint's like the dial-up Internet of flavors. Or a fax machine."

"Fax machine," repeats Rain. "That's funny. How come you don't add real captions to your Instagram pictures? Don't people want to know what this stuff tastes like?" He holds up the foil-wrapped dome. "Forget the sneakers or whatever. Tell me what's in one of these. What's the vibe?"

He's got a point.

"Pablo," he says, as if he's an uncle or something. "Don't be afraid of sincerity. Let people in. Let your fans get to know who you are. I know you have abandonment issues. I mean, look at us. There isn't a member of this family who isn't messed up, but intimacy's the shit."

"Where are you getting this?"

"Dad's meditation app," he says. "Whatever, man, I spend a lot of time alone. Mindfulness is that energy I'm trying to bring into my fourteenth year on this planet. Open the snacks."

I toss him my phone.

"All right, I'm gonna do an unboxing," I tell him. I unwrap the puck, hold up the wrapper. "So this is a Tunnock's *milk-chocolate* teacake." I survey the cookie and take a bite. "It's like a Mallomar."

"Pablo," interrupts Rain. "Elaborate."

I read the packaging. "All right, so it's from Scotland. And, I guess, if you've never had a Mallomar before, they're like s'mores. You've got your cookie, marshmallow, except this one's a little bouncier, more *toothsome*, and it's all enrobed in chocolate." I take another bite. "And for all of you who keep kosher, it's not unlike a Krembo."

I hand it to Rain to try.

"Nah, these are creamier than Mallomars," he says with his mouth full. "Reminds me of meringue."

The kid's a natural.

We shoot a video of the Hula Hoops and the Monster Munch, and even though the Flake's all broken, we crack open the yellow wrapper and taste test that shit.

"You think I should add a tag for the deli?"

"Yeah," says Rain. "Prices, too."

"When did you get so bossy?" I ask him.

"When I started having sex," he says, grinning.

I gag.

"Gross. Really?" I hope to god the kid kept it covered.

"Nah," he says, nudging me. "But this time next year I will be. I think I'm good at it."

I make him dinner, breakfast burritos with Korean red pepper paste and pickles, and kick him out. I feel better. Enough that I'm compelled to take a shower. I'm relieved that my brother's forgiven me. I love that little shithead so much.

As I settle into my personhood under the spray, I feel better than I have in days. I'm also chewing on something. What he said. About sincerity. Snack reviews are cool, but they don't reveal enough about me. Who I am. Where I come from. What I love. Plus, that teacake needed something. If the Hula Hoops were original flavor, the ones that come in a red bag, the crunch and salt mashed into a Tunnock's would have been superb. And Flakes, even though I love them better than Twirls (though nothing beats a Mint Aero), they're only spectacular when you add them to sundaes.

I shave, drink some water, and wait for the roommates to return so I can join civilization, but when no one's home by ten thirty, I cave and text her. Again. I don't know why. I guess I wanted to add yet another blue bubble to the unanswered message pileup.

I download the Instagram app again. Under the guise of posting these new videos since I deleted it from my phone three days ago, but when it opens back up it goes to her immediately. And that's when I see it. She got it. The movie.

The Big One.

Plus, according to the tabloids, she's been shooting in New York for a minute.

With Teddy Baptiste.

There's a picture of her with blond hair in Prospect Park.

My park.

I sit on the floor.

Her life has continued. She took the next step. I expect to feel sadness. Loneliness. Anger. Jealousy. I zoom in on Teddy, and while that doesn't feel great—he really is so handsome—I look at Lee. Truly look at her. I recall our talk in the bathtub. The way she sounded when she told me she'd sent the second tape—the one for the lead. How afraid she was. But she's done it. There will be new pictures and newspaper clippings for her abuela to add to the album of the next chapter in Lee's life.

The overwhelming emotion is joy. I'm elated for her. I'm thrilled to find that I'm capable.

I lie in bed and summon Tice's advice of doing the next right thing. I look around my room. And I start cleaning. I throw on another episode of *Watershed* as background noise. This one's about a guy who created Shazam for sneakers with a store. He's a good-looking kid from Long Island with one of those butt chins that immediately make you look distinguished in an eighties way. He's wearing those kinda ugly anniversary Air Max 1s that only, like, fifty people got with the animal-print patches on the mudguard.

As I gather laundry I wonder if this story's going to leave me in a bad mood. The way watching workout videos while eating trash makes me feel guilty, but when he says he dropped out of college he has my attention.

Dude doesn't look a day over twenty-five, but he's way older. He worked at a Foot Locker for years, commuting to Times Square. On his days off, before the sneaker market blew up, he'd go upstate and plunder random stores' dead-stock and resell it on eBay. Half the time they didn't know what they had.

He's yacking about how much he loves Times Square *because* of the tourists, so I have to assume he's a nut. But his encyclopedic knowledge collided with a Mexican television magnate with a yen for Nike Monarchs (aka

Air Dads) and this CEO type offers to seed his business.

Then Butt Chin meets some genius nineteen-year-old from Switzerland who was in New York on vacation, of all things, and then *he* winds up as the company's lead developer.

So this dropout is well on his way to making billions and then he goes, "No finite moment is responsible for my success. There wasn't a fork in the road. Some monumental inflection point where my life changed. It was the accumulation of totally normal, regular-ass days where I worked hard, followed my better instincts, and did the right thing. You don't get to start over every day; you get to keep going."

I get chills. It's basically exactly what Tice said. And this time I really hear it. I get why the creeping dread that hangs over my life never goes away. I am doing regular days, average minutes, all wrong all the time.

I want to love something as much as he loves sneakers. He says sneakers are wish fulfillment. It's everything you wanted as a kid, realized as an adult with the same trapped-in-amber joy that you can't find anywhere else. It's like magic. Or fantasy. But one that you can keep holding on to and return to. It's fucking Rooster and his fucking cheese. Tice and his acting. And Lee with her world domination. It is honestly so terrifying—so intolerably humiliating—to want anything and to declare it.

I fling open my window and look out.

I really do live in the best place on earth. That's when I figure it out. What I want to do. But I have to finish this.

I root through my dirty clothes to search for it. The bane of my existence. That niggling irritation that colors my world perspective. I find it. That goddamned sock with a goddamned hole in it. I toss it.

And wouldn't you know, I feel a little better.

Chapter 34

Tice comes over and it's weird that we have to buzz him up. We're going to watch my dad's theater debut at FiddleStick Playhouse in the Village.

It's awkward. Or not awkward but we're nervous. Me and Wyn cleaned up the living room, and Wyn even put a framed subway map of New York on the wall as if we've graduated to being those kinds of people.

"You didn't have to come," I tell him as he lint brushes crisp sweatpants with a mini roller that telescopes to full size. He looks great. All his tees got an upgrade from Target to Uniqlo. Me and Wyn lock eyes when he pulls the roller from his jacket, but neither of us says anything.

I won't lie; it still bums me out that he doesn't live here. His room's empty, and we keep the door closed because it feels wrong when we're sitting in the living room. It's like a missing tooth. Wyn's cousin Ross is moving in, and the slumlord finagled $750 from him, so I get a discount, which I'm grateful for. I borrowed a grip of money from Rain who's a little miser with his savings and I'm working on paying back the month and a half of rent I owe. I talked to Wyn's parents on the phone and they were really nice about me setting up installments.

"I definitely had to come," says Tice. "Your dad was straight spamming me for three months. He wants my professional opinion." He tears off a linty sheet and applies it to my shirt. "How do you attract visible lint on a white tee?" he asks me.

The three of us take the train, and when we get aboveground it's balmy and bright, and everyone's dressed for vacation. Fluttery sundresses, patterned shorts, sunglasses, and iced coffees. It's barely spring and in the fifties but warm enough in the sun. It's that instant when the cold snaps for the first time in the season, and we all deceive ourselves into thinking it's golden now.

It's almost the best season—summer—when you're never, ever lonely in New York. The city keeps you company, especially when everyone you know is hanging out outside, sitting on stoops or eating off folding tables on the street. You can hear every song you're in the mood for from passing cabs, and when you leave the house first thing in the morning and if you have a little walking-around money, you can stay out until it's dark. If I just get to summer I'll be okay.

Mom and Rain are already there when we arrive. She throws me a tight nod. Mom's the one I'm working up to.

I know we have to talk, but I haven't figured out what I'm going to say.

It's great to see her. Especially since I know we won't have it out in front of everyone here. Bless noonchi for life. She's dressed prettily in a short-sleeved blue shirt and matching skirt. And when she tilts her head down, to discreetly check her teeth in a mirror hidden in her purse, my heart squelches. I want to beg for forgiveness.

Rain calls my name.

We walk over.

"Tice," he says, smiling wide, grabbing his hand to initiate a complicated handshake that Tice immediately slips out of.

"Quit," he says, smiling.

"Hi, Mrs. Rind . . . ," says Tice, and falters, remembering my parents are separated, but mom doesn't correct him.

She pulls him in for a hug. "I saw you on *The Agents*! When they blew you up with the pelicans on the docks, I teared up. You were so good."

"Thank you," he says, bashful for the compliment.

"Hey, mom."

"Pablo."

Wyn bounds over. "Hey, Pablo's family. You saw Tice on the show, right? He's such a legend." He slings his arm over Tice's shoulders.

"You should have seen this kid last week when we went to the deli." Wyn slaps Tice on the chest. "A girl actually walked up to ask for a selfie with him."

"Shut up," says Rain.

"Deadass." From Tice's grin I can tell this really did occur.

"But then this motherf . . ." Wyn's eyes flit to my mom. "This *guy* goes, 'Of course.' And then, get this—*he* asks to take a selfie with *her* so he can send it to his mom. He's all, 'Thank you for watching!'"

"Stop."

It's so Tice. He talks to his mom and aunties every other day.

"It was unmitigated."

"I don't think that word means what you think it does," says Tice.

"Whatever."

There's a refreshment stand, so I line up to get a water for my mom so I'll have an in to talk to her, but of course they only have Pellegrino, which costs six bucks a bottle. I retreat. I'm trying not to use my cards.

"Ay, Selwyn!"

I turn my head. A wiry kid with a grown-out Caesar pulls Wyn in for a pound. Holy shit. It's Cruzo, the dude who'd be my nemesis if he knew I was alive. The graffiti kid who stole my crew name and rode it off into the sunset. Can sworn enemyship run one-way?

"You see Pablo?" says Wyn.

"Ayo, Esco!" says Cruzo, dabbing before walking toward me.

"Hey, Salvatore." I nod. It takes me everything not to call him Scolio. Sure enough, he says, "You can call me

Cruzo." And then, unconvinced that I'd heard, "I go by Cruzo now."

"Cruzo?" I can't help messing with him.

"Yeah, Cruzo. C-R-U . . ."

"Bet," I interrupt. "This is Tice. Selwyn you know—he goes by Wyn now. With a *W*." I pull Wyn in for a showy hug. "So many changes."

"No doubt," says Cruzo, and I notice kid's got gold grills, pretending like we're in Houston, Texas, in 2005. Still, his eyes are super-smiley. Dude might actually be happy to see us.

"What are you doing here?"

"Your dad invited me," says Cruzo. "He's very persistent."

What he is, is unbelievable.

Cruzo shakes his head. "It's amazing that you and Selwyn stayed friends. It's nice."

I look over at Wyn, animatedly chatting with my mom and Rain. He really is a good dude. "It is nice."

"Isn't it wild how much harder it is to make friends when you're older?"

"Cruzo, we're twenty."

"I know. It's just . . . ," he says. "It's different." He sighs. Dramatically. Enough so that I can smell cinnamon on his breath. "Don't you think?"

"Sure."

"You know after my moms passed . . . You heard she died of cancer this year, right?"

I'm such an asshole.

"I didn't, man. I'm so sorry."

"Thank you. Thank you," he says, bowing. "It's been rough. Couldn't leave my house. You never know who's going to look out for you through something like that."

There's a chime and a hush and it's time to go in.

"Anyway," he says, "it's nice to see you cats."

I catch the outline of my mom's head walking into the darkened room. I really have to talk to her.

The theater isn't that big. Just a mess of red velvet seats with a balcony above. Still, it's legit. There are programs and ushers, plus a fair number of people. Dad's saved us half a row near the front. It's blocked off with a piece of duct tape and a sheet of printer paper that reads "reserved" in black marker. It's totally dad's handwriting. The *e*'s have tiny eyes. I unstick the piece of tape as we file in and sit down.

"Pab," hisses a voice from the back. It's Dara. Miggs is with her. Dara's in work clothes, while Miggs wears a bright pink sweater I've never seen before.

"Hey." She sits down and gives me a sideways hug. "Hi, Pab's mom." Mom, who's sitting two seats over, waves.

"Hi, Pab's mom," says Miggs.

Cruzo's sitting on the other side of Miggs, and I watch as they give each other a polite nod.

Rain's sitting next to me, digging gum out of mom's purse, and the way they're whispering and laughing makes it clear they're on the mend. I know he's been on his p's and q's. Up for school early, doing his homework, sorting the laundry, preparing the occasional breakfast-dinner—which in his case is making fried rice with egg and cut-up Spam. "She can't stay mad at me," he told me yesterday. We've taken to calling each other, which feels so bizarre but is a nice way to end a day.

"Did my dad invite you?" I ask Dara quietly.

When Tice overhears this, he laughs and leans over. "Did he Facebook message you every day for a month?" he asks.

"Not me," says Dara, nodding at Miggs. "Him."

"Jesus." My father is relentless.

"There's apparently a comedic monologue he wants his professional opinion on," whispers Dara.

I groan.

"He didn't invite me," says Wyn, and he sounds genuinely hurt about this.

"He didn't have slumlord legislation that he needed your professional opinion on, I guess," says Miggs, and we crack up. But when a woman turns to shoot us a dirty look, we simmer down.

"This is official," whispers Dara, looking around. When the lights dim, I notice that the room is completely full. Who *are* these people?

My dad walks out under a small spotlight, wearing an oversize red V-neck. He clears his throat three times. His voice is quavery, and he shakes his head slightly while talking, as if to refute his own words.

"The show is seventy minutes without an intermission," he says. I panic at the prospect of having to sit here for more than an hour without a break. "I wrote it. Uh, I'm Bilal Rind. Anyway, it's called *Winner, Winner*. I hope you enjoy it." He shades his eyes from the lights to find us, waves, and then does a little bow and walks off.

I hear him clear his throat again from backstage and realize I'm shit scared.

There's something about seeing your dad's work that creates preemptive built-in embarrassment. It's too revealing. Your entire spine wants to curl to make you smaller and disappear. It's worse than seeing your dad have sex. It's akin to seeing your dad have sex while looking at you dead in the eye and singing an Adele song. Dads are awkward. Especially sensitive ones who you can read like a book. You get to a certain age where you start seeing their shortcomings and weaknesses bumping around in them like plankton floating inside a jellyfish. It's too much to bear.

It's worse than seeing your patriarch in a woman's sweater. Or watching him eat sad, old-man sandwiches or catching him stealing food from a wedding. I am dreading my dad revealing his play to the world. I fully expect to be disappointed, despite his hard work and efforts.

All I can think about is how unremarkable the main guy is. How he could be any old Chinese delivery dude off the street, a person you wouldn't give a second thought to as he whizzed by.

But ten minutes into it, as the Asian father celebrates

his windfall, watching him dance an erratic jig and then playing it dead-cool in front of the others when he walks back into the kitchen, I forget that this play is my dad's. I'm engrossed.

Snippets from rehearsal echo in my memory.

"This week no good," says our hero in heavily accented English. He's talking to his money-grubbing children over the phone. All while the local news swarm him.

He nods and *tut*s sympathetically. "Next week also no good."

He pats the winning lottery ticket in his shirt pocket. "Last week was good, but . . . *aiyah* . . . last week, *last week* . . . you know?"

The audience chuckles, eyes shining, smiles plastered on their faces.

My dad's play is apparently funny. It is nothing short of astonishing.

The acts move fast, and at the end the man splits his winnings equally among his three children, but not before torturing them mercilessly in that annoying dad way. Unsurprisingly, there's an individual life lesson for each. Humility. Restraint. Hard work.

When it ends, applause thunders around me. And I'm confronted by an alien emotion. Pride for my father. I've bristled whenever people say they're proud of me. It's so patronizing and presumptuous—as if their satisfaction was chief among the reasons to do anything—but I'm proud of my dad. There's a sense of relief to it. That my ingredients are tied to his and I'm hopeful for once witnessing what they can develop into.

I remember him calling me in Korea. How he couldn't sleep. How I'd doubted him then, too.

"Holy shit," says Dara, clapping her brains out. "I should call my mom."

Miggs is applauding on his feet and hooting and Tice does the same, and then our whole row rises—even that idiot Cruzo, who wolf whistles way more times than is necessary. Then everyone creakily delivers a standing ovation as dad and the cast hold hands and do a big bow. They walk offstage and return for a splashy encore, and I hope he feels this surge of love as much as I do. I glance at my mom, who's dabbing the corners of her eyes, and Rain looks at her and then at me.

We wait for dad in the lobby.

"Thank you for coming," Rain announces to my friends, as if he's dad's manager now. "It's clear we're the artistic ones of the family." My mom laughs and grabs him by the shoulders.

"So," I ask the roomies, "in your professional opinions, what do you think?"

"His dialogue was great," says Tice. "Crotchety and believable. Like every paper-towel-saving, sewing-kit-in-the-cookie-tin-having old person in my life."

"And funny," says Miggs. "That part when the daughter's white husband showed up, I lost it."

"He'll be so happy to see you guys," I tell them.

"I wouldn't have missed it," says Miggs, and then he pounds me on the shoulder. "Plus, I'm going to start bugging the hell out of him to come to *my* shows."

Dad steps out, but he's intercepted, and watching him smile and bob, at one point throwing his head back to laugh, I'm struck by how much I don't know about him. How comfortable he is around others. How certain aspects of him don't belong to us.

He stops to chat with someone else, and I realize I recognize who he's talking to. Wouldn't you know, it's desi guy with the redheaded wife from the Kims' store. He and my father talk for a while and then dad points over to us.

"Hey," says the desi guy, walking over. Then his eyes widen. "Yo," he says, pulling me in for a hug. "Holy shit. Pablo, from the deli."

"Yeah." I'm stunned that he knows my name.

"Where you been, man?"

"What a wonderful coincidence," says dad as I continue to have an aneurism from the glitch in the matrix. "I guess what they say about all of us knowing each other is true. Don't tell the goras."

Dad's pulled into another conversation with a silver-haired couple in matching windbreakers.

"Nil. Nil Mehta," says the desi dude, whose name is apparently Nil Mehta. "So, that's your dad. Fucking wild."

"How do you know each other?"

"I commissioned this," he says, running his fingers through his graying hair. "I'm the programming director at

Breuekelen Rep in Dumbo. I teach over at the New School."

So two Beck's tallboys, aka Freckles McGee's husband, is a theater programming director?

"Tell me honestly," he says. "I look like shit, right? I gained all this weight. . . ." He pats his belly. "I had a kid. I mean, my wife had a kid. Rachel. You know her. With the red hair. So what happened to you? Where'd you go? Me and Rachel were *just* talking about you. You head back to school?"

I imagine them over takeout pad thai talking about me. Bizarre.

"Nah," I say. "I wanted to, but . . ."

"Where at?"

"Well . . ."

"What's your major?"

"I don't know," I tell him honestly. "I don't know about any of it."

"Well, then, it's probably not a good time to go back. Yo, it's gnarly how expensive it is."

Gnarly? Nil Mehta is not at all how I'd envisioned him.

"Fuck knows I'm going to have to sell organs to send my kid.

"Anyway," says Nil, patting my shoulder. "It's good to see you. I'll tell Rachel you said what's up. She says hi. I mean, not literally but definitely in spirit."

"No doubt," I tell him.

Then he digs around in his jeans pockets, pulls out a fat leather wallet, and hands me a thick white card. "Hit me up if you need any help. I didn't figure my shit out until I was almost thirty. My parents were wild *pissed*."

Dad comes back over to all of us.

"Hello!" he says, arms wide. "The gang's all here."

"Baba," says Rain, and hugs dad first. My mom hangs back, but he searches her out.

"That was something else," she says, kissing him on the cheek. Then she does this cute thing where she claps a few times right at him to indicate how much she means it. "I don't know anything about the arts, but that was so funny. I could practically hear your voice coming out of the actors' mouths."

My dad beams and pats both my shoulders boisterously. I clear my throat. Suddenly tongue-tied.

"Thanks for coming."

"You were great," I exclaim breathlessly. "That was great."

We file outside as he tells us he got into the Fringe Festival.

"Oh, that's huge," says Tice. He tries for a handshake, but of course my dad pulls him in for a hug too.

"So, what did you think?" he asks my roommates. "Particularly, what did you think of the monologues?"

"It's all work with you lately, dad," quips Rain, and the artsy kids are off and running, talking about stage direction.

Dara hip checks me. "Happy?"

I nod.

"God, what if it sucked and you had to face your dad right now? Can you imagine?"

I laugh. "Yeah, I can," I tell her.

"Okay, I got to get back to work, but you guys should go out to eat," she says. "It'll be nice."

"Sure, mom," I tell her. For the crap I give Dara about being a mooch and being a know-it-all, in a lot of ways she keeps peace in the house. I know for a fact that she's the only one who replaces the toothpaste and toilet paper because it's always the same brand. Plus, she's kind. Truly kind and three steps ahead of any of us. Miggs is so lucky.

"And while I'm momming you," she adds. "We've got an opening for a busboy at work. A you-shaped opening. I can start you Monday. Sixteen an hour, no tips. And you have to get a haircut."

"Sixteen?" Sold. "I'm in."

I've checked the Craigslist jobs board on the hour and it's bleak.

"You have to do brunch until the end of time, but I'll be your direct manager." She air kisses me.

"Thank god, Dara," I say. "I mean it."

I join Wyn and Cruzo. "Yeah," says Cruzo. "We got this baby grand piano that is an exact replica of the *Millennium Falcon*."

I don't even know how to process these words or exactly what to picture. I go talk to my father.

"I could sleep for a month," he says. Dad's gaunt, I realize. With dark smudges at his eyes. I can't believe I didn't know he was such a good writer. The fact that my self-involvedness somehow missed this makes me sad in a kind of ache.

MARY H. K. CHOI

We're being the worst New Yorkers, taking up way too much sidewalk, but I love this moment between my family and friends. I love how creative these guys are and how exciting it is that they get to live in a place like this city. How the proximity to culture isn't wasted on them. What a gift to know your thing and apply yourself to it. Music or writing or acting and—even though I don't entirely respect it as an art— —even comedy. Or, shudder, *aerosol art.*

That night I decide I'm ready. I collect the envelopes that I've shoved to the back of my drawers and open them. Thank god at least half are repeats of the same main bills. My head swims with numbers.

I pin Nil's business card to the wall.

Chapter 35

"Water for sixty-nine," says Eduardo, an older, scarecrow-looking Puerto Rican waiter who smokes on breaks like it's a suicide mission.

"And twenty wants you to *remove* their breadbasket. I don't know why these rich pricks can't just not eat something."

Restaurants wring you out. Running around for punishing stretches. There's no dead time. It's like playing a really aggressive video game with a ton of screaming and fire. You never know what customers, or the staff, will throw at you.

The official title of the job is "back waiter," but for sixteen bucks an hour I show up at the crack of dawn in an ironed shirt and black slacks. It's a type of New York I used to never think about, and it astounds me how tourists, upon looking at the Freedom Tower, the memorial of where thousands of people died in a terrorist attack, get so hungry.

Lunch is always more demanding than dinner. That's when the offices disgorge their drones.

I'm always in the shit. Dara says it's six months in this business before you know your elbow from your asshole. I'm on day seventeen. Amber, a tiny waiter with a shaved head, screams at me for a full three minutes because the dishwashers ran out of espresso cups. This, on the same day I hand an office lackey the wrong nine-person pickup during lunch.

I meet Nil for coffee at six forty-five in the morning because it's the only time he has and I'm early. We talk about the future.

When I finally feel as though I have some semblance of a routine, the outline of a plan, I go and see my mother.

She's playing solitaire when I arrive. Eating sunflower seeds, wearing one of my old hoodies. It's enormous on her and covered in allover-print cartoon diamonds and dollar signs. I take off my shoes and hang my coat instead of dumping it on the couch. I don't even bring my laundry out of respect.

"Hey," she says, leaning over for a kiss.

"Hey." I take the seat next to her. "Rain here?"

"At your dad's. They're writing a play together."

She slaps another card down and surveys the lineup.

"Seven clubs," I tell her. I'm hovering.

Mom glares at me. It's her biggest pet peeve, when you help her at anything. Back-seat drivers, back-seat players, she loathes them all.

I place a bright blue foil brick in front of her.

Ace crackers. From Korea. Her favorite.

"We used to eat these at the beach," she says, cracking a seed in her teeth. Mom doesn't seem mad. But she doesn't seem happy either.

"So," she says. "You wanted to talk."

"Yeah." I clear my throat. "About college. And money."

"Okay," she says. "What about college and money?"

I stall. I want to play her three of hearts.

"I'm going to go back to school."

"What else is new?"

"Mom." I swallow.

"Where are you going back to school?"

"That's what I wanted to talk about. I didn't apply anywhere for summer. I missed the deadlines."

"I figured." I don't tell her about the part where I finally looked at the summer course selection for NYU to discover the program's only for visiting students.

She palms the crackers. Studies them. And then she sniffs and wipes her eyes.

Silence.

She sniffs again and clears her throat. My mother is crying.

"Mom?"

Still nothing.

"Umma?"

After a while she pulls herself together.

"So, what's the plan?" she asks. Finally she looks at

me. Her eyes swim with tears, but she's trying to smile.

"First I'll apologize to Dr. Houlihan and Mr. Santos."

"Okay," she squeaks.

Then silence.

I try again. "Mom." Attempt to get her to say anything more. To tell me why she's so sad.

"I'll get you the contacts," she says. "Is that where you want to go? Five Points?"

Her expression's guarded again. I finally see what everyone means when they tell me I'm withholding. That I'll talk about anything other than what's on my mind.

"Yes. There's a marketing course and a class on entrepreneurial finance. I want to start there."

"Okay," she says.

I wait for an addendum. A modification. An exasperated explanation as to why my idea is wrong, but it doesn't come.

"Then I'm transferring to the New School. There's a federal work-study program that will help pay for it." Nil's theater is an off-campus partner organization, and he's agreed to get me a job helping out.

"Great," she says in a strained voice.

Sometimes I wonder what would happen if we told each other the things we never say.

Mom opens the crackers and hands the first one to me. How she always does. I get the first since I'm firstborn. Rain gets the next, and only then does she eat. It breaks my heart in tiny ways how she considers us in all things.

I take it.

"I need help," I continue. "I tried being on my own, being an adult. But I screwed up, mom. . . ."

I place the cracker on the tabletop. I don't deserve it.

"I owe four thousand, two hundred dollars in credit card bills over three cards. And in thirty days from today some bill collectors are going to get a court order to sue for wage garnishment."

My voice shakes.

"Okay." She puts her hand on mine and pats it.

We sit for an interminable silence. "This is what we're going to do," she says finally and sighs. "We're going to pay them off from my savings."

"Mom," I protest. The thought of her reorganizing the stacks of notes and bills in her files breaks me. "You can't . . ."

"No, Pab," she says. "You're getting killed on interest. We'll figure out a direct payment plan from you to me. God, this country. It's so predatory."

I nod. I'm grateful and filled with shame but I have to keep going.

"Mom?"

"Yeah?"

I feel sick, but I have to ask her.

"What ever happened to my college fund?" There'd been talk of one when I was younger. Gripes here and there. Conversations over the phone between my parents, but as with the mysteries surrounding my family's extended family and why we don't talk to them, I've always been too uncomfortable to ask.

"There's forty-six thousand two hundred and eighteen dollars in there," she says. "We wanted more, Pab. We really did. But between our own student loans and what your dad could contribute . . . We couldn't do better. I'm sorry," she says, voice trembling again.

"Pablo, when you got into NYU, we didn't know what we were going to do. I couldn't sleep for weeks. It's a fantastic school, but it's also one of the most expensive in the world. I thought I could figure out a responsible way to manage, but then you just up and went. Like it was nothing. I wanted to kill your father for helping you."

She closes her eyes and takes a deep sigh.

"It was like watching a car crash in slow motion," she says, staring at the table. "I wanted to give you the money but I didn't trust you with it. Your dad wanted to. Said it was wrong to keep it from you." My mother looks at me finally. "And he was right.

"So what do we do?" she asks. "It's your money. Do we use a chunk to pay down your loans, defer, *and then* see what we have left over to pay for fall classes? Or defer, defer, defer, pay for as much school as possible now, and worry about the rest down the line? What do you think?"

While she breathlessly tallies options, I realize it's not rage my mom experiences most of the time. It's fear. It's never occurred to me that my mother gets scared.

"We can ask people," I tell her. I finally know how much I owe in student loans too. Nil will know who to consult. And if he doesn't, he'll ask someone.

"Okay," she says. I know she's pre-worrying about how she'll find time off work to meet with anyone about it, but that's okay.

I eat the cracker. Ace crackers are the best. Even butterier than Nabisco Waverlys. They'd be a great Hot Snack™ ingredient.

"I have something for you," she says, getting up. "Mrs. Kim came by." She grabs her purse. "She visited me at the hospital."

The thought of Mrs. Kim and my mom in the same place talking about me makes me instantly wobbly. And defensive. I'm not even sure in which direction.

"Okay," I say carefully.

"She's a lovely woman."

"Were you nice to her?"

Mom's brow furrows. "Of course I was nice to her. Jeez." She picks up her playing cards and reshuffles them. "Are you going to ask *her* if she was nice to me?"

"Mrs. Kim's a nice lady, mom," I tell her. "What did you guys talk about?"

"The Olympics," she says. "What do you think we talked about? She's worried about you. She wanted to know how you were doing. . . ."

"You told her I have a job, right? That I pulled it together?"

"Yes," she says, eyes watchful. "I told her you were a waiter at a very nice restaurant downtown. Which you still haven't invited me to, by the way."

"Okay." I relax. I don't know why, but I need Mrs. Kim to know that I'm not a deadbeat. Even if I screwed up at the deli.

"Did she say anything else?"

It's embarrassing to admit to my mother that what Mrs. Kim thinks of me matters. It's a gross hash of emotions. Like I'm cheating on my mom with this other mom.

"She brought your last paycheck." She nods at the door. "It's in the little tray."

I see a light-blue envelope. It's a greeting card.

"It's open!"

"Well, it wasn't officially closed," my mom argues. "The sticky seal wasn't licked."

It's a simple white card with a blue border that says "Thank You," and instantly my eyes prick with tears.

True to mom's word, my paycheck is in there, but Mrs. Kim has also written a note. Except the card's blank. The letter is written on a separate piece of paper.

"Dear Pablo," she says, and this is going to sound super ignorant or weird, but I think about how you can't see her accent in her perfect, tiny cursive. It looks like penmanship from a bygone era. "I hope you are well. We haven't seen you in a while and hope you will visit. The new freezers are working, but one is bigger than the other one. They're supposed to be same. Tina says hi. I don't want to give stress or ask too many questions (my sons always saying I ask many, many questions!), but I feel guilty because maybe me and Mr. Kim didn't ask enough questions before. We are wor-

ried about you. So I visit to your mother. Sometimes conversations are better from mother to mother. Here is your
last paycheck. We called you, but you didn't pick up. Call us
if you can. Mr. Kim says he has an issue with 'batch process-
ing' in the new software. We don't know what the problem
is. Jorge say hi also."

Then it's signed "Mr. and Mrs. Kim," even though it's
obviously all Mrs. Kim.

There's a fifty-dollar bill in the envelope. It's not every
day that you see a fifty-dollar bill, let alone a crisp one. It's
a small-face bill, which makes me think it came from some
stack of stashed cash that the Kims keep in their mattress
from ten years ago. Of course there's no mention of it.

I've never properly studied a paycheck before. I knew
they robbed you under the Federal Income Tax, Social
Security, and Medicare sections, but this is obscene.

"I'm probably nicer than Mrs. Kim, you know," says
mom after a sizable pause, which makes me laugh.

It's only when I get home that I realize why the card is
blank. Why Mrs. Kim never sealed it. It's so I can reuse it.
She's probably no walk in the park as a mom either. In the
best way.

Chapter 36

My favorite part of working at a restaurant is family meal. It's the ultimate Hot Snack™, where ingenuity and frugality melds to become a trough of nourishment diverse and delicious enough to satisfy some of the moodiest people I've ever met in New York.

I thought about putting up the videos that me and Rain shot, but going back through everything, I find the footage of the frittata and the affogato that I made the night Tabitha came over. I sort through all the Hot Snack™ footage and confirm that this is it. I knew there had to be a reason why I delete photos left and right but held on to this. This is my thing.

My heart will always belong to the bodega. Ever since I threw some of my dad's Junior Mints into the buttered popcorn at the movie theater, I knew I had a gift. It's not music, or theater, or anesthesiology, but it's mine. I will always love weird combos.

I edit and post a Shin Ramyun Black video set to music. My favorite instant noodles with three flavor packets and so much garlic. It's a classic Korean Hot Snack™, especially when you throw in cut-up hot dogs, frozen dumplings, extra kimchi—and this is where the artistry comes in—eggs, cheese, corn from a can, and a drizzle of sesame oil on top. And furikake if you're feeling wealthy.

The next night I put up a bacon, egg, and cheese not in a bagel but in a glazed honey bun. Laced with sriracha and pan fried on the outside.

Then it's chilaquiles with Spicy Sweet Chili Doritos and chorizo.

Jamaican beef patty casserole disrespected with a smothering of Japanese curry and broiled. With Crystal Hot Sauce over the top and pickled banana peppers. I'm trolling with that one but the controversy is berserk.

For the hit of sweet: s'mores with dark-chocolate Petit Ecolier cookies, toasted marshmallows topped with Rold Gold pretzels, crushed Flake, and a scoop of vanilla Heath bar crunch.

When I run out of old videos, I make saag paneer naanchos with Trader Joe's frozen Indian food, and it's a hit. Especially when I add yogurt and a thick layer of crushed-up Takis on top.

The comments come in hot and heavy. People love mash-ups as much as they hate them. A hundred likes have rained down. Way more comments than my best-performing sneaker × snack pairing. So many beefs about what's a better combo. Why glazed donuts are better than honey-bun bacon, egg, and cheeses. It's all so contentious. Everyone is a maniac. Exactly like me. There's so much genuine excitement that I feel as though I'm joining a pack. A tribe. The mixed kids are having a field day.

One morning when I'm on my way to work I scroll down, and that's when I notice it. The blue checkmark beside a name I know.

You should put these on YouTube.

It's Jessica Longworthy. If there's anyone whose business advice I'm happy to follow, it's hers. I double tap.

When I get home that night, I dust off my old YT account from the sad boy days, cut longer versions of the videos, and throw them up there with graphics. It's five a.m. when I'm done.

A few weeks later the craziest thing happens. I get a private message from a turkey jerky company asking if they can send me review samplers. They want to know what recipes I can come up with. I half expect it to be laced with anthrax or E. coli, but sure enough, it's a tiny outfit based out of Columbus, Ohio, and the founder writes me himself. He loves what I do.

The roommates gather to scheme on how to get me a Fit-Tea sponsorship, because that's when the real money happens.

"You only lose weight because it makes you go to the bathroom," Dara tells us. We're all eating the promo jerky, sitting around the table with Ross, Wyn's cousin, who's a pretty decent roommate considering he's not Tice.

"Isn't all tea a diuretic?" Count on Miggs to know about every diet and fitness supplement in the world.

"Sure," says Dara. "But I mean this stuff makes you pee where you poo."

"Ew," says Miggs, shaking his head.

"It's two large though," exclaims Ross, tipping back in his folding chair. "At least that's what the payments start at."

"What is a large?" I ask him. "Are you going talk about vigs now too?"

That's the only problem with Ross. He watches mob movies religiously every day. "Seriously, you talk like a bookie."

"But it's free money," he says.

"I don't know if I could do it," I tell him as I eye a piece of dried meat. What recipes can I cook up? Maybe if I reconstituted it in water . . .

"But you need money," he retorts. "I've seen your mail."

At the mention of mail, the roomie cipher goes quiet. I can hear Miggs, Dara, and Wyn's jaws working on the desiccated meat like cud.

"Twenty-two thousand dollars," Dara says, slamming her hand on the middle of the table.

Miggs catches her eye. "No way," he says. "A year of tuition alone at NYU is like fifty. Plus, he's got the credit cards."

"Those have defaulted," chimes in Wyn, leaning over to grab another piece of jerky. "So there's interest. He only did a semester. I say it's closer to thirty-six."

A month ago this conversation would have made me storm out of the room.

Ross's eyes ping back and forth. "I want in on the action. What's the buy-in?"

"They're guessing how much my personal debt is," I tell him.

"Shut up," he says, eyes wide. "You're thirty thousand dollars in debt?"

"Thirty-six," corrects Wyn. "Oh, and *Price Is Right* rules. Anything over is immediately disqualified."

"Well, I have to recuse myself. I know what the number is."

Dara shoots me a sidelong glance and squeezes my forearm like she's proud. Or else she's milking me for a tell.

"No way," Dara chimes in. "His mom's a doctor, so subsidized loans are out. There's only so much he could have borrowed. Right? Plus, he's not about to grab the merit-based grants."

"Hey, thanks a lot." She's right though.

"All right," says Miggs. "Dara, you're saying twenty-six. Wyn's at thirty-six. Ross is at thirty-eight *large*." He rubs his hands together. "I think it's closer to forty. All in."

"God, I can't believe you tried to go to private school," says Wyn, shaking his head.

"I mean, check his last girlfriend though," scoffs Dara. "He's not the best at reality."

"Ha ha," I remark. Dara had a full ride to Binghamton, and Wyn went to Hunter. Miggs always says he attended the Hard Knocks School of Life because he is a walking, breathing dad joke.

"Wait, who's your last girlfriend?" pipes up Ross, and god bless if the entire table doesn't say, "Nobody," at the same time.

Ross shakes his head. "Wait, private school? This isn't all credit card debt?"

"Nah," I tell him. "College."

"Oh, college?" says Ross, waving his hand in the air. "That's *good* debt. I'm a hundred and sixty thousand in the hole. My dumbass went to grad school."

Chapter 37

"**I want to** ask you about life," I tell my dad after I jump on the 7 on my day off.

"For that we'll need a walk." He's already putting on his cardigan.

I follow him down Main Street. The sunlight pours onto the sidewalk, and it's breezy enough that the pedestrians are squint-smiling straight into the rays, still defrosting from a brutal winter.

Main Street in Flushing is always hectic. As its name implies, it's the main thoroughfare of the Chinatown in Queens. We have three Chinatowns in the five boroughs of New York. Manhattan has Canal Street and Brooklyn has Eighth Avenue in Sunset Park. Unsurprisingly, all are mobbed with Asians. This part of New York may as well be a different planet from SoHo or Midtown. It's lousy with newcomers, but they're here to stay awhile. They're not tourists in Moncler coats taking macaron tours.

"Did I ever tell you about the time me and your mother went to Korea for our honeymoon?"

"No," I tell him, making a vow that I'll eventually come clean about the first time I went to Korea.

"Here," he says, fumbling with his wallet. My dad is the worst New York walker. He'll always stop short without pulling over. A Chinese dude almost collides into him and curses under his breath while tossing his cigarette butt into the street.

Rifling through an enormous wad of receipts from his billfold, he shows me a picture. It's curved from the wallet, but it's him and mom grinning into the camera, holding hands. It makes me wonder who took the picture. Mom's hair is braided in pigtails hanging down each side of her striped sweater, and dad's in this nineties look of a too-big shirt, sleeves rolled up under a sweater vest. They're standing on a dirt path with mountains behind them. It's a picture I vaguely remember but never knew where it was from. Honestly, they could have been in Montana. In the little windowed part of his wallet where his ID should go is a class picture of me from eighth grade, when I had horrible skin, and a picture of Rain that isn't a photograph but a matte printout on regular paper.

"Her parents didn't approve of me," he says.

"Maybe it was your tiny ponytail." I drive his elbow, so he keeps walking.

"Hilarious," he says. We stop at the light.

A crew of hoodied preteens join us. They're conspicuously passing a book of manga back and forth that's clearly porn since they're giggling and pushing each other. That's the nice thing about neighborhoods. Unlike Williamsburg or Gramercy, where everyone's in their twenties and thirties, you'll still find multiple generations out here that haven't been driven out by franchise gyms and Apple Stores.

We hit Northern and hang a right. It's where all the signage gets Korean. We walk for a while in silence and pass a music school.

"Remember when mom made me and Rain take piano?"

"Your mother loves music," says dad, crossing the street so we can walk on the median with trees. Dad's crazy about snatching as much nature as he possibly can. Even if it's a smattering of spindly saplings in the middle of traffic.

"She has perfect pitch and can play the piano from memory when she hears a song once. Did you know that?"

I didn't.

"No wonder she was such a Tiger Sociopath about those lessons," I tell him. "It only took thirty fights to break her down."

"Rain took the classes," he says. "Remember he won that award?"

I recall him bowing onstage in a blue blazer with gold buttons. Looking like a ventriloquist's dummy. Beaming. I'd erased the occasion from memory. All four of us had gone to Junior's afterward for lunch and cheesecake.

"We talked about the college fund," I tell him. I respect

that my dad didn't snitch on my mom. And that he'd never throw her under the bus in front of me.

"Productive conversations were had, I see," he says.

I swear, it's like talking to Yoda sometimes.

"Is this what you had in mind when you said you wanted to talk about life?"

I take a deep breath. "How did you know you wanted to be a playwright?"

"Ah, yes," he says, as if he's been expecting this question. "I wanted a purely collaborative creative process. And I like plays."

I like plays? That's how the muse struck? He *likes* them?

Dad looks past me to about middle distance. I wait for him to say something profound.

"Did you notice how mangos are a whole dollar cheaper over here?" He shakes his head, cutting across me to a fruit stand. "Two blocks away and you save multiple dollars for a few pounds . . ."

He picks one up and makes a high-pitched noise.

"It's criminal to me that there are so many types of delicious mangos all over the world and Americans only get these fibrous monster ones. There are mangos out there that are so juicy and taste exactly like custard. Bright haldi-colored ones." Still, he grabs a plastic bag to make his selection. "What is modern society's obsession with wiping out all diversity and nuance in favor of cheap, shoddy monoliths?"

He squeezes the fruit, tilts his head slightly, smells it, and changes his mind. As if he's diagnosed it.

"Dad?"

"Yes?"

"Writing? Plays?"

"Oh, yes, plays," he says. "I love them. Always have. And I knew that if I started learning to write them now, I'll be good in ten years. Great in twenty."

The woman at the stall knows a dawdling fruit squeezer when she sees one and sucks her teeth.

Twenty years? In twenty years he'll be a million.

I urge him forward.

"Aiyah," the woman mutters, rearranging the fruit.

"I want to be happy," says dad. "I want to be interested and challenged by whatever verb I elect to noun in any given moment of my life. If I am healthy, my family's healthy, and I am of sound enough mind to sustain curiousity around my work, then I'm blessed."

"I've started a video series," I tell him tentatively. "It's about food. . . . It's stupid. . . ." Dad's staring straight ahead, and I wonder if he's heard me.

"Nothing that is a manifestation of your creative energies is stupid," he says. "Doing nothing is the only stupid."

"I do these snack reviews."

"Alhamdulillah, that's beautiful," he says, clapping me on the back. "You're so good at video. The complicated one with Heather was excellent. Your mother came over for tea, and we watched it that morning at least twenty times. We were hoping you'd find a way to do more."

"You didn't tell me that."

"We don't tell you everything," he says. A pocket of foul-smelling air hits us as we pass a wet market, and I glance down in time to see a red bucket of frogs awaiting their destinies.

"Your mother and I were so worried," he says. "How you'd deal with the attention. You were always so anxious about any kind of audience as a child. And children these days seem to believe that fame is a birthright. What a blessing that it passed."

He pats my shoulder. "It's too emotionally expensive to be famous," he says.

I think of Lee.

"I'm going back to school," I tell him. "I'm still not totally sure about my major though."

"I know," he says. "Nil called me to let me know you were speaking. He's a fascinating man. It's okay that you don't know your major. Truth is you can learn anything through YouTube. YouTube and practice. It's not that mysterious."

"Easy for you to say," I tell him. "You have an engineering degree from Princeton."

"I didn't love engineering," he says. "I liked studying, but that was it. Tell me, do you love anything?" My dad looks at me tenderly. I know I'm in for some serious emotional outpouring. "Do you enjoy doing anything for the sake of doing it? Life isn't a destination. It's the continual practice of things that make you wiser and happier. Someday I hope to make perfect sourdough bread. I want to learn the piano.

I've made peace with the fact that I won't ever make a lot of money, but I make enough to live and eat. The rest goes to your mother. I know you boys think the way I live is depressing or strange, but in art the purpose is in the creation, not the result. Grow as you build. Autotelism. 'Auto' for self and 'telos' for goal. Find joy in the learning, Pablo, not in what it will get you. It took me so much searching to stop searching. Art is fueled by longing but you must learn to want what you have, not get what you want. It's the only way to stop suffering. I pray that you'll know this meaning by the time you're my age."

My dad hugs me roughly, then steers me to a different fruit stall.

"Now, this is a champion snack," he says, picking up a purple circle that resembles a tiny hand grenade with a bow tie. "The queen of fruit. Mangosteens. Review this. You'll go viral. Or more like antiviral, beta. They have so many antioxidants."

We buy a few for me to take home. The Chinese woman with lips so puckered she looks as though she's holding pins in them even throws in a few lychee. My dad acts as if it's the best thing that's happened to him. Ever.

Chapter 38

"You 5C?" A dude with tattooed hands and a bike helmet is posted up on my stoop.

"Who you looking for?" I ask him. 5C's us, but I'm not about to go advertising that. After everything I went through to sort out the bills, the calls, the letter-writing campaign, and setting up automatic payments, I'm still paranoid I'll get subpoenaed for some blacked-out Bed Bath & Beyond purchase I don't even remember.

"Pablo," he says, and reads off his tablet. "Neruda. Rind. You Pablo?" It's a miracle he caught me. Between two jobs and school I'm hardly ever around.

"Why?" I ask him.

"A gift," he says. I brace myself as he hands over a flat black box. Normally we get our packages delivered to the twenty-four-hour deli on the corner since they get stolen otherwise, but we've never gotten a bike messenger.

"Sign," he says, pointing to his iPad. And then, "Cool name."

I get it upstairs. It's midafternoon, sweltering, and the apartment's empty. Dust hanging in the beams of sunlight. It's been over a year but by the time I pull the rose-colored tissue aside, I know what it is. The smooth fabric underneath is a cold hand around my heart.

P, I miss you. L.

It's the suit.

And with it five invitations to Leanna's film premiere.

I replace the lid. And carefully place the box in my closet.

"It's a little pedo, right?" Tice asks us. We're all sitting on the roof a few nights later.

Okay, so we're not exactly sitting. We're standing in a circle so we don't get our asses dirty since the roof is legitimately disgusting from the winter. We're not technically allowed up here, but that doesn't stop us from hauling cheap plastic chairs up in the summer. No one knows what happened to last year's plastic chairs, but aside from one broken one, we can't find them. It's just one of those New York mysteries, akin to how you never see baby pigeons.

"It's not pedo," says Wyn, shielding his eyes to look up at him. There's a floodlight installed to discourage loiterers, but it's no match for us. "If anything, you're going to have every hot young mom after you. And that show reruns like crazy. You're going to get paid."

We all agree.

After a long dry spell, Tice landed a job on a kids' show.

"It's true," says Ross, who we still sometimes call new Tice except when real Tice is here. "Plus, that show's good. I saw Questlove on as musical guest once. It's huge."

"Totally," I confirm. I'm relieved Tice won't be moving to LA, at least for the near future. "It's not my dream job," he says. "But I'm happy about it."

"I'm happy for you, man." I pat his shoulder and hand him the last beer. "I mean it."

"How's finals looking?"

"We don't discuss this," I tell him. At this rate I'll graduate in six years with a business degree but even with the lighter load I don't exactly shine under pressure.

"You'll be okay," he says.

He hands me some of the beer, and I sip it appreciatively and hand it back.

"Thanks."

He pats me on the shoulder.

"Awww," says Dara. "Do you guys need a moment? Hug it out for posterity without all these spectators questioning your masculinity?"

"Real ones hug and kiss all the time," bellows Miggs, encircling me and Tice in a massive embrace. "It's cosmopolitan."

Wyn gets in on the action.

I can't take it anymore. All these feelings.

"Okay, house meeting," I announce. "You know that movie Leanna Smart's in?"

"Yeah," says Wyn. "Looks stupid."

"Completely stupid. *The Big One?*" asks Tice. "What kind of title is that?"

"*The Big One?* More like *The Big Deuce*," says Miggs.

"Yeah, *deuce*, like steaming pile of shit," explains Wyn. Miggs duffs him on the arm.

"The one with Teddy Baptiste?" asks Ross.

"Yeah," says Dara.

"That trailer looks sick," he says. "I'll probably go see it."

The OG roomies shoot Ross the collective death stare.

"We're not watching that movie," says Dara tartly. "Not even to stream. Not even for free."

"Well," I tell them. "We're invited to the New York premiere."

"Wait? All of us?" asks Wyn.

"Yeah." There's no way I couldn't tell them. "Do you want to go?"

"I mean . . . ," say Dara and Tice with expressions that suggests they're already planning outfits.

"After-party too?" asks Miggs.

I nod.

"Shit," he says, rubbing his chin.

These turncoats.

"Nah," says Wyn, glaring at them. "I'm not going."

"Thank you," I tell him. "What happened to *The Big Deuce?*"

"I mean . . . ," starts Dara again.

"A premiere, dude?" says Miggs, and then, "But

you know what? You say forget it and we forget it. No regrets."

They all look at me expectantly.

As if I could let these losers down.

As if this wouldn't be like winning every stupid betting fantasy game in one fell swoop.

"Fuck it," I tell them. "Let's go."

Ross cuts in with a huge, baffled grin on his face. "Wait, who are you, man?"

We're sent cars and we head downtown to the Metrograph. There's a black carpet instead of a red one, but there are velvet ropes. There's a line of photographers. There's no mistaking it for anything other than what it is. A movie premiere in Manhattan.

The photographers couldn't give a shit about any of us as we open the car doors, and once we're in the lobby we run into Jess, who's wearing a white suit. She looks fantastic.

"Good to see you, Pab," she says, and gives me a hug. "Hey," she calls out to the gang.

Jess introduces herself to Ross, who we requested to be added to the list after he cleaned all our rooms. She guides the gang to the unlimited snacks before pulling me aside.

"I wasn't completely sure you'd come," she says.

"I didn't know for sure I'd come." I hand her the box with the suit. She eyes me. "I couldn't."

She nods. "I'll have them put it in the car," she says. "How are you?"

"Good. Better." Standing in front of Jess, I realize how far I've come to be able to say this honestly.

"I'm glad." She smiles. "Good looks on the food channel. I see you out here with your oat milk sponsors and ad hashtags."

"Thanks." It's killing me to make a new video a week but I can't complain. "And you, congratulations on the show." It's only a matter of time that Jessica Longworthy will have a chief of staff of her own and we both know it.

"Listen, she wants to see you downstairs."

"Okay." I figured I'd have to see her. I just didn't know where and when. My throat's dry.

"You know you don't have to go," says Jess lightly.

"It's okay. I want to." I exhale. Korea flashes in my head. The flight home. The sleepless blur of all the days that followed. "It'll only be a second."

I'll have to make it quick. Even after all this time I'm wary. I can't lose myself like that again.

"Okay. Take the stairs and follow the path to the left," she says.

As I make to leave, she stops me. "It's not deliberate, you know. What she does. I know she cared about you."

"Thanks."

"Have fun tonight, Pab."

When I get downstairs, her door's ajar. Lee turns her head and sees me before I can even knock.

"Hey." My heart, that Judas, thunders. I can't conceal my excitement.

"Hi," she says, smiling wide. "Get in here."

Her hair is short, at the nape of her neck. Platinum. It makes her appear older. Her dress is oversized, ruffled, and becomingly off-kilter. One sleeve hangs down to her thigh.

She hugs me, and it's fruit again. The fruit so intense it doesn't exist in nature.

"You look great," I tell her, breathing her in.

She sees my black jeans, and her thumb travels to her mouth. "You didn't wear the suit . . ."

"I couldn't."

I never even took it out of the box.

"Okay." She nods.

"Hey, you did it," I tell her. "Your movie exists."

"Yeah," she says. "I'm happy." And then another huge smile. "God, it's good to see you. You know my abuela's here?"

"Holy shit," I tell her. "That's awesome. I can't wait to say hi."

"Yeah, she's proud. I sat you guys with my family, so . . ."

That destroys me. It's amazing what time can't do.

We both stare.

"Thank you," I breathe.

"Man," she squeaks in a voice not at all her own. "I really thought I was kind of crushing it on the gift . . ."

She looks away.

"Lee." I take a step toward her, and she rushes in to hug me again.

She feels good there. Familiar even when she shouldn't.

Lee exhales, warming my chest. We stay there for a long time before I pull away. I kiss her temple as she whispers into my neck, "I miss you."

I won't lie. A fissure opens in my sternum. Light shines through. The urge to recharge is monumental. "I miss you," I tell her. It's the truth. The god's honest truth.

"I got rid of Luca," she says. "Finally."

"I don't know what to say."

"Don't say anything," she says. "Come with me." She looks up. There it is. The words that initiated all of this. The invitation to escape my own life for a hologram version of hers. Fleeting. Secret. Nebulous. Governed by forces larger than me. Contracts. Insurance claims. Management.

Thing is, I want to. Desperately.

"I can't," I tell her instead.

I pull away.

I can't because I won't make my way back. And I need to be back here. Chipping away. Living my own life.

"Okay." Her eyes shine.

"Hey, do you ever think about how we'll remember this?" I ask her, smiling. "A long time from now?"

"What do you mean?" She smiles to match mine.

"I don't know," I tell her. "I think about us sometimes and we're old as hell. Don't worry, you still look amazing."

"Obviously," she says.

"But it's like nobody's going to believe it. That this happened. That *you* happened to me."

Her hugeness is unfathomable.

Leanna Smart laughs. It's a humorless sound, but her grin is picture perfect.

"Yeah, well," she says brightly. "As you know, this isn't my hair. Or my boobs. Truth be told, this is only half my chin and these aren't even my teeth." She taps at a capped incisor with a gel nail. "I'll tell you what, Pablo. Give it a few years and no one's going to believe *I* happened to me, either."

She steps in for another hug, and I hold her.

We fit as we always have.

I don't want to let go, but I do.

ACKNOWLEDGMENTS

Wow. What they tell you about second books is not wrong. At all. I really did well and truly break my brain on this one. Books are about as big a thing as I've ever made and this one got a lot of help. Thank you, Sam. My partner. I'm grateful that musicians are masochistic enough to put up with writers.

To my family. Mike, mom, dad, Vicki, and Wylie.

Thank you, Zareen Jaffery. My editor and friend. I love our rambling calls about mortality, spirituality, and that you high-key laughed in my face when you remembered I was on Book Two and *that's* why I was acting bananas. I am constantly floored by your patience, wisdom, and honesty.

Edward Orloff, my agent. Best head of hair and bespoke bookshelf maker in the business. I will always be grateful to you and what you saw in both "Emergency Contact" and "Permanent Record." Penny and Pablo are lucky to have you in their corner. And to everyone at McCormick, particularly Susan Hobson—I'm still swooning over these foreign language editions.

My supportive and awesome team at Simon & Schuster. It's such a trip that I have any business in Rock Center. What a town. Justin Chanda, ugh, you're so good to me. I love how you ride for all of us and I love being a part of the roster. Thank you, Anne Zafian, Lisa Moraleda, and Chrissy Noh (all eight apples tall of you!) for continuing to believe in me. Andre Wheeler for the details.

Oh, singular gg. Thank you for creating these beautiful covers that make my heart ache. I am such a forever fan. And, of course, Lizzy Bromley. I will always be galaxy brain over how you and gg see things before I do.

This book is dedicated to my New York family. I live and work to see you proud. To my Marshall (you will always be my first reader), Asa Akira, Jubilee, Suze (Smarties note was so clutch), Naomi, Swoles, Becca, Christine, Phil Chang, Benny Guinness, Rem, Will Welch, Daniel Arnold, Caramanica, Maeve (and Shadow), Rose, Sooey, Keith, Maudie, J. Escobedo, Dap, Yasi (gather the wools), Brendan + Kenny, Film Club, K Bloc, C47 *Magazine*, Catchdini, Kerin, NCB, Minya, Kristin Iversen, Vivien Wang and Stone (you count as NY in spirit), and Chethan Jeong Bhan (full government in case you show your parents lol).

To Desus & Mero for being Desus & Mero and for deadass keeping New York relevant in a post–Hudson Yards world. Dana for the graf details, Jian for the sneaker/drip details, and Jake for Gallatin details. If I got anything wrong in any of these departments, it's on me. Jenny Han! I love you! You shine so we can all shine. And to my favorite energy healer and grounding force, Jenna Wortham (I'm going to leave you my true feelings in a pancake).

And for my book friends: Bobby Hundreds, Shea Serrano, Samantha Irby, Jami Attenberg. Rainbow Rowell for the kindness and the DMs, Mark Lotto for the notes, and Taffy Brodesser-Akner for the phone calls. And of course the greater society of incredible YA authors IRL and on social media. Siobhan, Dhonielle, Nic, DJ, Tahereh, Shuster-man, Julie, Jason, Emily, Ashley, Morgan, Jennifer, Maurene, Laini. You're all so inspiring I can't believe I get to sit with you. Sabaa Tahir for straight-up interventioning me on deadlines and teaching me how to ask for what I need. Your encouragement and generosity makes me so emo. That call when you were sick and I was on a road trip with my parents informed a draft that I didn't know how to get my arms around until I talked to you. Thank you.

To mixed kids. And their feelings. Thank you for shar-ing your stories with me.

My therapist, my sponsor, my twelve-step group. And everyone who reminds me that art is not linear. And that expectations are nothing more than planned resentments.

Jermaine Johnson and Sim Hothi at 3Arts (insert: a small galaxy of DJ Khaled GIFs). Jason Richman and Mary Pender at UTA—let's make movies!

And to everyone who read *Emergency Contact*. Thank you. I can't believe I get to stay on the ride.